The Shadow of Judex

IN THE SAME SERIES

Judex (translated by Rick Lai)
The Return of Judex (translated by Rick Lai)

The Shadow of Judex

Stories by
Matthew Baugh, Nicholas Boving, Thom Brannan,
Matthew Dennion, Romain d'Huissier,
Emmanuel Gorlier, Travis Hiltz, Vincent Jounieaux,
Rick Lai, Jean-Marc & Randy Lofficier,
David McDonald, Christofer Nigro, Dennis E. Power,
Chris Roberson and Robert L. Robinson, Jr.

Based on the character created by
Arthur Bernède & Louis Feuillade

Edited by
Jean-Marc & Randy Lofficier

Translations by
Matthew Baugh and
Jean-Marc & Randy Lofficier

Illustrations by
Michelle Bigot, Fernando Calvi, John Gallagher

BLACK COAT PRESS

Visit our website at www.blackcoatpress.com

ISBN 978-1-61227-178-1. Printing. July 2013. Published by Black Coat Press,
an imprint of Hollywood Comics.com, LLC, P.O. Box 17270, Encino, CA
91416. All rights reserved. Except for review purposes, no part of this book may
be reproduced or transmitted in any form or by any means, electronic or me-
chanical, including photocopying, recording or by any information storage and
retrieval system, without permission in writing from the publisher. The stories
and characters depicted in this anthology are entirely fictional. Printed in the
United States of America.

TABLE OF CONTENTS

LIRE DANS
Le Petit Parisien
JUDEX
(CRÉÉ ET FILMÉ
PAR LOUIS FEUILLADE
FILM
GAUMONT
G
Grand Roman Cinéma
PAR
ARTHUR BERNÈDE
ATELIER PLUMEREAU
IMP. CORNILLE ET SERRE

Introduction

In 1908, French filmmaker Victorin Jasset created serials when he filmed the adventures of the famous American detective, Nick Carter, in episodic format for Studios Eclair.

Because of its huge success, Jasset soon followed it with a serial adaptation of Leon Sazie's master criminal Zigomar: *Zigomar* (1910), *Zigomar, Roi des Voleurs* [*Zigomar, King of Thieves*] (1911), *Zigomar contre Nick Carter* [*Zigomar vs Nick Carter*] (1912) and *Zigomar Peau d'Anguille* [*Zigomar the Eel*] (1912).

Rival film studio Pathé quickly followed suit with serials based on the perennially popular character of *Rocambole*, and *Les Mystères de New York*, starring Pearl White, a French adaptation by Pierre Decourcelle of the three *Exploits of Elaine* American serials. For Pathé, director Maurice Tourneur also made serials of *Monsieur Lecoq* (1914) and *Rouletabille* (1914).[1]

Meanwhile, at rival studio Gaumont, filmmaker Louis Feuillade embarked on a serial adaptation of Pierre Souvestre & Marcel Allain's classic arch-villain *Fantômas* (1913-14): 1. *Fantômas* (1913), 2. *Juve contre Fantômas* [*Juve vs. Fantômas*] (1913), 3. *Le Mort Qui Tue* [*The Dead Man Who Kills*] (1913), 4. *Fantômas contre Fantômas* [*Fantômas vs. Fantômas*] (1914), and 5. *Le Faux Magistrat* [*The False Magistrate*] (1914).[2]

Success was immediate and encouraged Feuillade to launch *Les Vampires* [*The Vampires*], a ten episode serial, written and directed by Louis Feuillade, released in 1915 to compete with *Les Mystères de New York*.

Despite its huge popularity, due in great part to the character of Irma Vep, the head villainess, whose name is an anagram of "vampire" (played by Musidora, a voluptuous, dark-haired stage and music-hall performer who did all her own stunt work), *Les Vampires* was too anarchistic for the times' bourgeois sensibilities.

---

[1] Black Coat Press has published a compilation of *Rocambole* plays (ISBN 978-1-932983-57-9) as well as translations of Emile Gaboriau's *Monsieur Lecoq* (ISBN 978-1-934543-31-3) and Gaston Leroux's *Rouletabille: The Mystery of the Yellow Room* (ISBN 978-1-934543-60-3) and *Rouletabille at Krupp's* (ISBN 978-1-61227-144-6).

[2] *Fantômas* novels available from Black Coat Press include *The Daughter of Fantômas* (ISBN 978-1-932983-56-2) as well as spin-offs *Fantômas in America* by David White (ISBN 978-1-934543-07-8), *Sherlock Holmes vs Fantômas* (ISBN 978-1-934543-67-2) and *Nick Carter vs Fantômas* (ISBN 978-1-934543-05-4).

A critic in *Hebdo-Film* (April 22, 1916) wrote: "That a man of talent, an artist, the director of most of the great films which have been the success and glory of Gaumont, chooses to deal again with this unhealthy genre, obsolete and condemned by all people of taste, remains for me a real problem."

So, in order to show that he was not always glorifying villains, Feuillade teamed up with writer Arthur Bernède and, together, they decided to create Judex—whose name means Judge in latin—perhaps the first costumed hero in modern history.

The son of a wine broker, Louis Feuillade (1873-1925) began his film career as a screenwriter in 1906. The following year, he was appointed production chief at French studio Gaumont, but continued directing his own projects. Today, Feuillade is considered the father of the serial, the forerunner of German expressionism, and a master of suspense. In just twenty years, he directed and wrote over 800 films of various genres. He is, however, best remembered for his pulp fantasy serials.

Arthur Bernède (1871-1937) was a renowned playwright, journalist, screenwriter and the author of numerous popular novels. His best-remembered creations are Judex and the villainous Belphégor, the so-called "Phantom of the Louvre," created in 1927.[3]

The first Judex serial of 12 episodes was released simultaneously with a novelization, signed by both Feuillade and Bernède, published first as a serial in *Le Petit Parisien*, then in a collected edition by Tallandier.[4] To play it safe, Feuillade had the eponymous crime-fighter played by then-popular heart-throb René Cresté, while the character of the female villain, Diana Monti, was portrayed again by Musidora.

The success of Judex gave birth to a sequel, a second 12-episode serial entitled *La Nouvelle Mission de Judex* [*Judex's New Mission*], released in 1918, also with the simultaneous publication of its novelization by Bernède.[5]

Judex was remade twice—the first time, very faithfully, by Feuillade's own son-in-law, Maurice Champreux, in 1934. The second time by renowned filmmaker George Franju,[6] assisted by Champreux' son, Jacques Champreux.

Franju cast American stage magician Channing Pollock as Judex, and incorporated Pollock's own act—an eerie number involving doves and birds—as part of the film, in a very strange costumed ball scene where guests wear masks

---

[3] Available from Black Coat Press, translated by Jean-Marc & Randy Lofficier, ISBN 978-1-61227-110-1.
[4] Available from Black Coat Press, translated by Rick Lai, ISBN 978-1-61227-085-2.
[5] Available from Black Coat Press under the title *The Return of Judex*, translated by Rick Lai, ISBN 978-1-61227-159-0.
[6] Who also directed the 1959 horror classic *Les Yeux Sans Visage* [*Eyes Without A Face*].

fashioned like birds' heads. The role of Jacqueline was entrusted to actress Edith Scob (the mad doctor's disfigured daughter in *Eyes*), and that of Diana Monti to the very competent Francine Bergé, who struck a wonderful figure in her black leotard.

While Judex hasn't quite gained the level of fame achieved by Arsène Lupin and Fantômas, even today he remains a popular, timeless classic, as evidenced by the following anecdote: French comics readers of the 1940s were surprised to discover in a new comic series published in the weekly magazine *Hurrah!* (and later, *Tarzan*) that the secret identity of Judex wasn't Jacques de Trémeuse but Lamont Cranston! This was due to the fact that this new series was, in reality, a French translation of the American syndicated *Shadow* comic strip distributed by The Ledger Syndicate—retitled *Judex* in France to capitalize on the character's popularity, taking advantage of the obvious similarities between the two.

This anthology of stories penned by some of the regular contributors to *Tales of the Shadowmen*, our annual celebration of French heroes and villains, exists to celebrate this milestone of popular fiction, and is respectfully dedicated to those two great pioneers of the genre, Louis Feuillade and Arthur Bernède.

The stories have been arranged in chronological order and we have made no attempt at trying to explain the timelessness (or unnatural longevity!) of the character. Judex walks forever through the decades, unchanged.

Long live Judex!

Jean-Marc & Randy Lofficier

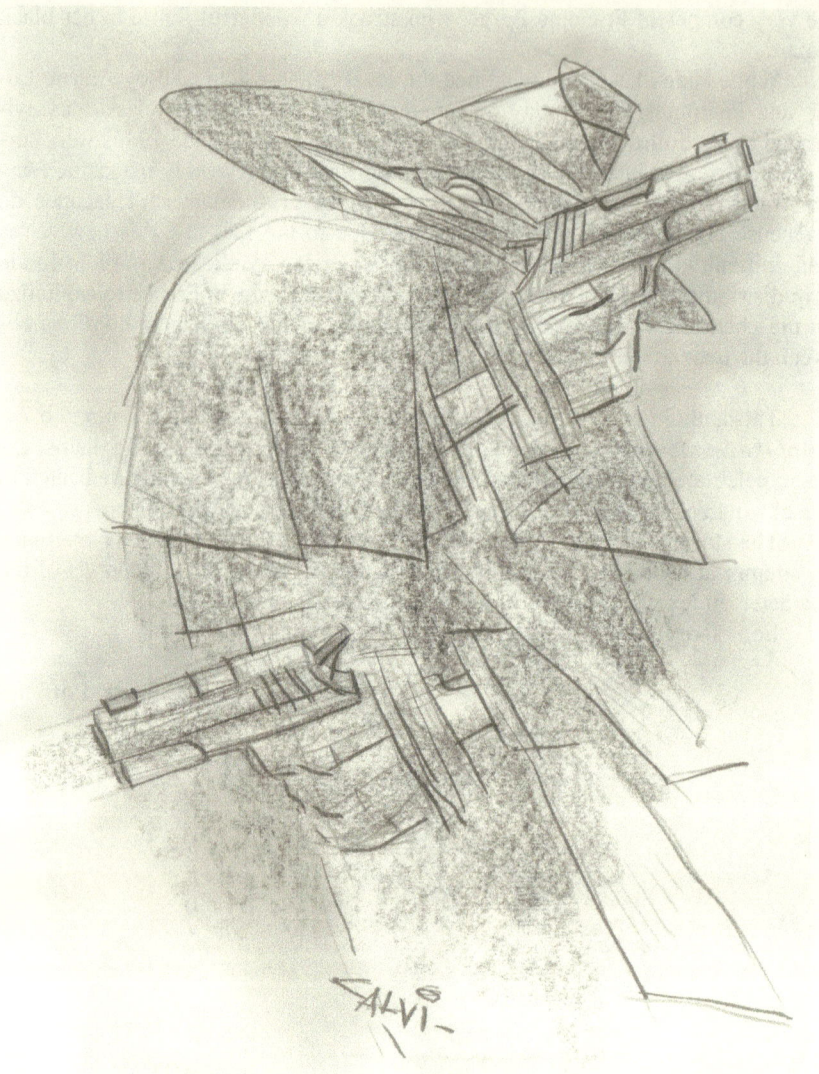

Judex by Fernando Calvi

Rick Lai: *A Brief Chronology of the Canonical Judex Saga*

1861. Birth of Julia Orsini.

1881. Julia Orsini marries Pierre de Trémeuse.

1883. Birth of Jacques de Trémeuse, the son of Pierre and Julia de Trémeuse.

1885. Birth of Roger de Trémeuse, the second son of Pierre and Julia de Trémeuse.

1893. Robert Bianchini discovers a mine in South America for Pierre de Trémeuse.

1897. Maurice-Ernest Favraux financially ruins Pierre de Trémeuse. Following Pierre's suicide, Julia de Trémeuse forces her two sons to swear an oath of vengeance against Favraux. Robert Bianchini restores the Trémeuse finances by discovering a mine in Africa.

1898. Robert Bianchini sells his interest to the South American and African mines to Julia de Trémeuse. Julia purchases the Chateau de la Ferté in the forest of Dreux.

1908. Birth of Jean Aubry, the son of Jacques Aubry and Jacqueline Favraux, and the grandson of Maurice-Ernest Favraux.

c.1910. Jacques Aubry dies in an automobile accident in the United States.

1912. Under the false identity of Vallières, Jacques de Trémeuse (alias Judex) becomes Maurice-Ernest Favraux's secretary.

1913. Events of *Judex*.

1914. (June-Mid-July) Events of *The Return of Judex*.

1914. (July 28) Outbreak of World War I.

X X

L E   J U G E M E N T

Judex by Michelle Bigot

Our first story deals not with Judex himself, but with his mother, Julia de Trémeuse née Orsini, a Corsican woman who has made vendetta *into an art form. After her husband's suicide, due to the schemes of the banker Favraux (whose amorous advances she had rejected), Julia fanatically devoted the rest of her life to molding her two sons into deadly weapons of vengeance. How such a woman came to be is the point of Rick Lai's tale, which connects Julia to a number of other French characters well known to readers of* Tales of the Shadowmen...

Rick Lai: *Acolytes of the Shadows*

The gaunt man was strangling the woman with his cravat. Darlla Rassendyll recognized the victim's face. She was Francine Letaine, Darlla's predecessor in the police force. Francine had been brutally slain by Gaston Morrell, the homicidal maniac dubbed the modern Bluebeard. Darlla knew that they were only wax effigies, but the sight of them disgusted her.

The Chateau of Wax was the rage of Paris in 1879. The museum capitalized on lurid murders sensationalized in the press. The proprietor, Antoine Dragone, erected displays of the most recent unsolved crimes. His reenactments contained details that the police had deliberately withheld from the public. Darlla's superior, Inspector Jacques Lefèvre, was convinced that Dragone had a private source of information in the department.

Darlla was determined to discover the source of these leaks. The ghastly depiction of Francine's demise only strengthened the detective's resolve. One year earlier, Francine's death that had prompted Darlla to join the police. Darlla's father had been a wealthy Englishman, William Rassendyll. He had frequently professed that no Englishman should pass through Paris without spending twenty-four hours there. During a trip to the continent in 1848, William had merely intended to waste an idle day in the French capital. On that day, revolution exploded in Paris. William's democratic beliefs had prompted him to join the rebels on the barricades. He became an ardent supporter of the Second Republic that sprang from the ashes of the monarchy. Caricaturing England as a corrupt land governed by aristocrats, William decided to spend the remainder of his days in France. Three years later, Napoleon III overthrew the Republic in a *coup d'état*. William was then arrested with other liberal activists.

He would have languished in prison if not for an extraordinary woman. One of the great mysteries of Marseilles was the antecedents of the beautiful Kent sisters, Armande and Arnaude. Arriving in France from parts unknown, they professed to be the daughters of an English officer and an Indian woman. The validity of this tale was highly suspect. Whereas Armande remained in Marseilles to become a notorious courtesan, Arnaude had migrated to Paris where she pursued a successful career as a stage actress. She fell passionately in love with William. Upon William's incarceration, Arnaude used his influence with a rising member of Napoleon III's regime, Eugène Rougon, to secure William's release. Grateful for Darlla's intervention, William married her. Abandoning politics, he prospered as a Parisian merchant. When a disastrous war with Germany led to Napoleon III's downfall in 1870, William supported the establishment of the Third Republic of France. The road to a new representative government became steeped in bloodshed when anarchists seized power in Paris in 1871. Their short-lived Paris Commune was destroyed by troops loyal to the new Republic. In the mist of the civil conflict, both William and Arnaude lost their lives.

Darlla, then eighteen, was left an impoverished orphan. Her father's business had been destroyed during the battle in the French capital. She supported herself by emulating her mother. Under the alias of Darlla Kent, she became a supporting player in the French stage. She was a statuesque woman with vivid red hair. Although attractive, Darlla had often been cast as villainess because of her wide mouth that suggested a cruel nature. Enjoying modest success as a dramatic performer, Darlla made the disastrous decision to also become an opera singer. Her debut as a vocalist was castigated by one critic as being a worse debacle then the French defeat at Sedan.

Darlla had first met Francine in 1877 when the police were probing a theft in the theater district. The pair became close friends. Darlla had encountered Inspector Lefèvre at Francine's wake in the following year. Hoping to avenge Francine, Darlla applied to become a member of the police. Lefèvre tutored Darlla to be Francine's replacement as an undercover operative. Darlla played no part in Lefèvre's campaign against Morrell. Before her training even began, Lefèvre's pursuit caused the strangler to drown in the Seine.

There had been numerous protests by relatives and friends of the murder victims depicted in the Chateau of Wax. Antoine Dragone's talents were in advertising and promotion. His partner, Henri Jaraud, made all the wax figures. Dragone had persuaded Jaraud, to make the images of the fatalities look exactly like the originals. This decision had been vociferously condemned as a shameful exploitation of the deceased. Nevertheless, the Chateau of Wax strived on the public controversy and continued to reap substantial profits.

In the course of a murder investigation, Darlla had noticed a young blonde girl loitering around the neighborhood. The sleuth spotted the same female later at the scenes of other crimes. Today Darlla trailed the petite blonde to the Chateau of Wax.

The blonde had been greeted by Dragone when she entered the waxworks.

"Julia, let's talk in my office."

As the pair left to confer, a crowd developed around Henri Jaraud, a tall distinguished man with a beard. It was said that Jaraud had artistic differences with Dragone. The sculptor was more interested in historical representations rather than glorifications of modern gore. Jaraud was standing before a tableau that must have been a compromise between him and Dragone. It was the representation of an eighteenth-century woman about to be branded on the shoulder with a hot iron. The iron was in the shape of the letter "V," an abbreviation for "*voleur*" (the French word for "thief"). Near the exhibit was another figure draped by a large white cloth.

"Behold the punishment of Jeanne Valois de La Motte. In 1785, she had engaged in a complex swindle. La Motte secured a valuable necklace by pretending to be a representative of Marie Antoinette. Despite her total innocence in this affair, the Queen was unjustly labeled La Motte's co-conspirator by the French public. It is universally believed that the resulting scandal sparked the Revolution four years later. The authorities named La Motte as the chief instigator of the fraud. The truth is that she was manipulated by another. She had been tricked by a detractor of the monarchy. His name was Joseph Balsamo, Count Cagliostro. According to novelist Alexandre Dumas, Cagliostro presided over a worldwide conspiracy that engineered the French Revolution.

"The legend is that Cagliostro discovered an elixir of eternal youth. There was evidence of this miraculous concoction nine years ago. Shortly before the outbreak of war in 1870, a mysterious woman appeared in Paris. She was Joséphine Balsamo, Countess Cagliostro. She used the facade of a fortune teller to spy for the Germans. Despite the appearance of a young woman about twenty-five, she avowed herself to be Count Cagliostro's daughter born in 1788. Her real age was closer to eighty-two. I am about to unveil the image of Countess Cagliostro."

Suddenly the exhibition hall was rocked by multiple explosions. Jaraud was knocked off his feet. The unveiled figure of Countess Cagliostro burst in flame. More fires ignited in other exhibits. Spectators ran in panic to the exits.

"Julia!" yelled Jaraud raising himself from the ground. The sculptor ran towards Antoine Dragone's office. He was followed by Darlla. Jaraud opened the door. Flames ran rampant in the room. Lying unconscious on the ground were Julia and Dragone. Without a thought for his partner, Jaraud picked up Julia from the ground and hurried to safety. Darlla pulled Dragone up from the floor. The promoter was dazed, but able to walk. With Darlla's help, he maneuvered through the burning building. The wax figures were quickly melting. Several people were screaming in agony as the flames enveloped them. As the fire brigade arrived, Darlla and Dragone left the burning structure.

A coach was parked some blocks from the inferno. Inside sat an attractive woman and a middle-aged man. The woman was thirty-four years old. She had flaxen hair, a delicate chin, deep-set eyes and high cheek-bones. On the fourth finger of her right hand, a ring bore the image of a golden ram. The man had an immense mustache and enormous side-whiskers that gave him the appearance of a cavalry officer. The blonde observed the carnage through a telescope.

"Are you pleased with the results, Gloria?" questioned the man.

"The incendiary devices of your Nihilist colleagues were effective, Dr. Villagos. Unfortunately, the principal human target appears to have survived the wreckage."

"It was through no fault of the timing mechanisms of the fire-bombs planted by my men."

"I don't doubt it. Dragone was rescued by a red-headed woman. I must learn her identity. She will suffer for circumventing my will!"

"Fifteen people perished in the blaze," pronounced Inspector Lefèvre in his office at police headquarters. "Three were employees of the Chateau of Wax. The other twelve were patrons of that ghoulish theatre of exploitation. We still don't know how Dragone learned so many classified details of our cases."

"I can answer that riddle," stated Darlla. "At the hospital, I listened to the injured girl whom I followed to the Chateau of Wax. She's in a state of shock and babbles randomly about her life. Her full name is Julia Orsini. She is only eighteen. Her family is prominent in Corsica."

"Dragone also is a Corsican."

"He used his powers of seduction to persuade her to flee their native island. The feverish Julia was begging her mother for forgiveness. She also prayed to God to forgive her for squandering her great gift."

"What great gift?"

"She's a lip reader. Years ago, an English teacher named Lee visited Corsica. He is an instructor of the deaf. The Orsini family is prominent in charitable works. They wished to fund a school for the deaf in Corsica. Lee trained the young Julia to read lips."

"She merely gathered information by secretly observing the conversations of our colleagues during their investigations."

"We could try to recruit her as a policewoman. The destruction of the Chateau of Wax has left her destitute."

"Your proposal is out of the question. I want nothing further to do with that abominable establishment. They shamefully capitalized on the tragedies of our dear Francine and countless others. Let Julia's lover ensure her livelihood. "

"I doubt very much that will happen. Dragone may have the dark handsome face of a Casanova, but he has the soul of Cesare Borgia. He was barely injured in the fire. In the hospital, he shamefully flirted with me even though poor Julia was in a state of delirium. He will surely abandon her."

"The fate of this Orsini girl should not concern you. Find the perpetrators of this devastation."

"This atrocity paralleled the outrages of the Russian Nihilists. There are numerous radical Russian émigrés in our city. The Second Bureau tracks their movements. Can I access the Bureau's records?"

"That will not be easy, Darlla. Our secret service is very jealous of its secrets. However, I am acquainted with Lucien Gévrol of the Second Bureau. His father was a prominent police inspector. He is generally sympathetic to our requests for collaboration. I'll arrange an interview."

The Callyx Bar was a restaurant that catered to the decadently wealthy. Its deed of ownership was made in the name of Josette Absalom. She lived on the premises in a series of upstairs rooms with her two young daughters. Josine, who greatly resembled her blonde mother, was eleven years old while her sister, the dark-haired Sabine, was nine. Wearing a purple robe, Madame Absalom was alone in her boudoir with her children and two men. Her lavender garment decorated with gold rams gave the impression of a high priestess of magical lore.

"Children," intoned Madame Absalom, "please go into the playroom with Léonard. My guest, Monsieur Nemo, has important business to discuss."

The young children were escorted outside by a somber bearded man. Madame Absalom was left alone with her visitor. Nemo was a tall ascetic-looking man with a large dome forehead. Both he and Madame Absalom were members of the Black Coats, the most powerful crime syndicate in Europe. It was an alliance of crime that spanned several countries and united such disparate organizations as the Gentlemen of the Night in London and the Camorra in Naples.

"I find it awkward addressing you as Josette. I prefer your English alias of Gloria Scot. "

"I am quite comfortable with that name, Jim."

"My power grows daily, Gloria. I already dominate the Gentlemen of the Night. With your help, I will control all the Black Coats. Your Nihilist friends will be a welcome addition to our ranks."

"The All-Father will resist any effort to seize his throne."

"He's a recluse in Corsica. His influence had gradually diminished over the last decade."

"The All-Father still maintains the support of Corbucci and his traditionalists in the Camorra."

"Perhaps a compromise can be arranged to placate Corbucci's faction. The British Empire is nominally ruled by Queen Victoria, but the true reins of power are exercised by her Prime Minister. The All-Father could easily be granted a ceremonial role in my own personal Empire."

"I doubt very much that the All-Father will concur. He has already sought to strike at you through me. One of his Corsican protégés, Antoine Dragone, was dispatched to hamper my activities. Dragone attempted to publicize my activities in 1870 by unveiling my wax effigy."

"Your earlier actions as a German spy must remain forgotten. We do not wish to compromise our sale of French military secrets to Bismarck's minions. This is not just a question of profits. We're playing for higher stakes. If our criminal network could be combined with the German war machine, then the Black Coats would be unstoppable."

"I have already forestalled Dragone. The All-Father does not view failure lightly. Dragone will find it prudent to leave Europe. There is another threat to our espionage enterprise. Our clients in Berlin have been careless. One of their couriers was apprehended by the Second Bureau. The resulting inquiry threatens me as well as my operative inside the Bureau."

"A modern version of Jeanne Valois de la Motte must appease the authorities, Gloria."

"Someone needs to *pay the law*."

Nemo was referencing a term popular in the Black Coats. "Pay the law" meant offering a dupe to the police to take responsibility for a crime.

"I have the perfect candidate, Jim."

Lucien Gévrol was a broad muscular man. Darlla conferred with him in the headquarters of the Second Bureau.

"When can I look through your files on known Nihilists residing in France?"

"You can start accessing them today."

"Thank you. If you ever need my cooperation, you have only to ask for it."

"Mademoiselle Rassendyll, there is a delicate situation in which you could be invaluable."

"Please elaborate."

"A serious breach of security exists. Recently we captured a courier of the German government. Under interrogation, he admitted that his mission in France was to purchase valuable military documents. The courier's contact was a woman. She acts as a go-between for the Germans and an unnamed informant inside the Bureau. For precautionary reasons, the courier's superiors did not entrust him with the woman's name. She was expected to contact him. In order to accept her identification, he was given a partial description. Her first name contains six letters and ends in an 'a.' Her last name contains four letters and concludes with a 't.' Additionally the entire name is an English alias that obscures the woman's true ancestry."

"Were you able to trace this Englishwoman?"

"Our suspicions focus on a socialite known as Gloria Scot. She frequently attends gatherings of the wealthy although her source of income remains unknown."

"Do you have any idea where she is meeting the traitor?"

"Possibly the Paris Opera House. She attended a performance there the night before we captured the courier. She will be attending the Opera tonight. I have instructed one of our best men to follow her there. Recently transferred from our Vienna office, my agent would not be familiar to the traitor. He should be accompanied to the Opera by a woman."

"I understand, Monsieur Gévrol. You're apprehensive that the traitor might recognize one of your regular female agents. You wish to employ my services because I am an outsider."

"Exactly. If you agree to assist me, there is one condition. We are dealing with secrets of the highest nature. You must not speak of these matters to Inspector Lefèvre or any other member of the police."

"I accept your restrictions. Is there a photograph of Gloria Scot?"

Gévrol showed Darlla a picture of a radiant blonde woman in her mid-thirties.

"May I keep this?" asked Darlla.

"No, it can't leave this office."

Darlla returned the photograph to Gévrol. He then left the room and returned with a brown-haired man.

"Mademoiselle Rassendyll, this gentleman will be your companion at the Opera tonight." asserted Gévrol.

"My name is Jean Lamotte," acknowledged the newcomer.

Before embarking on their mission, Darlla and Jean dined together. The redhead found the secret agent to be charming and debonair. She was strongly attracted to him.

Darlla and Jean sat in a private box at the Paris Opera that evening. They observed Gloria Scot, dressed in a stylish purple gown, as she sat in an adjacent box with a man who bore a large cane. Jean identified the man as Léonard Scot. He was allegedly Gloria's brother, but Jean harbored the belief that they were actually lovers.

After the performance concluded, Darlla and Jean spied on Gloria and Léonard as they left their box. Darlla and her associate followed their twin quarry. As they reached the main lobby of the Opera House, Gloria and Léonard veered into a side door.

"They're headed for the basement. It's a maze down there. They must be meeting the traitor."

Darlla and Jean also entered the basement. After an eternity of wandering through dark corridors, they finally reached a large underground lake underneath the Opera House. This lake had been discovered by architect Charles Garnier when he built the foundations of the Opera House in the 1860's.

Near the edge of the lake, Darlla and Jean saw Gloria and Léonard receiving documents from a man wearing a black silk hood. Jean removed a gun from the pocket of his coat.

"You're under arrest!" shouted Jean.

The trio of conspirators raised their hands in the air. Darlla approached the masked man.

"Let us see your true face."

Darlla pulled off the mask. The visage beneath belonged to Lucien Gévrol.

"Jean, you may recall that I supplied you with the gun that you're holding," remarked Gévrol. "Its firing pin is defective. It won't shoot."

"But this gun will," proclaimed Gloria removing a twin barreled derringer from her small purse. She shot Jean through the heart.

"No!" screamed Darlla as she leaped at Gloria. The second bullet in the derringer fired harmlessly into the air. Gloria fell backwards with Darlla on top of her. After they hit the ground, Darlla punched Gloria in the face. Her hands gripped Gloria's throat

Léonard drew a concealed sword from his cane. He grabbed the top of Darlla's hair and put the blade of his sword against her throat.

"Release Gloria or I'll slit your throat!"

Darlla relinquished her hold on Gloria's neck. Léonard pulled Darlla away from the murderess. Gévrol assisted the stunned blonde in rising from the ground. Gloria's hand rubbed against her lower lip.

"You drew blood, Rassendyll. I was going to kill you quickly like Lamotte. Now I will make you endure a lingering death."

"Why did you and Gévrol engage in this masquerade?" asked Darlla.

"We need to *pay the law* with two victims. You and your late escort were condemned by your names," crackled Gloria. "I couldn't resist the temptation to entrap Lamotte. His name was too reminiscent of Jeanne Valois de La Motte, the female scapegoat from the Queen's Necklace Affair. Jean Lamotte will be fed to the government as the turncoat inside the Bureau. "

"The story about the German courier was true, Mademoiselle Rassendyll," volunteered Gévrol. "You can easily be portrayed as the courier's contact. You're a woman with an English name. Your first name contains six letters and ends in an 'a.' "

"Imagine if your parents had employed a single 'l' in the spelling of your first name," Gloria speculated. "Five letters would have exonerated you."

"You slipped up," argued Darlla. "My last name doesn't have four letters concluding in a 't.' "

"You've forgotten your stage name. It was Kent, your mother's maiden name. I researched your background after you foiled my attempt to kill Antoine Dragone."

"You were behind that outrage!"

"It was Lucien who put me in touch with the Nihilists. Infiltrating the Bureau has its advantages. I have access to all their data on foreign exiles. The Nihilists massacre rather well."

"You have the soul of a devil."

"Such religious talk. I assume that you were baptized. As you were baptized at the start of your life, so shall there be a fitting baptism at its end."

Gévrol extracted s series of shackles from a sack that had been lying on the ground. He put a pair of handcuffs on Darlla's wrists. He encased her ankles in leg irons connected to a large ball and chain.

"We will move Lamotte's body to another portion of the Opera House's cellars," predicted Gévrol. "These documents will be planted on him. My official investigation will conclude that you and Lamotte were partners. You murdered him during a quarrel over the spoils of your combined treason. Your disappearance will prompt everyone to conclude that you fled the country."

"You could have snatched victory from the jaws of defeat," ridiculed Gloria. "You effectively rendered me *hors de combat* with your fist. If you had then turned your attention to disabling Léonard and Lucien, you could have triumphed. Instead you tried to throttle me. They always say that redheads are prone to fits of violent passion."

Gloria stroked Darlla's hair in feigned affection. The blonde waved the ring with the golden ram symbol defiantly in her rival's face.

"Before you perish, Rassendyll, heed these words of advice. If a god of the Netherworld ever permits your soul to return from Hell, be a more worthy opponent next time!"

Gloria pushed the enchained Darlla into the lake. The metal ball caused her to sink rapidly. Water congested her lungs. Her mind drifted into oblivion.

With Lucien and Léonard carrying Lamotte's corpse, Gloria departed from the scene.

She never saw the cloaked figure who detached himself from the shadows. He leaped in the water. Swimming downward, he found Darlla Rassendyll. He removed a lock pick from his black jacket. He opened Darlla's leg irons. The phantom rescuer carried the unconscious Darlla to the surface of the lake. He placed her form gently on the shore. He left her to retrieve a gondola which was hidden further down the edge of the lake. Placing the slumbering Darlla inside, the apparition paddled the gondola across the water.

Darlla found herself lying on a bed in a small room. A candle on a table illuminated her surroundings. Standing over her was a figure clothed in a black suit and cape. A red hood covered his entire head. Yellow eyes gazed at Darlla through the mask.

"Am I in Hell?"

"No, Darlla Rassendyll, you are still underneath the Paris Opera House. This room forms part of my home. I am Erik."

"Your home?"

"I was originally a native of Normandy. Years ago, I left France to travel throughout Asia. I mastered many arts—architecture, music and assassination."

"Assassination!"

"Life has always been governed by death. You should know that dark truth from your recent experience. I made a considerable fortune as a hired killer. The Thugs of India, the pirates of Indochina and the Afghan priests of Erlik Khan have been among my mentors. My patrons have included the Shah of Persia and the Sultan of Turkey. Eventually I returned to France and retired from my bloodthirsty career. As a sub-contractor for Garnier's great masterpiece, I constructed this clandestine retreat. You are wondering about my mask. If you saw my true face, you would understand my reasons for solitude. I was born with a hideous countenance."

"I was drowning. How did I survive?"

"I secretly watched your confrontation with the blonde woman and her allies. When they left, I fished you out of the lake."

"You just stood there and did nothing! Why didn't you interfere! Jean could still be alive!"

"You ungrateful wench! There was nothing that I could have done to save him! You would be dead if not for me! I merit your gratitude! Not your scorn!"

"I'm sorry. I must leave. I need to return to police headquarters."

"That is impossible. You have been comatose for three days. Much has happened in your absence."

Erik handed Darlla a pack of recent newspapers. They all reported the discovery of Lamotte's corpse. Gloria Scot's scheme had reached fruition. Gévrol had used his influence to brand Darlla both a murderess and a traitor.

"As you can see, Darlla Rassendyll, your departure will only result in your arrest and inevitable execution. There is an escape route from your current plight."

"What are you proposing?"

"I want you to become one of my two Disciples. I am well into middle-age and wish to leave a legacy. My desire is to train two people with the special talents that I have learned in my wanderings. One will be a Disciple of Life. I intend to train a woman to be the greatest opera singer of all time. She will be the embodiment of my love of music."

"You could never transform me into this ideal woman. I was always a bad singer. When I performed a small part in *Faust* inside this very Opera House, I was lambasted by the critics."

"I saw the performance. Leon Fauchery's column rightly skewered you for vocally imitating a frog."

"Due to your low opinion of my musical talents, you must hope to adopt me as your other Disciple."

"I initially envisioned that personage to be a man, but the possibility of a woman in the role intrigues me. My other adherent will be a Disciple of Death. I will implant in this individual all my lethal skills. My substantial wealth will also fund this individual in missions of vengeance. I have traveled the path of destruction for too long. If I transmit my knowledge of assassination to another, then perhaps I can purge my soul of these dark desires."

"You talk as if you're transferring a supernatural curse to me. Does your proposal have any conditions?"

"First, you must never try to remove my mask. Second, you must be willing to dislodge people who wander too close to my abode. Too many drunken patrons wander recklessly around the cellars during gala evenings."

"I will not kill for you!"

"I'm not asking you to take their lives. You can merely render them unconscious and then deposit in some distant corner of the Opera House."

"Are there any other conditions?"

"The third and final condition is that you must never hamper my efforts to create a Disciple of Life. Let me be brutally frank. I am quite willing to exterminate anyone who interferes in that great endeavor. You may be agreeing to condone murder."

"And if I refuse your proposal? Would you kill me to prevent my divulging your existence?"

Erik chuckled. "Your reputation has been so blackened that no one would believe your ramblings of a rescue by a masked man. If you decline, I will not hamper your departure. The life of a hounded fugitive will be punishment enough for a foolhardy refusal."

Darlla contemplated quietly for several minutes before answering.

"I accept."

Many weeks of arduous training followed. Erik instructed Darlla in the lethal Punjabi lasso and the Pickaxe of Burial. She learned how to employ a long weed as a snorkel under water. Darlla navigated through the labyrinth that Erik had constructed in the Opera House. Erik taught Darlla the art of throwing and catching .knives. The technique of blending into the darkness by wearing dark clothing was demonstrated. She learned to modulate her voice in order to sound like a ghost-like male apparition.

One day Erik presented Darlla with a black costume consisting of a mask, a shirt, pants and boots. She was also given a cape and a large felt hat.

"Everyone will think that I'm a man, Erik."

"Your enemy must never discern the reason for your animosity. Gloria Scot must never discover that you were once Darlla Rassendyll. Examine the cowl."

Darlla held a black hood that had the design of a small red skull on the forehead

"What's the purpose of this emblem?"

"I have long been an admirer of Poe's *The Masque of the Red Death*, Disciple. It's my tribute to a master of the macabre."

"I will need to disguise my hands."

"Wear any of the special gloves that I tested earlier. They are all red and match the skull crest."

Erik was referring to two different pairs of gloves that secreted chemicals. One pair gave forth chemicals that created a blinding flash when combined. The other pair released chemicals that would combust into flames minutes later.

"We are about to have a special guest. You must have wondered how information is received from the outside. I have a friend who sometimes functions as my agent. I let him visit here on occasion. I always take the precaution of blindfolding him before escorting him to my home. Only you and I know all the hidden passageways."

"Does your comrade have a name?"

"He prefers to be addressed as El Hichmakani."

"Is he an Arab?"

No, he's a Persian. He was once a *daroga*, a sort of police chief in the Shah's employ. Due to our friendship, he disobeyed a royal edict to execute me. For his disobedience, the Shah exiled him."

"Can he be trusted with my true identity?"

"No, he espouses a philosophy that questions the wisdom of vengeance. We'll use him to test the effectiveness of your male impersonation. You will need to pin your hair to fit entirely under the hood. Please retreat to your sanctum to put the final touches to your disguise. I will ring the bell when your presence is warranted."

Darlla retreated to a special room that Erik had given her. After making the final touches to her apparel, Erik's pupil amused herself playing with a disappearing ink provided by Erik. She wrote the name of the object of her hatred: GLORIA SCOT. As the words vanished, an inspiration quickly possessed Darlla. She wrote down another name: CAGLIOSTRO. Gloria Scot was an anagram of Cagliostro! The motive for the immolation of the Chateau of Wax was unveiled. Gloria Scot was really Joséphine Balsamo, Countess Cagliostro. Her wax effigy needed to be destroyed. The resulting publicity surrounding her earlier espionage in 1870 could have endangered her current schemes. Jaraud mentioned that Joséphine Balsamo was an immortal with the appearance of a woman in her mid-twenties. Gloria was clearly over thirty. These stories of an immortal Countess were pure hogwash. Joséphine had merely pretended to be an ageless sorceress in 1870. Perhaps there was a Joséphine Balsamo really born in 1788, but she couldn't possibly be Gloria. Darlla conjectured that Gloria might be the granddaughter of the original Countess Cagliostro.

The bell rang in her room. Darlla put on her hat and opened the door. Standing next to her Erik was a swarthy man wearing an astrakhan cap. His brilliant green eyes narrowed.

"Who are you?" demanded El Hichmakani.

"I am the Man in the Felt Hat," responded Darlla in a masculine voice. "I am Erik's Disciple of Death."

"Then you're a fool. Do you hope to slaughter the innocent?"

"No! I hope to avenge the persecuted."

El Hichmakani turned towards his host.

"This is madness, Erik. Now that you found a man to act as your Disciple of Death, what's your next project? Abducting some poor girl to be remolded into your Disciple of Life?"

"Don't you have faith in your old friend from Mazenderan?" pleaded Erik.

"The safest way of life is still to doubt," pronounced El Hichmakani.

"Enough of your Sufi moralizing!" roared Erik. "Disciple, remove this man from my presence."

Darlla hesitated before obeying Erik's command. She delivered a sharp blow to the Persian's neck. As he lost consciousness, El Hichmakani fell into her arms.

Holding the slumbering philosopher, Darlla looked to Erik for guidance.

"Is there any special place that you wish me to deposit him?"

"Take the secret passageway to the manager's office."

"But the office will be locked for the rest of the night. When he wakes up, no one will open it to free him until the morning."

"El Hichmakani can waste his time composing poetry."

"Won't the Opera employees wonder how he got there?"

"They're a superstitious lot who visualize me as a mischievous ghost, Disciple. There will attribute his materialization to one of my so-called supernatural pranks."

The next night, Box #5 of the Paris Opera House was officially vacant. This was not true. The managers had received an ultimatum years ago to reserve the box for their resident ghost. The frightened managers had always complied. To the rest of the spectators, Box #5 seemed dark and unoccupied. They were mistaken. Erik and Darlla were seated in the shadows watching the performance.

Darlla was wearing her mask, but not the rest of her costume. Tonight she was celebrating her femininity by wearing a black dress. Impressed by his pupil's progress, Erik had given Darlla a corsage of roses. It decorated her right wrist. Erik was extremely gracious tonight.

"Disciple, would you want a footstool?"

"No thank you, Erik, my feet are fine. There is something else that you can bestow on me: a more dramatic title than the Man in the Felt Hat. It's a very dull name."

"Gloria joked about your returning from the dead. In a metaphorical sense, you have. The resurrected dead are called revenants. You are henceforth the Revenant."

An idea floated into Erik's brain. He had long desired a mate. His original plan had been to make his bride the future Disciple of Life. Perhaps he should grant this honor to his Disciple of Death. Erik quickly dismissed the idea. Darlla did not fulfill his vision of an ideal woman. Her voice alone disqualified her

"You need to recruit a surrogate to be your principal agent outside the Opera House."

"Why only one? Several agents will be preferable."

"A personal spy network. You are extremely ambitious, Disciple. Concentrate on a single recruit for now. I recommend that you emulate Vautrin, the real-life policeman fictionalized by Balzac."

" Not exactly a compelling role model, Erik. Vautrin was actually a criminal before joining the forces of law and order."

"True, but an ingenious strategist in his illegal period. He once prevented a poet from committing suicide by drowning. Vautrin made the man a pawn by offering him a reason to live. You must locate a similar unfortunate dealt a disastrous hand by fate."

Henri Jaraud wandered the streets of New York. Both he and Antoine Dragone had fled France for America in the wake of the ruin of the Chateau of Wax. Dragone had hoped that Jaraud would continue their partnership, but the sculptor had severed all his ties with the Corsican. He would find another financial backer for a wax museum. The schism between the former partners had nothing to do with their debate concerning the horrific aspects of the exhibits. The origin of their feud was Julia Orsini. Jaraud had fallen in love with the young girl, but she had eyes only for Dragone. Just as Dragone had exploited Jaraud's genius, the handsome businessman had shamefully manipulated Julia. The consequences of the fire had prompted Dragone to desert Julia in order to romance a rich American heiress from Baltimore. The fruits of Dragone's romance had been the acquisition of financial backing for a new wax museum in the United States. Jaraud had attempted to comfort the heartbroken Julia. He even proposed marriage to her. She had refused, and the distraught Jaraud left France. Entering a local church, he muttered a prayer for the welfare of Julia Orsini. What would happen to the girl alone and friendless in Paris?

It was long past midnight when Julia approached the railway track. She was determined to end her life. She once read the newspaper account of a Russian aristocrat who committed suicide by throwing herself in the path of a locomotive. Julia knew the train schedules. A train should be coming by in five minutes. She stooped forward and rested her neck on the edge of the rail. It was universally believed in France that decapitation was a swift and merciful death.

Julia heard the roar of the train. She closed her eyes and waited for the impact. Hands grabbed her shoulders and pulled her away from the track. Julia found herself being held by a masked personage wearing a dark cloak and hat.

Julia struggled to break the grip of her captor as the train speedily passed by.

"Let me go! I want to die! I want to die!"

"You have been reprieved, Julia Orsini!" decreed a guttural voice.

"I have nothing to live for! My family has disowned me! My lover has deserted me! I want to die!"

"What about the people who perished in the fire at the Chateau of Wax! Did they want to die?"

Julia burst into tears.

"Three of them were my friends. There's nothing that I can do for them."

"You can avenge their deaths!"

Since the train had moved safely away. The dark figure released Julia. The young Corsican turned to face her rescuer.

"What sort of man are you?"

"I am the Revenant of the Shadows!"

"The Shadows?"

"The Shadows of Death hang over us all. They are the great equalizers dispensing justice."

"Who caused the fire?"

"A woman whose face is known to you!"

"What woman?"

"Did not Jaraud show you his last figure?"

"Countess Cagliostro! Then the legends are true. She's immortal!"

"The legends are false. She's a charlatan."

"But Jarred showed me the ring that he had duplicated for the figure. It bore the golden ram crest of the Cagliostros!"

The Revenant recalled Gloria Scot's ring. Julia's comments confirmed the Revenant's speculations about Gloria's origins.

"It is merely a family heirloom that she inherited. The Countess is no sorceress! Like a snake, she has adopted a new skin. She answers now to the name of Gloria Scot. "

"Cagliostro must pay for the evil that she had sowed!" pledged Julia.

"I will grant you vengeance if you accept my tutelage!"

"I'll do whatever you want!"

"Kneel before me, Julia Orsini!"

As Julia knelt, the cloaked apparition's gloved hands touched the supplicant's shoulders. The Revenant looked upwards to the sky.

"We are the Acolytes of the Shadows! We are the dispensers of justice! We are the punishers of the guilty! We are the executioners of the sinful!"

The Revenant then looked down into Julia's eyes.

"You were born Julia Orsini. As an Acolyte of the Shadows, you must adopt a new name. Just as I, the Supreme Acolyte, call myself the Revenant, you must choose a name that strikes fear into the souls of the wicked."

"I chose the Latin word for judge…Judex!"

"Arise, Lady Judex! You have a new mission!"

Outside the office of the Second Bureau, Gévrol was returning from lunch at a nearby restaurant. He brushed by a bearded man with a cane.

"Gloria will meet you tomorrow at Bozzo-Corona's tomb," whispered Léonard. "Be there at eight o'clock."

Gévrol nodded his head in acknowledgement. He was quite confident that no one overheard his associate. The only other person nearby was a young girl selling flowers. She was too far away to catch any words.

Some hours later, the same flower girl entered a building in the Rue de Provence. She proceeded to a locked office that was marked with a simple nameplate: "A. L. Lard." The girl slipped a note through a slot in the door and then departed. Returning to the boarding house where she resided, the girl went to bed.

The same evening, a cloaked figure prowled the halls of the same building. The shadowy visitor opened the door with a key and picked up the envelope.

"Lady Judex!" summoned a harsh voice.

The flower girl instantly awoke in her bed.

"You read my message."

"Your written report was extremely profuse in its details. Why did you request a personal meeting?! Explain!"

"You must be planning to ambush Gloria when she meets with Gévrol. I want to be there when you kill Cagliostro!"

"Your performance as a lip-reader is admirable, but you lack the skills to combat Gloria Scot. Request denied!"

"I served you faithfully! I watched Lucien Gévrol for days! I recognized Léonard Scot from your description! I am not your slave! I deserve to be treated as an equal!"

"Request denied!"

"I'm not the fool that you take me for! Drop the charade! You're no more a ghost than you are a man! You are Darlla Rassendyll!"

The Revenant was astonished by this disclosure.

"How did you learn the truth?" mumbled Darlla using her real voice.

"There is one flaw in your disguise. When you raise your head during my initiation as an Acolyte, your neck was exposed. A woman has a much smaller larynx than a man. Your lack of a pronounced Adam's apple divulged your true sex. Your cowl needs to be redesigned more like a hood. It has to have a piece that slips under the chin and covers the neck. I designed costumes at the wax museum. I knotted this for you."

Julia handed Darlla a black hood bearing the red skull crest.

"I accept your gift. I understand how you deduced my sex but not my identity."

"A. L. Lard, your alias on the office door, .is an anagram of Darlla. I heard at the hospital that a woman named Darlla Rassendyll had been visiting me during my delirium. Before his departure for New York, Jaraud mentioned that you had rescued Antoine during the fire. You became rather infamous when the papers painted you as a traitor."

"Do you doubt my innocence?"

"No. Being from Corsica, I know the true nature of the evil that you are opposing."

"Explain."

"What did you know of Colonel Bozzo-Corona?"

"Upon his death in 1842, he was venerated as a philanthropist. Later evidence linked him to many criminal societies."

"Those societies are beholden to the Black Coats. We know of these monsters in Corsica. Their trademark is to fool the police into arresting the innocent. Bozzo-Corona was their leader, their All-Father. Some say that he never truly died. He still haunts Corsica."

"If an All-Father currently exists, I suspect he's no more immortal than Countess Cagliostro."

"Regardless of the myths surrounding the Black Coats, you'll need my help to combat them tomorrow."

"I have talents that you haven't even glimpsed. I may have underestimated your intelligence, but your fighting skills are another matter. You would be more a liability than an asset at the cemetery. Request denied!"

Near a mausoleum at the Père-Lachaise cemetery, Gloria Scot was waiting. The monument had gold letters bearing this inscription: "*Here lies Colonel Bozzo-Corona, Benefactor of the Poor. Pray that his soul may rest in peace.*" The form of Lucien Gévrol moved towards the tomb. A briefcase was in the spy's right hand. As Gévrol greeted Gloria, a cloud of smoke erupted near the Colonel's tomb. As the smoke dissipated, a tall figure in a black coat emerged. His head bore a black top hat. The bottom of his face was shrouded in a black scarf.

"Are you the Colonel?" inquired Gévrol. "The All-Father?"

"The reigning All-Father is an impostor," dictated the man with the black scarf. "I am the legitimate heir of the Colonel. I am Jim Nemo, Lord of the Night."

Gévrol laughed before replying.

"Your theatrics are entertaining, but unimpressive. A smoke bomb is a mere magician's trick. Your *nom de guerre* of Nemo is uninspired. I know my Latin, Monsieur 'Nobody.' You speak with an English accent. Your title of Lord of the Night implies a connection with the Gentlemen of the Night, the London branch of the Black Coats. I assume you derived the Nemo pseudonym from *Bleak House* by Charles Dickens."

"Your comments are astute, Monsieur Gévrol," noted Nemo. "When you informed Gloria that you insisted on meeting her superior, I sought to test your intelligence. Forgive my little farce. Too many of my subordinates are distracted by illusions and meaningless ceremonies. I prefer to be served by practical men of ambition."

"Money is no longer enough to satisfy my desires, Monsieur Nemo. I crave power!"

"And I will grant it. Your new merchandise will consolidate an alliance between my forces and the most formidable military power in Europe. You will be my chief lieutenant in France."

Gévrol opened his briefcase. He removed a folder of papers.

"These are the complete mobilization plans of the French army.'"

A caped figure detached itself from the shadows of the graveyard. The enigmatic creature waved a large knife.

"Die, Cagliostro!" yelled the spectre of the night.

Gloria seized the knife-wielding wrist of her attacker. She slammed the assailant into the wall of the mausoleum. A black felt hat dropped off the intruder's head. Gloria's enemy fell unconscious to the ground. The blonde picked up the knife of her vanquished nemesis.

"Let me see the face of the man who has interrupted our meeting," ordained Nemo.

Grabbing her unconscious foe from behind, she raised the defeated aggressor to face Nemo.

"A red skull insignia," commented the Lord of the Night.

"We're dealing with a woman," concluded Gloria. Her left arm gripped the masked woman across the chest. Gloria raised the dagger in her right hand. "She tried to kill me. I demand satisfaction."

"Delay your revenge," decreed Nemo. "Lucien, remove the mask."

Lucien lifted his hand towards the face of the hooded woman. Before he could touch the mask, a noose fell over his head. The rope tightened cross his neck as he fell backwards

"No one move!" shouted the Revenant as she leaped out of the darkness. Her right hand held the end of the noose. Her left hand held a pistol.

"And now a male intruder," interjected Nemo. "From your garb, Monsieur, I assume that you are the mate of the prisoner."

"I am the Revenant of the Shadows. I am the Disciple of Death. Release my Acolyte."

"Let me applaud your expertise with the Punjabi lasso. The techniques of Thuggee are not unknown to me. I gather that Gévrol's neck is broken."

"Cease your banter! Release the prisoner!"

"Gloria's knife is pressing against the neck of your Acolyte. A bullet might not prevent the severing of her jugular vein."

"But my bullets will definitely dispatch both you and Gloria to Hell."

"I'm banking that you value your Acolyte's safety more than our deaths. You're bluffing."

"We seem to be in a stalemate," declared Gloria. "I suggest a compromise. We stroll together to the cemetery's gates where my coach awaits. There we will surrender your Acolyte in exchange for our freedom."

"Agreed!" vowed the Revenant.

"There is one more condition, Revenant, hand Monsieur Nemo the documents that Gévrol dropped when he expired."

The Revenant released the noose to lift the papers from the ground. Her gloved hand presented them to Nemo.

"For a Disciple of Death, you put a high premium on human life," taunted Gloria.

The various combatants marched toward the gates .Julia remained asleep as Gloria dragged her. A four-wheeled carriage manned by Léonard was awaiting them. Nemo opened the coach door. Gloria withdrew the knife from Julia's throat. As the Revenant breathed a sigh of relief, Gloria pushed Julia's body against the Revenant's left arm pushing her gun aside. Gloria threw the knife at the Revenant's heart.

The Revenant caught the hilt with her right hand before the point of the blade hit her chest. Erik's lessons in knife-catching had saved her life. Nemo and Gloria leaped into the carriage. Under Léonard's command, it pulled away rapidly. The Revenant let the senseless Julia drop to the ground. She raised her gun and fired three times, but the vehicle was out of range.

As the four-wheeler raced into the night, Nemo perused the papers.

"Gévrol's death was a misfortune, Gloria, but we have secured the key to the mastery of Europe."

The Lord of the Night screamed. The papers burst into flames. He threw the burning documents out of the window.

"Jim! Your hand!"

"Merely minor burns. I will recover. The Revenant outwitted us. That masked man used an old Thuggee trick. He secretly rubbed the papers with a chemical that caused them to ignite minutes later."

The Revenant had used Erik's special chemical-secreting gloves in order to contaminate the documents just before delivering them to Nemo.

Back at the cemetery, the Revenant sought to revive Julia. The Corsican girl finally woke up.

"What happened?"

"You miserable bungler!" scolded the Revenant. Darlla Rassendyll spoke not in the manly tones of her alter ego voice, but with her real voice. "I was waiting patiently to launch an assault before you blundered into the open! Both Nemo and Cagliostro escaped due to your meddling!"

"Forgive me! I wanted to…"

"I will not listen to your excuses! You deliberated disobeyed my orders! You created a duplicate of my costume without my permission! You must never wear that travesty again! Your mistakes will be forgiven, but not forgotten! You have seen the fruits of your defiance! If you are to continue as my Acolyte, you must swear now to follow my instructions faithfully!"

"I swear!"

"Come with me, Lady Judex. You must bear witness to a ritual."

The Revenant led Julia back to the mausoleum and pointed at Gévrol's corpse.

"Behold the corpse of a betrayer,"

The Disciple of Death removed her lasso from Gévrol's neck. She then ripped open his shirt. With Julia's knife, the Revenant cut a "V" in the flesh of the dead man's shoulder.

"*Voleur!*" gasped Julia. "The mark of the thief!"

"An appropriate badge of dishonor, Judex. He stole many things including the life of Jean Lamotte."

Darlla Rassendyll raised the knife to the sky.

"Let this cadaver be a warning to Cagliostro! I will one day carve the same mark on her lifeless carcass!"

1900. After his father's suicide three years earlier, young Jacques de Trémeuse—now 17—struggles on how best to gain revenge on the banker Favraux who ruined his family. He has not yet become Judex, and indeed, other far more sinister paths suddenly open before him. Will he have the strength of spirit to turn away from the dark side and embrace his true vocation...?

Matthew Dennion: *The Quality of Vengeance*

> *"Please allow me to introduce myself,*
> *I'm a man of wealth and taste."*
> Mick Jagger

He jabbed the pen onto the paper with disgust as he completed the last word of the document. His hand hit it with such force that the lone candle in his bedroom wavered and nearly blew out, causing a shade to flash across the room.

Jacques de Trémeuse folded his hand in front of his face and reviewed the information he had collected: over 100,000 people financially ruined, 9 people wrongly convicted for crimes they did not commit, 29 suicides, 15 people burned to death as a result of arson at the Universal Funds building, and the ruin of his own family. These were the crimes that his months of investigations had connected to the banker Favraux.

Jacques pounded the table in anger, and swore once more on his father's soul that Favraux would not go unpunished for these crimes. He stood up and nearly fell over as the room spun around him. He grabbed the back of his chair to steady himself, and reflected that he had not slept in two days. He stumbled over to his bed and crashed down into it. He noticed a chill in the room and pulled a blanket over himself. He closed his eyes with his mind fixed on revenge as he drifted to sleep.

Jacques could see both himself and Favraux in his dream. He was standing in the middle of the room while the banker sat behind his desk in his office counting the money he had stolen from his clients. The banker laughed as he placed each shimmering gold coin on his desk. The anger over all of the people the banker had forced into poverty began to swell in Jacques's breast. He cursed Favraux and, suddenly, felt a surge of power course through him.

As Jacques's anger grew, a dark cloud began to swirl around and expand outward enveloping the room. He stared at the banker, who stood up from his desk, surprised by the sudden darkness. Jacques focused his attention on the coins and smiled as one of them slowly rose off of the desk. It hovered in mid-air. The banker stood still, awed by what he was witnessing.

33

The levitating coin slowly began to spin and then shot forward like a bullet burying itself into Favraux's shoulder. The banker howled in pain as a second coin rose from the desk and tore through his arm.

Jacques felt no remorse as every coin on the table rose and began to shred his nemesis to pieces.

The banker fell to his knees in pain.

From the corner of the room, Jacques saw a cloaked figure emerge from the darkness. The figure glared at Jacques with a look that burned him to his very soul.

Jacques sat up in bed, composed himself, and then pulled his blanket across his body. The night was exceedingly colder than he had realized.

The following night, Jacques entered his bedroom, and was immediately hit by a cold draft. He was exhausted and frustrated from his experience with the Parisian Police. He had foolishly assumed that, once he showed them the evidence he had collected, they would arrest Favraux and place him on trial. He was shocked when the police had dismissed him as if he were a raving madman. Their comments still echoed in his head. All of Favraux's financial transactions were legal. The banker's handling of his client's money was ethically questionable, but there was nothing about it that contravened any regulations. As for the evidence connecting Favraux to the arson at the Universal Funds building, it was purely circumstantial.

The police smirked when Jacques brought the suicides to their attention. They bluntly stated that Favraux could not be blamed if these weak-willed people had taken their own lives. Jacques broke out in a fit of anger and was removed from the police station.

Jacques kicked over his chair, and punched the wall. The law may not hold Favraux accountable for his actions, but he found him responsible for the suffering of thousands. He lay down and saw his breath freeze in midair. He closed his eyes and drifted off to sleep.

In his dream, he saw himself and Favraux standing atop the observation deck of the Eiffel Tower. A cold wind whipped across the tower as the two men gazed down from the monument. At the base of the tower, they could see the bodies of the people who had committed suicide as a result of the losses they had suffered due to Favraux's theft. The banker gazed unconcernedly at the corpses. Jacques's spark of anger grew into a blaze.

Once more he felt a surge of power swell within him and was enveloped in a cloud of darkness. Jacques lifted his hands upwards and watched as Favraux's arms imitated his motion. Jacques swung his arms from side to side and fluttered his fingers. Jacques every movement caused Favraux's body to move against his will. Jacques was the marionettiste and Favraux his puppet.

He began to direct Favraux to walk to the end of the observation deck. When the banker realized what was happening, he begged Jacques to spare his

34

life. The young man thought of all the bodies lying at the base of the tower, and how each of them must have pleaded with the banker to spare them as he ruined their lives. Jacques' face twisted into a sneer as he continued to direct Favraux to the edge of the platform.

When the banker reached the ledge, tears rolled down his face and he continued to beg for mercy. Jacques was about to direct him to jump off the monument when he saw the cloaked figure approaching him from across the platform. Jacques stood still as the figure walked up to him, placed its hand on his right shoulder, and pointed across Jacques's body.

Jacques turned to his left and saw a horrid creature standing next to him. The abomination had the head of feline and the body of man, with massive bat like wings protruding from his back. Jacques screamed when he realized the creature's claw-like hand rested on his shoulder.

Jacques awoke and found that his room was freezing. Despite the cold, Jacques was sweating profusely.

Several days later, Jacques was exhausted. He hadn't slept or left his ice-cold bedroom since his last dream. His body ached, and any attempt at eating resulted in horrible vomiting. Jacques looked at himself in the mirror. His face was pale and scars were beginning to appear across it. His eyes had changed color and become sunken in his skull. The physical anguish he was in did nothing to change his mental state. His mind remained fixed on exacting revenge on Favraux.

He knew that his dreams were more than just his mind processing information about the crimes the banker had committed. The figures in his dreams were trying to tell him something about how to punish Favraux. Jacques resigned himself to finding an answer of how to carry out his crusade. He climbed into bed and closed his eyes for the last time.

Jacques found himself with Favraux standing amid the inferno that was the Universal Funds building burning to the ground. The fifteen men who died were pounding on doors and windows trying to escape, as heat burned their skin and smoke seared their lungs.

He watched as the ceiling collapsed on the men, setting their bodies aflame. While they burned, Jacques saw the darkness begin to form around him once more. Prepared for what he would see, he turned to his left and found the creature with its claw on his shoulder. The beast did not talk, and yet, somehow, Jacques could sense that it was communicating with him.

It was a demon called Pazuzu. It offered Jacques power—power enough to punish Favraux a hundred times over for his crimes.

Through Jacques, Pazuzu caused the burning corpses to rise from the flames. More than a dozen of them thus rose from the ground and stumbled toward the terrified banker.

Favraux fell, curled into a ball, and cried as the fiery corpses approached him. Each of them laid a burning hand on the banker, searing his flesh with every touch. The banker cried out in pain and Jacques smiled. He knew what Pazuzu was offering him. All of the dreams Jacques had experienced could become reality. Favraux could be made to suffer for each of his crimes individually. The demon had the power to make Favraux endure the pain he had caused others to the point of death—and beyond. Pazuzu could resurrect the banker night after night. He could suffer a terrible death and not enjoy the escape of the grave. Each death would only lead to more punishment. All of this, Pazuzu offered Jacques in exchange for his soul.

Jacques was reveling in the banker's despair as he considered the demon's offer. Then, he noticed the cloaked figure approaching him from the flames. It walked up to Jacques and removed his cloak.

Jacques' eyes filled with tears as he gazed upon the face of his father.

Pierre de Trémeuse placed his hand on his son's shoulder.

"My son, do not accept what this foul demon offers you," he said.

Jacques shook his head in disbelief.

"Father, he offers me the opportunity to make Favraux pay for what he did to all of those people!" he replied. "The demon offers me vengeance for what Favraux did to you!"

"My son, he offers you an empty vengeance at a very high price. The vengeance you seek must be your own, if it is to mean anything. Accepting this demon's offer will punish him, but it will not avenge our family. I offer you another choice, my son. It is a long and difficult path that will require much sacrifice. It will consume your life, but will save your soul, and the vengeance you extract will be truly yours. Not that of some demon from the pit."

When his father finished speaking, a plan formed in Jacques' mind. He saw himself infiltrating Favraux's home, destroying him from within, slowly, before finally ending the banker's life. He knew that the plan would take a few years to evolve, but, as his father said, the vengeance would be his own.

For a moment, Jacques weighed this course of action against the offer made by the demon. Then, he took a deep breath and pushed the demon into the blazing fire. After Pazuzu had returned to Hell, Jacques turned to his father and nodded, indicating that he understood the path he had chosen.

Suddenly, a light flashed before his eyes and he awoke. The room was warm and he felt invigorated. He could sense that the demon, his father, and even Jacques de Trémeuse, were gone.

All who remained was Judex.

Sometime between 1900 and 1910. Having made up his mind to become Judex, and inspired by his mother's fanatical devotion to revenge, Jacques proceeds to lay the foundations for his future crime-fighting career. This will take him on an extraordinary journey that will only reinforce his faith...

Emmanuel Gorlier: *Judex ab Chaos*

Jacques de Trémeuse lit his lantern and held it so it illuminated the stairs plunging into the darkness ahead of him.

The day before, he had purchased the ruins of Château-Rouge, a medieval redoubt overhanging the banks of the Seine and the surrounding countryside.

He had already explored the rest of the building, which did not offer great opportunities as far as accommodation was concerned. He thought, however, that the cellars would be better suited to conceal the secret facilities he planned to build. During the preliminary visit of the castle, which he had made with the solicitor a few days before, he had only seen the entrance to the cellars, but he had ascertained the existence of a series of large, deeper caves and tunnels that lay beyond. It all seemed very promising and he had been looking forward to exploring them in greater detail once he was the owner of the Château.

The stone staircase penetrated into the ground like a screw into wood. The stone steps were mostly regular and dry, despite some damp on the walls. After descending about three meters, Jacques entered the first cellar—the only one he had already visited. It was spacious, safe, and ideal for housing some of the scientific equipment he planned to order. It needed, however, to be cleaned of the clutter that filled it: dilapidated furniture, broken bottles, old firewood...

To the left, Jacques saw another, smaller, room that must have once been a storeroom or a wine cellar, and that could become a bedroom.

On the opposite side, a corridor led to a large room that could be turned into a series of cells if he decided to imprison his future foes.

To the right, another smaller storeroom could be used to keep the rest of the equipment.

The location seemed perfect for establishing a secret base from which he could safely undertake his vigilante activities.

Entering the smaller storeroom, Jacques noticed the remains of an old bookcase. He approached the piece of furniture which almost fell apart under his fingers, being completely rotten due to water infiltration.

Jacques's eye was then drawn to a different piece of wood that had appeared between the moldy, decomposing planks that made up the back of the bookcase. He slipped his hands between two of them and easily pried them apart, revealing a hidden door that had been concealed behind the bookcase.

It was a massive oak door, still in good condition, reinforced by a metal frame, with a large iron lock.

Jacques smiled at the challenge. He went to fetch a package from his car and returned a few minutes later. It contained a variety of small locksmith tools and some lubricant. In no time, he was able to open the secret door.

Behind it, he found a room filled with medieval-looking furniture. Given the dust, one could easily believe that no one had entered it for hundreds of years.

Long wooden chests had stood inviolate for centuries. Antique, gold-embroidered tapestries adorning the walls were likely worth a fortune. They all told the glorious history of a noble family, now all but forgotten.

In a corner of the room, a black metal armor caught Jacques's eye. The knight who had once worn this marvel must have been a colossus amongst men, as it was large and extremely heavy.

Above it, carved into the wall, a partially faded coat of arms showed a sword and a pair of scales, beneath a motto starting with the word "*Judex*," but the rest had been erased by time.

"*Judex!*" exclaimed Jacques, impressed.

Then he saw another door partially concealed by the tapestries on the right wall. He tried to open it, but it resisted, probably because of age. Eventually, he managed to open it and discovered a small room plunged in darkness. He stepped forward holding his lantern carefully to light the way.

Suddenly, he became dizzy. Trying to regain his balance, he stepped into the room. Far from making him feel better, this had the effect of forcing him to breathe in the stale and pungent atmosphere from inside. He fell to his knees. After flailing about for a few seconds, he fainted.

After what seemed a long time, Jacques slowly regained his senses. He got up painfully as if he had been dealt a blow to the head.

This is not the time to falter, he thought. *Today may be the most important day of my life, and I must be strong. I should have been careful when entering that room. I must have hit the door frame with my head.*

Still, he did not remember banging his head.

Jacques reentered the main room he had just left. But it now looked very different: it was brightly lit, clean, and all its furniture and tapestries seemed new, as if time had reversed its course.

Everything also seemed smaller, as if he had grown taller. The black armor against the wall was now his size.

Above it, the coat of arms was intact. It did indeed bear a sword and the scales of justice, and its motto was *Judex ab Chaos*, A Judge out of Chaos.

This sentence resonated with him and mingled with his own personal demons. Yes, the Judge would soon render justice and avenge his father...

Suddenly, he felt an alien thought in his mind which, surprisingly, echoed his own thoughts: *Yes... Avenge my father. I have waited for this moment for months...*

Jacques realized that he was no longer in control of his own body. For a start, it was bigger and stronger, dressed with a quilted, padded tunic. He walked towards a stool and put on the coat of chainmail that he found there.

The foreign thought continued:

Damn you, Enguerrand! You have dishonored my father and murdered my mother after subjecting her to the worst outrages. You have stolen my land and besmirched my name! For months, I have hunted you, killed your villainous vassals, destroyed your possessions, struck at your allies! Today, by attacking she who is promised to me, you finally gave me the opportunity to kill you. May the Lord be thanked!

Jacques was disturbed by these thoughts which so closely mirrored his own. After all, hadn't Favraux dishonored and caused the death of his father? Had he not decided to punish him in the most merciless fashion?

Meanwhile, his body approached the black armor and paused for a second to look at it.

This is the last time the Black Knight comes out, said the thought. *This afternoon, I shall have to reveal my identity in order to take part in the battle! I will remove this helmet and fulfill my destiny!*

The Black Knight? Jacques realized that his spirit now inhabited the body of a medieval knight, one who had once lived at Château-Rouge and was preparing for a fight... He wondered if he was dreaming!

The Black Knight began to don his armor.

Yolande, my beloved, your father's honor will not be tarnished like mine! When my friend Quentin Durward proposed this duel, Enguerrand could not refuse. He was even delighted! Your father is suspected of collusion with Charles the Bold, the Duke of Burgundy, the King of France's worst enemy. He can't expect any help from anyone at Court. Nobody would dare face the wrath of Louis XI. Nobody—except I, who saved his life and cannot be suspected of treason.

Helmet in hand, the Black Knight stepped through the front door and into a small chapel to the side. There, he knelt and prayed before the Cross:

O Lord, and you, too, Lady, grant me victory in this fight for the sake and the triumph of Justice.

Jacques understood that the Black Knight was going to face a trial by ordeal, otherwise known as God's Judgment. The cause of the winner would be recognized as just and true, blessed by the Will of God.

The Black Knight rose and walked along an underground tunnel that let out near a small stone farmhouse, where he had concealed his horse. This was the secret passage that allowed the castle's occupants to flee in case of a siege.

The Knight mounted his war horse, also armored in black, and trotted toward a nearby meadow where he knew that the King and his Court had set up their tents.

After a short ride, he saw the royal camp. The brightly-colored tents surrounded a clearing where the duel was to take place. Standing above all the other banners, unfurling in the breeze, was the royal standard of golden lilies on an azure field. King Louis XI had come to enjoy the defeat of Sigismond de Beauséjour, father of the Black Knight's fiancée, who was accused of felony and treason in favor of Burgundy.

Among the banners, the Black Knight saw that of Quentin Durward, his best friend, and that of Enguerrand de Sombreval, his arch-enemy.

From within the Knight's mind, Jacques watched the scene, transfixed. He did not understand why this was happening to him, but was beginning to think that it might have a hidden meaning, as if someone or something was trying to impart a message to him.

The noblemen were installed in a wide circle around the clearing. Surrounding that space, there were ten crossbowmen with orders to kill any combatant who might decide to flee or be guilty of a felonious act.

The royal herald sounded his horn and asked the prosecution to present its champion.

Enguerrand de Sombreval, dressed in a shining armor, appeared and bowed before the King, seeking to court his favor.

Louis XI, sitting on his throne, gave a smile that looked more like a grimace. He trusted no one, save for himself and the Virgin Mary, to whom he prayed every night, kneeling before the holy medals that he wore on his hat, in an image forever immortalized in history books.

The herald then called the champion for the defense. The King smirked, watching Sigismond de Beauséjour and his daughter Yolande, both sitting near the battlefield.

No one moved. Enguerrand threw the King a triumphant smile. Sigismond and Yolande looked on in anguish, as their fate was about to be sealed.

Suddenly, they heard the gallop of a horse, and the Black Knight entered the clearing. He came before the King and bowed. Louis XI frowned and made another grimace.

The armed men of Sombreval, recognizing the enemy who had plagued them for months, moved to attack him. But the Black Knight then raised his hand and said:

"Sire, I am the champion for the defense. I am granted immunity in order to take part in God's Judgment."

With a gesture, the King stopped Sombreval's men.

"Sir Black Knight," said Louis XI, "Enguerrand, my trusted liege, has often complained to me of your attacks against him. Whosoever attacks one of my vassals, attacks the King himself. What have you to say to hold my arm?"

"Sire, Enguerrand used treachery to destroy my family. My actions against him were an expression of the Lord's own revenge—the same God who will decide on the rightness of our causes here and now. After today, no more will need be said about this."

The King looked at him doubtfully and, in an unconscious gesture, touched his holy medals, then seemed to relax.

"Yes, perhaps you are right. But to be a champion here today, you must be worthy. What is your name and quality, Sir Black Knight?"

"I am Hugues du Puy, Comte de Rochefontaine."

Enguerrand paled when he heard a name he had long thought buried in the past. He intervened:

"The Rochefontaines are all dead. You can't rely on this identity..."

"True. Therefore, I do not..." The Black Knight took off his helmet and added: "I am also Hugues de Château-Rouge, knighted by our good king in person on the day of the Feast of Saint-Jean, after I saved his life from a sneak attack by the Bourguignons."

It was probably one of the very few times in his life when Louis XI was taken by surprise. How could this most deserving knight who had rescued him also be the dreaded Black Knight? But he pulled himself together quickly and ordered:

"Château-Rouge, your titles of nobility cannot be challenged. You are indeed worthy, and under the protection of God's Judgment. Join your opponent on the battlefield and let everything be done according to our Lord's will."

Jacques was beginning to get used to the situation, observing the scene closely and yet, at the same time, as if through a distorted glass. He saw himself move into the clearing. The herald signaled the duel could begin.

The two men began to slowly circle each other. Enguerrand struck the first blow. With a series of powerful strikes of his sword, he tried to gain the upper hand. The Black Knight parried every time with his shield.

Jacques felt the effort exerted by his host. The armor, sword, shield, were heavy and exhausted the combatants quickly. But the Black Knight was a force of nature. He tired less quickly than his opponent, whose blows were becoming less powerful. The Black Knight was preparing for a decisive action when, suddenly, after an unexpected feint, Enguerrand managed to strike his opponent's face. The blow was given with such force that it suggested that the villain had faked his premature weakness in order to lure Château-Rouge into a false sense of security.

The Black Knight's helmet was broken and the man behind it seriously injured. With blood in his eyes, Hugues could no longer see his opponent clearly. He interposed his shield to parry the blows which rained down on him mercilessly.

In less than a minute, the shield was smashed and the temporarily blinded Knight was left without protection.

Jacques, too, was blinded. But not having to fight for himself, he was able to concentrate on listening to the sound of footsteps on the gravel. He heard Enguerrand approach from on the left, intending to strike a fatal blow.

In his mind, he screamed: *To the left!*

Then—by miracle or by chance—the Black Knight seemed to hear the message. Jacques would never know if a higher power had intervened that day, or if it was merely the result of his host's battle-honed instincts. At the very moment when Enguerrand prepared to end the battle with a devastating blow, the Black Knight brought his sword up and stabbed forward—a technique rarely used in the Middle Ages when side blows were preferred.

Although blinded, Hugues had kept all his strength. The sword pierced Enguerrand's breastplate, then his heart, and exited from his back.

The fight was over. The Comte de Sombreval lay on the ground, bathed in his own blood.

The Black Knight had avenged and restored the honor of two families: the Beauséjour and the Rochefontaine.

The public remained silent. This outcome was entirely unexpected and had surprised everyone. An old woman murmured:

"God Himself intervened today. Praise His Holy Judgment."

Such seemed to be the general opinion. The King's face, frozen in stupor, showed that he shared this feeling.

Slowly, the Black Knight left the battleground.

The King stood and declared Hugues de Château-Rouge the winner.

The Black Knight was dizzy because of the blood loss he had suffered. He put one knee to the ground and fainted. Jacques, whose fate appeared linked to his, did the same.

When he woke up, he found himself back in the cellar of Château-Rouge. It was dark, except for the small light still shining in his lantern.

He stood up and returned to the small room where he believed the polluted atmosphere had caused him to faint. The air inside was now breathable.

The room turned out to be an ancient chapel. In front of the door stood a stone cross that resembled the one he had already seen in his dream.

On the left, he found the entrance to the secret passage that had once led to a stone farmhouse. On the right, along the wall, were two recumbent tombs that he had not seen in his dream.

Two names were engraved in the stone: Hughes and Yolande de Château-Rouge. The two faces carved upon the tombs seemed familiar, as if they stood for the features of two people that he might have known once...

After a few moments of contemplation, Jacques left the room.

He thought: It was not a dream. He did live—a long time ago. A black knight who struck terror in the heart of his enemies, an avenger of wrongs... no, a judge rather...

"Judex!" he exclaimed, looking at the coat of arms on the wall.

"Yes, I, too, will smite my enemies dressed in black... I'll make Favraux and the forces of evil know the meaning of fear! Yes, I will become... Judex!"

(translation by J.-M. & Randy Lofficier)

1912. Jacques de Trémeuse has now been Judex for two years and is gaining in experience. He has perfected his tools, and is ready to take on even the deadliest of challenges. The disastrous World War I is still two years in the future. The streets of Paris are in bloom, the sweet smell of flowers is in the air. No one yet has an inkling of the massive slaughter looming just over the horizon. Justice is simple and Science is wonderful—or are they? Already, cracks are beginning to appear in the social edifice...

Matthew Baugh: *Mask of the Monster*

In all of Paris, perhaps the last place you would expect to hear a woman screaming at 3 a.m. is in the fashionable quarter of Auteuil.

The screams came from the upper floor of an isolated home on the west side. They were loud enough that some of the closest neighbors could hear them, but they stopped so quickly that no one assigned much importance to them. Not until the following morning.

After the screams stopped, the lights began to come on in the house. A second story window burst open and a large man in dark clothing stepped out. He carried a bundle wrapped in bed sheets across his shoulder. The bundle was the size of a human body.

Inside the residence, there was commotion. The master of the house was awake and shouting the name "Louise" over and over. The servants were stumbling out of their quarters, looking frightened or confused.

The large man paused a moment and a trace of a smile crossed his scarred face. He stepped over the rail and dropped to the ground. There was something ungainly about the man, an oddness about his movements that suggested deformity. Despite this, he moved quickly to the garden wall. It was ten feet high and topped with iron spikes but the giant clambered across it in seconds.

There was a soft grunt from the bundle as the man landed outside the fence. The ugly smile crossed his face again, and then he jogged off into the darkness.

Half-a-mile distant, a milk wagon was making its morning rounds. The driver was a heavyset man with a hard face and white hair. A lean youth sat on the cart with him. An observer would have guessed they were father and son, or master and apprentice, out on their morning route. The two were silent as their mule pulled the wagon along. The older man smoked a pipe, the younger a cigarette. Neither had heard the woman's screams or the distant commotion.

There was a movement from the brush at the size of the road. The large man stepped out in front of the wagon. The driver tugged on the reins forcing the mule to stop. The younger man tossed his cigarette to the pavement and hopped down. He moved to the back of the wagon. The big man followed him. The youth was tall but the giant topped him by more than a foot.

The youth opened the back of the wagon, there were cases of milk bottles, but the compartment was far from full. The giant placed his bundle into the opening, then eased his bulk in beside it. The youth shut the door and headed back to his seat by the driver.

"Let's go."

The driver grunted and flipped the reins. The mule moved forward, falling into that steady rhythm that all mules seem to have.

"I don't like this much."

The younger man grinned at his companion's words. He took out a fresh cigarette and lighted it.

"What don't you like? The boss's plan is running beautifully."

"You know who we've got. The police will be crawling the streets within the hour. If they stop us, there's nothing to keep them from finding her."

The young man sniggered.

"I pity the gendarme who does stop us. You've seen what our friend can do."

The older man grunted. The wagon continued in silence.

"What's that up ahead?" The driver asked suddenly.

The young man squinted into the pre-dawn darkness. Ahead there was a silhouette of someone standing in the middle of the road.

"You think it's a cop?"

"Quiet!" The older man snapped. "Whoever it is, he doesn't need to hear anything."

As they drew closer, they could see that the man wasn't wearing a police uniform. He was tall, with a stony visage mostly hidden by shadows and a black slouch hat. He wore dark clothes under a long cape; the kind gentlemen wore to the opera. As they drew near, the man raised his hand for them to stop.

The driver reined the mule in.

"Good morning, sir."

"Open the back of your wagon."

"Is this a robbery?" The driver asked. He tried to make his tone light but only partially succeeded. "You won't get much I'm afraid. We have only milk."

"You have something much more valuable than that," the stranger said. "I want the girl."

The driver swallowed and glanced at his companion. The youth's hand slipped to the small of his back where he kept his knives.

"I don't know what you mean, sir. It's just me and young Gaspard." The driver forced a chuckle. "If you're looking for a girl at this hour, you're in the wrong part of town."

As the driver spoke, Gaspard worked a finely balanced throwing knife out of his belt. At 19, the youth was already an accomplished knife fighter.

"If you'd really like to find some nice girls..."

The driver stopped in mid-sentence as Gaspard threw his knife. It happened so smoothly and quickly that the driver could barely catch the motion.

The man in black shifted his body and the knife shot past him.

"I am here for the girl that you took from the Léonard house."

With a cry of anger, Gaspard leapt to the ground, another knife already in his hand. The driver moved to join him more slowly. He held a heavy wooden cudgel. They advanced on the black-clad man from opposite sides.

Gaspard struck first, thrusting at the stranger's ribs. The man slipped out of the way and caught Gaspard's wrist with one hand. A quick twist and bones broke. The dark man threw the youth away from him casually as the knife went spinning off.

The driver rushed in with a slashing blow. The man dodged the blow and brought his foot up in a *savate* kick. His toe caught the older man in the elbow. The club fell to the ground as his arm went numb. The stranger followed up with a neat punch to the point of the chin that left the driver stretched out on the cobblestones.

Gaspard had managed to sit up and was cradling his broken wrist.

"Gouroull!" he screamed, "Help us Gouroull! The devil's come for us!"

The man in black moved toward the youth. Before he reached him, the back of the wagon burst open and the big man stepped out.

Big was a sorry word for it, the stranger realized. Gouroull was well over seven feet tall.

The giant surged forward with a suddenness that would have done a bantamweight boxer proud. Only the dark man's quick reflexes allowed him to duck past the huge arms. The man's fists shot out, landing a powerful combination of punches against Gouroull's kidneys.

Gouroull showed no signs that he had even felt the blows. He spun and caught the stranger's neck in his massive hands, bearing him to the ground.

The man in black was pinned. His throat crushed by the inhuman strength in those hands. He tried several jujitsu holds, and struck at the pressure points on Gouroull's wrists. There was no effect.

In desperation, he reached into the folds of his cloak and produced a small revolver. He pressed the barrel into the giant's massive chest and fired four shots.

Gouroull screamed in pain and staggered backwards. He clutched at his bleeding chest, but he didn't fall. He looked around for a weapon and spied a rock, as big as a horse's head half-buried in the ground at the side of the road. With one motion, he tore it loose and raised it above his head to crush his foe.

The man in black was gone.

"He slipped into the trees." Gaspard nodded in the direction the stranger had taken. Gouroull started to move in pursuit but the youth raised his good hand.

"No! We've got to get out of here. That was enough noise to bring the police."

Gouroull glared at the youth for a long moment, then nodded his massive head. He picked up the young man and placed him in the driver's seat, then stuffed the unconscious body of the driver into the back of the wagon and climbed in himself.

With the steady rhythm of the mule's steps, the wagon moved on into the dark.

Nearby, the man in black watched from his hiding place. His throat throbbed with pain and his breathing was ragged. He wanted to follow but it had taken all his strength to get away from the monster. Silently, he swore that the kidnappers would see him again, and soon.

Etienne Léonard was storming around his garden when the detectives arrived. He was a fierce-looking man of 50 with white hair and a pointed beard. His dark eyes blazed with emotion but his face was calm. A quarter of a century as a *juge d'instruction* had given him a grim dignity that even this crisis couldn't erase.

"Sir! We came as quickly as we could."

Léonard nodded to Inspector Gauthier as he entered. The anger in his eyes flared when he saw that the inspector had brought his protégé, Jules Maigret, along.

"They left a note." Léonard said, and handed a piece of paper to the detective. Gauthier read it while the taller Maigret read over his shoulder.

M. Léonard,

We have taken your daughter. She has not been harmed, but if you wish to see her safely again, you must raise a quarter of a million francs by tomorrow evening. We will contact you to let you know where and how the exchange will be made. If you value her life, you will cooperate!

"My God." Maigret whispered, "My poor Louise."

"Your Louise?" The anger in Léonard's eyes was frightening. "She is my daughter, young man! How dare you say such a thing? You are no part of her life. You are only here because you happen to be a policeman!"

Maigret flushed, but he managed to keep most of the emotion out of his voice.

"Forgive me, Monsieur le Juge. You are right of course. We will do everything possible to recover your daughter safely."

Maigret's face had settled back into its usual impenetrable expression. Léonard knew that look well, and hated it. He could see no refinement in that broad face, no hint of passion or gleam of intelligence.

"Sir," Gauthier said. "Time is of the essence. Please tell us everything, in as much detail as you can."

Léonard's anger seemed to drain out of him. He nodded and sank down into a wrought iron chair.

"It must have been half-an-hour ago. I was awakened from a sound sleep by screaming. It took me only a moment to recognize the voice as Louise's. The screams stopped, as if a hand had been clapped across her mouth. I was on my feet in an instant and seized my pistol."

"Excuse me, Monsieur le Juge," said Maigret. "You keep a pistol in your bedroom?"

"Of course I do!" Léonard snapped. "A man in my position has many enemies. I've led the investigations of many of the most dangerous gangs in the city."

"It's just an unusual thing to do," Maigret persisted, "unless there have been specific threats, of course."

"Gentlemen," Gauthier cut in, "we must focus on the heart of the matter. Maigret, these tangents won't help us to find Mademoiselle Léonard."

He turned back to Léonard with an apologetic smile. "Please continue, sir."

"Very well." The magistrate gave Maigret a poisonous look then resumed his story. "I ran to the room as quickly as I could. It couldn't have taken me more than half-a-minute. When I arrived, the window was open and Louise was gone."

"So quickly, sir?"

"Yes, Inspector. I didn't see how it could be managed either. I hoped the kidnappers might still be hiding in the house so I roused the servants and put on all the lights. We searched everywhere, but we found nothing. I don't understand how they could have escaped in such a short time."

"There was no one else in the house?"

"My wife and my other daughter are staying with relatives in at our house in Alsace."

"The first sound you heard was Lou—" Maigret paused, "was Mademoiselle Léonard screaming. Is that right, sir?"

"I've already said so, haven't I?"

"Of course, sir, but that surprised me. Don't you keep dogs to guard your house?"

"I keep two mastiffs if that's any of your concern."

"It's just that it seems strange. Why wouldn't the barking of the dogs have roused the house before your daughter's screams."

"The dogs were killed, young man."

"Killed? How, sir? Were they poisoned?"

"They were not. The gardener tells me that their throats were cut."

"Cutting the throats of two large dogs must have been a very difficult feat for these kidnappers," Maigret mused. "Especially without making any noise."

A look of disbelief crossed Léonard's face. "My God, man! Are you a detective or a veterinarian? My daughter is missing! I would think that you, of all people, would see some significance to that! Yet, here you are, wasting time worrying over two dead dogs!"

"Excuse me, Monsieur le Juge." Inspector Gauthier's voice was calm and quiet. "Please allow me to consult with my young colleague for a moment."

He took Maigret's arm and walked with him through the garden gate to the street outside.

They made an odd contrast. Gauthier was a slender man of medium height who moved with elegant precision. Maigret was taller, bulkier and called to mind the image of a Bernese mountain dog plodding along next to a whippet.

Once they were outside, Gauthier turned to Maigret.

"It's not going to work," he said.

"But, sir, I know I can help!"

"Any other time, I'd say yes, but you see how he is."

"I have to try, sir. I can't stand by while Louise is in danger."

Gauthier sighed. "I know how you feel, Maigret. Honestly, I do. But we're not going to make any sort of progress if I have to separate the two of you every few minutes. He is at his wits' end, and you are at yours."

Maigret's big shoulders sagged and he nodded. Louise's disappearance was affecting him. The taciturn patience he could usually call on was a shambles.

"Besides," Gauthier continued, "you know who he is. He could have you removed from this case in a minute. He could even have you demoted, and where would I be then?"

The Inspector smiled affectionately and clapped Maigret on the shoulder. "Don't look so glum. I'm not taking you off the case."

"What do you want me to do?"

"I've sent for Doctor de Grandin from the Faculté de Médecine. He'll be arriving shortly and I'm assigning you to assist him. You were a medical student once, weren't you? Who knows, maybe there's something to your idea about the dogs after all. In any case, that's what I want the two of you working on."

Maigret knew that the medical evidence was often critical in prosecuting a case. Every part of him wanted to help find Louise, but he could see why that was impossible. He nodded and received another clap on the shoulder from his superior.

"Don't worry, we'll find her." Gauthier turned and strode back to the house, leaving Maigret at the curb. The younger man sighed. He took a large pipe out of his pocket, loaded it with tobacco and began to puff as he watched the eastern sky lighten.

The milk wagon had left Auteuil at its slow pace and had used the Pont Mirabeau to cross to the left bank. It had turned onto the Quai d'Orsay and followed the course of the Seine into the heart of the city. As the wagon passed by the Ile de la Cité, it turned south into the neighborhoods of the fifth arrondissement. The shops and restaurants of the scenic Rue Mouffetard were just coming to life when the wagon turned into a small building with the sign *Crémerie*.

A few of the dairy workers glanced at the wagon, but their eyes didn't linger. All manner of items came in and out of the dairy in those trucks and the workers never took any notice. It benefited them not to know too much.

Once the wagon was parked out of sight, Gaspard opened the back. The towering Gouroull joined him with the sheet-wrapped bundle in his arms. Gaspard opened a hidden door for the scarred giant and the two went down a stair. They came to a set of passageways at the bottom of the landing. Most of these were blind alleys, designed to delay a police search if the secret of the dairy ever became known.

Gaspard knew the passages well. He followed a twisting route that emerged in a good-sized chamber. Bright lights came on revealing the two men while the far portion of the room was left in impenetrable shadow.

"Report."

The voice from the shadows was cultured and business-like, with just a trace of a foreign accent.

"We have the girl, sir." Gaspard indicated the bundle the giant held.

"Your partner is not with you and you are injured?"

"Gouroull too, sir. He's been shot in the body several times. Philippe is unconscious. I left him upstairs."

"The police?"

"No, sir. It was the work of one man."

"A stranger?" A second voice asked. It was similar to the first, though it lacked even the trace of an accent. It seemed less business-like than the first, yet sharper at the same time.

"He was a tall man, sir," Gaspard said. "I couldn't see him well because he wore a long cape or cloak, and a big hat to hide his face. He fought like a devil, but that didn't help him against Gouroull."

"Was he killed?" The first voice asked.

"No, sir. Gouroull hurt him, but he managed to give us the slip."

"I am aware of this man," the first voice said. "It is regrettable that Gouroull didn't kill him. He has become a thorn in the flesh of the Red Hand recently. It is good that you escaped from him. Go and see to your injuries."

Gaspard bowed to his unseen masters and left the room.

"Gouroull," said the second voice, "the girl is unharmed?"

With a small nod of his head, the giant indicated that it was so.

"Please uncover her."

Louise Léonard gasped as the sheets came away and she saw the scarred face of her captor. She started to back away, but a giant hand closed on her arm. When she felt the iron strength of those fingers, she made no effort to struggle.

"Don't be frightened. Mademoiselle," the first voice said. "Gouroull may look like a monster, but he won't hurt you. Not without cause."

"What do you want?" She tried to sound brave though her voice trembled.

"It is better for you if you don't know too much."

"My father won't rest until he's found you!"

"It's true your father is a hard man," the voice replied. "It's also true he loves you deeply. He will behave intelligently."

"Why are you telling me this?"

"We wanted you to have a good look at Gouroull. You have felt his strength. You have seen what he can do. The police cannot stop him, your dogs couldn't stop him and even bullets mean little to him. We want you to know that, even after we release you, you will always be in the palm of our hand. Let your father know this so he doesn't entertain foolish thoughts about us in the future."

Louise looked up at the towering man who held her. Her eyes held as much curiosity as fear.

"I expect you find him hideous," the second voice said. "His face is a veritable mask of scars, isn't it?"

"A mask," she repeated. "I'm not frightened of masks."

She reached up tentatively. When Gouroull didn't pull away she touched his face.

"Skin as white as snow, lips as red as blood, hair as black as ebony."

Gouroull's brow furrowed as he let the girl's slender hands brush across the mass of scars and crude stitches.

"These stitches," she murmured. "It's as if you had been..." She turned toward the darkened part of the room. "It can't be!"

"Congratulations, Mademoiselle," the second voice said, "You may have a better deductive mind than your father. You are correct about what and who Gouroull is."

She turned toward the voices. "You've shown me his face. Are you afraid to show me yours?"

"That is as much for your safety as for ours, Mademoiselle," the first voice replied.

"Gouroull," the second voice said, "please escort Mademoiselle Léonard to her room. Then return to me and I shall attend to your wounds."

The scarred giant released Louise's arm and gestured for her to follow him. The two left the chamber the way they had come.

When they were gone, a remote mechanism shut and bolted the door. The spotlights went out and a diffuse glow filled the room. The chamber was empty except for two well-dressed gentlemen sitting behind a large table.

"What do you think, Cornelius?" the first man asked. He seemed to be the older of the two. He wore a conservative suit and round spectacles. His heavy moustache and unruly mane of greying hair gave him an air of dignity. He looked like someone's stern but kind uncle.

"She seems an interesting girl," Dr. Cornelius Kramm answered. He was smaller and thinner than his brother, with the kind of massive head that suggested genius. He was mostly bald with a fringe of dark hair. He was dressed in a black suit as well. Behind his round glasses, his black eyes were lit by a fierce intelligence.

"She is quite pretty, too," Fritz Kramm replied. "I wonder what Gouroull would do with her if we weren't guiding his actions."

"I think you know the answer to that, Fritz, and it's an ugly picture. The rules of human society have no meaning for such as our friend." Cornelius paused. "It would be interesting though. I should certainly want to study any offspring that might result."

The elite of society in Munich, Paris and New York would have been shocked to hear this conversation. Fritz Kramm was one of the wealthiest and most reputable businessmen on the continent. His brother, Cornelius, had an even more spotless reputation. A famous surgeon, Doctor Cornelius Kramm was as well-known for his philanthropic gestures as for the brilliant procedures he had pioneered.

"What was that she said about his skin?" Fritz asked.

"She was quoting a story from the Brothers Grimm. Mademoiselle Léonard is a great admirer of fantasies and fairy tales. She is an avid reader of Féval, Radcliffe, Edgar Poe and, of course, Mrs. Shelley. I believe her special favorite is Madame Jeanne-Marie Leprince de Beaumont, and that is most interesting."

"Interesting? In what way?"

"Interesting, my dear brother, because one of Madame Leprince de Beaumont's most famous stories is of a young woman held captive in the home of a monster. By her goodness and beauty, she eventually breaks the Beast's curse. It seems his hideous nature is only a mask and he is really a charming prince underneath."

"Hmph!" Fritz Kramm grunted. "I wonder if Gouroull has read that one."

Cornelius smiled coldly. "I suspect the fantasies of the Italian, Collodi, would be more to his taste. He wants to be a 'real boy' after all. As for Mademoiselle Léonard, she may not be expecting the sort of tale the Brothers Kramm have written."

"I'd best go up and find out how the police investigation is proceeding," said Fritz.

"See if you can learn anything of our mysterious man in black."

"I will. It bothers me that we know so little."

"Yes." Cornelius' voice was frightening in its lack of emotion. "We'll just have to be prepared when he turns up at our doorstep."

52

Fritz nodded and rose. He crossed to a folding door, which opened, into a small elevator cage. He touched a button and rose from sight, leaving Cornelius alone in the large room.

Maigret had met Jules de Grandin about four years earlier, during his abortive stint at medical school in Nantes. De Grandin had come as a visiting lecturer and Maigret had been impressed with his energy and encyclopedic knowledge.

The forensic doctor hadn't changed. He was a tiny man, full of energy and strange oaths, who had set the young detective to gathering evidence at the crime scene. He had been commanded to take what seemed an absurd number of samples and to make measurements in precise detail. Now, back at his laboratory, Doctor de Grandin was dissecting the bodies of the slain dogs.

"Move closer, man." De Grandin's tone was impatient. "I need you to angle the light so I can see."

Maigret complied, though he didn't understand why the forensic man was so intent on seeing deep inside the gash on the animal's throat.

"Surely, Doctor, there's no doubt about what killed the poor brute?"

"Ah bah!" the little man snapped. "You know the general cause, but not the particulars. We mean to catch a devil, my young one, and the devil is always in the details."

"I'm afraid I don't see much point. How is any of this helping to find Mademoiselle Léonard? I feel I should be out helping in the search."

"The search? That is a charitable description of what is happening. At this moment, Inspector Gauthier and his men are kicking down the doors of known criminal establishments and rounding up wagonloads of street apaches in an effort to pick up the trail of the kidnappers. All in vain. No, my friend, what we do in this room will be of much greater help to your Louise than all the frantic activity of the Sûreté."

Maigret started to protest, then realized what de Grandin had said.

"Why did you call her that?"

"Your Louise?" the Doctor's eyes twinkled. "Do you think that I have never been in love? How could I mistake your sighs, your long face unless I was blind? You are her lover, or else you hope to be."

"We had hoped to be married."

"But her father forbade it?"

"Yes. How did you know?"

"I have met that pompous ass of a magistrate on several occasions. His daughter must be a rare beauty indeed if you would even consider him as a father-in-law. Tell me, what pretext did he use to forbid a wedding?"

"He says he won't have his daughter marry a common policeman. He tells me that I am too crude for Louise." Maigret smiled sadly and opened the back of his pocket watch. "I confess, I sometimes agree with him about that."

He showed the picture in the watch to Jules de Grandin. It showed a sensitive round face, framed by a wealth of brown curls and dominated by wise, black eyes.

"She is lovely."

"She is more than that. She is an angel." Maigret shrugged and looked embarrassed. "I know that is what a lover is expected to say, but you would understand if you met her. She is sensitive and gentle, and not only to those in her social circle. I've seen her talk to servants, shopkeepers and beggars, always with the same respect she shows her father's friends. She often goes to the orphanage as a volunteer and reads her fairy tales to the children."

"And she loves you."

"Yes, sir, she does." Maigret shuffled his feet awkwardly. "I am a lummox compared to the elegant gentlemen her father introduces her to. Yet she says she sees something in me..."

Jules de Grandin grunted and ran a critical eye across the young detective.

"I think she must be more discerning than the silly girls one often meets. It is a shame her father sees you so differently."

"Even if he liked me, there are religious differences." Maigret said. He was surprised at himself for revealing so much. There was something about de Grandin that inspired his trust.

"Ah," Maigret saw a look of pain cross the older man's features. "The old intolerances will raise their ugly heads. I once loved a girl, but she was a Catholic and my mother forbade the match. The good God cannot be pleased when young lovers are kept apart for such reasons."

"Still, I must agree with Monsieur le Juge on one point." De Grandin's tone was suddenly lighter. "Why should a lovely and refined girl want to marry a man who insists on moping when he has such an excellent chance to rescue her?"

"Rescue her?" Maigret brightened. "Do you mean you have found something?"

"Something?" the little man looked scornful. "I have found many things, and you, my friend, are clever enough that you could have found them yourself if you were not so occupied in wishing you were somewhere else. I saw much more potential in you than that in medical school."

"What have you found?"

"Let us start with the footprints," de Grandin replied. "You took the casts yourself. What do you think?"

"I think that I failed to do a good job. The man's foot must have slid, distorting the print. As a result, it looks much larger than a human foot could possibly be."

"Not so!" De Grandin crossed to the table that held the plaster cast of the single footprint that had been recovered from the garden. "Look at the sharpness of the edge of the sole, especially here, at the heel. If the foot had slid, the sharpness of the print would have been blurred."

"Are you saying that is really the size of his foot?"

"Of his shoe, yes." De Grandin replaced the cast. "We have only the one good print but there were other marks to show where he went. By using the measurements I had you take, we know the length of our man's stride. I compare it to the stride of a running man whose height is known, a little math and we learn that our man is eight feet in height."

"But surely that's not possible?"

"I tell you it must be possible. The evidence is not like an eyewitness. It cannot forget or tell a lie. What it says must be believed."

Maigret frowned, as important as evidence was his inclination was to probe the people involved first.

"Then, we must find a giant," he said. "Surely a man like that can't hide in Paris."

"Not by himself, but look at this." De Grandin pointed to the plaster footprint again. The well-formed shape, the nail marks on the heel, they all indicate that this is a shoe of the highest quality. For such a colossal foot, it must have been custom-made. It would have cost a small fortune."

"Then, the giant has a friend?"

"Very good, my young friend. We would certainly know it if there was an eight-foot-tall millionaire walking the streets of Paris."

"So, this giant has a wealthy friend," Maigret said slowly, "And he is involved in a well-planned, well-executed crime. Does that mean that his friend is a criminal?"

"I believe it does. What else do we know?"

"We know that our giant is athletic enough to climb the high garden fence." Maigret paused to think. "Before he climbed it though, he must have lured the dogs to the gate and killed them."

"That sounds reasonable, but we must be cautious of what sounds reasonable if it is not supported by the evidence. The bodies of the dogs, and the blood from their wounds, were found well inside the garden."

"So he climbed the fence before he attacked the dogs?"

"It seems strange, but the evidence does not lie."

Maigret shook his head in wonder.

"Sir, you make it so clear. It's as if you were Sherlock Holmes."

De Grandin frowned. "Fah! That one is overrated. I should prefer to be compared to the great Dupin."

"Or perhaps the brilliant Rouletabille?"

De Grandin thrust out his chin. The points of his waxed moustache seemed to stand at attention.

"That puppy? He is the one who should be flattered to be compared to Jules de Grandin!"

Maigret had to smother a laugh. His new friend wasn't lacking for ego, comparing himself so favorably to two men who were arguably the greatest living detectives. He decided that it was probably a good idea to get back to the topic of the crime.

"Is there anything else you have learned, sir?"

Jules de Grandin nodded.

"There is something strange and most disturbing about the wounds on the dogs. Look at this..." De Grandin moved to allow Maigret a clear vision of the mastiff's body.

"His throat has been slashed."

"Yes, but no knife made these wounds. See?"

Maigret bent closer.

"Teeth marks!" he exclaimed. "I don't understand. No one saw or heard any other dog."

"Perhaps that is because these are not the teeth marks of a dog," de Grandin said. "These marks were made by human teeth."

"My God! What sort of man could do such a thing?"

"I would like to know that as well," said a voice from the shadowed section of the lab behind them.

Maigret and de Grandin spun to see a dark-clad man standing in the center of the room. He wore a black cape and a slouch hat, which hid much of his face. He had entered without a sound.

"Who are you?" Maigret demanded. When there was no immediate reply, he started forward.

"No." Jules de Grandin laid a restraining hand on Maigret's arm. "This man isn't our enemy."

Maigret looked back and forth between his friend and the mysterious newcomer.

De Grandin nodded to the stranger.

"You're Judex, aren't you?"

Judex! With the mention of that name, Maigret understood. For two years, the Paris underworld had been haunted by a mysterious figure who acted as self-appointed judge over the criminals the law couldn't reach. Gauthier had mentioned the cloaked figure several times, always with anger and a touch of awe. The Inspector had little use for vigilantes. An infallible vigilante who seemed able to appear and disappear like a ghost was even worse.

Others had a more charitable view of the cloaked man. Maigret had heard some compare him to a modern Rocambole, a figure of superhuman cunning and strength who acted outside the law but who targeted only the worst of criminals.

Maigret had suspected the reports of the cloaked figure had been exaggerated, or even manufactured by the older members of the force as a story to tell to rookies. Now, facing the stranger in black, he realized that it was no fabrication. Judex, the self-appointed judge of the underworld, was real.

"I am Judex," the man said, "and you are Constable Maigret and Doctor de Grandin. The same Jules de Grandin who studied for a time under Sâr Dubnotal, if I am not mistaken."

"You are well-informed, Monsieur," de Grandin said with a little bow. "I did spend six months with the Sâr, though I am hardly the psychagogue that he is."

"I fought the man who took Mademoiselle Léonard," Judex said. "I call him a man for I don't know what else he could be. The criminals working with him called him 'Gouroull.' "

"What sort of name is that?" Maigret asked.

"An appropriate one," Judex replied. "I don't know what it means but it sounds like 'ghoul,' 'gargoyle' or 'gorilla.' I can see how any of those names could be applied to the creature I fought. He was bigger than any man I have ever seen, with a hideous face and the agility of a devil."

"Could he have actually been a gorilla?" Jules de Grandin asked, "Or an orangutan? It wouldn't be the first time an ape committed crimes in Paris."

"I don't believe the creature I fought was an ape. It stood upright and its face was human, though terribly scarred."

"Perhaps it was an ape-man," Maigret suggested, "Like that creature Balaoo who terrorized the city only months ago."

De Grandin nodded.

"I was not involved in that case, but I did help in the arrest of the madman Otto Beneckendorff. He experimented to create a hybrid of ape and man. Could this creature be the successful result of such an experiment?"

"As I said," Judex replied. "He isn't like any man I have ever seen. I had hoped you could tell me what he is."

He produced a sealed test tube from the folds of his cloak and tossed it to de Grandin.

"I wounded Gouroull when we fought. I shot him four times in the chest with my pistol, but he didn't fall. This is what bled from his wounds."

Jules de Grandin's brow was furrowed as he smelled the fluid.

"This is not blood."

"No," Judex replied. "It is not blood, and I don't believe Gouroull is any natural creature. I'm hoping you can tell me what he is. This ichor is beyond my ability to analyze."

"But not beyond the ability of Jules de Grandin, eh? Don't worry, Monsieur; I will justify your faith in me. Maigret, bring me the microscope."

Jules de Grandin placed a single drop of the dark fluid onto a glass slide and applied a cover. He slid the specimen under the microscope and peered at it intently.

"Name of the Devil! I have never seen anything like this before. It has a cellular structure like that of blood but it doesn't seem to be organic. It will take me some time to be certain, but I think this is a synthetic blood."

He looked up from the microscope. Except for Maigret the room was empty. Judex had disappeared as mysteriously as he had come.

A small red light came to life on the surface of the mahogany desk. Fritz Kramm noticed it at once, but didn't acknowledge it. He was sitting in his brother Cornelius' office at the charity clinic on the Rue Mouffetard, listening to one of the staff doctors.

Fritz raised his hand to interrupt the young physician.

"Forgive me, Doctor Lorde. I'm afraid all this medical terminology is my brother's domain and not mine. I'll be happy to ask him to speak to you but beyond that..." He raised his palms face up.

"Of course, Monsieur Kramm." The young doctor smiled. "I'll appreciate it greatly."

Fritz rose and showed Lorde to the door. Then, he crossed the room to a set of bookcases. He pressed a hidden release and one of the cases slid aside revealing the hidden elevator. As it did, the light on the desk winked out.

"Who was that?" Cornelius Kramm asked as he stepped into the room.

"That was that Lorde fellow. He's hoping to do some research and wanted to talk to you about carrying on a study in the clinic."

"He has a first-rate mind," Cornelius replied. "I'd like to see where his research goes, but I can't allow it. The studies he would like to do would result in unaccountable deaths and I can't have the reputation of my clinic sullied."

"How is your patient?"

"He was resting comfortably when I left him." Doctor Cornelius reached in his coat pocket and produced four light caliber slugs. "His ability to withstand damage is astonishing. And his recuperative powers are greater than those of any natural animal. Victor Frankenstein was a genius!"

Fritz nodded.

"If we had a few more like him, there is nothing we couldn't accomplish. If only we could count on his loyalty."

"You worry too much, Fritz. After all, we have the thing he desires most in the world. The Monster wants to look like a man, to walk among normal humans and attract as little attention as possible. Who else could give him that except the 'sculptor of human flesh?' My carnoplasty techniques can make even a monster into a matinee idol."

"And then what, Cornelius? You know what happened to his creator. The same thing has happened to every human who has tried to use him since."

"Technically, Gouroull didn't kill Frankenstein," Cornelius shot back. "It was the man's mania to destroy his creation that did that. But your point is well-taken and I have already planned for it. I am certain Gouroull would betray us as soon as he had his new face. That's why he will never wake from the anesthetic."

"Really? You aren't completing the surgery?"

"I'm afraid not. It's a shame too. Making that face into something human would have been a wonderful challenge," Cornelius shrugged. "Unfortunately for him, there's so much I can learn by doing a vivisection. His amazing vitality should keep him alive for days, possibly weeks. In that time, I'll be able to learn all of Frankenstein's secrets. Then, I can create your army, dear brother. Undying, superhumanly strong and possessing much more tractable minds than our unhappy Gorouoll."

Fritz brought out a decanter of cognac and two glasses.

"We should toast the success of your studies."

He poured the liquor; never suspecting that every word they had said had been heard. Behind the bookcase, in the hidden shaft, a huge form dangled from the elevator cables. Gorouoll's eyes twinkled with hatred and inhuman cunning.

It was early morning when the two investigators made their report to Inspector Gauthier. His face paled a bit when they mentioned Judex's appearance.

"That outlaw!" Gauthier snapped. "I'll be certain to have two gendarmes ready to catch him if he tries to approach you again."

He listened patiently to their estimates of the size of the kidnapper. De Grandin left out the details about the synthetic blood and his suspicion about what that meant. The two had discussed the matter ahead of time and decided to hold back some information until Gorouoll was captured. Telling the Inspector that his men were looking for the Frankenstein Monster wouldn't help them at this point.

Gauthier listened patiently until the report was done.

"Thank you, gentlemen," he smiled tolerantly. "We have not found such a giant yet, but I now know we have our prime suspect as soon as we do."

He had asked Maigret to stay for a moment after de Grandin had left.

"So, Maigret, how are you getting on with the good doctor?"

"He is a remarkable man."

"He is certainly full of remarkable theories," Gauthier said with a chuckle. "We're to deliver the ransom tonight so you have only a little longer under his tutelage. It will be good to have you back doing real police work soon. Monsieur Léonard has raised the money and I think we will have Mademoiselle Louise safely home by late tonight and the kidnappers behind bars soon after that."

Maigret had gone home and slept for a few hours. He arrived at the laboratory to find the little doctor still working on the bodies of the dogs. They worked together through the early afternoon, until Maigret managed to persuade the older man to take a break. They walked to a nearby café that de Grandin knew and had a late lunch and a glass of calvados.

After lunch, de Grandin lit up a fat cigar. He offered one to Maigret, but he politely refused and loaded his pipe.

"There is something to be said for this, my friend," the forensic doctor said. "Sometimes, I become so obsessed by the evidence that I forget the needs of the body."

"This is the only way I can think clearly," Maigret replied. "I have to let things sink into my bones before I really understand them."

De Grandin nodded and the two sat in companionable silence until the little man's cigar burned down.

"I thank you, my friend, but now it is time to get back to my laboratory."

"I'll go with you."

"No, it may be better for you and your bones to stay here and ponder a little longer," de Grandin grinned. "No, I am not making fun of you. What you said is right. Each man thinks best in his own way. For me, it is in the close study of the evidence, but not so for you. Not every man can think like Jules de Grandin, but there is great value to thinking like Maigret too, I think."

They said goodbye and the little man hurried off.

A peculiar man but a good one, Maigret thought. He thought of his other new ally, the mysterious Judex and wondered what drove a man like that. Surely, it wasn't some abstract concept of justice. More likely he had suffered a very specific injustice in his own life and had brooded on it so long that he could no longer bear to see injustice anywhere. He preyed on criminals to avenge his own wrongs by proxy. What a grim life that must be.

The mention of Judex had provoked an unusual reaction in Gauthier. It was as if the Inspector actually feared the man. Was it just that the caped man was an unpredictable element in the investigation, or was there more to it than that? Also, it had seemed to Maigret that his superior had actually believed the story of an eight-foot man. Had he simply not known what to do with such an odd detail? Perhaps now that Monsieur Léonard had agreed to the ransom, he was focused on other things.

Maigret paid for his meal and began to trudge the streets. The afternoon breeze was warm and brought the aromas of the nearby park to him. There were young couples out, holding hands. He thought of Louise and felt a stab of worry. How foolish he was to risk losing her to something as foolish as her father's displeasure. When he rescued her, he should marry her as quickly as he could.

Who had taken her, and why? She wasn't the sort of person a reasonable kidnapper would go after. Her family was well-off, but there were many wealthier people in Paris, most of whom would make much safer targets than the daughter of a juge d'instruction. It didn't make sense.

Then, Maigret realized that it did make sense.

His meanderings had brought him back near the laboratory. That was good, but he had spent several hours walking and thinking and the Sun was nearly down. He and de Grandin would have to hurry.

"So this kidnapping is not what it seems?"

Jules de Grandin sat next to Maigret in the carriage as it sped along the boulevards. He had taken the young detective at his word and left his examinations behind to accompany him.

"I don't believe so," Maigret replied. "You said that the supplier of the giant's shoes must be wealthy. Why should someone like that blackmail a man like Monsieur Léonard for money?"

"But what if he were being blackmailed for something else?"

"I believe that is indeed the case," Maigret said.

"Then, perhaps the money is a way to distract the police. They will focus all of their attention on the ransom, leaving the kidnappers free to play another game."

The carriage pulled up to the Léonard house. All of the windows were dark.

"I knew he had sent the servants away during the investigation," said Maigret, "but where are the police?"

"They may have left to try to apprehend the criminals when the ransom is delivered," de Grandin offered. "Still, to leave the house empty is strange." Abruptly, he pointed as a light came on in an upper window.

"There is someone here!"

The two left the carriage and hurried to the house. The doors were unlocked and the foyer was empty. De Grandin motioned Maigret to silence as they went up the stairs. The door to the study was ajar and de Grandin caught Maigret's arm before he could enter.

Inside the room, Etienne Léonard stood, tears streaming down his face. It shocked Maigret to see the stoic man with the fierce eyes so vulnerable. In one hand, Léonard held a sheaf of papers; in the other, a small revolver. As they watched, he opened the grill and thrust the papers into the fire. He pulled another paper from his pocket and read it through before dropping it into the fire as well. He shut the grate and raised the pistol to his head.

"Name of a blue man!" Jules de Grandin hissed. "We must stop him."

They burst into the room.

"Monsieur Léonard, stop!" Maigret called. "There is another way to save your daughter!"

The magistrate froze in place, a look of pain and confusion on his face as Jules de Grandin opened the grate and pulled the burning scraps of paper onto the carpet, then tried to stamp out the flames.

"Maigret? Doctor de Grandin? What are you doing?"

"We know the truth, Monsieur," Maigret said. "The true ransom has nothing to do with the quarter million francs, does it? Your silence will not save your daughter. Only your cooperation can help her now."

Léonard slumped heavily into a chair. The pistol fell from his fingers.

Maigret turned to his friend.

"The papers?"

"A loss, I'm afraid," the small man answered. "We may be able to piece together a little from the fragments, but I don't hold out much hope."

"Monsieur le Juge can tell us." Maigret turned back to the stricken Léonard.

"The last paper you tossed into the fire. That was the note that told of the kidnappers' true demands, wasn't it? What was it you were investigating?"

Léonard raised his eyes. All of his defiant anger was gone.

"Do you know of the criminal syndicate called the Red Hand?" he asked.

"Of course," Maigret said. "They're one of the most dangerous organizations on the continent. I've heard that their influence extends even as far as America."

Léonard nodded.

"I've been investigating them for years and recently learned the names of the two individuals who lead them. I was going to prosecute them, but I had to be sure. They are powerful men with impeccable reputations. To accuse them without final confirmation would have been folly."

"And this confirmation?" de Grandin asked.

"It came yesterday evening," the magistrate said. "The night Louise was taken."

"You received two ransom notes?"

"Yes, the first was for money. It was to occupy the police so they wouldn't suspect the real demands. I was to burn all the evidence against the two men, and then I was to take my own life. They can't afford for anyone who knows what I know to live."

"You must tell us what you know, sir." Maigret's voice was agonized. "If we're to have a chance to save Louise, we have to know everything."

"The Red Hand will kill her whether you take your own life or not," de Grandin added. "You must know this."

Etienne Léonard nodded his head.

"I do. I hoped that somehow this could save my little girl, but that hope is gone."

"Tell us the names, sir."

Léonard raised his head. Whether he intended to answer Maigret's question or not wasn't clear. When he looked at the doorway, a fresh look of surprise crossed his face.

Then, there was a gunshot. A small round hole appeared in Léonard's forehead and he sagged into the chair.

"I beg your pardon, gentlemen." Inspector Gauthier stepped into the study, pistol in hand. "I'm afraid the names of my employers must remain a secret."

"Gauthier!" Maigret had half-suspected his mentor. Even so, it was a shock.

"I am sorry to admit it, but I have a passion for betting. Sadly, I am not very good at choosing the best horse or the fastest dog."

"But the Red Hand told you they could make your debts disappear, didn't they?" Jules de Grandin's voice was contemptuous.

"Your deduction is correct, Doctor. I've always regretted that you chose medical investigation over the regular police force. We could have used you." He turned to Maigret with sad eyes. "And you, young Maigret, you have the makings of an outstanding detective. It's a shame such a promising career must be cut short."

He raised his pistol.

"Maigret, be ready to rush him," de Grandin hissed. "He can only shoot one of us, then the other will be on him."

Gauthier looked worried. He backed into the doorway, trying to cover both men.

"Don't try it. I'm an excellent shot. I can kill two men as easily as one."

"What about three?" said a voice from the darkness.

Gauthier started to turn to face the speaker. Before he could move, a black-clad arm chopped against the side of his neck and he fell senseless.

"Judex!" Maigret cried. "What perfect timing."

The black-cloaked man stepped into the room.

"I'm glad to have gotten here when I did," he said, "but if my timing had been perfect, Monsieur Léonard would still be alive."

He scooped up Gauthier's gun and tossed it to Maigret.

"You'll need this before the night is out."

"But it's evidence."

"If you want to save Mademoiselle Léonard from Gorroull, you'll need more than evidence."

Maigret looked to de Grandin. The little investigator nodded and picked up the pistol Léonard had held.

"Now that her father is dead, your Louise's life can probably be measured in hours. We must act immediately."

"But how? We are no closer to knowing where she is being held than before."

"On the contrary," Judex nodded to Gauthier's unconscious form. "He will tell us."

The ride to Judex's lair had seemed to take hours, even in the mysterious man's powerful motorcar. He had sworn Maigret and de Grandin to secrecy before driving them to the ruins of Château-Rouge. On the way, he had told them of his investigation of the Red Hand. He had learned of the plan to kidnap Louise too late to do anything more than try to intercept her abductors.

Château-Rouge had been a stone castle overlooking the Seine Valley. It sat at the top of a sheer cliff and had been an impressive stronghold in its time.

Now, it was a crumbling ruin, but one which still functioned as a stronghold. A hidden hatch led to a maze of passages that Judex had outfitted with the most modern equipment.

Gauthier sat in a small, windowless cell. The men could watch him using an electronically-controlled mirror. The room held some rudimentary furniture including a chair, a cot and a glass screen of a type Maigret had never seen set into one of the walls.

"He will wake soon," Judex said. "I've given him a hypnotic drug to make him more susceptible to my methods."

"I never thought I would be a party to such things," Maigret said softly.

Judex gazed at the policeman.

"I do as I must to find justice, Monsieur Maigret. If you believe that police methods will have a better chance at saving the young lady's life, I will gladly hand over the prisoner."

Maigret said nothing. He was willing to go along with Judex in these extreme circumstances but he couldn't help but sympathize with the man in the cell. Inspector Gauthier had been his superior and his friend. It was painful to see him like this.

"This is a remarkable place," Jules de Grandin commented. "And that cell, I've never seen anything quite like it."

"It is as much as a monk's cell as it is a place of confinement," Judex replied. "In that room, a man must face his sins. He is made to see all that he has done so that he can seek atonement. I designed it for another, but his time of judgment has not yet come."

"He's awake!" Maigret pointed at the mirror. The others saw that Gauthier had risen and was looking around the cell.

Judex crossed to a desk where a futuristic-looking typewriter sat. As he typed, words formed on the screen in glowing red letters.

ROBERT GAUTHIER, YOU ARE MY PRISONER. FOR THE CRIMES YOU HAVE COMMITTED, I SENTENCE YOU TO CONFINEMENT IN THIS CELL FOR THE REST OF YOUR LIFE.

"What is this?" the Inspector cried, "You have no right to hold me! I demand to be handed over to the police at once!"

THIS IS NO LONGER AN AFFAIR FOR THE POLICE. I HAVE TRIED YOU AND FOUND YOU GUILTY. I NOW PASS SENTENCE ON YOU.

"Who are you?" Gauthier's voice rose with the beginnings of panic.

I AM JUDEX.

"Judex? The madman who has been terrorizing the underworld?"

THOSE WHO HAVE KNOWN TERROR AT MY HAND HAVE BEEN
DESERVING OF JUDGMENT. LIKE THEM YOU HAVE BEEN JUDGED
AND FOUND WANTING.
NOW, BID FAREWELL TO EVERYTHING YOU HAVE KNOWN.

"You cannot frighten me!" the Inspector shouted. "I will never give in to
these childish tricks!"

"He's telling the truth," Maigret said. "I know him, he's too strong to
break."

"Perhaps not," Judex replied. "But it may be that you underestimate me."

For hours, it continued and Maigret watched his former friend's sanity slip
away bit by bit. The drug made it impossible for him to ignore the flaming letters promising just punishment for his crimes. At one point, Jules de Grandin
whispered in Maigret's ear.

"This Judex is relentless. It is only a question of whether Gauthier's will
breaks first, or his mind."

It was past midnight when the end came. Gauthier hadn't spoken for an
hour. He had simply sat and stared at the screen with its fiery messages of judgment.

Finally, the policeman let out a loud wail.

"No! Please! Is there nothing I can do?" Gauthier sounded desperate.
Maigret shook his head in sorrow. The man he had trusted and admired was re-
duced to something barely coherent, wild eyes filled with panic.

WHY DO YOU DESERVE MERCY?

"Because I repent!" the Inspector was sobbing now. "I will do anything I
can to atone for my sins! I will tell you everything I know!"

WHERE IS THE GIRL?

"She is being held at the Red Hand's headquarters. It is a secret basement
beneath the dairy on the Rue Mouffetard!" He paused, breathing raggedly. "I've
told you. Will you show me mercy?"

I RESERVE JUDGMENT. I WILL RETURN SOON. IF THE GIRL IS
UNHARMED, YOU WILL GO TO THE AUTHORITIES. IF SHE IS NOT, I
SHALL PASS SENTENCE ON YOU.

Judex left the final words glowing on the screen as he turned to the others.

"Our course is clear, gentlemen. We cannot call the police, they are not prepared to deal with Gouroull, and Mademoiselle Léonard would certainly be killed the moment they approached the building."

Jules de Grandin held up his revolver.

"I am not certain that we are any better prepared to fight that monster."

"I have thought of that." Judex reached into his desk and pulled out a strange weapon that looked like an oversized version of an automatic pistol. It had a very long barrel and was obviously hand-crafted.

"Among my allies is a gunsmith of considerable talent," the caped man said with a trace of a smile. "When I realized that we faced the Frankenstein Monster, I asked him to make this. It has the compactness of a pistol, but it fires the rounds of a high-powered hunting rifle. I thank God for his efficiency and speed."

"You knew that we were facing the Monster?" Jules de Grandin seemed slightly put out that he was not the only one to reach this conclusion.

"What else was I to think after your comments about synthetic blood?" Judex crossed to a file cabinet and produced a folder. He dropped it on the desk in front of the detectives.

"Once I knew what to look for, I had my agents comb the newspaper morgues. Here is his trail. Frankenstein created the Monster at the end of the 18th century. The events of Mary Shelley's novel seem to be accurate in most regards.

"After the Monster's supposed death in the Arctic, his body was recovered by an Ulsterman named Blessed. Blessed returned to his homeland where he made an exhibit of the body. In 1875, the Monster revived and killed a man. It was lost in the bogs and was thought dead until it turned up in Scotland several years later. The records are confused, even hysterical, but it seems that the Monster was involved in a string of horrible deaths in the village of Plosway.

"The last appearance I have found was in the Swiss Alps, near Ingolstadt. The Swiss are usually so meticulous about times and dates but my men haven't been able to sort out whether this was 10 years ago or nearly 20. In either case, Gouroull had taken up with a mad clergyman named Schleger. Their activities together are too horrible to relate. They eventually had a failing out. Gouroull murdered the pastor and fled into the mountains."

"Frankenstein... It's so hard to believe." Maigret shook his head. "But, if it is true, will even a weapon like that be enough?"

"I am told that it would kill a tiger, an American grizzly bear or even a Cape buffalo. As for Gouroull," Judex shrugged, "we will know that soon enough."

Doctor Cornelius Kramm sat at his desk in the clinic on the Rue Mouffetard, reading through a great pile of notes on anatomy, biology and the alchemical treatises that had inspired Victor Frankenstein. Suddenly, the red light on his desk came on.

Cornelius frowned. Fritz was away on other business and none of the members of the Red Hand knew of the secret elevator. Best to be safe. He pressed a hidden button on the underside of the desk. The soft swishing sound of something large sliding filled the room. He smiled and pressed the button that caused the bookcase to slide back.

Gouroull stepped out, his massive form nearly filling the elevator.

"Ah!" Cornelius said, "I thought it might be you, my friend. It was very clever of you to find my conveyance. What do you want?"

The creature gazed at the surgeon with hate-filled eyes and his thin red lips pulled into an ugly grimace.

"I see," Cornelius' voice was as calm as if he were discussing the weather. "You're here to kill me then?"

The Monster surged forward, giant hands reaching for the doctor's throat. A few feet from the desk, he stopped abruptly as he collided with something that was invisible but very solid.

"If you found the elevator shaft, I suppose you must also have been eavesdropping on my conversations with my brother Fritz. That was very careless of me, I'm usually much more discrete."

Gouroull ran his hands across the unseen wall. He began to pound at it with his mighty fists. This produced a loud, vaguely musical "bonging" but had no other results.

"Useless, I'm afraid," Doctor Cornelius said pleasantly. "Even you can't beat your way through my barrier. It's a bulletproof glass of my own design. The transparency is marvelous, don't you think?"

Cornelius' hand slipped beneath the desk again.

"Were you going to ambush Fritz after you'd killed me? Or perhaps, you were going to take the Léonard girl and disappear into the countryside?" The doctor shook his head. "You seem to be forever trapped into repeating the same patterns."

Cornelius hand slipped beneath the desk and his finger pressed another button. There was a quiet hiss as a dozen tiny jets began to fill Gouroull's side of the room with a greenish gas that smelled of mimosa.

"It's a shame it has to end this way. I would have preferred your cooperation."

The giant covered his mouth and nose with one hand while the other flailed around, smashing bookcases and hurling their contents against the unseen barrier. As Cornelius watched, he noticed that the books were forming a large pile against the center of the glass wall.

Gouroull stopped his rampage and pulled a box of wooden matches out of his pocket. He bared his teeth at Doctor Cornelius in what might have been a grin as he struck a match and dropped it on the pile of books.

"Very clever!" Cornelius murmured. "Even I have underestimated you it seems."

It was raining heavily when Judex's car pulled to the side of the Rue Mouffetard and stopped. The three men had a good view of the dairy.

"How do we get in without raising an alarm?" Maigret asked.

"We need a distraction," Judex replied. "I wish I had thought to bring my hunting hounds. If we sent that pack into the building, the Red Hand wouldn't know what to make of them. We could slip in easily."

"We may not need any such thing. Look!"

The others followed Jules de Grandin's pointing finger. Smoke was starting to pour out of the second floor of the charity clinic next to the dairy.

"My God," Maigret cried. "Those poor people."

"The two of you see that the clinic is evacuated," Judex snapped. "I'll use this opportunity to find the way down to the Red Hand's headquarters. Join me there as soon as you can."

Maigret and Jules de Grandin raced to the clinic where a slender man with fierce black eyes and a high, bald head was directing the evacuation.

"Monsieur, we are here to help."

"Excellent!" the man said. He was admirably calm. "Are you with the police?"

"I'm Constable Maigret."

"Good! I am the clinic's director. The fire broke out on the second floor so the patients are safe for the moment. All the beds are on the ground level. Just the same we need to get them out quickly."

"Why is that?"

"We store a great deal of ether on the upper floor. When the fire reaches it, there will be a terrible explosion. Can you send for help?"

"I'll do what I can."

Maigret managed to round up several gendarmes. The pouring rain hampered their efforts but it also slowed the progress of the fire. Before long, the building was evacuated and the fire brigade was setting up to fight the blaze.

Maigret and Jules de Grandin regrouped at the door of the *crémerie*.

"We had best see what Judex has found."

Maigret nodded at his friend's comment and the two turned to go in.

The explosion threw them both to the ground. The fire had finally reached the volatile materials and the effect was much greater than Maigret or de Grandin could have expected.

The next day, the newspapers reported that the blast had shattered windows for a quarter mile in every direction. Thanks to the heroic efforts of the police and Dr. Cornelius Kramm, no lives were lost. Unfortunately, the clinic was blown to bits. Nothing remained of it to show that there had ever been anything like a bulletproof glass barrier or a hidden elevator.

Inside the building, Maigret and de Grandin found the unconscious bodies of several men, including Gaspard, the young knife fighter. Judex had found the hidden door and was struggling to force it. Maigret added his shoulder to the job and the barrier slowly gave way. They hurried down the hidden stair, Maigret in the lead.

When they reached the bottom, they discovered a maze of passages.

"By all the Devils of Hell!" Jules de Grandin swore. "It is a labyrinth, with a beast more terrible than the minotaur at its center!"

They heard a woman's scream through the passages.

"Louise!" Maigret raced forward.

More through luck than anything else, the three managed to follow the girl's cries through the maze.

"I hear running water!" Judex said in a low voice.

"The Rue Mouffetard sits above a section of the old Roman sewers of Lutetia," de Grandin whispered back. "The Red Hand must have connected their passages to it as an escape route. But the sewers are small. A brute like Gouroull would scarcely fit."

"Then we have him."

Maigret redoubled his speed and nearly left the others behind. Moments later, he saw the entrance to the old sewer and stepped through.

It was much larger than he had expected. Whether through ancient design or later modification, this section of the sewer was clearly meant to be easy to traverse. The arched ceiling was 12 feet at its highest. Water ran through an eight-foot channel in the center of the tunnel and a narrow walkway flanked it on either side.

All of this, Maigret registered in the fraction of a second before a huge hand closed around his arm and another caught him by the neck. He heard Louise scream his name as the creature lifted him like a child and flung him across the sewer. He hit the stone wall on the far side and fell to the walkway.

He heard pistol shots and cries. Then, there was a louder retort followed by an inhuman howl of pain. Maigret forced his eyes open to a bizarre tableau.

De Grandin was down and Maigret couldn't tell how badly he might be hurt. Judex stood over him protectively, an electric torch in one hand and his strange pistol in the other. The heavy bullet must have hurt Gouroull. He held Louise in front of him like a shield against Judex's bullets. His clothing was burned away in many places but his flesh seemed unharmed. Louise was still wearing the pale nightgown she had worn the night before. Maigret thought, absurdly, that it made her seem an angel in a crowd of black-clad devils. Her face and the Monster's were very close, the warm olive of her skin against the dead pale of his.

Maigret shook his head and tried to think more clearly. Gouroull's eyes were locked with Judex's and his mouth was clamped on Louise's neck. He remembered the dead mastiffs, their throats slashed by those teeth. Lower the gun, those inhuman eyes said. Lower the gun, or I will kill her as I killed the dogs.

Maigret raised his hand. Somehow, he had managed to hold onto his pistol. He aimed as best he could, said a quick prayer and pulled the trigger.

The bullet struck the Monster in the head. It failed to pierce his massive skull but Gouroull cried out with pain and let go of Louise. She twisted away as she fell. He tried to bite her but his teeth merely carved a bloody gash down the side of her face and neck.

Judex fired two more shots. Gouroull clutched his chest and fell backwards into the water. The current was swollen by the heavy rain and began to carry him away. Judex fired another shot and moved after the floating body.

"Louise!" Maigret called, stumbling to his feet.

"I have her," de Grandin said. "You go with Judex. Try to catch the Monster."

Jules de Grandin bent over the young woman and daubed the blood from her face.

"It's not a serious wound, Mademoiselle, though I'm afraid it will leave a scar."

"It's all right." Louise's voice was distant with shock but still lucid. "A scar is only a kind of mask and masks don't frighten me." She tried to smile. Pain and shock were making her giddy.

"There are many kinds of masks, aren't there, Monsieur?" she added. "I thought his concealed his true nature but the mask was his real face after all. His soul was more horrible than his face could ever be."

"Perhaps so, little one," de Grandin said, "but there is no need to think such morbid thoughts. You are safe and Gouroull's moments are numbered. You should think only of getting better."

"What about...?"

"Maigret? Your young man will be all right I think. And I believe he would love you no matter what your scars. Happily, there is no need to put that to the test. You have the promise of Jules de Grandin that your face shall be as lovely as ever. Tomorrow, I will call on the greatest surgeon in Europe. He is a German living in Paris and they say he is a veritable 'sculptor of human flesh.' "

Maigret had kept pace with Judex as they had moved down the walkways, but neither man could keep pace with the current. Maigret saw the giant raise his arm to grab at the embankment but he failed to get a good grip.

"He's still alive!" he shouted.

Judex fired another shot. It was impossible to tell if it struck home.

"No!" Maigret shouted.

"Are you insane?" the caped man shouted back. "You want to save this thing's life?"

"If we can."

The look in Gouroull's eyes had chilled Maigret to the soul. There had been intelligence there, but no sign of the higher qualities of compassion or empathy. He sensed that this was a creature that would kill without remorse for its own, strange purposes. There was no room for dialogue with such a creature.

Still, it was alive, and he couldn't help but sympathize with its struggle to continue living. In his own way, Gouroull had even reached beyond the need for survival and sought some kind of meaning in his existence.

"We must turn back!" Judex yelled. "The water is rising too quickly."

"But the creature," Maigret returned, "we may still be able to catch him!"

"He'll drown soon. We'll join him unless we go back now."

Maigret nodded. He had mixed feelings about giving up but he saw the necessity of what his companion said.

Judex trained his light on Gouroull's bobbing form again. As the two men watched, he was soon borne away by the waves and lost in darkness and distance.

1912. Judex has now entered the service of his nemesis, banker Favraux, under the disguise of his elderly private secretary, Monsieur Vallières. This short-short tells of a small incident characteristic of Jacques's campaign to ruin his employer...

Jean-Marc Lofficier: *Lost and Found*

Jacques de Trémeuse had sworn to destroy the banker Favraux, responsible for his family's ruin. Whatever he could not achieve by day under the guise of Favraux's discreet secretary, Vallières, he undertook by night as the black-clad Judex, an identity he had come to relish.

It was Vallières, however, not Judex, who sat across from the corpulent, sweating, 30-year old German in the *Brasserie d'Alsace*.

"I will come straight to the point," wheezed the interloper. "Information has come into my possession, Monsieur Vallières, that your employer, Monsieur Favraux, has purchased an important consignment of rare *objets d'art* from Turkey. Worth a veritable fortune, but only if properly appraised and sold to the right parties, of course."

"You are well informed, Herr...?"

"Gutman. Kaspar Gutman. That consignment happens to contain a treasured heirloom, which had been in our family for generations until the great earthquake of Izmir in 1883... I would like you to arrange for that special item to be sold to me privately. Of course, there would be a gratuity for you, Monsieur Vallières. A considerable gratuity, I might add."

"I am not in the habit of doing those kinds of transactions, Herr Gutman. I am sorry but you will have to talk to Monsieur Favraux yourself."

Gutman had told Jacques de Trémeuse what he wanted to know, which is why he had agreed to the meeting. Properly auctioned off, that mysterious consignment, the contents of which Favraux had kept secret, could provide an unexpected boost to the banker's fortunes, just as they were beginning to flag. That could not be allowed to happen. A plan was forming. As Vallières, he had access to all the shipping information, and it would be child's play, as Judex, to let these details fall into the hands of the Vampires, for example...

The news that the consignment had been stolen in Marseilles was a shock to Favraux, although not as much as Judex expected. The wily banker had gotten wind of the underworld's interest and purchased some last minute insurance.

"It's out of my hands now, Herr Gutman," Favraux told the German. "What was that item again?"

"A black statue in the form of a bird... A falcon..."

"Well, I'm sorry, Herr Gutman, but it's probably lost again. Forever, this time, I think."

72

Late 1912. According to Louis Feuillade, the character of Judex, contrasting with those of Fantômas or The Vampires, was meant to "exalt the finest sentiments." But, in reality, Judex is anything but tame. Robert L. Robinson (who wrote a Judex screenplay for an updated remake, published by Black Coat Press) highlights the merciless side of the character, never as evident as when our cloaked avenger teams up with another hunter just as fierce as he is...

Robert L. Robinson, Jr.: *Two Hunters*

The sounds of the Parisian streets trickled through the slightly opened windows in the main office of the Banque Favraux, as street vendors, strolling lovers and the honking horns of new motorists created an opera of sorts. The sweet cascading scents of perfumes, pastries and cigarettes mixed in the air as they formed a new smell, unique to the City of Lights. Within the marble walls of the building, the hum of commerce filled the air as men diligently followed the financial markets in Europe and abroad.

Entering the magnificent building of the bank, in a brisk walk, his large frame covered in a fine overcoat and hat, with the brim over his face, was a man with eyes like those of a beast. They blazed mercilessly at all who met his glance. For weeks, he had lived in the shadows; those who knew him thought him dead. But the time had come for his return. The time had come when justice—or so he believed—must be served. Or more precisely, vengeance would serve in lieu of the justice he craved.

Coldly, the man approached a receptionist, a proud-looking woman who sat behind a desk. Her hair was tightly pulled back in a bun, her face expertly wore the latest in makeup, enhancing rather than detracting; she sat there in her tailored blue dress, her stern, yet beautiful, appearance complementing the décor of the office. She looked up at the man and was not put off by his eyes, as she had seen those kind of eyes almost every day for a year.

"I am here to see Monsieur Favraux," announced the stranger, handing her his calling card. "I have an appointment. My name..." The man suddenly paused; he had kept his name silent for months. Then, he announced with arrogance: "My name is Nikolas Rokoff."

The receptionist took his card and placed it on a silver tray, its edges wonderfully ornate, then signaled to an office boy. Upon the simple wave of her hand, the boy—no more than 12—ran over to stand before her.

"Louis," she ordered the youth, "bring this to Monsieur Vallières. At once."

The boy walked quickly away.

"You may have a seat, Monsieur Rokoff. It shall be a few moments."

Rokoff removed his hat and sat in a chair, his eyes always scanning the room, never once stopping. After a short time, the boy came back down. He nodded to the receptionist, who looked at Rokoff. "Monsieur Vallières will meet you upstairs," she said.

Rokoff rose and followed the boy to the elevator cage.

The boy held the gate open, waiting for the larger man to enter. Once inside, his hands skillfully manipulated the levers, operating the car as they rode together to the top floor of the building.

Neither spoke during the ascent, the boy enjoying the wondrous ride as if it were its first again, Rokoff quietly anticipating the meeting at the top. As they came to a halt, the boy again opened the gate, revealing a gentleman standing before them. His hair and beard betrayed his age as they sparkled shining silver. For an elderly man, he was tall, although slumped over from age; his eyes shone with signs of the youth he once had been. Rokoff exited the elevator. The boy smiled at him before manipulating the levers to bring the car back to the ground floor.

"Monsieur Rokoff," began the man as he extended his hand, "welcome to the Banque Favraux. I am Monsieur Vallières, personal secretary to Monsieur Favraux. Please, come with me." The elderly man led Rokoff down the hall to the outer chamber of an office. Knocking once, then opening the door, Vallières entered, with Rokoff following, into the office of Monsieur Favraux.

The huge corner office was one of opulence, fine art and comfortable furnishing filling the room.

"Monsieur Rokoff," said a voice from behind a large marble desk. "I don't often meet with strangers."

Rokoff walked towards the desk. "It is in both of our interest for you to do so, Monsieur Favraux," replied Rokoff.

"Please sit," said the banker as he motioned to the chair before his desk. Vallières took the seat beside Rokoff, then opened a leather-bound portfolio to take notes.

"I was under the impression that we would speak alone," began Rokoff as he glanced at the secretary. "What I have to say is most confidential."

"Monsieur Vallières is my right hand," said the banker. "If you want to work with me and make use of my resources, you must learn that he is amongst my most treasured ones. It is that simple. Now, what do you have for me?"

Rokoff rubbed his bald head for a moment as he decided which course of action he would take. He had come too far to back out now. "I believe that there's an absolute fortune to be found in Africa."

"That is nothing new. Men every day travel to the dark continent to find their fortunes."

"Listen to me, Monsieur Favraux, and listen to me well. I'm not a man to be trifled with, nor dismissed casually. I've come to you for a simple reason: I need the funds to accomplish two things. Mount an expedition to a city called Opar, and get the services of a certain English Lord to guide us."

"Then why ask to speak with me? There are men in my employ here who could evaluate your project and make a decision."

"It's not that simple. First, only one man knows where Opar is located. I believe that it is the reason for his fortune. And he won't be easily persuaded. Second, and this is more important for you, the pay-out for this is beyond anything you might imagine. Gold, gems of untold value... We could fill ten ships and still not have dented this treasure."

Favraux rose from his desk and walked to a bar located along the wall. He reached in and took out a bottle of brandy, of which he poured two glasses. Walking back, he handed one to Rokoff. "Why haven't you already made this English lord some kind of offer then?" Rokoff raised his glass in thanks to Favraux, and then drained the contents in one swift sip.

"Why? This man is not like you or I. He is a demon, with the strength of ten men. Believe me when I tell you this. I've had my hands on his throat, and he's had his on mine, and we've looked into each other's eyes with hate. I know for sure, he is more beast than man."

"I wasn't told you were a madman, Monsieur Rokoff. Our mutual acquaintance, Alexis Paulvitch, said you were a man to be listened to."

"Then listen to me, you pompous ass. Lord Greystoke is no normal man. He was the son of an English lord, born in Africa and raised by apes. Do you understand what I am saying? He was not raised by men, suckling on the milk of his proper English mother, but at the tit of a hairy ape. He ruled a herd of them, along with a tribe of natives. In the jungle, he is seen as some mystical god... a warrior of unequalled skill and strength. They call him Tarzan."

"My God," said Favraux. "I'd heard that story, but I thought it was legend."

"It is not. I know this man. We're sworn enemies, but each time he returns from Africa, his estate grows. I paid his banker for information, a man in Switzerland, and he told me that Greystoke's deposits are all in gold and jewels. And each one larger than the one before it."

"If this jungle man is your enemy, then how will you get him to lead you to this fortune?"

Rokoff walked to the bar and refilled his glass. "Ah," he exclaimed, "there is only one thing that makes Greystoke a man and not a beast. His woman. He has a wife and a son. And they're in Paris as we speak."

Favraux rubbed his chin, and then looked at his secretary. *It was tempting*, he thought, *but fantastic*.

"Monsieur Rokoff," asked Vallières, "if this man hates you, why would he help you?"

"To regain what he wants," said Rokoff.

"And that would be?" said Vallières.

"His family. I will take his family. You will keep them hidden, until we return with the treasure."

Favraux stood up. "You ask me to commit a crime, Monsieur Rokoff? Kidnapping, coercion, possibly more. Are you mad? I run a bank!"

"You run more than a bank, Monsieur Favraux. Do not think that I do not know your business. Your fortune was made by stealing from others, throughout Europe. You've blackmailed officials, embezzled millions, help the Vampires launder their loot... Yes, you're more than a banker. But all that doesn't matter now... the kind of fortune I'm talking about will erase your past, make you as respectable as the families you've ruined."

Vallières' eyes blazed as he listened to the two men, but he said nothing.

Favraux laughed out loud as he took the bottle from Rokoff's hand. "Good, we understand each other. Now, where is this ape man?"

Across the City of Lights, at the Royal Palace Hotel, two men stood on a balcony looking out at the skyline. The smaller of the two wore the uniform of the French Navy. His name was Paul d'Arnot. A slim cigarette in his left hand twirled to and fro as he spoke, like the baton of an orchestra conductor. He held a glass of Burgundy in his right hand. Beside d'Arnot was a bronzed god, a full head and half taller, with a body that would rival the sculptures of the Louvre. That was his friend, John Clayton, Lord Greystoke. Paris was a regular stop on the annual trips he took with his wife. "This is a jungle of a different sort, eh, John?" Paul asked his companion. "The predators that come after a man here, come with a smile and a desire unknown to all but them."

"My world was simpler before I met you," said Greystoke. "My enemies were so for no other reason than I was a meal to them, or they were a meal to me. It was easy. No anger, no hatred. Since becoming a civilized man, I have discovered emotions that my brothers, the Great Apes, would find humorous."

"Ah, this is true, but would you have known the wonders of love? To see a rare beauty and know that she is the one for you. Do you think your ape friends know that?"

Greystoke looked out over Paris with his grey eyes, and thought back to his youth, to a love named Teeka, but chose not to mention her. Paul, while he accepted much of his life prior to their friendship, would never understand his love for this beautiful creature. The female who filled his heart with longing, until the day he first saw the golden tresses of the one who would become his mate, his wife, Jane Porter. "No Paul," he replied. "They don't. But neither do you, calling on a different lady every night."

The two men laughed, then sipped their wine in a moment of silence.

"Your wife took your son shopping in Paris," said d'Arnot. "There goes that amazing fortune of yours." It took Greystoke a long time to understand the value of wealth and the importance that other men put on it. He only saw that the jewels of Opar provided him and his family with security.

76

"Jane should return shortly with her litter carrying her treasure," he laughed. "She loves to hunt in the shops of the Left Bank as I in the jungle. But she left Jack here, with his nanny."

"What a quiet child," said the French Lieutenant. "I did not even know he was here."

"From what I understand, it is common trait among men of my bloodline. My mother told me I never cried as a baby."

"Your mother?" exclaimed d'Arnot. "But I thought she..."

"Kala," said Greystoke gently. "The mother who raised me."

Suddenly, the Jungle Lord turned his head. His eyes narrowed as he tried to identify the source of a sound he had just heard.

"John..." started d'Arnot before a quick hand signal from Tarzan silenced him. Without a word, the civilized man the world knew as Lord Greystoke vanished as the creature called Tarzan of the Apes hurtled off the balcony skyward, scampering towards the rooftops.

He jumped across the span of the boulevard to the roof across the way where a man in black stood tall. He was an imposing figure, as tall as the jungle lord, dressed all in black, with a matching hat covering his face.

"I mean you no harm, Lord Greystoke," said the man in black.

"Who are you?"

"My name is Judex. I'm here to help you. A man whom you believe to be dead is alive, and at this moment, he has taken your wife as his prisoner."

"Rokoff!"

"Yes. Unfortunately, I arrived too late to stop him..." Judex watched Greystoke sizing him up, deciding if he was telling him the truth or not.

"They could be holding her anywhere," muttered Tarzan to himself.

"True," said Judex. "But in this case, they're not. They've taken her to a building near the Moulin Rouge. We must hurry. My car is down there."

The two men swiftly made their way to the street and entered Judex's large, black sedan. The crime-fighter wove his way through the bustling streets of Paris just as Tarzan wove his way across the branches high above the ground of Africa.

"I should have made sure Rokoff was dead," said the Jungle Lord. "Until one of us is dead, he will always threaten my family."

"His goal is two-fold," said Judex. "Your death, but only after you show him the location of the lost city of Opar."

"How do you know this? No one knows of Opar."

"Rokoff does. A man as evil as he named Favraux now does too. But don't worry, your treasure is your own. I only serve Justice."

"I care nothing for gold and jewels, only my wife."

"Then, let us make haste," said Judex as he drove even faster.

In silence, the two avengers rode, as if on the wings of a chariot to the field of battle. The stars came out as the car slowed behind a warehouse. Judex pointed to a building with a windmill on it. "She is in there. It's a club with song and dance, which is good for us, as it will cover the noise. Once, it was the center of all society in Paris; now only those chasing a dream go there, and become lost in absinthe. We must go quickly."

Inside the building, Jane Porter sat in a large room, her arms bound behind her, a blindfold over her eyes. "Where am I?" she had pleaded for the length of time she had been held captive. But no one ever answered. No one, until now.

"You are my guest Lady Greystoke," said a booming voice which she thought she recognized.

"You!" she gasped. "But you're..."

"Dead? Hardly. It takes more than an ape man to kill Nikolas Rokoff."

"Why? We meant you no harm. Will this nightmare never end?"

"When the treasures of Opar fill my coffers, and the head of your husband hangs over my fireplace, like a wild beast, then it will be over."

Rokoff walked over to the bound woman and pulled off her blindfold. They glared at each other, eyes locked in hatred. "When John finds me..."

"Finds you!" shouted Rokoff. "He will find you only when I choose to let him find you, and that will only be so you can watch as I take his life before your eyes. But only after he has shown me the secrets of Opar!" Rokoff ran his hands through Jane's golden hair. "And then, I will decide if you will become my mistress." Jane spat at him as he laughed and walked to the door. He called one of the five men who were waiting in the other room. "Go to the hotel where Greystoke is staying. Give him this note," he instructed, handing the man a slip of paper.

Walking away from the building, the apache whistled a popular tune, unaware of the two men coming towards him. As he walked past them, Tarzan stopped and sniffed the air. In a single lunge, he turned around and grabbed Rokoff's henchman, his hands squeezing the apache's throat.

"My wife! Where is she?"

The man could barely speak, his eyes bulging in horror. His shaking hand pointed to the building. Judex knocked the apache unconscious as Tarzan growled at him. "If she is harmed, you will be the first to die."

They entered through the back way. Judex smiled as he pointed out a high window to Tarzan. The jungle man took a prodigious leap and vanished. Then a strange sound was heard through the building. A roar in the night. The war cry of the Great Apes.

Inside, Rokoff stopped in his tracks, sweat breaking out on his brow. "Impossible. He can't be here." He took a look at the outer room. The men had pulled their pistols as a bronze blur entered. Before they could react, Tarzan was on them. Shots rang out, blasting holes where the ape man was.

Rokoff retreated from the carnage and looked for Jane, but she was no longer there. He looked in absolute fear at the empty chair that had once held his prisoner—but no more. He had to escape before Tarzan could find him. Running into the hallway, he made his way outside but stopped as a dark-clad figure sprang before him.

"You have sinned against this man and his family, Rokoff," said Judex. "It is time to face Justice."

Rokoff's answer was an explosion of gunshots as the villain fired madly at the spot where his enemy stood. But before he realized, the figure in black had vanished in the night, his laughter left behind. The alley was empty, filled only with the empty clicks from his gun and, from inside, the sound of Tarzan finishing off his men.

Suddenly, a body crashed through the wall, followed by the Ape Man, his shirt shredded, his steel body glistening in the dim light.

"Rokoff!" challenged the Jungle Lord. Rokoff snapped a switch blade open and charged. His knife slashed frenetically but kept missing Tarzan, who eventually caught him with a massive fist across the jaw, breaking it in two. Roaring in pain, mad with blood lust, Rokoff came on harder, trying to plunge his blade into his foe's body, but it was not to be. In one, swift movement, Tarzan lifted the villain's huge frame and brought him crashing down on his knee, breaking the back of his mortal enemy, killing him.

Judex stepped out of the shadows. "He is dead. Justice is served."

"My wife..."

"I have her. While you attacked Rokoff's men, I went to get her. Desperate men do desperate things and I did not want any harm to come to her."

Judex led Lord Greystoke around the corner where Jane rushed into his arms. Neither could speak as they held each other. "We must hurry," said Judex. "The gunshots will have alerted the police and while they move slowly, they move surely."

The black car raced off into the night, returning Tarzan and Jane to their hotel where d'Arnot waited with young Jack and his nanny. As they left the sedan, Tarzan turned to Judex. "You have my thanks, Judex."

"And you have my friendship, Lord Greystoke. If we can't protect our loved ones, justice will be replaced with revenge. Farewell."

The black car sped off into the Paris streets.

The next morning, at the Banque Favraux, the banker was having his morning coffee. Vallières sat before him, going over the reports from the financial markets in America when he stopped short. A tall stranger had just appeared in the halls of the top floor and walked into the office unannounced.

"Who the hell are you and how did you get in here?" demanded Favraux.

"The window was open. I am Lord Greystoke."

"Greystoke..." stammered the banker. "What do you want?"

"You allied yourself with my enemy in his quest for Opar. He is dead. If my family is ever threatened again, you will become my enemy and incur the same wrath. Do you understand?"

"I do," said Favraux.

"Never forget that. There is no place on Earth I wouldn't hunt you down."

Vallières rose from the chair, his old bones making it a slow task for him. "Please, Lord Greystoke," he said, "allow me to show you to the elevator... It is easier than the window, I assure you."

Greystoke followed the old man out.

"Again, my thanks," he said, before taking the elevator.

"You know it is me?"

"Despite your disguise, your scent is known to me. Why you serve that man, I don't know, but you must have your reasons."

"I do. But the time for my justice is coming. So, I wait and learn."

"Then may your hunt go well, my friend," said Tarzan extending his hand.

"And may peace find you and your family," said Judex, taking his hand in friendship.

Both men smiled at each other as Greystoke entered the elevator, to ride the cage down to the street. Vallières returned to a shaken Favraux. "He has left."

"Thank God," said the banker. "A crazed madman like that, I don't need. Not when there is other, easier money to be made."

Judex looked at Favraux and smiled faintly.

1913. This story takes place soon before the events of Judex, *when our cloaked hero is about to exact his revenge on his nemesis, Favraux. Yet, Jacques finds the time to protect Paris from a variety of unsuspected menaces. This time, he is not alone, but allied with the powerful mystic known as Sâr Dubnotal. (A collection of the Sâr's adventures is available from Black Coat Press.) Matthew Baugh wrote this story to accompany Genkis & Sev's beautiful cover...*

Matthew Baugh: *The Gargoyles of Notre-Dame*

"I feel a spiritual presence," Gianetti Annunciata said. "It is drawing closer."

Vallières glanced around the circular table which held a crystal ball, a lit candle, and a stack of tarot cards. To the distinguished, white-haired man's left sat Madame Beaudin, a plump, matronly woman who held his hand. Next to her was her attorney, Monsieur Moubray, then her companion, Mademoiselle Denault, followed by the tall, turbaned figure of Sâr Dubnotal. Finally, at Vallières' right hand was the medium, a beautiful Italian woman with a wealth of dark hair.

"Is it Raymond?" Madame Beaudin asked. She sounded so eager that Vallières' heart went out to her. He had no use for spiritualists and it was difficult for him to watch his employer's clients defrauded by such charlatans. Then again, it was difficult for him to see them defrauded by Favraux, his employer, but that was a necessary evil. The man, who only called himself Vallières, had spent a lot of time and effort infiltrating Favraux's financial empire. One day, very soon, he would use all that he had learned and the corrupt banker's many victims would be avenged. But that was still in the future. For now, he was playing a role, and that meant accompanying a wealthy client to this absurd ritual.

A white mist began to gather over the table.

Ectoplasm, Vallières thought. Without seeming to, his keen eyes searched for the source of the mysterious substance. He was surprised when he couldn't find it; Annunciata and her cohort must be exceptionally skilled.

"Celeste," the medium said. Her voice had changed to the deep and cultured tones of a Frenchman with the trace of a Gascon accent. The gray-haired man marveled at her talent for mimicry.

"Raymond; it is you!"

"Why have you summoned me?" the medium asked.

"I... I have to ask you a question. The bank has come to me with some investments. It will cost forty-thousand francs, our whole savings, but Monsieur Favraux has guaranteed me that there will be a great profit. Isn't that so, Monsieur Vallières?"

The gray-haired man fought to keep from grimacing. He knew that his employer's investment opportunity was a sham and had been glad when she had asked to consult some friends before signing away her money. He had been disappointed to learn that the chief person she wanted to consult was her late husband. Unable to say much without giving himself away, he simply nodded his head.

"The banker's secretary?" Annunciata asked in the man's voice. "No, you are deceived."

Vallières' eyebrows drew together. He was not what he seemed to be, but there was no way for the medium to know that. He remained silent, trusting that this was part of the ruse on the widow.

"What do you mean?" Madame Beaudin asked with a confused expression.

"No matter," Annunciata said. "Celeste, you must not invest a cent in Favraux's schemes. Not now or ever."

The woman gasped and Vallières felt the tension in his muscles relax a bit. A glance at the lawyer showed that he was also relieved to hear those words.

"But... why, Raymond?" the widow said.

"You asked and I have answered. That is all I can say."

"Very well, my dear," she said, gathering her courage. "Now there are some other..."

"No!" boomed the bass voice from the pretty woman's mouth. "I answered one question because I loved you in life and love you still. But I have passed beyond the concerns of this world and you must accept that."

"You... you're leaving me?"

"Use your own wits and the advice of those you can trust, Celeste. Do not call me again by this medium or another for I will not come."

The widow sank into her chair, looking stunned. As she did, Annunciata's gaze shifted to the Sâr and she spoke. The voice was harsher this time and more guttural. Gone were all traces of Gascony. The new voice sounded vaguely German.

"*El Tebib!*" she growled, "if you wish to find me, you must go to the holy place where the grotesques gather. Tonight, as the midnight hour strikes," she said. "You must face your foeman's wrath and lust."

Sâr Dubnotal's bearded face reflected surprise, then anger. He rose and faced the medium with one palm thrust toward her.

"Enough!" he said in a low voice. "By Mitra and thrice-great Viritrilbia, I command you to release her!"

The deep voice growled and a cold breeze swept through the room, scattering papers and extinguishing the candle.

The medium spoke and it was Monsieur Beaudin's voice again.

"You must not go alone," she cried. "There is another who must accompany..."

The sentence ended in a cry of pain, this time in the woman's own voice. The wind stopped and the tarot cards shot into the air and scattered through the room. A pair of the cards fell onto the back of Vallières' hand.

In the dimness that followed, the gray-haired man found the gaslights and turned them up. In their glow, he looked bewildered while Madame Beaudin and her companion huddled together in fear; Sâr Dubnotal supported a very pale Gianetti Annunciata. He noticed that he had unconsciously held onto the tarot cards and glanced at them. One was *The Magician*, and the other *Justice*.

He hesitated a moment, shocked, then tucked the cards into his jacket and moved back to the others.

"Forgive me, my friends," the Sâr said, as he helped Gianetti to her feet. "A powerful force has interfered with our séance; fortunately, the danger to you is over. Please, go home now for I must tend to Mademoiselle Annunciata as well as… other business."

The group was distraught and confused, except for Vallières who, gently but inexorably, led the others out of Sâr Dubnotal's apartment and into the Avenue de l'Opéra. But as the doors closed, the gaze he cast behind him was anything but gentle. Something was happening here, and he would be back to discover what it was.

It was half past eleven when Sâr Dubnotal stepped out of his building and into a waiting taxi. Down the block, the man who had been Vallières was instantly alert. No one looking at him now would have recognized the kindly old man. A white wig and makeup had been stripped away to reveal a charismatic, youthful face partly obscured by the collar of his long cloak and the shadows of his wide-brimmed hat. The mysterious man sat behind the wheel of a powerful modern sedan, which slipped out after the taxi into the moonlit streets of Paris.

He followed without headlights and at a distance; for traffic this time of night was almost non-existent, and he didn't want the Sâr to know he was being followed. He used parallel streets when he could, and hung back when it became clear where his quarry was going.

He waited until the taxi had crossed the Pont d'Arcole onto the Ile de la Cité before he followed. He saw Dubnotal disembark onto the steps of the Notre-Dame Cathedral and dismiss the cab. As he watched, another man stepped from the shadows to greet him, a priest in a black cassock and a red sash. The two shook hands and spoke in voices too low for Judex to understand. After a moment, they walked to the entrance of the South Tower. The priest unlocked the door and the two men entered.

As the door closed, Judex was already in motion. Moving silently and almost invisibly under the cover of night, he reached the door quickly. He checked to make certain he wasn't being observed then quietly opened the portal and slipped inside. He could hear the two men's footsteps clanging on the narrow spiral stair as they ascended the 387 steps to the top.

The man in black followed and his footfalls made only the faintest whisper of noise. When he reached the top, he paused, listening to the two men who had stepped onto the tower's narrow walkway.

"…and you are certain this is the place that was meant?" came a voice. It sounded like a man past the prime of life and somewhat out of breath. Judex assumed it must be the clergyman.

"Where else?" replied a voice he recognized as the Sâr's. It was deep and resonant, and not the least winded. "The message said 'the holy place where the grotesques gather.' I knew at once that it had to be the Cathedral and its *Galerie des Chimères.*"

"I do not understand," the priest replied.

"I have an enemy who I have been pursuing for months," Dubnotal said. "He has challenged me to come here tonight."

"My son, I owe you a great debt, but I cannot allow your fight to enter this holy place."

"It is not my choice, Monsieur l'abbé. Herr Doctor Von Meyer does not respect sanctity of any kind. Whatever he is planning, it would happen tonight whether I had come or not."

"If that is true, then I can only pray you are able to stop him."

"Thank you," Dubnotal said. "Fortunately, I will not face him alone."

"I don't know what I can do to help," the priest said.

"Thank you," Monsieur l'abbé," the Sâr replied. "But there will be another to help me. Perhaps he is already here."

He glanced around, and Judex withdrew deeper into the darkness. His fingers brushed the handle of one of the Steyr automatic pistols he carried. His brow furrowed as he wondered who this man was and what sort of game he was playing.

"Is there anything different here?" the turbaned man continued. "Anything unusual?"

"Only these," the priest said, gesturing at a pair of hideous statues. One had the head of a tiger and the wings of an eagle, the other had a satyr's face and bat wings. Beyond that, Judex couldn't make them out.

"New gargoyles?"

"Actually, they're *chimerae*," the priest said. "We have them on loan from the cathedral in Vyones. They've had some damage from the German shelling and had to move their statuary and relics to safer locations."

"Very sensible," Sâr Dubnotal said. "If you don't mind, father, I'd like to be alone to commune with your gargoyles and *chimerae* for a while."

"I do not understand."

"I believe my enemy will strike at me tonight. If that happens, I don't want you to be in harm's way."

"But, what about you?"

"I've taken steps to protect myself," the Sâr replied. "Come back at dawn. If I am successful, I will be able to tell you much more."

The priest hesitated, then nodded. "Very well. I don't like this, but I do trust you, my friend. May Our Lady and all the saints and angels watch over you tonight."

When the priest had gone, Sâr Dubnotal took a long look around the interior of the tower. "He's gone," he called. "You may as well come out; I know you're here."

Judex didn't believe that the man could have seen him, but he saw no reason to remain concealed. He stepped from the shadows, his long cloak folded around him.

"Ah!" the Sâr said, a thin smile forming on his lips. "You are a stealthy one. But are you one of the Herr Doctor's agents, or the one Gianetti predicted?"

Judex raised his left hand. With a stage magician's flourish, he made the tarot card seem to appear in his hand. Then he tossed it to land face up near the mystic's feet so the word *Justice* could easily be read.

"That tells me what you are," Dubnotal said, raising an eyebrow. "I still don't know who you are."

"I call myself Judex."

Judging by his expression, Sâr Dubnotal was hoping for more of an answer, but Judex wasn't inclined to give him one. The man in black relied on knowing more than his enemies—more even then his potential allies. He likes having enough information to be the master of the situation. Unexpected happenings, like the séance, and mysterious people were a frustration and always a potential source of danger.

"Very well, Monsieur Judex," Dubnotal said. "Did you hear what I said to the abbé?"

"That a rival magician with a German name sent a message to draw you here and strike at you? I heard that."

"You sound skeptical, my friend," the mystic said.

"I don't hold with mummery and hocus pocus," Judex replied. "I may not know how you managed everything at the séance..."

"So you *were* there!" Dubnotal's eyes narrowed in thought, then opened wide. "Of course! You were the old man, Vallières. That is an impressive disguise, Monsieur."

Judex kept his face blank with effort. The man's shrewd deductions had rattled him more than he wanted to show.

"If you're going to continue this guessing game, I'll be on my way." Judex turned to go.

"Please," Dubnotal said. There was something in his voice that made Judex pause—a trace of vulnerability in his confident façade. He turned back to face the mystic.

"Stand vigil with me until midnight," he said. "If something happens, I will need your help."

"And if nothing happens?"

"Then you have my word that I will never trouble you again."

Judex nodded. "Until midnight."

"Thank you, Monsieur," Dubnotal said. "Then it is time to prepare."

He took a piece of chalk from his pocket and began to draw patterns on the floor of the tower.

"Come into the circle," he said.

"What is it?" Judex said.

"A form of protection," Dubnotal replied. "It will shield us against any magical attack."

"Thank you, but I'll see to my own safety," Judex said. He drew back into the shadows and watched as the Sâr continued his drawing. First, he made a large circle, then at each of the points of the compass he wrote something in Hebrew. Halfway between each set of words he drew a five-pointed star, then a smaller circle within the first. He drew four more Hebrew letters at the cardinal points and finally two interlocked triangles, forming a six-pointed circle, with himself in the center.

"What do you do if you need to counter-attack?" Judex asked. He found himself both amused and vaguely troubled by the mystic's preparations. He seemed so sincere about his mummery.

"I have this," Dubnotal replied. Reaching into his jacket, he produced a short, straight dagger with a three-edged blade and a hideous, demonic face on the pommel.

"This is a Tibetan *phurba*," the mystic said. "It should suffice against anything my enemy can send at me."

Hearing footsteps on the spiral stair, Judex faded back into the shadows. A few moments later the door opened and a tall, dour looking man in the dark cloak of a sacristan emerged, followed by three younger assistants. The sacristan nodded curtly to Sâr Dubnotal and led the group to the platform where the four bells in the tower hadn't been rung since before the days of Quasimodo. They took their seats and began working a system of foot-pedals to get the huge bells ringing. Judex glanced across to the South tower where the massive Bourdan Emmanuel hung silent. The colossal bell was only rung on high holy days.

The clamor of the bells was deafening but mercifully brief. As the twelfth stroke rang out and then began to fade away, Judex heard a new sound—the scrape of stone on stone. He turned to the two grotesques and saw something that chilled him to the core. The two hideous statues from Vyones were moving. Their eyes were lit with a hellish glow and their limbs had gone from stony immobility to fluid, animal grace.

The sacristan crossed himself and his helpers froze in horror as the monsters moved toward Sâr Dubnotal. They reached the edge of the circle and stopped as if they had encountered a wall. Inside his ring of protection the mystic raised his strange dagger and began to chant something in some language Judex didn't recognize.

The cat-headed gargoyle opened its mouth in a silent roar. It bared terrible fangs at Dubnotal and swung a taloned paw. The claws struck sparks of blue flame as they encountered the invisible barrier and failed to reach their target. Judex noted that the creature's other hand was missing, apparently broken off sometime in the past.

The second grotesque, which he now clearly saw to be a bat-winged satyr with the upper torso of a leering, horned man and the lower body shaped like the hindquarters of a goat, didn't waste any effort on the barrier. It turned toward the cringing bell-ringers and began to stalk them.

"Stay back!" Judex shouted as he drew his pistols and emerged from the shadows. He fired both weapons and the bullets struck the monster's torso side-by-side.

Surprised, the gargoyle stepped backward and clutched its chest. Then it moved its hands and a triumphant leer lit its face. The bullets had barely made a mark on the solid granite of its body.

"Run!" Judex yelled to the terrified men. "Get to the stair; I'll hold this thing here!"

He fired as he spoke, this time striking the creature in the forehead. Again, the damage was negligible, but the shot managed to focus the gargoyle's attention on him. He lost track of the ringers and Sâr Dubnotal's fight as it sprang at him. Judex dodged by the narrowest of margins.

As the creature turned on him again, Judex shot it point blank in one glowing eye. He heard the bullet ricochet away with a whine as the gargoyle's clawed hand caught the front of his shirt. With frightening ease, it picked him off his feet and tossed him away. The force of the throw carried Judex out of the tower into the open space, two-hundred feet above the ground. His back struck something solid and he lost his grip on one of the pistols. He grabbed frantically and his hands caught something. With a start he realized that he was hanging from a gargoyle, one of the Cathedral's many hideous waterspouts. With a surge of effort, he managed to pull himself atop it and lay there, gasping.

The monster didn't give him a moment to rest. It lunged at him. Judex had managed to hold onto one of his pistols and fired once at point blank range to no effect. As the thing's stone fingers encircled his throat, he grasped his wrist and heaved backward, thrusting his foot into its midsection as he did. The improvised throw worked; using his leg as a lever he thrust the monster up and over. Judex struggled for a moment to keep from joining his foe in its plunge into space. A moment later he rose and looked down.

"Impossible," he whispered.

The gargoyle hadn't struck the ground. Somehow—defying physics and common sense—its outspread wings had caught air, and it glided beneath him like a monstrous bat. It swung away from the tower and gained altitude.

Judex knew that, if the gargoyle gained the tower again, his chances of beating it were next to nothing. Taking careful aim he fired all his remaining bullets in quick succession. The first punched a hole in the monster's wing. Like the rest of the monster's body, the membrane was stone—or stone-like flesh—but here it was thin enough to puncture. The second and third bullets also made holes from which fine cracks extended. When the fourth shot struck, a large chunk split away and the gargoyle's flight became erratic. The final bullets fairly shattered the wing, sending the monster down to the cobbles with a shattering impact.

He stared down on the broken remains of the monster for a moment, then clambered back into the tower. The ringers were gone, he saw, and Dubnotal still stood in his protective circle, though he was too busy dodging to do anything else. Apparently, the cat-headed gargoyle was helpless to pass the barrier, but nothing prevented him from tearing up boards, metal rods, and loose pieces of stonework and using them as missiles.

"Judex, look out!" the Sâr cried. It was an unnecessary warning and one that cost the mystic dearly. The monster hurled a chunk of rock the size of a big man's fist. The projectile caught the Sâr in the torso and sent him reeling out of the circle, the *phurba* falling from his grip. The monster's lips pulled back from its fangs in a snarl of pleasure, and it stalked toward him.

Reflexively, Judex raised his pistol before remembering it was empty. The gargoyle had turned its back on him in its single-minded desire to kill Sâr Dubnotal and he used that. Racing after the monster he leaped on its back, locking his legs around its waist and one arm around its neck. He used the other to hammer at its head with the pistol.

The creature staggered, but quickly recovered. It was immensely strong and his weight impaired it no more than a housecat's would have slowed him. Worse, his hammering blows with the pistol barely scratched its head. The gargoyle flexed its wings, crushing him between them. Judex gasped in pain, but tightened his grip. Then the creature reached back, over its head. He felt the talons pierce his cloak and clothing to tear into the flesh of his back as it gripped him. Then the thing pulled him loose with frightening ease and slammed him down.

Ignoring his pain, the man in black tried to roll away but the monster was too fast. It placed a knee in his belly, crushing the wind out of him. The monster's talons dug into his chest muscles as it pinned him to the tower floor. Judex struck at it with the pistol and managed to break off one of the thing's fingers, but it swung the stump of its other arm, smashing the weapon out of his grasp. The cat's head lowered, fangs bared and Judex thrust up both hands in a futile attempt to hold it back.

As the mouth opened, ready to tear out his throat, Judex heard chanting from behind the creature. Sâr Dubnotal had risen and held the *phurba* in his hands as he murmured strange words. As the jaws descended on his throat, he saw the Sâr let go of the ritual knife. Amazingly, it did not fall but hovered for a moment before shooting toward the gargoyle's back. He heard the rasp of iron against stone then the monster reared back, its face a mask of pain and rage. It toppled to the side, as stiff and unmoving as stone should be.

As Judex rose, he saw Dubnotal kneel by the fallen gargoyle to inspect it. The handle of the *phurba* projected from the monster's back, between its shoulder-blades.

"Is it…dead?" he asked.

"Yes," Dubnotal replied. "At least, as much as that word can be applied to a creature like this. I should have recognized these gargoyles sooner. They were the work of a stonecutter named Reynard. Legend says that his wrath and lust were so great that they somehow animated the creatures and that neither magic nor the protection of holy symbols was any use against them. It is as I feared, my enemy has discovered the ancient magic of Averoigne and will be almost impossible to stop."

Judex shuddered and took a deep breath to steady himself. He had seen things this night that he didn't want to believe but, having seen, he couldn't turn his back on them. Evil such as this couldn't go unchecked, even if it meant delaying his own plans of vengeance.

"You saved my life, Sorcerer," he said.

"No more than you saved mine, my mysterious friend."

"If you need me again, will you be able to reach me?"

"I will." Dubnotal turned his attention back to the gargoyle for a moment. "The authorities will come soon," he said. "I will stay to deal with them, and to see to the final disposal of the gargoyles, but it may be best if you are gone when they arrive."

But when he looked up, Judex had already disappeared.

1916. Judex accomplished his vengeance on Favraux in 1913, and defeated a ring of spies in 1914. He is now 33, happily married, with at least one child. But World War I has been raging for well over a year. We do not know what role Jacques de Trémeuse played during the Great War. Unlike the Nyctalope ,who served in uniform, with the rank of commandant in the French forces, he was probably acting behind the scenes, like Arsène Lupin and Joseph Rouletabille, who both undertook secret missions for French Intelligence. Meanwhile, as Judex, he continued to serve justice, both behind the lines, as well as at the front. We begin with the former...

Chris Roberson: *Penumbra*

The morning papers all carried the story on their front pages, most with huge banner headlines above the fold. Perhaps the various editors thought their readers needed a diversion from another day's litany about the numbers of young French servicemen dead in a recent military action, or about ground lost to or won back from the Boche. Or perhaps they knew that glamorous crime, particularly so close to home, would always sell newspapers. Either way, over breakfast all of Paris was buzzing.

Ironically, of all of the reporters covering the event, Philippe Guérande of *Le Mondial* was the one most skeptical of the proposed connection to the infamous gang, the Vampires. Guérande had been writing about the suspected activities of the Vampires since the spring, even if his reports were buried in the back pages of the metropolitan section before the decapitation of Inspector Dural made front-page headlines. The editors at *Le Mondial*, though, knowing full well how many copies a Vampires-related lead story could sell, had commissioned one of their staff artists to do a somewhat hasty sketch of the figure clad in skin-tight black slinking away across the rooftop, alongside an inset photo of the victim's body lying on the pavement, the crushed remains tastefully covered in a white sheet the instant before the photographer had taken the shot.

Through the black-and-white grain of the photo, faint shadows could be seen appearing on the impromptu shroud, where the blood pooled on the body had begun to seep through the fabric. The editors then placed above the photo and pen-and-ink sketch a headline reading, *"VAMPIRES THROW VICTIM FROM HIGH WINDOW—FLEE SCENE."*

Guérande's article, however, left open the question of whether the infamous gang was or was not truly involved, stating merely that a man had fallen to his death from a high story window of a residential building, and that a figure clad in skin-tight black from head to toe had been seen fleeing the scene of the crime, running across the rooftops.

At the home offices of the banker Favraux, the topic was mentioned in passing, dispassionately, as one might discuss the weather or the quality of one's dinner of the previous night. Not 200 miles away, war raged, and young men bled out their last strung up on wires in No Man's Land, or huddled for shelter in trenches and hastily-dug foxholes, dreading the whiff of gas that might come drifting across the lines—chlorine, phosgene, or worse yet, mustard gas—but within the cool confines of Favraux's wood-paneled study, all was peaceful and serene. Favraux and his guest had business to discuss, and the concerns of the wider world dwindled in comparison.

Favraux's personal secretary, Vallières, an older man with snow-white beard and hair neatly trimmed, was on hand as he always was on these occasions; but he kept to the shadows at the corner of the room, silent, unobtrusive, never noticed unless and until he was needed. Vallières was the most trusted of all Favraux's servants and employees, and the only one to whom the banker entrusted his most guarded secrets. Favraux never kept notes during his meetings, or a personal diary. Instead, he looked to Vallières to monitor what was discussed, and to recall specific details on demand. So it was with great care that Vallières followed the conversation between Favraux and his young guest.

Dr. Wayne, a young American in Paris on an extended honeymoon, had opened discussions with Favraux a few weeks previous about potential European investments for his family fortune. The sole heir of a considerable estate, Wayne was eager to see his fortunes grow, and Favraux had convinced the young American that he was best qualified to assist. On that morning, Wayne and Favraux were in the midst of yet another in a seemingly endless series of meetings about investment opportunities.

Wayne was prepared to invest some considerable capital into a number of funds selected and managed by Favraux, but he had need of a short-term loan while a cashier's check was drawn up and sent from the States. In return, he would provide an extremely valuable piece of jewelry as collateral. After feigning reluctance for an appropriate span, the banker Favraux quickly agreed to the arrangement. Vallières well understood why. The gem, which Wayne's wife was bringing from their rooms at the Park Hotel, was a fire-opal of immense value, mined in the Xinca region of the Republic of Guatemala some years before. Famously known as the Gotham Girasol, it was easily worth one hundred times the loan that it secured. If Wayne paid back the loan—along with the exorbitant interest rate Favraux was charging, compounded weekly—it was all to the good, but if he should default, and the gem remain in Favraux's possession, so much the better.

Favraux's distress was obvious and genuine, then, when Mrs. Wayne arrived in tears and without the gem in her possession.

"Oh, darling," she said, throwing herself into her husband's arms. "You simply must forgive me. I... I no longer have the Gotham Girasol."

Dr. Wayne stiffened, and cast an uncomfortable glance to his host before turning his wife's face upwards and looking her in the eyes.

"Martha," he said, trying to sound calm but his voice audibly strained, "whatever do you mean?" His French was as good as hers, which is to say passable, but pronounced with a thick-tongued American accent that fell hard on Gallic ears.

"It was stolen from me nearly a week ago," Mrs. Wayne answered, her voice quavering. "I was wearing it when we attended that ball on Avenue Maillot, and when I was woken by the police the next morning, I found it gone." She bit her lip, her eyes flashing. "I wanted to tell you, but I was simply so overwrought by its loss that I couldn't bring myself to mention it before now."

Dr. Wayne held onto his wife for a moment, as his gaze drifted and settled on the middle distance, thoughts racing behind his eyes. Then he released her, and slumped into a chair. Mrs. Wayne, sobbing vocally behind a handkerchief, kept stealing glances at her husband, almost as though gauging his reactions.

The Waynes did not need to explain to Favraux or to Vallières about the ball on Avenue Maillot the week before. All Paris knew about that night. It had made the front pages of all the papers, just as the murder had done that morning, and in both cases the Vampires were suspected.

Several days earlier, the Baron de Mortesalgues had held a grand ball at his home on Avenue Maillot, in celebration of his niece's birthday. Over 100 of the brightest lights of Parisian aristocracy, from financiers to artistes, rushed to the reception. At the stroke of midnight, the doors were locked from the outside and, by all accounts, a strange gas entered the salon. All of those trapped within found themselves succumbing, passing into unconsciousness and not waking until the authorities arrived in the morning. No one was hurt, but the Baron, his niece and all of the jewelry and valuables in the room were missing. Neither the Baron nor his niece had been seen since that night. Authorities feared the worst, that they had fallen prey to the infamous Vampires, or to the criminal organization led by the villainous Moreno, only recently escaped from jail. Parisians had not been so fascinated with criminal exploits since the days of Fantômas, as the circulation figures of the daily newspapers certainly proved.

After a long moment, Dr. Wayne composed himself, and rose from the chair, straightening his waistcoat.

"Mr. Favraux, you must accept my apologies," he said, turning to his host. "It appears that I will not be able to provide you collateral, after all, and as a result my wife and I might be forced to cut short our stay in Paris."

Favraux bristled visibly. Vallières knew his employer's moods and tempers well, and could see that the banker was pained at the thought of not laying hands on the precious gem, to say nothing of the interest he had planned to collect on the loan. However, if Dr. Wayne were to return to the States without first investing in the banker's funds, Favraux stood to lose a great deal more. Just a few days' grace, and the cashier's check would arrive in Paris, but without the short-term loan to cover expenses, Wayne and his wife would have to leave almost immediately.

"Well, my dear Dr. Wayne," Favraux answered, visibly pained by what he was about to say, "we cannot allow the criminal element and the capricious whims of fate to interfere with the business of men, now can we? Absent the security of the gem as collateral"—he paused, his face flushing red with suppressed anger and anxiety—"I am still willing to loan you a small sum, sufficient to allow you to stay on in Paris until our business is concluded."

Dr. Wayne took Favraux's hand, visibly relieved.

"I cannot thank you enough for your generosity, Favraux," he said. "It would have been most... unfortunate, if our long negotiations would have been for naught."

The hard glance Dr. Wayne gave his wife made it clear to Vallières for whom such an outcome would have been the most unfortunate. Wayne was not the most doting husband, and for all of his wealth and refinement, he had a certain rough edge that Vallières found unsettling. No wonder his wife spent so much of their honeymoon by herself at cabarets and restaurants, while he whiled away his hours in business meetings with Favraux.

Once the arrangements for the loan were completed, and polite words were exchanged all around, Dr. Wayne and his wife took their leave.

When they had gone, Favraux dismissed Vallières for the rest of the day. The banker's daughter Jacqueline, had convinced him that his grandson needed more masculine attention, since her own husband had died nearly three years before. As a result, Favraux had reluctantly agreed to take his daughter and grandson to the circus for the afternoon, though it was obvious that he regretted the decision.

Vallières, unaccustomed to being at his liberty so early in a working day, saw nothing for it but to go home. Pausing only to pick up a copy each of the day's papers from the newsagent on the corner, he returned to the apartments he kept in another quarter of the city.

Once safely in his study, Vallières dropped the newspapers on his cluttered desk, piled high with papers, notes and photographs. He laid his coat carefully across the back of a chair, and crossed the floor to an armoire with a full-length mirror set in its door.

With practiced motions, Vallières removed his snow-white beard and mustaches, and pulled off his wig of snow-white hair. Dropping them into a bowl on a side table, he stood straighter, an intense scowl on his young, lean face. He smoothed back his short black hair, and regarded himself momentarily in the mirror. Having put aside the mask of the ever-loyal, always patient Vallières, he stood revealed for who he truly was: Judex!

Of course, Judex himself was something of a mask. Not the name with which he was born, he chose it by necessity, to help him fulfill the oath he made to his mother, so many years before. An oath to avenge the death of his father, the Count de Trémeuse, who took his own life after losing the family fortune to bad investments. Investments made on the advice of an eager young banker, Favraux.

That his father died just as news arrived that a gold claim he had in Africa had come through, making him the owner of a fabulously rich gold mine, was an irony almost too cruel to bear.

Instead, fate had decreed that Judex would own a gold mine, along with his brother, who was currently in Africa overseeing its operations. His brother would return before the year was out, to help put into motion the next and final stage of their revenge against the banker. For the moment, though, Judex would continue to play the faithful servant, learning everything he could about Favraux and his dealings before making his terminal move.

And at the moment, Favraux's dealings included the young American couple, the Waynes.

Judex sat at his desk, and looked over the piles of newspaper clippings, bank records, notes, photographs, medical documents, receipts and vouchers. Ephemera and trivia, bits of information discarded in the wake of the young doctor and his wife. A portrait of a life painted in tiny bits of data, like the points in a Seurat painting.

Judex had been investigating Dr. Wayne and his wife as a matter of course, these past weeks. If the Waynes were good people, Judex would by subtle means attempt to steer them away from investing their money with Favraux. He could not stand idly by and watch another family ruined as his was. If the Waynes themselves were dishonest, unethical people, though, then they deserved whatever fate befell them.

Before that morning, Judex had found no reason to suspect their sincerity, nor to believe they were anyone but who they said they were. He had initially suspected that the couple might not be the Waynes at all, but might instead be Raphael Norton and Ethel Florid, Americans who had embezzled $200,000 from American millionaire George Baldwin and fled to Europe. Through careful investigation, though, he had been able to confirm that was not the case. They were, indeed, Dr. and Mrs. Wayne, and their fortune was their own.

Why, then, did Judex feel so strongly that something was amiss? Mrs. Wayne's recounting of the theft of the Girasol this morning, though emotional, was not convincing. It had too much the air of a rehearsed speech, of a dramatic address delivered on queue. She was lying, but about what?

The answer, Judex found, was right in front of him.

Amongst the piles of research materials on the Waynes was a recent clipping from the front page of *Le Mondial*, just starting to yellow with age. The headline boasted of the poisoning of a dancer named Marfa Koutiloff while onstage performing in a ballet entitled *The Vampires*. The story had caught Judex's eye, as in a photo of stunned theatergoers accompanying the article Dr. and Mrs. Wayne could be seen, eyes wide with shock and horror.

Judex drew a jeweler's loop from the desk drawer and peered at the photo through its magnifying lens. Around the neck of Mrs. Wayne, he could make out the Gotham Girasol, suspended from a silver chain.

Judex laid beside that photo another, clipped from the society pages of *La Chronique de Paris* just a few days before. It was of Mrs. and Dr. Wayne, taken the evening of Baron de Mortesalgues' ball on Avenue Maillot. In the photo, the young couple were smiling happily, unaware that in a few hours' time they would be rendered helpless and unconscious by assailants unknown. Judex studied the photo through the jeweler's loop, as though seeing it for the first time. Dr. Wayne in evening wear, his wife in an elegant gown with a plunging neckline. Judex looked closer, to be certain.

He sat back, his brow creased. There could be no doubt. In the photo, Mrs. Wayne was clearly not wearing the Gotham Girasol. The gem had not been stolen that night at Avenue Maillot, because she had not been wearing it. That could account for why she didn't report the gem's theft the following morning, when the rest of the victims were reciting their losses and woes to the authorities. Why, then, concoct a flimsy tale about the gem's loss at the ball, nearly a week later?

Why was Mrs. Wayne lying?

Perhaps the Waynes were not all they appeared to be, after all.

Judex was convinced that the Vampires were involved in some fashion. There were simply too many points of congruence to dismiss them as coincidence—the Waynes in attendance at the ballet when Koutiloff is poisoned, and again at Avenue Maillot for the most daring robbery of the decade. What other connections might there be?

Judex was committed. He would investigate the Vampires in parallel with his ongoing researches into the Waynes, and determine whether the couple deserved his assistance, or whether they deserved to be damned along with the banker Favraux.

Judex was not the only one investigating the Vampires. The police were involved, naturally, their every available resource assigned the task of searching for the gang. Impatient at the progress of the investigation to date, though, the authorities had called in the assistance of private detectives like "Celeritas" Ribaudet and the famous Rouletabille, and citizens such as Cigale Mystère—a civilian adventurer who assisted the Parisian authorities from time to time, cruising the streets in his electric car, loaded down with futuristic gadgets and devices—and the Nyctalope—who prowled the nights for sign of the Vampires, his keen eyes seeing what others could. But so far no one had been able to track the Vampires to their lair, nor divine the mystery of who led the mysterious organization. There were whispers of a Great Vampire who directed his subordinates' movements from behind closed doors, and perhaps even higher echelons of power above even that, but they remained only whispers, nothing more.

But the police and the other mystery men could busy themselves tracking down the criminals. Judex was interested in matters only as they pertained to Favraux. What deviltry the Vampires did in the larger world was of no concern to him. Until his father had been avenged, there could be no justice.

It seemed to Judex prudent to begin his investigations into the Vampires at the site of their most recent crime. Their earlier exploits—the decapitation of Inspector Dural, the poisoning of Marfa Koutiloff, the mass robbery and possible kidnapping at the home of the Baron de Mortesalgues—he knew well enough from the detailed coverage provided each in the daily news. If there were hidden connections to the Waynes to be found, there might be secrets about this most recent case yet to be disclosed.

It took only a few hours investigation and a few francs placed in the right palms to turn up a number of interesting facts about the case. The victim, who had fallen to his death from a fifth story window, was one Jean Morlet, an associate a Monsieur Oreno who resided at that same address. However, Judex could find no record of this Oreno before the previous week. In addition, he was able to discover that Oreno had rented out the entire fifth floor of the building the day after the events at Avenue Maillot. Most surprising, Judex learned that the night before had not been the first attempted robbery at that address, but the second in less than a week. The police had apprehended the burglar attempting to break into Oreno's suite of room. The burglar, an American, was currently in jail awaiting trial.

The next day, once "Vallières" had completed his duties for the banker Favraux, Judex made for the jail, sure that he was feeling around the edges of some larger puzzle. It took only a few francs to learn the prisoner's name, and a few francs more to convince the policeman on duty that Judex should be allowed a brief counsel with him in private.

"I've already told the other inspector everything I'm going to say," the prisoner said, after Judex had been ushered into his cell. The policeman locked the door.

"Just call when you are ready to go, Monsieur," the policeman said, retreating down the hall.

Judex waited until the jailer was well out of earshot, and turned his attention to the American. He was young, just entering his twenties, with high, narrow cheekbones, a prominent hawk-nose and piercing eyes.

"I am not with the police, Allard," Judex said, drawing his cape tight around him, gazing at the American from beneath the brim of his hat. "I have questions of my own."

The American seemed to squirm beneath Judex's steady gaze.

"All right, then," he finally said, his eyes shifting to the ground. "What is it you want to know? It's not as if I've got anywhere else to be at the moment."

"You were arrested for attempting to burgle the residence of a Monsieur Oreno, which I will come to in a moment. But first, I'm curious to know why you are in Paris, Mr. Allard. Why come to a land in the grips of war, when you could easily live in safety at home?"

Judex could not help but think of Raphael Norton and his embezzled fortune. But if this were he, what had become of his female accomplice, Miss Florid?

"Look," Allard said, raising his chin defiantly, "I'm not about to sit out the war like those cowards back at home in the States, too fat and lazy to come to the defense of their European cousins. If all men don't act to stamp out evil at its root, it'll spread like a weed all across the globe. And then where will we be?"

Judex's mouth drew into a tight line, and he said, "I'm sure I don't know."

"Well, I couldn't sit idly by while others fought for the cause of justice," Allard went on. "I'm a... how do you say it in French?" He paused, and then said the English term, "barnstormer."

Judex nodded slowly, and translated into the French, "An aviator."

"Yes," Allard answered, "I'm an aviator. Anyway, I have relatives in Russia, and one of them, a Major Kentov, has agreed to arrange for me to be given a position in the Czar's air corps. Kentov was supposed to send word for me here in Paris, and then I'd go on and meet him in Russia. But I've been here a few weeks now, and I'm not sure if word is ever going to come. I'm starting to worry that Kentov might have died out on the Eastern Front, and then I might never get a chance to do my part against the Kaiser."

"If you already suspect that this Kentov will never contact you here, why remain in Paris? Why not just continue on to Moscow, come what may?"

Allard's gaze shifted, and a blush raised on his cheek.

"I have been... distracted," he finally said, a faraway sound to his voice.

Judex pulled his cape tighter, but nodded slightly.

"Very well," he said. "Now we come to the matter of Monsieur Oreno. Who is he to you?"

"He's a cheating bastard, and a liar!" Allard scowled, teeth clenched, his eyes flashing. "Oreno stole something of considerable value from me, and I was just trying to get it back."

"How did you know him?"

"I've been going to a cabaret called the *Veuve Joyeuse* a great deal these past few weeks," Allard said, a wistful tone creeping into his voice, "and I met Oreno there one night. We talked a bit about the art of mesmerism, which he claimed to have some special knowledge of. I don't have any proof of this, but I think that he might have clouded my mind in some way. How else could he have known about the..." He paused, and bit down on the next word he'd been about to say. "About the item, that is," he finished, lamely.

"What was it that he stole from you?"

Allard's expression was guarded, his lips drawn tight.

"Something very dear to me," was all he would say.

A few nights later, after fruitless investigations, Judex returned to his apartments late in the evening. He looked forward to the day when his brother returned to Paris. His mission was a solitary one, but it would be nice to pass the time with someone, on occasion. Someone with whom he could lower his guard, drop the masks and just be himself. Whoever that truly was.

Judex's rooms were darkened, but he knew in an instant that something was amiss. A subtle scent on the air, a tingling sensation on the back of his neck. Once the door was shut and locked behind him, he knew. He was not alone.

"Do not turn on the light," came a soft, sultry voice from the darkness. "Or, if you must, turn on only the table lamp. It is so much nicer that way, don't you think?"

Judex's fingers ached for the brace of pistols he kept in the armoire, a dozen steps across the room. He would never go out unarmed again. In a flash, he calculated the path and distance to the armoire, the seconds needed to reach it and open the door, grab and aim the pistol—if the intruder were armed, he'd never reach it in time.

"If you're thinking of these," the voice from the darkness said, followed by the distinctive sound of a pistol's hammer being pulled back, "I liberated them from the cupboard when I came in. I do hope you don't mind."

Judex stood in place, but reached down to the table at his knees and switched on the lamp.

Seated in his chair, with her feet up on the desk, was a woman wearing a skin-tight black jumpsuit. She was covered head to toe, with only her face left revealed. Her smoldering, fierce gaze caught Judex's, and she smiled.

"A pleasure to make your acquaintance, Judex," the woman said, gesturing him towards the couch with the barrel of the pistol, the other held casually in her lap.

"Who are you?" Judex stood his ground, arms crossed.

"Who I am is not of particular importance at this juncture, but whom I represent most definitely is."

"The Vampires," Judex hissed through his teeth.

"Got it in one." The woman smiled. "I have come to tell you something. This murder that you've begun investigating, the man who fell to his death from that building—the Vampires had nothing to do with it. Our leader has only recently become aware of your existence, and has ordered that you be left alone for the moment because he is not yet sure whether you can be of use to us in future. If you interfere in our affairs, though, and go from being a potential asset to being a nuisance, we will be forced to eliminate you."

"And to forestall this you deny one of your crimes? How do you benefit?"

The woman bristled, a cloud passing momentarily across her smooth features.

"We deny none of our actions!" The woman gestured with the pistol, and Judex tensed involuntarily, anticipating a shot. "Did we cut the head from that oaf Dural? Yes! Did we poison that bitch Koutiloff? Yes! But did we throw this Morlet to his death last night? Most definitely not."

"Why should I believe you?" Judex's eyes narrowed.

"Because if we were truly guilty of the killing, we wouldn't be warning you away. We'd just kill you for interfering in our business. But I prefer to kill those who deserve to die." Her mouth drew into a line, and she added in a hushed whisper, "Like that bastard Moreno."

"And what about the Avenue Maillot heist? Do you deny that one, as well?"

The woman jumped to her feet, tossing one of the pistols to the ground with a thud, and pointing the other square at Judex's chest.

"You mention Avenue Maillot to me?" She snarled, white teeth bared behind curled lips. "Would it surprise you to learn that even the Vampires can be victims, at least in this case? That the plunder from that night was stolen from us before we'd even reached the safety of our home?" The woman began to walk to the open window, her expression grave. "If ever I lay hands on that bastard Moreno..." she began, her voice trailing off into silence.

When she reached the window, her attention briefly turned away from him, Judex prepared to rush forward, intending to tackle her to the ground. As though she could sense his intentions, though, the woman spun around, and pointed the barrel of the pistol directly at Judex's face.

"Please don't try that," the woman said, sounding again all sweetness and light. "I don't want to have to hurt you unnecessarily, and it would be a shame to mar such a striking profile."

With that, the woman tossed the pistol to the ground, and stepped over the sill to the ledge beyond. When Judex rushed to the window to look out, she had already disappeared into the night.

Judex could not sleep that night. The information the woman provided, however unintentionally, was the last puzzle piece that he needed. He had only to confirm his suspicions, and all would be clear.

Returning to the night air, his cape wrapped around him and his hat pulled down low over his brown, Judex made his way to the scene of the crime. With ease, he did what Allard and the black-suited burglar had both failed to do, breaking into the home of Monsieur Oreno without once being seen. Oreno was not in, no doubt meeting with his associates at the *Veuve Joyeuse* cabaret at that hour. Crime does not keep workman's hours, after all.

In a locked bedroom in Oreno's suite, Judex found what he was looking for, and more besides, packed into several valises and a few small chests. It was the work of just a few minutes to transfer the contents of the cases and chests to his automobile, parked on the street outside. One item in particular he slipped into his pocket.

Driving to the Public Assistance Bureau to make a donation, Judex cursed himself for his earlier blindness. Monsieur Oreno. "M. Oreno." He should have seen it long before.

Mrs. Wayne was packing up her belongings in their rooms at the Park Hotel. Her husband had concluded his business with Favraux that afternoon, and they would now be returning home to America.

"Your pardon," said a voice from the shadows, and Mrs. Wayne leapt a few inches into the air, her heart in her throat.

"I mean you no harm," the voice continued, and Judex stepped out from a darkened corner, silent as a ghost.

"W-who are you?" Mrs. Wayne clutched a black leotard to her chest, wringing the fabric in her hands, her packing forgotten.

"You can call me Judex."

"Did you say... justice?"

Something like a smile played across Judex's mouth.

"No. Judex. But it is about justice that I've come. I know what you have done, Mrs. Wayne."

Judex pointed to the black leotard in her hands, with scalloped-edge bat wings attached at the shoulders and wrists.

"I see that you even kept the costume you wore that night."

Tears began to stream down her cheeks.

"I hadn't meant for anyone to get hurt, honestly. But that man chased me out onto the ledge, and then he fell, and then... But I just had to... I had to get it back..."

Judex held out his hand and opened his palm, revealing a fire-opal with a faint purple cast and lights dancing deep within. The Gotham Girasol.

"I broke into Oreno's rooms," Judex explained, "and found what remained of the loot from the Avenue Maillot robbery. Ironically, the Girasol had ended up in amongst the other pilfered goods, despite the falsity of your claims. I find that somewhat... amusing."

Mrs. Wayne looked with wide eyes at the gem in Judex's palm, and then met his eyes.

"You mean...?"

"Yes, Mrs. Wayne, I know that you gave away the Gotham Girasol some time before the night of the ball."

Mrs. Wayne struggled to take a breath.

"What will you...?" She paused, swallowing hard. "That is, what will you do with...?"

"I have given the pilfered goods to the Public Assistance Bureau, where they will no doubt serve society better than they ever could have done in the hands of their rightful owners. I am, however, prepared to return the Girasol to you."

"No," she said, turning her eyes away. "I could not bear to hold it. There is another who should have it, who should always keep..." Her words choked off in a stifled sob.

"Allard," Judex said simply.

Mrs. Wayne was shocked, but she nodded, slowly.

"You met him at a cabaret, unless I miss my guess," Judex went on, "and you found him a welcome change to your somewhat brusque and acerbic husband, the good doctor. You wanted to give him a token of your affection, one which you prized above all others. Otherwise, the gesture would be meaningless, no?"

Mrs. Wayne nodded still, as though hypnotized.

"No," she said, then shook her head, as if to clear away cobwebs. "I mean, yes. I mean..." She drew a deep breath, collecting herself. "I met... him... a few weeks ago. My husband had been so busy with his meetings that it was almost as if we weren't going to have a honeymoon at all. I started going out on my own, to the restaurants and cabarets. It was at the *Veuve Joyeuse* that I met... Mr. Allard. So intense, and an aviator. How dashing he was. I suppose you could say that we fell in love. I gave him the gem in a moment of passion, symbol of my feelings for him. But I'd soon have reason to regret it."

Mrs. Wayne glanced at the gem, still resting in Judex's palm.

"The next day, my husband told me that we might need the gem for collateral. I knew that any day he might come and ask me for it, and I wouldn't have it. As soon as I could, I rushed to see Mr. Allard, to get it back, but he told me that it had been stolen by this Oreno character. He promised he'd get it back from Oreno, but the next thing I knew Mr. Allard had been arrested."

"So you had no choice but to steal it yourself," Judex said.

"Yes. I'd heard all the stories about the infamous gang, the Vampires. I hired a costume from the Costumier Pugenc, the same I'd seen in the ballet weeks ago, with the idea that if anyone saw me breaking into Oreno's apartments, the blame would be cast on the Vampires gang. The man came upon me just as I was entering the room, though, and then he fell to his death. After that, I knew I'd never have another chance at stealing it back, so I told my husband it had been stolen that night at the Avenue Maillot ball."

Mrs. Wayne took a deep breath and sighed. She smoothed the fabric of the black leotard in her hands, and then set it gently back on the bed.

"I suppose you will turn me over to the police now," she said, sounding resigned. "I am wanted by the law, after all."

"I wouldn't give a bent *sou* for the law," Judex said, tightening his hand into a fist around the gem. "The law turns a blind eye while villains prosper, allowing a cancer to eat away at society's heart. No, I care nothing for the law. I care only for justice."

Mrs. Wayne shook her head, looking like she wanted to spit.

"Justice? Do you want to know about justice, Monsieur Judex? Then I will tell you. I have just learned today that I am with child. Pregnant. And I don't know whether my husband or my beloved is the father."

"You talk to me of justice? What are your sordid affairs to me or to Lady Justice?"

Mrs. Wayne lifted her chin, defiant.

"Because even if the law never lays a hand on me, I still pay the price for my deeds. My own life is ended here, for the sake of my unborn child. Were it otherwise, I would leave my husband, and my beloved and I would be together forever. But what kind of life would my child have, with a penniless aviator as a father? Always at the fringes of society, living forever in the shadows. No, better to return home with my husband, letting him think the child is his, so that my baby can grow up in comfort, with all the opportunity in the world. So what if my heart belongs to another, and I die inside a little every moment we are apart? I live now for the sake of my child."

Judex stood silent, appraising her, and found he had nothing to say. Justice, the only god Judex worshipped, indeed moved in mysterious ways.

Tucking the gem back into his pocket, Judex strode to the door, making to leave. He drew his cape around him, already seeming to blend into the shadows.

"Wait!" Mrs. Wayne said, stepping forward, raising a tremulous hand. "Will you see...?" Her breath caught in her chest, and she swallowed hard before continuing. "Will you see Mr. Allard again?"

Judex shrugged beneath his cape.

"I do not know, madam."

"If you should see him, could you give him the Girasol for me? As a keepsake to remember me by?"

Judex's expression remained hard, but he nodded. He turned to the door.

"Only," Mrs. Wayne said, taking another step forward, "please don't tell him about the child. He has his own life to lead, and doesn't need a shadow hanging over him."

Judex did not turn around, but nodded again.

"I will," he said softly, and then disappeared into the night, leaving Mrs. Wayne alone with her memories.

The next day, an anonymous party posted bail for the American aviator, and Allard was released on his own recognizance. When his possessions were returned to him, Allard was surprised to find among them an envelope containing a near-priceless fire-opal and a railway ticket. The train left Paris that afternoon, heading east. Allard would take it as far as the state of combat would allow, and make it the rest of the way to Moscow on foot, if need be.

That same afternoon, Dr. Wayne and his wife were already in Le Havre, boarding a luxury liner that would carry them back to the United States.

In the home offices of the banker Favraux, Judex hid behind the mask of Vallières, waiting for his moment to strike.

And in the streets of Paris, the Vampires still prowled the shadows, and the search for them continued.

1916. This time, the action moves to the blood-drenched front lines of the Great War. Judex and his erstwhile ally Sâr Dubnotal are once again called to action to thwart Herr Doktor Von Meyer's latest scheme, this time teaming up with a very superhuman fellow in order to stop a supernatural apocalypse...

Matthew Baugh: *What Rough Beast*

"Monsieur Danner?"

Hugo looked up from his novel. The nurse was an angular woman in her 30s who he had never particularly liked. He knew the feeling was mutual; with so few beds to spare for the wounded, she didn't think much of accommodating one uninjured Legionnaire.

"There is a man wanting to see you," the nurse said. "Will you follow me, please?"

He put down the book and rose with the ease of a gifted athlete in perfect health. He was handsome, with his tanned skin, and his hair and eyes so dark that many of his compatriots mistook him for a "Red Indian." More than that, there was a sense of power about him, as if his personality was charged with electricity that made him the center of attention.

With a sour look, she led him through the rows of cots crammed into the ruined church that now served as a field hospital. Outside, the day was sunny and there was no sound of the fighting in the trenches, not five miles away. She left him in the shadow of an oak where an elderly man dressed in formal black waited. On the lane, just beyond the tree, stood an expensive Peugeot touring car.

"Legionnaire Danner?" the white-haired man asked, extending his hand politely. Hugo shook it, trying to size up his visitor. He was probably in his sixties, and possessing a quiet dignity that impressed the younger man. He wore no sign of rank or service.

"My name is Vallières," the man said.

"Do I know you, Monsieur?"

"No," Vallières said, "and there is no reason that you should. I am not a terribly important person; outside of the mission I have been given."

"And this mission concerns me?" Hugo asked.

"It does... At least, if you truly are the one they call *le Colorado*."

"I come from Colorado, in the United States," he replied. "Some of the men in the Legion called me that as a nickname."

"I have heard some remarkable stories about *le Colorado*," Vallières continued. "They say that you single-handedly resupplied your post during the recent German offensive. You carried 1000 kilos of food and ammunition on your back through no-man's land."

Hugo shrugged.

"Is it also true that you went into the trenches alone and, when your rifle was broken, slew scores of men with your bare hands?"

Hugo didn't respond. He wanted to like the white-haired gentleman, but he wondered where this was going.

"You were shot?"

"More times than I could count."

"And bayoneted?"

"The *Boches* did their best. They managed to shred my uniform, for all the good it did them."

"You were not wounded?"

In response, Hugo stripped off his shirt revealing lean, hard muscles and unmarked skin.

"Why, then, were you in the hospital?"

"Exhaustion."

Vallières shook his head in wonder. "If all of this is true, then you are the man we need."

"It is true," Hugo said.

"Forgive me, but this is so remarkable. Can you show me something to convince me?"

Hugo walked over to the man's automobile. Taking a solid grip with both hands, he strained to lift the vehicle. The weight didn't bother him, but it was tricky balancing the big car, and he wanted to be careful not to damage it. After a moment, he found the right stance, and his feet sank ankle-deep into the grassy lawn as he raised the car over his head.

"How do you do that?"

"They grow us strong in Colorado."

Vallières smiled. "I think, rather, it has something to do with your father, the medical scientist, Abednego Danner."

Hugo scowled as he lowered the vehicle to the ground. He hadn't made a secret of his strength in his service with the Foreign Legion, but had never said a word about the treatment his father had used on him in the womb. He felt suddenly vulnerable, something uncomfortable for him.

"What else do you know?"

"You were liked in your hometown, even though your parents kept you rather secluded. You left to attend Webster University in Missouri where you excelled at American football. You left there…"

"I left when I accidentally killed another player in a game," Hugo said. "Monsieur Vallières, where is this leading?"

"Forgive me, Monsieur Danner, but it was necessary to investigate you. I regret that I have crossed the bounds of discretion, but I assure you, there is no need for concern. Your private history is safe with me; even should you refuse to accept my offer."

"What offer?"

"There is a mission you are needed for. It is most urgent and only you have the power to accomplish it."

What kind of mission was this?

Vallières had dropped Hugo in an abandoned farmhouse close to the front. He'd obtained the American's release from the hospital with a set of orders signed by General Broulard and brought him to this remote place.

"Wait here," the old man said. "You will be joined by three others shortly. Two men and a woman."

"Agents of the French government?" Hugo asked.

"Not exactly," Vallières said with an enigmatic smile. "I am a patriot, but trust me when I say that this is a greater matter than nation against nation. You will understand soon enough."

Hugo looked into the old man's eyes and saw the strength there. He could tell that he would not get any more from Vallières, except through force. He decided that he would rather trust that the man was an ally.

Vallières showed him where provisions and an oil lamp were kept, and the best way to blank out the windows so the enemy would not see his light and call down fire on him. Then he bade him good luck and drove away.

Hugo waited, impatiently, for several hours. There was some furniture still in the house, though most of the belongings had long since been looted. There were a round table and a few chairs, plain but made with painstaking craftsmanship. Hugo wondered about the hand that had carved them. He imagined a farmer, skilled with mallet and chisel, and the family he shared meals with, and wondered if they were still alive.

He made himself as comfortable as he could and ate some of the provisions, finding the bread stale, but the cheese good and the wine excellent. For a time, he tried to read his novel, but without much success. He was too anxious to focus his mind on anything for long.

Just past dusk, he heard the sounds of a car coming down the lane. Hugo extinguished his lantern and watched as the vehicle came to a stop and two shadowed figures emerged.

With the confidence born of invulnerability, Hugo opened the door and stepped out. The visitors walked into the light from the doorway and, if they were afraid, he couldn't see it. The first was a man as tall as he was; he wore a European suit but with the beard, turban, and sash of a Sikh. The woman looked to be well into middle age, though still very attractive. She had a wealth of black hair, shot with gray that framed a pale, lovely face.

"You are the people I am to meet?"

"Yes," the man replied.

"I was told to expect three."

"We are all here," said a voice from behind him. Hugo spun to see another man, this one dressed in a long black cape and matching slouch hat that partially hid his features. He had not heard or seen any movement, but the stranger had managed to enter the cottage.

"How did you…?"

"Pardon me," the turbaned man said, "but it would be more practical if we finished this conversation inside. Your light may be seen."

Hugo stepped aside, letting the man and his companion pass, then followed and shut the door.

"Now, perhaps you can tell me what this is all about," he said. "And who are you?"

"I am Sâr Dubnotal," the turbaned man said. "My companion is Mademoiselle Gianetti Annunciata. Our mysterious friend uses the name Judex."

Hugo scowled, puzzled by the men's odd pseudonyms. Still, this was secretive business and spies, he supposed, must have codenames. "Gentlemen, Mademoiselle," he said with a nod. "If someone can tell me what we are here for, I'd appreciate it. I've been on pins and needles all day."

"Of course," Sâr Dubnotal said with a polite smile. "Each person here has certain abilities that are needed to prevent the unleashing of a terrible weapon."

Hugo felt his heart begin to pump faster and his mouth tightened in a grim smile. This was the sort of thing he'd been looking for: a true challenge, a chance to make a difference.

Dubnotal produced a folded map and spread it out on the table. It showed France and the western front was clearly indicated by a red line.

"As you know, the war has been static for some time, with each side entrenched against the other. There have been offensives and counter-offensives, all without any real result. But recently something new happened, here."

The Sâr placed his finger on a point that Hugo judged to be about 20 miles north of the farmhouse.

"For the last three nights, the bodies of the fallen have risen from the trenches and walked."

Hugo glanced at the man's face, incredulous, but the turbaned man seemed completely serious.

"The dead walking? That's preposterous!"

"I have heard the reports," Judex said, his shadowed features grim. "They say that the soldiers walk or crawl in the same direction. It doesn't seem to matter whether the dead belong to our forces or the Germans. Some soldiers have tried to shoot them down, but short of blowing them to bits, nothing stops their macabre pilgrimage."

"Our enemy has strange powers, and strange allies," the Sâr said. "I have taken the liberty of procuring ammunition that should be more effective." He produced two boxes of pistol cartridges from his jacket and set them on the table.

Judex opened a box and took out one of the bullets to examine. It shone a bright pale color in the lamplight.

"This is silver?"

Sâr Dubnotal nodded.

"Your best target with these is the heart," he said.

Hugo stared at the men in disbelief. "Are you serious?" he demanded. "This story is insane! It's obviously nothing more than hysteria, or shell-shock."

Judex had taken out a pair of Steyr automatic pistols and was changing out his load.

"You're actually going into combat with silver bullets," Hugo said, feeling more disgusted with each moment.

The dark-clad man looked him in the face with such intensity that he took half a step back before he caught himself.

"Monsieur Danner," Judex said. "My homeland is threatened and I plan to fight. I believe, as you do, that we will face only mortal soldiers; silver will kill them as surely as lead. On the other hand, if our friend is correct, I do not intend to go into battle unprepared."

He handed his second pistol and a box of shells to Hugo, who tucked them in the pockets of his jacket.

"Thanks."

"For what? A man like you has no need of guns." Judex turned back to Sâr Dubnotal. "Where are we going?"

"Here." He indicated a spot on the map some distance behind the enemy lines. "This is a ruined fortress here, the ancient Château de Joiry. It is said to be haunted, and to contain passages that descend into Hell itself."

Hugo felt a stab of anger at this the man's melodramatics, but said nothing.

"Currently the Château is in the hands of Herr Doctor Von Meyer of Leipzig," Dubnotal said. "He is a powerful occultist with dozens of disciples, and may be the most dangerous man in Europe. He is the seventh son of a seventh son, and is 49 generations removed from the master magician, Simon of Tyre. More than that, he remembers the knowledge of every one of his incarnations."

Hugo's patience snapped.

"Look," he said. "You can believe in whatever kind of hocus pocus you want; that's your business. But, for pity's sake, get to the point. Is this man a mastermind? Then tell me where he is and I'll kill him. Show me his weapon and I'll break it to pieces. But, please, don't ask me to believe this nonsense about sorcery and past lives."

The Sâr seemed unperturbed by Hugo's outburst.

"I do not ask you to believe anything, Monsieur Danner," he said. "I simply offer information; it is up to you to decide how to use it. There is one more thing I must show you. If you will be seated around the table and join hands..."

"What is this, some kind of séance?" Hugo asked.

"Gianetti is one of the most gifted spirit mediums of our age," the Sâr replied.

Hugo nearly refused, but the appeal in the woman's dark eyes, and Judex's stern expression swayed him. He sat opposite Judex and joined hands with Gianetti on one side and Sâr Dubnotal on the other. The turbaned man began to chant quietly, using words that belonged to no language Hugo recognized.

A thin, faintly luminous mist was gathering on the table and dribbled off the edges. It thickened as Hugo watched and he seemed to see tiny figures moving through it. Slowly the insect-sized forms resolved into human beings—men in tattered uniforms—who trudged and crept through a landscape sculpted of mist."

"He calls them," Gianetti said in a hollow voice.

"Who?" Sâr Dubnotal asked.

"Von Meyer calls the dead to his home."

"Why does he call them?"

"That he may use their flesh and bone to sculpt a weapon; a colossus that will sweep away the forces of his enemies."

"By what power does he call them?"

"By the words of the grimoire."

"What grimoire?"

"The book of Nathare of Vyones."

The Sâr caught his breath. Even in the dim light, Hugo could see that his face had gone pale.

"Does he build the same abomination that once laid waste to Ylourgne?"

"He does, and no weapon forged of man shall be able to stop it."

"Show me!"

Gianetti gasped in pain. Her eyes rolled back and Hugo felt her hand spasm and grow cold. He looked at her in alarm, but the spell passed in a moment. When his gaze returned to the table, the scene had changed. The tiny soldiers lay in heaps while robed men and nude man-like things hewed the flesh from their bones with knives and cleavers. The flesh they gathered in a cauldron that simmered with a deep red glow while the bones they placed in a vat of sickly pale hue.

As quickly as the two vessels filled, huge bestial man-things ladled their contents into buckets which hooded men carried into another area where they dumped the contents on a great pile in the shape of a colossal, partially fleshed skeleton.

"The Colossus," Gianetti said. "Made from the flesh and bones of ten-thousand dead men. He will—"

Her words ended with a shriek of pain as she leapt to her feet, her limbs twitching with epileptic frenzy. Hugo and Judex both reached for her, but the Sâr's voice stopped them.

"She is in the power of our enemy," he said. "If you touch her, she could come to great harm. Please, leave this to me."

"*El Tebib?*" Gianetti's voice had changed into a deep and cultured male voice. "*El Tabib, ist dass Sie?*"

"I am here, Von Meyer," Dubnotal replied. Hugo was amazed at how calm he remained.

"*You seek to spy on me, my old friend,*" Gianetti said. Her limbs no longer twitched but Hugo saw that her feet hovered several inches over the floor. The sight sent a shiver of dread through him. He glanced at Judex, wondering if the same fear he felt had penetrated those unreadable features.

"Release the woman," Dubnotal said in a clear, reasonable tone. "She is an innocent; your conflict is with me."

"*An innocent?*" Gianetti threw back her head and peals of masculine laughter came from her mouth. "*El Tebib, don't you know how much joy it gives me to torment an innocent? The jaded are so tedious, but the naïve can provide us with such exquisite entertainment.*"

Hugo saw the Sâr's hand dip into his pocket and emerge with a thick piece of chalk. Out of the corner of his eye he saw that Judex had drawn his Steyr, but made no move to point it at the woman.

"Danner," Sâr said. "Seize Gianetti."

Hugo leapt forward, his arms closing firmly around the woman's slender form. She struggled with inhuman strength, clawing and biting, but might have been trapped in a steel vice for all the good it did her. His only concern was to keep her from harming herself in her frenzy.

Dubnotal didn't waste a moment. He bent low and used the chalk to draw an even circle around Hugo and his captive. Then he drew strange glyphs, fourteen in all, evenly spaced around the outer edge. When he completed the last one, Gianetti screamed in her own voice and went limp in Hugo's arms. As gently as he could, he powered her to the wooden floor.

"What did you do?" Judex asked.

"I did not think he was so powerful," the turbaned man said. "He reached out with his psychic powers and overwhelmed her mind. The circle should protect her, but…"

He stopped as the woman's body convulsed violently and her mouth began to foam. Hugo caught her arms to keep her from hurting herself.

"She's like ice," he said.

The Sâr stepped carefully into the circle, taking care not to scuff the chalk. He knelt next to Gianetti and forced her eyes open with his fingers.

"Von Meyer is trying to break through my defenses," he said. "I must save her if I can."

"What can we do to help?" Hugo asked.

"Thank you, my friend, but this is something only I can do," Dubnotal replied. "While Meyer is distracted here, the two of you must go to his base. The colossus must not be allowed to rise."

Hugo gazed at the dark terrain far below. In the light of the full Moon, and from an altitude nearly a mile, the French country looked serene and beautiful. It was hard to imagine that this was the same land that was the battleground for tens of thousands of men in the daylight.

He rode in the front seat of Judex's plane, a Morane Type-L spotter. His mysterious companion, ever prepared, had hidden it in the old barn by the farmhouse. He and Sâr Dubnotal must have been planning this even before they contacted him.

His reverie was broken by the roar of diving engines and the whine of bullets. He felt a series of mild stings across his back and saw holes appear in the fuselage around him, then the aircraft rolled sideways and several dark shapes shot past.

Biplanes, he realized. *The Germans have found us.*

He strained into the darkness and counted three of the planes circling to come at them again. Judex didn't seem interested in a fight. He turned them away from their pursuers and began to climb toward a bank of clouds, clearly hoping to lose them.

It was a good strategy, but Hugo quickly realized that it wouldn't work. The German planes were faster, and could climb better than the Morane. It was only a matter of moments before they were strafed again.

As the planes began to fire, Judex took the Morane into a dive, picking up speed. The Germans followed as he dodged and wove in an unpredictable pattern. Abruptly, the aircraft rose into a steep climb, losing speed rapidly but rising out of the line of fire. It took only a moment for the pursuers to adapt and begin the climb behind them, but, as the Morane came close the stalling point, Judex turned the rudder and the nose dropped. In an instant, they were screaming toward the ground.

The Germans scattered to avoid the diving plane and, with a half roll, Judex leveled out heading back in the direction they had just come.

For a moment, Hugo thought they had escaped, or gained a few precious moments, but the squadron leader was an unusually talented flyer. He was back on their tail in an instant, firing his twin Vickers machineguns. Several shots struck the engine, for it stuttered and caught fire. Hugo could see Judex fighting with the controls, but the aircraft didn't respond. Despite his best efforts, the plane went into an uncontrolled spin and plummeted toward the ground.

The spinning, tumbling fall disoriented Hugo, but he knew he had only seconds to act. He reached behind him and grabbed the fuselage, his fingers tearing through the heavy canvas to find a solid grip on the plane's metal skeleton.

He pulled himself from the cockpit, shredding his safety harness as he did, and made his way, hand over hand, back to Judex's seat.

He had just a moment to register the disbelief on the Frenchman's face before he ripped lose his harness. Gathering his ally in his arms, Hugo kicked out into space.

Once he was away from the plane, Hugo managed to orient himself. They were approaching the ground rapidly and he barely had the time to get his feet under him before they hit.

The Moon had risen to the peak of the sky, but its light barely penetrated the heavy canopy of forest. As far as Hugo was concerned, that was a good thing. It meant that the German planes couldn't see to strafe them on the ground, and even search parties on foot would have trouble finding them.

Judex stirred where he lay and opened his eyes.

"How are you feeling?" Hugo asked.

"Alive," he replied, rising cautiously to his feet. "Nothing seems to be broken, which is remarkable."

"I cushioned your fall the best I could."

"And how are you?" Judex asked.

"I'm right as rain. Jumping out of an airplane doesn't seem to be that much for me."

Judex smiled and shook his head. "Did you know you'd survive?"

"I suspected as much, but I couldn't be sure. That's not the sort of thing I do for a lark, you know."

"Your strength is an amazing gift."

"I suppose so," Hugo said. "I keep hoping I'll find a way to use it that'll make a real splash in the world, but no luck. I think I'd have been a lot happier without it."

"What do you mean?"

"I didn't have any real friends, or even pets, when I was a kid. My mother was afraid of my strength; afraid I'd kill someone. When I got away from home I thought it'd be easy to make my way in the world, but all I seem able to do is break things and terrify people.

"I thought the War would be the perfect chance to put all that destructive power to use. The thing is, as many Huns as I kill, it doesn't seem to bring the conflict any closer to ending, and the people around me still die."

"You have lost friends," Judex said. It sounded like a question, but Hugo could tell that the man already knew the answer."

"One friend, yes. Another American named Tom Shayne. He was a swell guy until the Huns dropped a shell on us. It deafened me for a bit but there wasn't much left of Tom...

"I kind of went crazy then. I went into the trenches and wore myself out killing them. Can you imagine? It's like stomping cockroaches until you're so tired you can't lift your feet. That's when they put me in the field hospital. You know the rest."

Judex was silent for a moment, then he took a small flask from his coat and passed it to Hugo. He caught the aroma of strong brandy and took a swallow. The liquor warmed his stomach but did nothing to lift his spirits.

Judex took the flask back and raised it.

"Tom Shayne," he said, then took a small drink and put the flask away. The sincerity of the gesture touched Hugo.

"Did it help?" Judex asked.

"What?"

"Taking vengeance on your enemies."

"Not really," Hugo said, after a moment of thought. "Tom's still gone, and I hate the bastards more than ever."

Judex was silent and Hugo could see that his words had stirred something deep within the man.

"Perhaps for revenge to truly make a difference, it must be applied carefully."

"Are you saying I shouldn't have killed those bastards?" Hugo asked, feeling a surge of indignation.

"No," Judex replied. "I would never deny any man his just vengeance. It is only that, if it is to achieve true justice, revenge must be applied as carefully as a surgeon's scalpel."

"Is that why you do this?" Hugo asked.

"This mission?"

"More than that. You have some amazing skills, and your own airplane, and there's this hat and cloak. What is all of this for?"

"Yes," Judex replied. "There is a man I must punish, not just for what he has done to my family, but for all those he has ruined."

"Maybe when this is over, I'll help you," Hugo said.

Judex smiled and nodded, but it seemed to Hugo that he was still troubled. The cloaked man pulled out a map and a compass and spent a few moments getting his bearings.

"Joiry is that direction," he said, pointing into the woods. "If we start now and walk through the night we should be able to reach it before dawn.

"We can do much better than that," Hugo said with a grin. "I can outrun a race car if I want to."

Half an hour later, the two men stood on an outcropping of rock where heavy forest opened enough for a clear view of the starry sky. The ruin of Joiry Castle stood on a jagged escarpment overlooking the countryside. An unhealthy red light shone through some of the gaps in the ancient stonework.

"There," Judex said pointing to a narrow trail that ascended the rock face. "Movement on the rocks."

Hugo followed the gesture. In the light of the full Moon, he made out an irregular trickle of human shapes shambling up the path.

"Men," he said, "but there's something wrong with the way they're moving."

"I wish I had my field glasses," Judex said with a rueful smile. "I'm afraid I left them on the plane."

"We were in a bit of a hurry," Hugo replied, returning the smile.

"The walkers aren't being challenged, but the forest has been cut back at the base of the rocks. I don't see a way to reach the place by stealth."

"There's no need," Hugo said. "There's no way they can keep me out of that place. You stay here; I'll go and smash their super-weapon."

"We should both go."

"No offense, but for all your skills, you're just a man. There's no danger for me, but you'd likely be killed."

"No danger?" Judex fixed an intense stare on him. "My friend, you are powerful, but it is foolish to make such an assumption. We need a strategy."

"I don't," Hugo said. "I hope you take my advice and keep to cover. *Au revoir*, my friend. I'll bring you Von Meyer's head on a bayonet."

He made a huge leap, which cleared the treetops and took him to the edge of the woods, then he ran toward the cliff-side path. Hugo heard shouts from the ruins and, a moment later, the sound of rifle fire. He barked out a laugh as a lucky shot caught him in the abdomen, the bullet flattening against his unyielding flesh.

Hugo slowed for the narrow, winding footpath. He could make out the figures ahead of him now, soldiers in German and French uniforms marching together in single minded determination to reach the Château Joiry. Some of the men bore terrible wounds. A one-armed German, half his head a wreck, marched almost proudly, while another followed at a slower pace, limping but otherwise untroubled by his missing right foot. Hugo felt the fear tickle his spine from bottom to top. He knew that the walking dead couldn't harm him any more than the living, but the sight of them was horrifying. He decided to bypass the macabre procession as much as he could. He stopped running and looked up to where the trail doubled back to pass over his head. Gathering himself, he leaped to the next section, then repeated the process, using the switchbacks like a set of stairs.

A few shots caught him before he reached the top, but they barely registered. The joy of battle was on him as he came over the edge, and he was disappointed to see only a dozen terrified German soldiers and two men in black hooded robes.

He raced toward them contemptuous of their rifles. When he reached them, he drove his fist through the first soldier's chest like a spear. Hugo felt a brutal satisfaction as he saw the others blanch with fear. Several of the soldiers continued to fire, but most turned and tried to flee into the keep. Hugo grabbed a man and pitched him far over the side of the escarpment. Seconds later, he sent two more screaming after him.

By this time, all of the others had abandoned their weapons and were scrambling over each other in a frantic attempt to get through the narrow door. Hugo picked up a discarded rifle and hurled it like a javelin to impale one of the men. He caught two more by their necks and banged their heads together with such force that their skulls exploded in sprays of red. He pushed through the throng, lashing out with his fists, crushing a spine, collapsing a ribcage, ripping an arm from its socket and discarding it.

Ignoring the three surviving men, Hugo surged forward and caught the robed leaders and pinned them against the parapet wall, one in each hand.

"Where is your leader?" he yelled at one of them.

"*Ich verstehe nicht!*" the man cried, his voice frantic.

"Wrong answer," Hugo said. He tightened his grip, just a little, and was rewarded by the crunch of the man's trachea and, an instant later, the pop of his spine.

"Your turn," he said to the other hooded man. "Where is the Herr Doctor Meyer?"

"*Der Meister?*" the terrified German pointed to an archway that had once been a door leading to the inner castle. "*Er ist dort, durch diese Tür.*"

"Thanks, pal," Hugo said. He slapped his palm against the man's brow, turning his head to a mix of red jelly and bone shards.

He gave a glance at the three surviving soldiers, who huddled against the wall, paralyzed by fear. He nearly turned back to kill them, but something in him didn't want to.

"Not worth my time," he said, then headed through the arch into a broad stair that spiraled downward. The passage was dark but, as he descended, he discerned the reflection of a ruby glow. A moment later, three guards appeared around the bend, carrying torches that gave off the unnatural glow. They were roughly human in shape, but with distorted, dog-like faces and hooved feet.

Their inhuman appearance startled Hugo, only for an instant, but enough for them to leap on him, attacking savagely. They were strong—much stronger than men—but that was nothing to Hugo. Their claws slid harmlessly across his flesh. He grabbed one by the hip and shoulder and found that its flesh was unnaturally touch and rubbery. With a powerful wrench, he pulled the creature to pieces. He lifted the second and slammed it into the stone wall with such force that the ceiling threatened to cave in.

The third monster backed away from him, growling uncertainly. Hugo sprang forward swinging his stiff-fingered hand horizontally, like a sword. The blow caught the creature in the side of the neck, releasing a fountain of gore. The doglike head fell from the body to roll down the stairs.

Hugo emerged into the room he had seen in Gianetti's vision. Black robed men and naked fiends paused at their grim work to stare at him. One man, tall and bearded, his robe embroidered with strange occult symbols, stood at the far side of the room, supervising. Hugo knew instantly who he must be and strode toward him.

He was met by a surge of inhuman bodies as more creatures like those he had killed on the stair leapt on him. Others joined them: a bat-winged reptilian creature shaped like a giant ape, a small-toad-skinned man with tentacles lining his mouth, and many others whose bizarre appearance Hugo barely registered before they were on him.

Hugo flailed at them as their fangs and claws shredded his clothes and left scratches on even his steel skin. This was like the trenches again, except these things were far stronger than men and did not die easily. Like ants, they continued to attack long after taking wounds that would have killed a human being. Still, for all their ferocity, he smashed them down, one by one, until the floor of the chamber was steeped with a mix of blood, ichor, and foul smelling fluids.

Then the small demon with the tentacled face rose up with a bowl of pale liquid which it dashed into Hugo's face. It blinded him and he swallowed a bitter mouthful. A moment later, he felt weak and dizzy.

Hugo tried to throw his tormenters off, but his muscles wouldn't obey him. Under the unrelenting attack of the demonic horde, he sagged to the ground and darkness claimed him.

He awoke in a different room, a huge chamber that must once have been the great hall of the castle. The ceiling had partially collapsed and he could see the moon through the aperture.

Hugo was bound to the wall by heavy chains that held his arms over his head; his feet dangled above the stone floor. He tried to test the chains, but discovered that his muscles were paralyzed. The room was dominated by a gigantic human form, the colossus of Gianetti's vision now completed.

"Master!"

He had just enough mobility to glance toward the voice. It was the toad-skinned creature which, with the winged ape-thing and two of the robed men, stood near him, apparently acting as guards.

"Master," the creature repeated, "he awakens!"

The man Hugo had seen earlier stepped up to him. He was tall and massively built, with close-cropped red hair and a full beard. The softness of his body was offset by his eyes, which were a pitiless blue that made Hugo think of an Arctic sky.

"*Wer sind Sie?*" the man asked.

"Go climb a tree," Hugo replied in English. Speech was easy for him so he reasoned that paralysis rather than weakness was what held him motionless.

"Who are you, *Engländer*?" The man's English was slow and heavily accented but Hugo could understand him.

"What's it to you, Herr Doctor Von Meyer?"

116

"Ah..." Von Meyer smiled at the sound of his name. "If you know that, then you are an ally of the Frenchman, Dubnotal. Was he the one who gave you such power?"

"Nuts to you."

"Are there more like you?"

"A whole regiment," Hugo said. "The 'Fighting Colorados,' they call us."

"But they only sent you?"

"One man is more than enough to take care of a freak show run by a two-bit sideshow magician."

Von Meyer's face darkened and he smashed Hugo across the face with a backhanded blow. He hardly felt the impact, but the sorcerer yelped in pain and nursed his hand.

"Ghouls," he yelled, "*Bestrafen Sie ihn!*"

Two of the dog-like men moved forward, heavy iron bars in their hands. They began to beat his torso with powerful, measured blows. After some time, they stepped back, breathing hard, and Hugo laughed.

"You are a challenge," Von Meyer said. "We must see if there are more vulnerable areas." He barked an order to the ghouls. They stepped away to return a moment later. One carried a sledge hammer, the other held a glowing poker. Hugo closed his eyes, tightly, and braced for what was coming. The red hot metal pressed against the skin of his eyelid and he felt the heat. It was unpleasant, but no worse than what a normal man might feel when the water in a shower grows too hot.

He could feel the ghoul trying to wedge the point of the implement between his eyelids and strained to prevent it. It seemed to go on forever, then the iron withdrew and he felt rubbery hands grasp his ankles and spread his limp legs.

Hugo opened his eyes in time to see the second ghoul swing the hammer in an upward arc to strike him squarely in the testicles. It wasn't a damaging blow, he knew, more what an ordinary man might feel if flicked with a fingertip, but he no longer felt like laughing. Half a dozen strikes later his eyes were watering and the creatures released him as Von Meyer stepped forward.

"You see?" the sorcerer asked. "Nothing can withstand the intelligent application of force. Even a diamond can be split when one knows how."

Hugo glared, but kept his mouth shut. As strong as he was, he knew that the man was right. Eventually they would break even his superhuman body and, long before that, the pain would break his spirit.

"Are there others like you?"

"No," he said, seeing no harm in the answer.

"Did you come alone?"

He thought of Judex waiting in the forest. It had been foolish to leave the man behind.

"I did. Sâr Dubnotal wanted to send others with me, but I thought I could do this myself."

"Perhaps," Von Meyer said. "Just the same, I have sent some of my ghouls out. They will sniff out anyone within five miles of the castle and tear them to pieces."

Hugo said nothing.

"I shall enjoy learning more about you, my friend," Von Meyer said. "A man who can slaughter ghouls and demons may be of great use to me. For the moment, though, I have far more important things to attend to. I leave you to the tender care of my creatures."

For the next quarter of an hour, the ghouls applied their ingenuity to the most vulnerable parts of Hugo's body. In the background, he could hear the sound of chanting in some language he didn't recognize.

Then it stopped.

As if someone had thrown a switch, the chanting, the torture, all sound in the movement in the great chamber went away.

Hugo opened his eyes and saw that everyone was staring at the colossus. The gargantuan body took a breath, then another, then opened its eyes; the same ice-blue eyes of Von Meyer's face.

The creature rose to its feet—Hugo guessed that it was at least 100 feet tall—and stretched its muscles. The thing raised its face to the sky.

"*Meine Stunde ist gekommen!*" The voice was the sorcerer's, but augmented by a chorus of 10,000 others. The giant laughed and strode from the castle, sending demons, ghouls and black robed men scurrying to avoid the falling debris as it tore through the walls.

Many of the fiends followed in its wake, but one man, the ape demon, the little toad skinned man, and two of the ghouls remained to continue their work on Hugo.

As he waited for the torture to resume, Hugo saw something like a shadow move from the shelter of the wall and come up behind his tormentors.

Judex!

The caped man came silently, his pistol drawn. When he was almost close enough to touch, Hugo saw the nostrils of one of the ghouls twitch. The creature spun, only to receive two slugs in the chest from Judex's Steyr. The pistol spoke again and the second ghoul joined the first on the floor.

The ape-thing sprang at the man, but he side-stepped and it caught only his cloak, pulling it loose. He fired a bullet into the demon's heart and the creature dissolved into foul greenish smoke.

The little demon sprang at Judex then, tackling him to the ground. Though only four feet tall, with a scrawny build, the toad-skinned horror seemed to have inhuman strength. It slapped the pistol away and began to strangle him. Fortunately, for all its strength, the creature only had the mass of a child. Judex spun to the right, throwing it off balance, and swept its feet from under it with his leg.

The demon lost its grip and was thrown nearly a dozen feet. It sprang back up in an instant, but Judex was just as fast. He dove for his pistol and rolled to his feet in one smooth motion. As the demon leaped, he fired two shots, and it burst into flame and vanished.

Judex turned, gun still in hand and strode toward the black-robed man who was the last of Hugo's tormentors. He placed the muzzle of the weapon against the man's forehead.

"There is an antidote for the paralysis drug, is there not?" he asked in a calm voice.

"How did you get in?"

The antidote the lackey had produced seemed effective. Hugo had recovered his movement in a matter of moments and easily broken free of the chains.

"It was not hard," Judex replied. "I overpowered one of the walking dead and took his uniform. I copied the unfortunate creature's gait and entered the castle unchallenged."

He paused for a moment.

"I saw what you did to those soldiers outside."

"Do you have a problem with that?"

"It was not necessary. They could not have harmed you."

"They were enemy soldiers," Hugo said. "They're responsible for killing Tom, and thousands of other good men."

"They were soldiers in war. Our own troops have done as much."

"Why are you criticizing me? I hate those sons of bitches and I'll avenge my friend's death every chance I get. I'd think you, of all people, would understand that."

"We have different ideas," Judex said, "but now is not the time. We have to stop the giant."

"I don't think even I can do that," Hugo replied.

"We must try."

The colossus was moving fast, but Hugo was faster. He carried Judex through the woods at the same breakneck pace, only stopping when they reaches a clearing a quarter of a mile ahead of the giant's path.

"Stay hidden," he said. "A silver bullet won't do anything against that monster." Hugo moved to the center of the clearing where an ancient glacier had scattered an assortment of granite boulders. He lifted one that must have weighed five tons and, as the colossus entered the clearing, threw it.

The rock sailed at the giant's chest, only to be batted away like a tennis ball. The monster bellowed out his eerie chorus of laughter and stomped with a colossal foot. Hugo saw it coming, but not in time to dodge. The weight stunned him and drove his body into the ground like a tent peg. He thrashed and struggled himself free of the earth, only to feel a great hand scoop him up and lift him high.

He drove his fist into the palm of the hand, piercing the flesh and breaking a metacarpal bone thicker than his torso. The colossus cried out and flung him to the ground with stunning force. Hugo lay there unable to move, waiting for the final attack that would snuff out his life, but it didn't come.

"Can you stand up?"

Judex was at his side, helping him to his feet.

"I was afraid you were dead," he said.

"Too close."

Hugo shook his head to clear it and became aware of the sound of howitzer fire around them. "What's happening?" he asked.

"Several German artillery placements have begun to shell the creature. That was what distracted him from you."

"The Germans? But he's one of them."

"All they see is a monster," Judex said. "They do what anyone would do."

"Can they kill him? Is it even possible?"

Judex shook his head. "I don't know, but we must try to help them."

The big guns were still firing as the two arrived. Dozens of soldiers tried to augment them with small arms fire. The Germans had set up their position in an old stone church and the attached parsonage. As they watched, the colossus tore open the roof of the smaller building and scooped out a handful of screaming infantrymen. He raised the soldiers to face level, then caught one with his other and popped him into his mouth. Hugo looked away as the giant began to chew.

One of the howitzers fired. Hugo turned back to see an explosion open a gaping hole in the monster's chest. For a moment he felt a surge of hope. Then the wound began to knit itself closed and, in moments, it had disappeared.

The colossus laughed and tossed away the remaining soldiers. He strode to the big gun seized it by barrel and lifted it like a toy. He tossed the howitzer into the woods and set about stamping on the gun crew like ants.

"Keep him busy," Judex said. "I have an idea."

He darted away in the direction of the buildings leaving Hugo to stare incredulously after him.

Keep him busy? That's insane.

Judex ducked into the old church but the colossus saw him. He abandoned lone survivor of the gun crew and moved toward the building.

Hugo muttered a string of curses and looked around for something to use as a weapon. His gaze settled on an officer's staff car. He raced to it and hoisted the big vehicle to his shoulder just as the giant bent to peer in the church windows. He threw it with all his might and caught the colossus on the jaw, staggering him.

"Here I am!" Hugo shouted, throwing a German motorcycle good measure.

And here we go, he said to himself as the giant rose and began to move toward him. He raced toward it, avoiding a clutching hand and running between the towering legs.

He pushed himself to the limit as the colossus gave chase. With its long legs it could cover ground faster, but it couldn't turn or stop nearly as fast as he could. He moved into the woods, darting through clumps of trees like a rabbit while the giant stumbled after him, leaving a trail of destruction.

It must have been a dozen times that Hugo narrowly dodged a trampling foot; then he saw something ahead of him. He only caught a glimpse but he could tell it was a little town, with people in the streets. He couldn't lead the abomination there.

Hugo hesitated as he tried to change his course. It was only for an instant, but that was enough. A mammoth hand scooped him up. He struggled against the grip and managed to apply a variation of a wrestling hold to one of the fingers. He pulled as hard as he could and heard the gratifying snap of tendons.

The giant let out a bellow of pain and threw him with such force that he nearly blacked out. The ground shot past at blinding speed until he came to earth with shattering impact.

Hugo lay still for several moments before he could raise his head. His entire body throbbed with pain unlike anything he had ever known.

He looked around and realized that he had been thrown back to the artillery placement at the church. The colossus apparently wanted for all of his victims to be in the same place. Colossal footsteps echoed through the forest as the monster approached. Hugo rose, his limbs barely able to support him, but he wanted to fight, or at least to die on his feet.

The colossus came into sight, towering above the tallest trees. When it saw him, its mouth twisted into a bestial leer and it headed in his direction. Hugo found himself watching his approaching death with an odd sense of detachment. He was too weary to be defiant, angry, or even frightened.

The voice of a howitzer sounded and, a second later, a wound appeared in the giant's chest. Hugo waited for the hole to close, but it didn't. Instead, black blood began to flow from the wound as a look of confusion spread across the colossal features. It raised its head and ten thousand voices shouted as one, "*Nein!*"

The colossus collapsed with the sound of a toppling building. Hugo followed a moment later, sinking to his trembling knees. He heard someone calling his name and turned to see Judex and several German soldiers racing toward him. Then he breathed deeply and let darkness carry him away.

He woke in the same field hospital. His old nurse seemed a little more pleased with him this time, now that he was covered with cuts and bruises. The second day, Sâr Dubnotal came to see him.

"Is he dead?" Hugo asked.

"Von Meyer?" The Sâr stroked his beard thoughtfully. "It is possible," he said, "though with a thaumaturge of his power it would be foolish to assume so."

"I know that Judex found a way to kill him—the giant—but how?"

"He remembered what I said about the silver bullet and went into the church to try to find something made of that metal."

"He must have succeeded. What was it?"

"I believe it was a statue of St. Dunstan. He gave it to the gun crew and it became their bullet."

"So I own my life to the enemy?" Hugo chuckled bitterly. "At least, now I know there's some use for religion."

"I have a note for you," Sâr Dubnotal said, and passed him a folded piece of paper.

My friend,

I am grateful that you survived. What you did took great power and greater courage and I am proud to have fought by your side.

As for your generous offer to help me in my mission, I fear I must decline. The vengeance I seek must be dealt out coolly and precisely and you are a man of passion and turmoil.

A man of your gifts has much more to offer than to act as an instrument of revenge or a weapon of destruction. I hope that you discover a way to build up rather than tear down. More than that, I hope you find peace.

Judex

The nurse announced that Hugo needed his rest so the Sâr shook his hand and left. He didn't rest though. He remained awake staring at the note and wondering if there could be anything in his life that would mean more than death and destruction.

For the life of him, he couldn't think of a thing.

1917. Following the ill-fated demise of the secret French Martian colony set up in The Nyctalope on Mars, *Léo Saint-Clair, a.k.a. The Nyctalope, returned to Earth to serve his beloved France in her fight against Germany. He was then entrusted with a variety of secret missions. In this one, his path crosses that of Judex, who helps Léo seal the traumatic events he experienced on Mars deep within his mind...*

Christofer Nigro: *Justice and Power*

Justice and power must be brought together,
so that whatever is just may be powerful,
and whatever is powerful may be just.
Blaise Pascal.

Leo Saint-Clair's mind was virtually devoid of coherent thought as he hurtled towards his home planet in a small but sleek spacecraft, powered by a unique energy source known as "heliose," the creation of a mad but brilliant scientist named Korrides. He had pre-set the coordinates to take him from the now dead French colony on the Red Planet to Earth in less than two weeks' time.

The craft shuddered a bit under the spatial equivalent of atmospheric turbulence. That sudden jolt brought the Nyctalope out of his blissful reverie, as he tried—unsuccessfully--to forget the horrific events that had transpired the day after he, his twin children, and his fellow French colonizers had celebrated Bastille Day on Mars, incorrectly believing that it would mark a new era of exploration for his native country. But Mars was named after a cruel deity, and it appeared that the dreaded war god had been lying in wait for those ill-fated colonists.

As a commandant in the French army, and an inveterate soldier, Leo believed he knew war, and could handle anything this merciless deity could throw his way. He was wrong. Dead wrong.

They're all gone now, he mused to himself wearily. *My wife, Xavière... my little children... everyone... gone. We didn't know what infernal forces were waiting for us there. We had no control over our own actions. None of us could resist that overpowering evil... I cannot... I must not hold myself accountable for any of that...*

With the auto-pilot safely on, Leo fell into a fitful sleep, his slumber haunted by the faces of the dead colonists, his two precious children standing in front of all the rest with Leo's own blades jutting out of their abdomens, their internal organs spattered on the marble-like floor before him...

One month later, Leo awakened to a bright sunny morning in the military hospital in Paris, where he had been staying for the past few weeks, being treated for what would someday be called "post-traumatic stress syndrome."

He was under the care of a meticulous physician, Dr. Cerral, who had the annoying habit of not looking his patients in the eye while speaking to them, and instead writing all of his observations down on a pad.

"Bonjour, Commandant," Cerral said in his usual detached fashion. "Did you sleep better last night?"

Stretching and yawning, Leo replied:

"*Oui, très bien, Docteur.* When can I be released so I can resume my work? I am very aware that there is a war being fought right now, and my talents are no doubt needed."

Dr. Cerral held up a pencil and waved it to emphasize his words.

"Not so fast, Commandant. In my judgment, I believe you should remain here for a bit longer. What you suffered was..."

Leo interrupted the doctor with a stern reply:

"What I suffered is over, Doctor. I am a soldier, trained and experienced in dealing with loss. I want—no, I *need* to return to the front and do my duty. France can no longer wait. Do you understand?"

"Yes, yes, I do, of course, but what occurred to you back on... you know where... was not a typical loss for a soldier, and your, er... participation... in that tragedy may well have left you, er, a bit unwell—from a mental standpoint, I mean."

Leo's iron grip was suddenly around Dr. Cerral's wrist, squeezing so tightly that it caused the physician to drop his prized pencil and yelp in pain.

"Doctor, you may not have heard me clearly enough. I am telling you that I am fine, and eager to return to my military responsibilities."

Before Dr. Cerral could either acquiesce, or protest further, an older French officer entered the room and wasted no time in getting down to business after the customary salutations.

"Commandant Saint-Clair," the officer said, "I am Colonel Gilles Fontaine. Your wish to return to the front is about to be granted. General Foch himself has sent me to recruit you for a clandestine but crucial mission that only someone with your combination of talents could possibly execute."

"Excellent!" Leo exclaimed.

"I'm sorry, Colonel Fontaine," Doctor Cerral said, matter-of-factly. "But as the Commandant's physician, I must protest. I still need to make a professional assessment regarding his mental fitness to serve..."

"That will be enough, Dr. Cerral," the Colonel said with heavy authority. "General Foch himself has decreed this. While your concerns are noted, they must presently be ignored in the interests of France."

The doctor still seemed undaunted.

"I have final authority when it comes to matters such as these..."

"Doctor, your authority ends where the best interests of France, and the troops who so valiantly serve her, are concerned," Colonel Fontaine noted brusquely. "Now kindly take your ministrations to other patients. Commandant Saint-Clair and I have business to discuss. Do not make me say this again."

Visibly withholding the words he wanted to say, Dr. Cerral abruptly walked away. *This is in God's hands now, not mine,* he thought to himself. *May the Lord do what is best for Saint-Clair—and for France.*

Minutes later, Leo sat across from Colonel Fontaine at a table in the hospital commissary. The Officer sipped a mug of steaming hot tea as he briefed the Nyctalope on what was expected of him.

"This will be one of your most difficult missions to date, Commandant."

"With all due respect, Colonel, I've fought some of the deadliest menaces from two worlds. At this point in my life, I doubt there's anything you can throw at me that could faze possibly me."

"You are as brave a man as I've ever seen, Saint-Clair," the Colonel commended. "If only the Hun knew what was coming their way, they would flee in terror."

Leo suddenly displayed a blank expression despite the compliment he had just received.

"Saint-Clair? Are you unwell? Should I summon Dr. Cerral?"

"No, Colonel, I was just… reminiscing. What does the mission entail?"

"This is the situation. Our government is working with Great Britain to launch a third offensive on Ypres a few days from now—a locale that you are quite familiar with, due to your earlier participation in previous military operations there. General Francois Anthonie requested you for a mission of the utmost importance that will be France's contribution to that offensive—a mission that will require all of your legendary skills, and particularly your famed powers of nyctalopia.

"The Germans have recently developed a new type of deadly gas that is worse than chlorine. We call it 'mustard gas' because of its horrific effects on the men who come in contact with it: the color of their blisters all over their skin take on a mustard-like hue. It is invisible and nearly odorless, and its effects do not appear for many hours following exposure. Other effects include swelling of the eyes that results in blindness, frequent regurgitation, and the deterioration of one's mucous membranes to the point that many slowly die an agonizing death over the course of several weeks as their throats close up on them."

"My God!" Leo exclaimed. "Mars never ceases to perfect the horrors he unleashes on the warriors who walk his path."

"Pardon?"

"Excuse me, Colonel, I was speaking in metaphor."

"I see. To conclude, a combined British and French military force is planning to launch an assault on a town in the vicinity of Ypres known as Passchendaele. Recent intelligence reports have revealed that there is a large storage base on the outskirts of that town, filled with over 50 canisters of mustard gas, which is more than enough to wreak bloody havoc on the entire Allied unit when it arrives. That base is well guarded, so a full-scale attack on it would give the Boche ample time to release the gas. This is why we need one man to travel several miles on foot in the dead of night and approach the base surreptitiously, despite all the enemy patrols in the vicinity. It will be your job to neutralize every German before they can release the gas, and to sabotage all the canisters."

"It will be done, Colonel."

"You should know that the meteorological conditions would be atrocious. The entire area has been besieged by enormously inclement weather lately. The ground will be muddy and flooded in many places, thus making travel hazardous in the extreme. However, the overcast skies will ensure that no Moon will be visible. But of course, you won't need a lantern."

"They don't call me the Nyctalope for nothing, Colonel. The absence of light will be no impediment to me."

"What about the other hazards?"

"I am also called a soldier for good reason too, Monsieur. Overcoming any obstacles—natural or man-made—is what I do."

"Good, good. You will be based at the camp located left of the Ypres Canal, where our men are now sequestered with a new regiment of the French First Army. You will be given the name of a contact answering directly to General Anthoine who will provide you with further instructions upon your arrival. Godspeed, Commandant Saint-Clair!"

"It will be the Boche who'll need to worry about God that night, Colonel."

Leo Saint-Clair sat up on what passed for a bed at the military camp in Ypres, sweating profusely as the result of another one of his nightmares. He could have sworn that he'd seen the bodies of his children lying at the foot of his bed with his blade thrust through their bellies for a brief moment. His abrupt awakening caught the attention of his bunkmate, a fat Belgian wearing glasses named Remy Baudouin, who was unaware of his identity.

"Léon, are you all right?" asked Remy.

"I am. I just thought a scorpion had crawled into my bunk."

"There's no scorpions in Belgium," said Remy, firmly.

"Yes, but..."

"Don't worry about it, soldier. We're all on edge with the way things have been here, especially after the cookhouse was flooded and all the food was drenched. That stuff the cook fed to me yesterday morning looked like something he'd scraped from the bottom of his shoe—and it tasted even worse. It was probably just something you ate, is all."

"I *am* a soldier," replied Leo, stiffly. "I'm accustomed to adverse conditions in the field, and you should be as well. We must all sacrifice comforts for the greater cause."

"Well, yeah, of course, but that doesn't mean some of us wouldn't rather be back home relaxing at the Gai-Moulin, watching a revue where the girls shake their cans to the can-can, if you know what I mean."

"Such good things would not exist for anyone back home if not for what we soldiers sacrifice here on the field, Remy. Now, I beg your pardon, but I must get some fresh air."

"I'd bring an umbrella, if I were you, Leon. 'Course, we weren't issued any luxuries like umbrellas, and as soldiers, we don't need any such luxuries, right?"

Ignoring Remy's sarcasm, Leo emerged from his tent in the hope of enjoying the morning air. He saw his fellow soldiers, none of whom enjoyed the benefits of his synthetic heart, diligently going about their various duties while drenched in the rain, their feet ankle deep in mud. Many had a grayish cast to their faces, due to constant exposure to the squally weather; several were visibly shivering, a condition caused by the fact that these men had to wear the same clothing for weeks, and their shirts were infested with lice.

Leo reminded himself again of the necessity for sacrifice. He was a soldier, and knew that it was not his place to question the way of the world; he simply had to perform his duty to the best of his abilities. That was what a warrior did. He told himself that the hardship and suffering that came with war emboldened his nation, and made those who survived all the stronger. He didn't believe in an easy world that bred a soft and lazy civilization. But he couldn't help recalling how many of the high-ranking officers enjoyed comfortable lodgings well away from enemy lines, whereas the enlisted men had had to give up all amenities, many of which they could ill afford even back home.

What are these men truly fighting for? he asked himself. *The liberty of our fellow Frenchmen? Or the continued privilege of the few who make all the decisions?*

Leo quietly admonished himself for thinking such thoughts, and tried to focus on the mission he would be undertaking at nightfall.

As he walked about the camp, the Nyctalope was unaware that another soldier—or at least a man who appeared to be a regular member of the infantry unit—watched his every move, with a concerned and calculating expression on his face...

No sooner had the sun set that Leo began his difficult trek through the rain-filled darkness towards the German base in Passchendaele.

Few men would have had the endurance to make such a trip on foot, and fewer yet could have done so under such conditions. But the darkness was no obstacle to one gifted with night vision. Leo endured the constant rainfall and the frigid wind by reminding himself that every trial just made him a stronger and better soldier.

For the purpose of his mission, he carried a specially modified Luger and a razor-sharp, tailor-made hunting dagger, both ready for use at a moment's notice. During the long trek, the Nyctalope met two German patrols that were wandering about the area, looking for enemy combatants. But they did so under the assumption that these would be subject to the same visual limitations as themselves. As a result, no grenades were hurled at Leo with anything near accuracy as he trod towards his goal. Whenever a German soldier approached him, expecting to find the scattered remains of his human target, the Nyctalope would either put a bullet through his skull or slash his throat, whichever struck his fancy for the moment. He deliberately allowed a few of the Germans the time to scream in agony in order to attract their fellow soldiers, so that they, too, could promptly fall before the fury and might of the night-thriving warrior.

Finally, after a seeming eternity, and with no more than two hours of nightfall left, Leo approached the base where the canisters of mustard gas were being held. Quickly, he dispatched the two sentries who had been unable to detect his approach. Leo savored the thrill of his enemies falling before him with their blood staining his blade as his inner rage built within him like carbonated liquid under pressure in a bottle.

Picking the complicated lock on the front entrance with ease, the Nyctalope entered the base. He found the interior gently lit by several lanterns. He knew that there were eight guards inside, so he proceeded with caution. However, as he moved about, he suddenly found himself plagued with the same visions, as if it were his children whom he had just put killed with his blade, instead of the sentries...

As a consequence of the shock, Leo carelessly kicked a wrench lying on the floor as he strode through the edifice. He might as well have set off a stick of dynamite! Two guards immediately came running in his direction to check the source of the noise.

Leo pointed his Luger at them and let off two blindingly quick shots, killing both as the deadly bullets pierced their chest and skull respectively.

The sound alerted the other six guards, and all of them simultaneously advanced upon Leo. As the Nyctalope turned his gun in the direction of the men to his right, one of the guards, attacking from the left, leapt upon him from behind, drawing a bayonet in preparation for puncturing his left kidney. Leo deftly countered the move by backing into a crate, catching his opponent's arm as he thrust the blade at him, and disarmed the enemy soldier before he could skewer him. He then quickly shoved his dagger into the man's throat, blood spattering from the wound as the man died instantly.

Two other sentries swiftly moved in for the kill, but Leo disemboweled the first with a quick slash of his dagger across the man's lower abdomen, and split open the other's skull with the butt of his Luger before the unfortunate soldier could react.

Now acting in a frenzy, realizing that he needed this conflict as a catharsis, Leo shouted: "I'm here! Come and get me, you boche bastards!"

No longer taking any chances, the last two guards each leapt in front of Leo from a different direction, both expertly aiming their Mauser rifles at him, ready to unleash the full complement of five bullets from each of their magazines. Reacting at the speed of thought, Leo simultaneously fired at one guard with his Luger, killing him instantly, and hurled his dagger at the other, sending the sentry to the ground vomiting a torrent of blood as the blade penetrated his throat.

However, that last soldier managed to get off one stray shot, which failed to hit the Nyctalope, but punctured two of the canisters, sending twin streams of mustard gas into the atmosphere.

The Nyctalope bellowed a scream of victory as waves of adrenaline continued to saturate his system; he then struggled to catch his breath, as his artificial heart had been taxed almost beyond even its formidable limits.

Leo suddenly became aware of an imposing presence behind him. He turned around and discovered a tall, dark-clad figure standing near the entrance to the base. This mysterious man was not dressed like a member of the German infantry, and instead appeared to be covered with a specially designed charcoal-colored outfit intended to protect its wearer from the extreme weather conditions now afflicting the area. He also wore a mask over his face and gloves designed to protect against mustard gas. A distinctive black hat and cloak completed his raiment. Presently, the man was pointing a large pistol of unclear design at Leo.

"I'm afraid I must ask you to come along with me, Commandant," the dark man said in a grim-sounding voice. "You were clearly not mentally fit for undertaking such a mission, and because of your recklessness, this area is now contaminated with mustard gas. You must face justice for these actions."

It was then that Leo realized exactly who confronted him.

"Judex," he said aloud. "The much feared vigilante of Paris. What are you doing here?"

"Let me just say that I, too, have been called to the front," Judex replied. "I know all about your recent travails. I was at the base incognito, and I observed your erratic behavior all day. I know one with a precarious grip on their sanity when I see them. With the use of these special lenses, designed to compensate for the lack of light, I followed you to make sure that you carried out this mission correctly. But you did not. You appear to be harboring some sort of death wish. Allied soldiers can no longer approach this area now, and the threat of mustard gas has not been averted. I cannot sabotage the canisters myself since this mask only gives me limited protection. Come with me now. This is not a request."

"Really? You're hardly a military tribunal. I'm wagering you don't even have a true officer ranking. So I strongly advise you to lower your weapon and go back from whence you came, while I'm still in a good enough mood to give you the option of getting out of here in one piece."

"You wish to escape justice? You think you can intimidate me into letting you walk free?"

"You're not Justice itself, Judex. You're only a man who has the pretentiousness to think he is. You need to be taught the error of your ways, and I can't think of a better teacher than I."

With a lightning swift move, Leo delivered a swinging kick that disarmed Judex, much to the latter's surprise. However, the vigilante trapped Leo's leg after he tried a follow-up kick to the face. Judex lifted the Nyctalope in the air and hurled him to the ground. Leo expertly recovered, landing on his hands and flipping himself back onto his feet, landing in a classic fighting stance. Judex followed suit in a fighting stance of his own.

With a series of blinding moves, the two warriors began facing off, each blocking a flurry of the other's blows, with a few connecting from time to time. The two men soon realized that they each faced a foe the likes of which the other had ever encountered before.

This seeming stalemate went on for several minutes, until Judex managed to dodge one of Leo's blows and struck him hard on the jaw. He then cracked his clavicle bone with a brutal elbow thrust, grabbing the khaki-clad soldier by the collar and smashing him up against one of the crates. Before the vigilante could deliver what he hoped to be the finishing blow, the Nyctalope quickly recovered, blocked Judex's strike, and side-kicked him to the sternum, knocking the wind out of him and sending him sprawling to the ground.

Managing to regain his wits, Judex saw Leo recover his dagger and hurl it at him. Reacting automatically, the vigilante caught it in his left hand and quickly hurled it back at the Nyctalope, who ducked out of the way a microsecond before being skewered in the shoulder.

Somersaulting towards the area where his gun lay on the floor, Judex knew that he had but a few seconds to act. He grabbed his pistol and pointed it at Leo just as the Nyctalope, who had done the exact same thing with his own Luger, took aim at him.

"It would appear we find ourselves at a deadlock, Judex," Leo observed aloud. "So I strongly suggest you allow me to leave, and in return, I will let you do the same. *D'accord?*"

"Non, Commandant," Judex icily replied. "Despite all you have endured, despite all the good you have done for our nation, and the world itself, I cannot in good conscience let you go on in your mental state and ignore what you did here. You must face justice."

"And you think you have a right to judge me? After all I have been through, all the tragedy I have endured? After all I have accomplished for

France? After all the sacrifices I have made? You see yourself, and yourself alone, as being worthy of judging me?"

Judex's bright gray eyes tightened under his face gear. "Yes, for it is what I do."

Judex suddenly rolled out of Leo's line of fire and let off a shot, having very carefully aimed at a thick metal pipe above the Nyctalope's head. Leo shot at the same time, his bullet barely missing Judex due to the latter's suddenly rolling dodge. The vigilante's bullet struck and ricocheted off the pipe in precisely the right direction to crease against Leo's skull, giving him a concussion and knocking him unconscious.

Running over towards the dazed Nyctalope, Judex realized that, despite his foe's injury, he had to act quickly, while Leo Saint-Clair was still unconscious.

"Long ago, I had some very special training courtesy of our common friend, Sâr Dubnotal," Judex said quietly as he pressed his fingers against Leo's forehead and concentrated. "He helped me develop my powers of mesmerism. What I am going to attempt now is difficult, and potentially dangerous, but the risk must be taken. It is the form of justice that I believe should properly be meted out to you. Our country—the very world, in fact—greatly needs one such as you among us, but you cannot be allowed to go about these tasks in your current state of mind. Moreover, you do not deserve to suffer as you have for an act outside of your control. Now, please remain relaxed...

"I am going to suppress all conscious memory of your role in the recent tragedy that occurred on Mars, including the very knowledge that you once had twin children. You will only remember the son who yet survives..."

This memory will not stay suppressed forever, Judex thought, *but it is my hope that it will remain buried long enough so that, by the time you do remember it, you will have gained enough time to be able to properly deal with it.*

A few moments later, the deed was done.

Leo recovered moments later, with Judex helping him to his feet.

"What happened?" the Nyctalope asked weakly. "What are you doing here, vigilante?"

"I was sent here to provide you with some back-up, Commandant. I was able to dispatch the last of the guards, who delivered the head wound you are now suffering from. Regrettably, your mission wasn't entirely successful, as two canisters of mustard gas were breached by enemy fire, and you have been exposed to it. We must get back to the base quickly and have you report to the infirmary."

"I must be really concussed, as my memories of the past few hours are vague at best, and as for the last few months...damn, my head is really pounding the more I try to think back."

The Nyctalope looked at the imposing figure of Judex, smiled appreciatively, and continued speaking.

"Needless to say, I must thank you for your timely assistance. As you said, I had best get back to base now, and hope General Anthoine will show a bit of mercy for my inability to prevent this area from being contaminated. Let us be off."

While returning to the base on the opposite end of the Ypres Canal after another long trek, concern for the possibility of mustard gas infection, and being lamented for the partial failure of the mission, were the only two matters weighing upon Leo Saint-Clair's psyche.

Late 1917. Judex is once more pitted against the evil Dr. Cornelius and his ne-farious criminal organization, the Red Hand, last seen in "Mask of the Mon-ster." This time, it is not the Creature of Frankenstein whom the mad scientist schemes to use for his own nefarious purposes, but another classic monster, one with fangs and claws...

Christofer Nigro: *The Beast Within*

Dr. Cornelius Kramm stood as the head of a five-strong group of Red Hand operatives surrounding a rather important tombstone. This grave was situated in a private cemetery connected to the Dumas Hospital of Mental Health. All their occupants were former patients, conveniently laid to rest here as an option for family members to avoid having such unfortunate individuals buried alongside the more "respectable" members of their lineage—and another option for the institute to make a profit from the affluent families who had a patient confined there.

The grave in question had a rather elegant tombstone engraved with the words: *Here lies Bertrand Calliet, beloved nephew of Aymar Galliez and family, (1851-1872).*

"Are you certain this is the one, Doctor?" queried a large-framed hench-man called Trelane.

"Of course, I'm certain, you fool!" Cornelius spat in response.

"I meant no offense, Doctor, I just wanted to make sure before we, er, started to, well, you know..."

"Yes, I know! Just make haste with it, for grave-robbing is no small of-fense in France!"

Following the Doctor's instructions, Trelane led the other three men in ex-huming the body buried within this grave for so many years. They found the oaken wood coffin, heavily chained, as anticipated, sequestered several feet un-der the moist earth.

"Can you pick those locks?" Doctor Cornelius asked Franz, one of his henchmen noted for his acumen in that area.

"I can try, but they are quite expensive and sophisticated," the man replied nervously. "They will be difficult to crack."

"Then use the acid to corrode them so they can be easily broken."

With that order given, another of the henchmen, Benoit, produced a vial of highly volatile acid designed by Doctor Cornelius himself. He carefully pulled the cork from the top and poured several drops of the viscous yellow liquid on each lock chamber. The strong metal sizzled and putrefied before their very eyes; in just a few minutes, the weakened metallic bonds were easily cut from the coffin by a simple wrench.

"Now see to the lid," was Cornelius' next order.

Each of his men placed a crowbar in the crack where the lid was held shut, and all put their full efforts into lifting it open. Due to their combined strength, the closure was promptly thrown open with a loud cracking sound. The sight greeting them was the vague outlines of a body covered under many branches of a brownish plant.

"Wolfsbane, no doubt," Cornelius surmised. "Remove all of it."

Hastily doing as the Doctor commanded, the four men quickly cleared the branches to reveal a male corpse that looked remarkably well preserved for one said to be interred in the earth for so long.

"*Mon dieu!*" Trelane exclaimed at the sight. "The body looks sort of mummified, but not as decayed as one would expect. As if it went into some state of... of..."

"I believe 'preservation' is the word your limited intellect was struggling for," Cornelius interjected. "And that is quite correct. It's also what I expected, given the reported nature of Monsieur Calliet's affliction. He is not actually dead, but his body is in a death-like state, simply awaiting direct exposure to the rays of the full Moon to revive...or the beams of the lunar simulation device I have created. Let us remove him back to my laboratory before we are seen by a member of the security staff we did not pay off. Benoit, make sure that the empty coffin is re-interred, and the grave is completely filled in before you return to the headquarters."

"*À vos ordres, Docteur*," said Benoit.

He then quietly complied and began his tedious job while Doctor Cornelius led the other three with their precious cargo back to his laboratory.

Approximately one hour later, the Doctor and two more of his henchmen, Hervé and Louis, stood in the scientist's elaborate laboratory with the shriveled but intact body of Bertrand Calliet lying on a large operating table. Above him, a one-half-meter in length lamp-like projection was maneuvered in place.

"If my theory is correct, bathing this man's body in the simulated lunar energies produced by my device should restore him to full active life," the mad scientist said aloud. "And my theories are rarely wrong."

"Why did ya make such a device, Doctor?" Louis asked in his typically dullard-like manner. "It couldn't 'a been just for this mook."

"Of course not," Cornelius curtly retorted. "It was designed to provide stimuli for inducing certain mental states. But upon learning of Monsieur Calliet's story, and then confirming his burial location, I realized that I had found another marvelous use for this machine."

"How so, Doctor?"

"I do not think Monsieur Calliet is fully human; I believe he is an actual specimen of the changeling species we call *loup-garou*. If that is the case, I am about to gain a very important operative for the Red Hand."

Without further ado, Doctor Cornelius depressed the on-switch on his lunar-simulation lamp. A loud, unsettling hum began vibrating the molecules of the air as an intense yellow beam enveloped Calliet's emaciated form. The cadaver started twitching its fingers and opening and closing its dried mouth, as if gasping for air, prompting an expression of sheer horror on the countenances of the two henchmen, contrasted by a triumphant grin on Doctor Cornelius' face.

Within a few minutes, the leathery skin had lost its coarse, wrinkled texture and taken on a color and vibrancy resembling normal living flesh. The dryness of the mouth and throat gave way to functioning salivary glands, and, within seconds, its barely discernible grunt escalated into genuinely human-sounding pleas of agony. In short order, his opaque, milky eyes took on their original blue appearance, and his arid, crumbling dark hair returned to its original satin-like luster. A loud scream of both relief and terror ushered forth from Calliet's wide open craw, showing that his lungs and larynx were fully functioning again.

"Welcome back amongst the living, Monsieur Calliet," Doctor Cornelius said, a wide grin on his face. "The world outside the grave greets you warmly."

Calliet's reaction to that salutation was an even more hysterical, animalistic howl. His incisors began visibly enlarging. He then started flailing about like some madman trapped in a box.

"Restrain him!" Cornelius commanded.

The two bulky henchmen leapt upon the berserker before them and struggled to keep him from leaving the table and running amok in the laboratory. Unfortunately, he proved too difficult to hold, as his strength was surprisingly great for such a normal-looking man. Worse, his screeching persona displayed even more beast-like traits. He sunk his fangs into the upper part of Hervé's right arm, tearing out both a chunk of flesh and a swath of cloth from the man's long-sleeved shirt.

The guard screamed in pain and shock as a fountain of blood spurted from his wound, and he fell back against a nearby counter, losing his grip on Calliet.

Louis shouted a series of expletives and did his best to restrain the raging man-beast by wrapping his left arm around the creature's neck. However, Calliet executed a shockingly brutal move, grasping each of Louis' ears in his hirsute palms and simultaneously tearing both clean off in a spray of crimson. The man's screams surpassed those of his colleague. He was forced to let go of his captor so he could clasp his hands over the bloody holes where his ears had once been.

Calliet hungrily stuffed both of Louis' ears in his mouth, and voraciously chewed the gullet-full of cartilage to bits. He then leapt off the table and landed in a crouched position, as if ready to attack again.

However, the man-beast's plan was abruptly interrupted by two darts that punctured his back. He turned and saw that the projectiles had been fired from an odd-looking gun wielded by Doctor Cornelius.

"Those darts have enough anesthetic to send an elephant to sleep, Monsieur Calliet," the scientist informed the creature. "You're not even in a quarter of your full lupine state, so you *will* fall."

As if determined to prove the scientist wrong, Calliet spent several more seconds throwing various lab equipment around in a desperate effort to fend off the powerful sedative. Ultimately, though, Doctor Cornelius's prediction proved correct, and Calliet let out one last throaty snarl as he collapsed to the floor with a loud thud.

"Fret not," Cornelius said to his severely injured and bleeding henchmen. "I will fix you both; you'll soon be good as new, and you will be receiving hazard pay, as well as a controlling interest in a Paris café of your choice."

Their joint reply—if that is what it could be called—was a series of agonized moans.

About an hour earlier, Benoit was busy re-burying the coffin which had held the body of Bertrand Calliet, once known as the infamous "Werewolf of Paris." As he whistled lightly to himself, endeavoring to do nothing less than a perfect job, he failed to notice a dark form moving into his vicinity a few yards away.

"A fine night for grave robbing, *mon ami?*" queried a mellifluous but icy voice from behind.

Drawing his firearm with impressive speed, Benoit turned towards the voice, only to have the weapon shot clear out of his hand by another piece that was drawn even quicker. The henchman held his bleeding hand as he gazed fearfully upon the tall, imposing, black-cloaked figure standing before him. It resembled nothing more than a roughly human-shaped silhouette outlined against the darkness, with the visible features of a wide-brimmed hat and a long cloak billowing softly in the night wind.

"*You!?*" Benoit managed to choke out.

"I'm afraid it is I, indeed," the figure replied with no trace of irony. "Now, will you be so kind as to tell me why you are robbing this particular grave, and for whom you work—though I am guessing the Red Hand by your choice of fashion."

"How could you have known...?" the criminal pleaded, struggling to staunch the bleeding from the area of flesh where the bullet had torn across his hand.

"Do you think your employer is the only one who has contacts in this hospital, and other similar places in Paris? The arrogance of your ilk in thinking otherwise has never failed to work to my advantage. But you can rest assured that, contrary to Doctor Cornelius's belief, he doesn't yet rule this city."

"You'll get nothing from me!"

"Then allow me to teach you the error of choosing fealty to the cause of evil rather than the forces of justice."

With that declaration firmly made, the man called Judex began slowly walking towards the tremulous Benoit. This was followed by the sounds of the henchman shouting in pain and terror as the dark-clad vigilante began his interrogation.

Back in Dr. Cornelius' laboratory, located in a large building in the fashionable business district of the city's 1st Arrondissement, Bertrand Calliet slowly regained consciousness. He now found himself securely strapped to an upturned surgical table, with the exquisitely attired scientist standing before him, holding a firearm in his hand as a precaution.

"Please pardon these restraints, Monsieur Calliet, but you were hardly in a hospitable mood when you last awakened here."

"Who are you? Where am I?"

"I, my dear boy, am Dr. Cornelius Kramm, renowned scientist, surgeon, and researcher. I can be credited with reviving you from your state of suspended animation, one that even the best doctors of today would have mistaken for clinical death."

"Why did you bring me back? I tried to get out of that place... I had Sophie in my arms... I wanted us to escape and resume our life together..."

"Monsieur Calliet, I did some research on you, some of which were acquired from Dr. Dumas' own notes taken during the interval when you were in his rather dubious care. This included his records of a very telling conversation he had with your adopted 'uncle,' Aymar Galliez. You are, of course, a *loup-garou*, a man gifted with the power of metamorphosis, in your case, the alteration of your physical and mental state to simulate the attributes of a wolf. When in that form, you possess strength and regenerative capabilities far surpassing any actual member of the *canid* family, but also a few unique weaknesses.

"I'm not yet certain of the precise biological mechanism behind this power, but I am rapidly learning, and you will help me in that study now that you're in my... employ. But I have learned through my various studies and experiments that this ability is very real, however rare and overlooked by conventional science. I believe I can teach you to control that power, to harness it on behalf of... humanity."

"You are truly insane if you think you can do that. I tried so hard to control it myself; I really tried. My uncle tried. My Sophie tried. How did I get here, and where is Sophie...?"

"I'm sorry to be the one to inform you of this. Bertrand—may I call you Bertrand?—that woman in your arms when you leapt from the upper floor of the hospital over 40 years ago wasn't your paramour. It was a deranged Oriental woman whom you mistook for your true love due to the mental state you were in at the time. Sophie, I fear, committed suicide following your disappearance, and even if she hadn't, she would be either quite elderly or deceased at this point in time."

"No! That cannot be!"

"My dear Bertrand, I am someone who—unlike so many whom you met in your previous life as a fugitive and member of the Foreign Legion—will not lie to you. I'm not certain how your lycanthropy was triggered, but it seems to have had difficulty emerging full-blown due to a variety of factors. This is why you were in human, or mostly human, form when the psyche of the beast took over on so many occasions, and why the full wolf form manifested relatively rarely. Ordinarily, the energies of the full Moon would have caused the beast to completely emerge, but its powerful psyche still managed to periodically rise to dominance over you, regardless of the time of month. Its needs and dark desires became yours, even when you were in your human form.

"Your uncle tried to help you suppress the animal inside you, but in the end, he had no choice but to abandon you to your fate. I will never do that, because unlike all others you have known, I am a scientist, and I believe your condition will prove quite controllable with proper treatments. Would you like to learn how to control your bestial side, Bertrand? I ask for but the smallest of remuneration in return…"

Calliet began sobbing incessantly. "Sophie used to let me feed on her own blood… she and she alone in this world cared for me… she didn't hesitate to love a beast in human form. She was that angelic of a soul."

"Are you listening to me, Bertrand?"

"*Oui, Docteur.* I'm sorry. What is this small remuneration you ask in exchange for helping me control this god-forsaken beast?"

"Simply a generous donation of blood samples for research purposes and working as a special operative for my firm. This is a very good deal in accordance with what you will receive in return, do you not agree?"

"Please don't… don't let it control me anymore… I'll give you what you ask if you help me stop the beast."

"*Très bien!* Then let us begin what I am certain will be a mutually beneficial working relationship, Monsieur Calliet."

The following day, Judex stood quietly in the office of his close ally and friend, Prosper Cocantin. The private detective was rifling through a stack of files, almost frantically searching for the right ones. He felt relieved when he ascertained that he hadn't misplaced that which he sought. He knew his dark-clad associate disliked being kept waiting.

"So you believe that was the reason Doctor Cornelius' crew of malcontents robbed that grave?" Cocantin asked the tall figure standing next to him.

Judex looked impassively at the file his friend had just handed him.

"If this information you've just given me proves true, yes. And I find this very disturbing."

"Everything about the Red Hand is disturbing."

"Agreed, but this new development is particularly so. I hope you can trust your contact…?"

"Of course! This information comes straight from my adopted son, the Licorice Kid. When he sticks his nose in something, he seldom pulls it out again without a useful bit of information being attached to the tip of it."

Cocantin looked down for a moment, thankful that Judex wasn't the sarcastic type, and thus would avoid making a comment about the detective's very prominent proboscis.

"And you would certainly know the quality of noses, *mon ami*."

Sacrebleu! *Did he make a joke after all?* Cocantin wondered to himself.

"But you're correct," Judex continued, smiling. "You know that I trust the Kid entirely. This may explain why Cornelius was collecting information on the Pitamont family."

"French genealogist generally believe the Pitamonts to be a 'cursed' family. And though I do not believe in peasants' superstitions like werewolves, legend has it that a curse brought down on this clan long ago resulted in lycanthropy running rampant through the family line, just waiting for one of their children to be subjected to the proper catalyst to trigger it."

"I wouldn't discount the possibility out of hand, Prosper."

"Oh, come now, my friend! What a thing to contemplate in this era of high regard for reason and science!"

"Such high regard, as you put it, might result in our society becoming lazy and overlooking the reality of some phenomena that do not fit the present materialistic worldview. Previous generations often avoided the misuse of 'reason' to ignore the reality of the fantastic, and allow its dangerous manifestations to thrive under their prominent noses."

Mon Dieu! *Did he just make another such joke?*

"Reason should not lead to rationalizing, remember that. I have already encountered many fantastic creatures in my time, and thus, I cannot afford to assume that others such as werewolves do not dwell on the periphery of reality."

"The Kid tells me much the same, but when I see a grown man utter such nonsense…"

"Perhaps that means you should have more respect for the Licorice Kid, who doesn't allow so-called maturity to obstruct his thinking, much as I do not allow 'reason' to do the same with my own."

"Humph."

"No need to take that as an insult, my friend. Merely consider it constructive advice."

"Humph."

Judex's generally impassive expression appeared to actually come close to smiling at that moment.

"In any event, it would appear that the Red Hand managed to trace the Pitamont lineage to the young man buried at the Dumas Institute's private cemetery. His last name was Calliet, but according to this file, Bertrand Calliet's mother may have been impregnated by a member of the Pitamont family, and her son given a false surname to hide his illegitimacy. I suspect there was more to it than that, but this is all we have on such short notice."

"So you're thinking that Doctor Cornelius stole the body because he was..."

"That is *exactly* what I'm thinking. If the Pitamont legend is correct, then Calliet could very well be a *loup-garou*, capable of being revived under the right conditions."

"After more than four decades in the grave? Come now, even your open mind can't possibly be considering..."

Suddenly, Judex lifted another paper from the manila folder and perused it carefully. One particular passage caught his attention. After reading it, the vigilante was filled with a surge of unremitting horror, the likes of which he had rarely experienced.

"A project to create 'superior soldiers'..." Judex read aloud. "Dear God, no."

"Why so much concern, *mon ami?*"

"I know exactly what Doctor Cornelius is up to now. He plans to exploit Calliet in the worst way imaginable, both for him and for the world: The creation of an army of superior soldiers by synthesizing the blood of a *loup-garou*, possibly selling that formula for massive amounts of money to the Great Powers of Europe!... Where did you say the latest headquarters of the Red Hand is located?"

"My word, I just cannot believe this could be possible..."

"*Where*, Cocantin?"

"Let me look ... yes, 18 rue de l'Arbre-Sec, behind Saint-Germain l'Auxerrois, in the 1st Arrondissement. Do you require any back-up?"

But Cocantin looked up to discover that he was now alone in his office. Judex had already departed to counter this new, monstrous threat.

A few days later, Cornelius was placing another vial of blood he had just extracted from Calliet in its proper holder on the lengthy middle laboratory table. The young man himself was ravenously devouring a large piece of bloody raw meat that the scientist had the local butcher provide for him.

"You can eat slowly, my friend; that meat isn't going to run away on you," the Doctor said with a chuckle.

Calliet simply ignored his benefactor and continued to voraciously devour the meat as if he hadn't eaten anything raw in decades; and, in truth, he actually *hadn't*.

Turning his blood-covered face to the scientist, the *loup-garou* asked:

"Have you deduced how I'm able to lift things while in wolf form if I have paws instead of hands?"

"*Oui*, Bertrand. You see, my studies of lycanthropy and other metamorphic humans claiming to have come by their attributes by means of 'magic' or some sort of supernatural 'curse' have uncovered the fact that there appears to be different breeds of lycanthropes. They tend to vary in the requirements for their transformations, such as dependence on the reflected light of a full Moon, or in vulnerability to substances such as silver and wolfsbane. Moreover, they vary in what specific phenotypic form they take, with at least four such forms appearing in the various reported accounts.

"Their specific breed, and the specific means by which they acquire their condition, seem to influence the anatomical phenotype in which they manifest during their metamorphoses. However, it's quite clear that most lycanthropes are potentially capable of taking any of the four reported lupine phenotypes, be they bipedal, quadrupedal, or a hybrid thereof. Hence, you may have retained your hands in lupine form, and could switch at will from mobility as a biped or quadruped, or even shifted between paws and hands depending upon your needs, maybe without consciously realizing it."

"This is all quite fascinating, Doctor, but that serum you gave me doesn't seem to have calmed my lust for flesh, nor my urge to run free and hunt other living creatures. You said you would help me, and I am enough of a wretch as it is without the love of Sophie to temper the beast…"

"*Patience, mon ami*. I devised that preliminary serum over the past few days only. Even one with my skill must be given sufficient time through trial and error to perfect a treatment. I believe this chemical should at least allow you to shift more easily into your full lupine form when needed, regardless of the lunar phases, so you can act more effectively in your capacity as an agent of the Red Hand…"

A moment later, the loud clanging sound of several bullets striking and cracking the reinforced glass of the laboratory window startled both men, as well as the two guards present in the room. Another moment later, the broken glass completely shattered and the dark-clad Judex leapt through the window, landing on one of the tables a few meters across from Cornelius and Calliet.

"*Bonjour, Docteur*," the vigilante said in his usual cold monotone, with both of his specially designed firearms brandished. "Are you ready to settle your account with justice?"

"Judex!" Doctor Cornelius bellowed at the upper limits of his larynx. "You won't ruin another of my special projects! Bertrand, this is the man who seeks to prevent me from helping you!"

Hearing that accusation, Calliet's eyes grew pitch black just as his teeth elongated in tandem with his tongue. Judex was certain he could see multiple tufts of hair sprouting from the young man's face and body, even as his ears began to become more pointed.

"You!" the young man shouted in a garbled voice, with puddles of drool flying from his maw. "You will not harm Doctor Cornelius! He is my only hope of controlling the beast!"

Steeling himself against the difficult confrontation that was surely to come, Judex retorted, "I know who you are, Monsieur Calliet. Cornelius is a vile criminal, and he has no intention of helping you, only of exploiting you. Help me stop him, and I will commit all my considerable resources to helping you in his place."

"Don't believe him, Bertrand!" Cornelius yelled in response, as he surreptitiously pushed an alarm button hidden on the leg of a nearby table to summon more men. "He dresses like the Devil, just like the legends tell us. He represents all the evil you are fighting in yourself. He is here to prevent me from quelling your own bestial side. Kill him!"

Howling in rage under Cornelius' verbal manipulation, Calliet completed his metamorphosis into wolf form in a matter of seconds. Dropping to all fours, he began running towards the vigilante with remarkable speed. Reacting quickly, Judex pumped four bullets into the huge, snarling, grayish-black creature rushing towards him. The werewolf let out a distinctly canine whine of pain as the projectiles struck, but his charge was not halted. Leaping several meters into the air, the hellish beast smashed into Judex, knocking him clear off the table.

Cornelius turned to his two men and shouted orders at as high a volume as his lungs could muster:

"Get those vials of blood over there and take them to the safehouse! If they are damaged, I will exact horrific retribution against you and your families! For *three* generations!"

As Judex landed on the floor, he used the werewolf's momentum to flip him off his own body with his legs, effectively hurling the beast several meters across the room. The creature slammed into the far wall, yelped in pain, but landed on four legs. He then stood up, measuring well over two meters in height. He growled at his adversary, waving his furry, taloned hands. The vigilante knew the beast would attack again within seconds, but he was loathe to engage it unnecessarily. He realized that he had to try to appeal to the man within.

"Calliet, listen to me! There must be some of you left in that wolf! Cornelius has been using you to acquire blood samples! His aim is to create an army of *loups-garous* with *your* blood! All for war profiteering! You were a soldier, you fought against the Commune, you know how horrid war is! Imagine hundreds of men with your curse released upon unsuspecting villages!"

"Not... true!" the wolf managed to utter through a partially lupine throat.

142

He once more dropped to four legs and charged at his nemesis. Acting quickly, Judex grabbed a vial of acid off a nearby table and splashed it in the werewolf's face. The beast was stopped in his tracks, and howled in agony as the searing fluid blistered his eyes and muzzle.

Judex executed a swift turning kick to the wolf's jaw, momentarily stunning him. He then lifted a heavy wooden chair and began beating the creature with it mercilessly.

However, none of these attacks were enough to dispatch a supernatural beast of this nature. Calliet quickly moved past the pain, jumped back into a bipedal stance, and swatted Judex across the length of the room. The lycanthrope's strength was immense, and the vigilante found himself hurled over 15 meters. He landed on a distant table, knocking its assortment of vials and beakers into a mass of shattered glass on the floor.

Before the beast could resume his attack, however, the creature's ultra-keen hearing overheard Cornelius shouting his main concern to his men again:

"Get those vials of blood out of here! Their safe extraction is paramount to all other concerns!"

The werewolf then turned towards the scientist in whom he had put all his hopes and trust. His extended fanged muzzle began growling and dripping saliva, as the anger within him swelled up into a volcanic rage.

"You… lied!" the beast managed to articulate. "You… used me! The… Dark one… was right!"

"No, Bertrand, you're wrong!" Cornelius shouted in desperation. "Don't listen to the lies of this devil!"

Growling and foaming like a rabid dog, the werewolf began approaching the scientist with murder in his glaring eyes.

"Damn it!" muttered Cornelius. Then, he ordered: "Shoot that creature!"

The two guards released a salvo of hot lead into the werewolf, which caused the beast to cry out in pain, but it wasn't sufficient to stop his charge. Taking an astounding leap several meters forward, the creature landed on the guard carrying the vials of blood. His weight alone crushed the man. The *loup-garou* ripped the guard's esophagus from his throat with minimal effort. The wolf's paws then morphed into furry human-like hands, grabbed the vials of blood from the dead man, and hurled them against the wall. A loud tinkling sound was heard as the vials were smashed to pieces, their precious liquid contents spattering on the wall and the floor beneath.

Cornelius was now beyond livid. "No! You imbecilic beast! I'll kill you for this!"

The wolf then turned towards the scientist and snarled viciously, as if challenging him to try carrying out his threat. A second later, however, a cadre of armed guards entered the room, each with firearms drawn.

"These men have guns loaded with silver!" Cornelius boasted with haughty anger. "You think I failed to come prepared for this eventuality, you freakish monstrosity?"

Before the men could open fire, however, one of them had the left side of his head blown off by a bullet fired by Judex, who quickly followed up with a second shot that opened a gaping hole several centimeters wide in the gut of another guard.

Taking advantage of this surprise attack, the werewolf leapt on two of the other men, quickly ripping them limb from limb with full bestial fury before they could fire a single projectile.

The remaining guards aimed their weapons at Judex, and discharged several shots, all of which failed to hit their target when the vigilante somersaulted behind a large wooden storage shelf. The dark-clad avenger then ran out of hiding and returned fire, delivering fatal shots to two guards. Judex then looked up to see the werewolf rising to a bipedal stance with the severed limb of one of the two remaining men in his mighty jaws, and the decapitated head of the other in his left hand-like paw.

"Calliet, try to control yourself now!" Judex yelled. "We need to find Cornelius before…"

But even as the werewolf's ears perked up at the sound of Judex's words, he was cut down by a silver bullet that struck him from behind, fired by Cornelius who had retrieved one of his men's discarded pieces.

The wolf yowled in agony before falling to the floor in a massive furry heap, this time not rising again.

"May you rot in Hell where you belong!" was the last thing the mad scientist shouted before quickly running through an escape door. Judex fired at him, but Cornelius managed to slam the bullet-proof access shut before the projectiles could find their mark.

Judex then heard the blaring alarm that signaled the initiation of an evacuation protocol. This headquarters would be forever abandoned, and all items left behind would be written off as a business loss. Thankfully, though, Cornelius' nightmarish plot to create his own army of *loups-garous* had been defeated.

The vigilante rushed over to the fallen form of the werewolf, and saw that he had reverted back to human form. He was barely breathing, and his pulse was on the verge of halting.

"I'm… sorry," was Calliet's scarcely audible statement. "Sophie, I am…coming to be with you… at last…"

The young man then went silent, and his breathing and pulse ceased entirely.

"I am the one who is sorry, Calliet," Judex said quietly, with considerable remorse in his tone, "for failing to save you from the beast within. But sometimes the hand of Justice is harsh, and she did not look upon you favorably this day."

1919. World War I with its 2.3 million dead and crippled buried the 19th century and sapped France's confidence, creating deep wounds in the collective psyche: on the one hand, the French had won the war, and chauvinistic pride and xenophobic arrogance reached an all-time high; on the other hand, things would never be the same again. This schizophrenic conflict between the illusion of superiority and the desire to preserve traditional values, on the one hand, and the emergence of new, and therefore threatening, ideas intending to break with the past on the other, was played out, with most dramatic results, in the field of popular fiction. We now follow Judex as he struggles to find a place in the new world that lies ahead...

Thom Brannan & Matthew Baugh: *Every Rose*

The man in the long black cape and slouch hat stood in the rain outside the barred windows of the city jail. Inside, he could make out a hulking prisoner sitting on a narrow cot. The sight surprised him. Judex was unused to surprises, and his annoyance manifested itself in a crease between his eyebrows. No other emotion showed on his face.

He had come to Padua, drawn by news of a series of killings that seemed as familiar as they were brutal. He had been certain he knew who must be responsible; someone he had faced before… someone the Italian authorities had no chance of catching. Now, to his surprise, not only did they have a suspect in custody, but it was someone who looked physically capable of the crimes. The man in the gaol was large, well over six feet tall, and his shoulders strained the cheap fabric of the shirt he wore, a shirt which should have been billowy and loose. He sat, ill at ease, constantly shaking his head.

The rain began to let up and Judex moved away from the window. The downpour had helped him approach the gaol unseen, but soon the guards would resume their rounds. Drawing his black cloak around him, he faded into the night.

The next morning, an English dandy appeared before Magistrate Buratti with an odd request.

"What is this?" the Magistrate proclaimed in heavily accented English.

"See now, old boy," the Englishman said, smoothing back an errant lock of black hair. "My name is Roland Smythe-Thorpe and my purpose is quite plain. I wish to speak to your monstrous prisoner. He's to be executed, isn't he? I don't see the harm." The Englishman waggled thick eyebrows at the magistrate, who sat back, mustache twitching.

"It'll make great copy for the ladies in England, what? Ooh, I can see them clutching at their heaving bosoms now, reading in awe about the Italian Ripper!"

"*No, no, questo non sarà,*" the Magistrate said, momentarily losing his English. "This is all very irregular."

Smythe-Thorpe shrugged eloquently. "Oh, well. I suppose the ladies will have to forego the experience of reading about your keen mind, as well."

"What is this?"

Waggling his eyebrows again, the Englishman leaned forward. "You're the chap in charge, aren't you? Anyone who receives the credit for snagging such a monster should find their name quite famous across the channel, I would think."

Buratti stroked his bushy mustache. "And the pale ladies, with their heaving bosoms?"

"Would have your name on the tips of their tongues."

"Federico!" the magistrate called. "*Scortare quest'uomo per vedere il prigioniero, Maciste.*"

"Well," Smyth-Thorpe said, slapping his gloves on his thigh. "You certainly are a brute, aren't you?"

The large sullen man looked up at the Englishman with something in his eyes, a look that hovered between disdain and violence. It made the journalist think of a lion he had once seen in the zoo; weary of being placed on display.

Turning to the guard, Smythe-Thorpe waved him away. "*Sei secure, Signore?*" the guard asked, and was answered with a nod. Shrugging, for who can understand Englishmen, the guard left.

"That look tells me you speak English," the man said.

Maciste did not move, nor did his stare change. "I speak many languages, *Signore.*"

A hint of something came into Smythe-Thorpe's that was previously absent. "And the guards?"

Maciste shook his head.

"Good," the Englishman said. He leaned down to speak in a lower voice. "I know you did not do what you stand accused of."

Maciste's eyes widened. "For truth? How is this that you would believe me when my own countrymen do not?"

"I've seen this before. I know the *creature* who is truly responsible."

"Say this again, if you will? You said 'creature.'"

At the reporter's nod, Maciste stood and stretched his massive arms. "Ha ha! At last, someone who will believe me!"

The Englishman waved reassuringly to the guard, then turned back to Maciste. "Tell me."

Maciste, nearly drunk for having imbibed most of a bar's inventory, was walking to his home. It was very late, the new moon lending no light to the dark streets of Padua. He turned a corner, only a block or two from his home, and a scream tore through the night.

His blood singing to him already, Maciste ran in the direction of the scream. He turned into an alley and beheld a nightmare.

A monstrous man-like creature, perhaps eight feet tall and chalk white, stooped over the still form of a lithe woman. Her arm had been wrenched from its socket, and though she was lying prone, her neck was so badly twisted that her face looked up to the dark sky. The thing was holding something to her shoulder; it looked like a shepherd's waterskin that he was using to catch the gushing blood.

With a cry of rage and horror, Maciste rushed into the alley, arms wide, and smashed into the creature. It staggered back a step, then braced itself and pushed back. For a moment, the pair of brutes were locked together, each pushing but neither gaining an inch. With a surge of strength, Maciste broke his hold and shoved against the monster's chest with all his strength. Both of them staggered back, eyeing each other with shock. Then the moment was over, and they closed again.

Quickly, Maciste wrapped his corded arms about the monster's waist, kicking hard at the legs. Maciste's lower center of gravity gave him the advantage and the pair of the tumbled to the cobblestones with him on top. The monster moved with amazing speed and grabbed Maciste's shoulders with a grip like fire.

Feeling the strength in those hands, in the torso he squeezed which refused to bend or break, Maciste's mind begin to whirl. Everything, from the creature's pale face to the dark alley, was turning red. Here was a challenge for him!

Then the monster arched his back and used his grip to hurl Maciste over his head. The big man slammed into a wall with shattering force to shake the house. He scrambled to his feet but the creature was already ready and a massive, stone-like foot smashed into the Italian strong-man's face. The blow opened a cut on his forehead, and a sheet of blood quickly covered his face.

Wiping his eyes, Maciste climbed to his feet, looking for the pale creature. But it was gone, and all that was left was the poor girl.

Maciste got down on his knees next to her. The emptiness of her face, and the extreme disfiguration of her neck, told her everything. He picked up her arm; it seemed such a frail thing. With care, he put it next to the body, more or less where it should go.

And that's when the police came into the alleyway.

After the interview, the foppish Englishman returned to the magistrate's office.

"Did you find what you wanted?" Buratti asked.

"Splendid, splendid!" the reporter said. "Now I only need some background to tell the story properly."

"Background?"

"You know; information about the murdered girls, the part of the city where it happened, the significant history of Padua. I want people to see the canvas on which the story of your heroism and Maciste's villainy is painted."

"Ah, of course," the Magistrate said. "But, I was only doing my duty, you understand."

"Your patriotism and humility will cause me readers' hearts to flutter."

"Within their white bosoms?"

"Precisely!"

"How can I help, *Signore*?"

"If you could take me to the crime scenes and answer my questions about the crimes, it would be invaluable."

"I would like to, *Signore*," Buratti said, glancing at his pocket watch, "but my wife will be expecting me for lunch. I fear my absence will upset her."

"I see," the Englishman said, producing a fat wallet. He opened it and took out several bills. "Perhaps you should buy the *Signorina* a new dress, by way of apology."

"You are a true gentleman," the Magistrate replied with a smile. The bills disappeared quite suddenly.

"The other thing that occurs to me is that I would love to know something of the legends of the city, particularly the more sinister ones."

"Sinister, *Signore*?"

"This Maciste is very strong, is he not?"

"It is true," the Magistrate said. "During the War he fought as one of our Alpine troops. They say that he recaptured a castle that those dogs of Austrians had taken. By some accounts he defeated a battalion of their soldiers, alone and unarmed, though that is surely an exaggeration. I have heard other stories of him doing other things, lifting a car so the tire could be remounted, carrying a grand piano up a flight of stairs on his back, and so on."

"It must have taken several squads of *carboneri* to arrest such a man."

"No," Buratti said. "He came meekly enough, and has made no attempt to escape. I believe that the enormity of his crimes weighs heavily on his soul."

"His strength makes me want to investigate some of the lore of Padua," Smythe-Thorpe said.

"How so?"

"Such wondrous feats are often associated with the alchemists of yore and their experiments. I can think of examples associated with men like Paracelsus, Praetorius, Cagliostro, and Frankenstein. I wonder if there is a legend of such a man from your fair city."

"I know a man who could tell you," the Magistrate said. Professor Teone from the University is an expert on the city's history and legends. I could invite him to dinner this evening and he could tell us."

"Capital!" the Englishman said.

"Alas," Buratti continued, "I had made plans to dine with my mistress this evening. She will be cross with me, I fear."

The Englishman smiled and took several more bills from his wallet. "Perhaps a pretty dress for her as well?"

"You do understand, *Signore*! But my mistress... unlike my wife, she is very beautiful... and perhaps a little vain."

"So it would take a prettier dress?" The reporter withdrew another bill and the Magistrate's eyes twinkled. "But we would not want your wife to be jealous, would we?" he asked, passing yet another banknote across.

"Ah, *Signore*, it is a pleasure to meet such a man of the world!" the Magistrate said.

"It is in this area the bulk of the attacks have occurred," the Magistrate said. He kicked at the street. "Cobblestones, everywhere still. It feels as if we here are the poorest in all of Italy. During the War we were the center of government and military action, but now poverty has emptied entire areas of my little city."

Buratti indicated the buildings bordering the *palazzio* where they stood with flicks of his hand. "Just look about you."

The Englishman did so, eyes narrowing.

"It is sad," he agreed. "I can see the grandeur of the arcaded walkways, yet I can also see how such shadowed spaces would make a grand stalking ground for the killer at night."

"It is true," the Magistrate said. "And it is not hard to find an isolated spot, where screams will not be heard."

"Thank you so much for all the color, my good man. It certainly helps me gain perspective on your community. It is an ancient city, is it not?"

"The oldest in Northern Italy," the Magistrate said, puffing out his chest. "Virgil writes of its founding in his *Aeneid*, and for nearly 800 years it has been home to the greatest University in Europe, where Galileo himself lectured."

"Less than a mile from where we now stand, is it not?"

"Indeed," Buratti replied. "Though there is certainly no connection. Maciste is an untutored man; a common laborer. I doubt he has ever set foot on those hallowed grounds."

"I'm certain you are right," Smythe-Thorpe agreed, "but will you humor me anyway?"

"But of course!"

Linking arms with the Englishman, the Magistrate led him to one of the covered walkways that led to the University.

"A wonderful meal!" Smythe-Thorpe said, pushing himself back from Buratti's table.

Buratti beamed and translated the compliment for his wife, who smiled in turn. Then he rose and ushered his guests into the study for brandy and cigars. Professor Teone was a stout, middle-aged man with thinning hair and a quiet manner.

"My friend Buratti tells me that you are looking for legends of a Paduan Frankenstein," he said.

"Aptly put," the journalist replied. "Is there such a man?"

"Why do you want to know?"

"I can tell by your answer there is. You simply must tell me now, my good sir."

"It is nothing," the Professor said with an entirely European shrug. "There are always such stories; I can't see how it would be of importance to you."

A sparkle lit the Englishman's eyes. "Try me."

"Professor, I am certain we can trust *Signore* Smythe-Thorpe's discretion," the Magistrate said.

The Professor turned his eyes away and looked up. He brushed his mustache with both hands before speaking in a low voice.

"Rappaccini," he said. "Oh, over a hundred years ago, there was a man, a doctor famous for his method of distilling plants into medicines. He was, by all accounts, a cold man, more interested in the advancement of science than his fellow man."

Glancing at the Englishman, Teone detected no signs of boredom or impatience.

"*Signor* Rappaccini had a daughter. He brought her up in the most usual way, with a singular exception. In her maidenhood, she was locked away in the lush garden, kept there by her father. She tended the garden, and having spent her entire life around these plants, which were, as it turns out, infamously poisonous... she was not only immune to their harm, but poisonous herself!"

He turned, as if defying the newsman to dismiss his story.

"You have my undivided attention," Smythe-Thorpe said, in a voice so cool it seemed to the Professor to have come from a frozen hell.

"Yes. Well, there was a young man in residence, a student at the University of Padua, and he fell regrettably in love with Rappaccini's daughter, Beatrice. And upon discovering her poisonous nature, he endeavored to cure her, for he found her to be full of innocence, even with the killing touch, the killing breath. The young man attempted this with a powerful antidote.

"It did not cure her. Instead, *Signore*, it killed poor Beatrice, who was only poisonous in her body. You can see the ruined mansion, not far from the University. It is rumored to be haunted by the ghost of Beatrice and the young man. Giovanni was his name."

A dark look fell over the Professor's face.

"And the garden is in bloom."

"What?" Buratti said. "But you said yourself that the home has long been abandoned."

"Nevertheless, it is true," Teone replied in a quiet voice. "I have looked over the all myself and seen the garden."

"When did Rappaccini die?" The Englishman asked.

The question shook the Professor from the melancholy he seemed to have fallen into, and he looked up in the direction of the University and the old mansion.

"I do not know for sure, *Signore*. Surely, he is dead. It has been, after all, over a hundred years."

"Very well," the Englishman said, again gay and careless, almost as if overcompensating for his quiet attention earlier. "Thank you so much, my good man. I shall be sure have my publisher send you a copy of my article."

On leaving the Magistrate's home, the reporter caught a carriage which took him to the little farmhouse on the edge of the city. He had rented the isolated home for the privacy it afforded him.

Once inside, the man removed a wig and stripped off the theatrical makeup. The Englishman's foppish features gave way to the lean, handsome, yet somewhat predatory countenance of Jacques de Trémeuse. He put on black clothes, a long cape, and a slouch hat and was transformed again into the mysterious Judex.

Moving to the old barn, he took a tarpaulin from a powerful automobile. The vehicle purred to life and moved into the darkness.

On the rooftop, the man in black watched the dark and winding streets and alleys of Padua. The Magistrate's exclamations of poverty were not exaggerations. Even now, at the end of the Great War, when electricity was available in most metropolises across the globe, it remained dark here.

A bit of movement caught Judex's eye. There was a woman, coming down the darkened street. She was tall, singing as she walked; a French song that he recognized. She had a beautiful voice, yet her face was lined with sadness. Judex had seen her earlier, at her own place, a tavern where she sang in the same lovely voice for her patrons. Her name was Gina and she was the widow of a pilot, killed in the late War.

As she passed the open mouth of the alley, Judex saw he was not the only creature of the night in the area. A great shape rose up from beneath a canvass covering and darted large hands to grab the woman!

Judex was momentarily frozen by the horrible visage of the creature, one he had confronted before in the sewers of Paris. His paralysis lasted only a second; then, without further thought, he launched himself from the rooftop, plummeting three stories to land with both feet on the creature's right shoulder.

Yellow, unblinking eyes turned up to meet his at the last moment before impact, and the man in black leapt away as soon as he had landed. Already knowing of the creature's prodigious strength, he knew his only chance was to stay out of its considerable reach.

But the girl needed to *run*.

"Get out of here," he hissed, dancing back on light feet as the chalk-white creature swiped a huge hand at his face. Though it was dark, Judex could see the dull yellow of the creature's sharp teeth shining in his face. There was a flurry of movement behind, and the girl was gone.

"So you remember me, Gouroull. Do you remember everything about me?"

Judex shifted back again, this time drawing a Steyr automatic from beneath each arm. He aimed them at Gouroull, and the creature sneered in disdain.

"You are strong and fast, monster," Judex said, his voice low and even. "But even one such as you cannot stand against an angry mob." He turned one of his pistols sideways so the creature could see it. "This is nothing to you. But sixteen gunshots will certainly get the attention of the police, who are particularly alert because of your exploits."

Snapping its mouthful of jagged, razor-sharp teeth once, the creature cast a last baleful glance at Judex and it bounded away with absurd grace.

Quickly, Judex holstered his weapons and ran to the end of the alley where, with all his skill, he scaled a drainpipe to gain the roof. Alighting there, he sprinted to the other side of the building in time to see the glaring white skin of the creature disappear around the corner. He smacked his gloved fist once on his other.

He knew which way the monster was headed.

Judex made his way quietly back to the gaol, putting the pieces together in his rapacious mind. The creature's methods and motives were alien in the extreme, not to be understood by ordinary men, but one thing was consistent: Gouroull desired a mate. It had been so at his creation, and had been so ever since. Was it a desire to fit in with the humanity he so despised? Or was it a simple need the creature itself did not fully comprehend?

It did not matter. All that mattered was the rest of the puzzle.

"The garden is in bloom," Judex whispered to himself as he snuck past the roaming guard to approach the rear of the gaol. Clearly, the creature had heard the story of Rappaccini, and had somehow coaxed the poisonous plants back to life. But why did he need the blood?

He stood again outside the barred window where he had first stopped when he came to Padua, looking in at the hulking mass of Maciste, who sat rubbing his neck. Judex got close to the bars.

"Maciste," he said, and the large man's head shot up.

"Who is it?"

"Who I am is of no concern of yours, my strong friend. But know that I believe your protestations of innocence."

"First, the Englishman, and now you. But my own people?" Maciste raised his head, pointing at his neck. "They tried to hang me today!"

"Fear not," Judex said. "I know how we can clear your good name. But you will have to be on this side of these bars for us to do so."

With a sigh of relief, Maciste stood and yanked his iron chain from its anchor in the stone wall. Judex had expected him to be able to do it, but the ease of the action astonished him. This was more than a strong man, this was a force of nature. He walked quickly to the bars in the window. "I would have done this earlier," he said, placing his heavy hands on them, "but they would have just brought me back here."

Jaw set, Maciste tensed his massive arms. Corded muscle stood out on his forearms, and his knuckles went white. Judex stepped back as the iron creaked, then covered his face when the bars Maciste gripped screamed in protest and broke free from their moorings.

"Quickly," Judex said. "We must away from here."

"Just a moment," Maciste said, bending to grip the irons around his ankle. "I can't find purchase."

Like an oily shadow, Judex moved to kneel at Maciste's foot. A pair of thin metal rods appeared in his hands, as if by magic, and he went to work on the lock. A scant twenty seconds later, the metal released and fell from Maciste's leg.

The man in black stood, looking up into the larger man's face. "You know of the old mansion in the northern part of town, the one rumored to be haunted?"

The giant shrugged. "I do."

"Meet me there in an hour." He looked Maciste up and down. "And try to disguise yourself. We don't need interference from the police."

Maciste nodded, then looked back to the ruined window. "Not bad, eh? Sometimes, I—"

There was a rustle of cloth, and when he looked back, the figure in black was gone.

Not long after, Maciste was walking along the old deserted street which led to the dilapidated mansion. He wore the same pants and shirt as he had in jail, but had added a false beard as well as a hat with a large, floppy brim. He nodded to the few persons he met, satisfied he was completely unrecognizable.

Along the way, he paused as he encountered beggar. The poor man sat with his poncho draped over a wheeled platform; he had no legs. He looked blind, to boot. Maciste was overcome with compassion, and stooped to drop a coin in the man's cup.

"Is that your disguise?" the beggar asked, and Maciste jumped back several feet. The beggar looked up and down the street. "Never mind. We're not too far. I thought you were never going to show."

Maciste's brow lowered. "I was working on my disguise."

Judex, standing, folded his wheeled platform with quick motions. It disappeared under his voluminous poncho and he tilted his head towards the great castle. "Come on."

As he moved that way, Maciste noted a blued-steel barrel poking from the bottom of the poncho Judex wore.

"What are you expecting to find here?" he asked. "How do you know of this place?"

Judex shook his head, holding his hand up for silence. Stealthily, with the greatest care, he parted the hedge with his gloved hands. Beyond lay the fabulous garden of Rappaccini, filled with exotic flowers and shrubs from around the world, and hybrids found nowhere else, all. In the center stood a fountain which, against all expectations, still poured out sparkling streams of water to feed the lush foliage.

Near the fountain stood a massive urn—at least four feet high and ten across—in which had been planted a bush unlike any either man had ever seen. It was a good-sized shrub covered with a profusion of remarkable flowers, each the color and luster of an amethyst. Judex glanced back at Maciste, then indicated the remarkable bush with his eyes.

There was a pod growing from it.

It was long, just over five feet. It pulsed with life, the fleshy covering veined in dark green. Even from their distance the pair could make out the ground beneath the bush, oozing and dark with stolen blood.

"*Dio mio*," Maciste whispered. He pointed as the pod began to shudder. Judex's eyes widened as a black seam formed along the side of the growth, and with a wet sound, it widened and opened, spilling forth a girl.

Pushing Judex aside, Maciste tore through the hedge, running towards the girl, who seemed completely insensate.

"Maciste, no!" Judex hissed. His eyes darted around the garden, but there was no sign of the creature.

"She's alive," Maciste near-shouted, and Judex cringed. He followed, but cautiously, fearing the big man had given away their position to their enemy. So far there was no sign of Gouroull, but the uncanny nature of the pod still worried him, especially in light of the stories of Rappaccini's experiments.

"Don't touch the bush, Maciste," he called in a low voice, "and don't touch the girl. There is danger here."

But where Judex saw danger, Maciste clearly only say a helpless innocent. He gathered the naked girl in his arms and began to rise, then a look of shock came over his features. He put the pod-girl down and staggered away a few paces, then gave a gigantic twitch and fell over.

Judex cursed under his breath and rushed over. The great form of Maciste was stretched out on the garden ground next to the girl, who was beginning to stir. For a moment, Judex looked at his own gloves, as if considering their worth versus poison.

But only for a moment, because Gouroull dropped from the balcony above to land behind and lashed out with his massive fist. Judex rolled away, feeling the draft of the blow. The rifle under his poncho hampered his ability to move, and he shook the garment off his shoulders.

He parried the next two blows with the rifle, an elephant gun, and leapt back. Gouroull pressed forward, swinging his arms in a fury, his glaring yellow eyes full of malice. Pointed teeth gnashed with every missed blow; Judex knew he couldn't keep this up for long. He blocked another hammering fist with the elephant gun, only realizing at the last second it was a feint!

The rifle was ripped from his hands, leaving his fingers numb. He watched in near-despair as the creature took the elephant gun in both hands and wrenched it apart.

Judex reached under his cloak, arms crossed, for his Steyr automatics. The creature rushed forward in a blur, grabbing Judex in a bear hug, trapping his arms! The pointed teeth made another appearance, and then the great moon face came smashing down on Judex' own.

When Judex was next aware of the world, he found himself chained to a great crucifix. He continued to breathe shallowly, keeping his eyes squinted, looking around the room. It was the chapel of the old castle, lit by hundreds of candles. The woman from the pod, now clad in a white wedding dress, sat in the first pew, head down and sobbing.

"Why do you cry?" the creature asked from the rear of the chapel. His voice sounded as if it was ripped and torn as it came through his jagged mouthful of teeth. "This is the happiest day of your life, woman."

Yellow eyes flicked up to Judex on the cross. "I can smell that you're awake."

Gouroull stepped out of the shadow. He was draped in black robes, yet still wore a white tie. His pasty white flesh peeked out from under his hood. His bulging eyes seemed to dance with mirth. He pointed at Judex. "You. Preside." He laughed, throwing his head back.

He began to hum a mangled version of Wagner's *Bridal Chorus* as he walked down the aisle.

"No," the woman said. "No, no. You... you are not my Giovanni."

Judex' head came up. How could she know that name?

Gouroull snarled and rushed down the aisle at her. He picked the woman up bodily and held her so that her face was inches from his. "No choice, you!" He bared his teeth and laughed as she slammed her little fists into him over and over. Her eyes widened, and she looked at her hands.

155

"What manner of creature are you, that my touch has no effect?"

"He is no man," Judex said, struggling with his bonds. "He is completely inhuman, madam, and the weird black liquid in his veins is not blood."

The creature dropped the girl, turning to Judex. "You," it growled. "You don't preside anymore."

As Gouroull stepped onto the chancel steps there was a great tumult, and the side door of the chapel blew apart in a storm of splinters.

"Monster!" Maciste shouted, and he ran headlong into Gouroull. The pair of brutes smashed through the altar and rolled to the other side of the dais, both howling without words and pounding at each other.

Judex redoubled his efforts to get loose from his chains. Maciste was strong, undoubtedly so, but Judex could tell already from the man's movements, he had yet to fully overcome the effects of the girl's poison.

"Let me help you," she said, suddenly in front of Judex. "None of this is right." She struggled with his chains.

Maciste and Gouroull came to their feet and squared off. Almost absently, the creature kicked over the first pew, sending the rest of the rows falling in a domino line. Eyes still dull, Maciste followed the movement and the creature dove at him.

The giants met again. Maciste caught the attack with barely any time to counter; his great arms, sinews cracking with effort, strove to fend off the inhuman strength of the creature. The pair of them strained, staring into each other's eyes. A gruesome smile blossomed on Gouroull's face as he realized the titanic strength of Maciste was not at its fullest.

"Hurry, girl," Judex said. "If there's a key…"

"I don't know," she said, looking back. "I didn't see—ow!"

She drew her hand back, looking at cut which had opened on her palm. Where the blood landed on the chains, it spat and sizzled. She hesitated for barely a second, then slashed her hand on the same rough burr on the chain, slathering her blood on the hasps of the locks holding Judex down.

He looked up at the steam rising from the metal where the acid-blood burned. "Better find a place to hide," he said. The locks failed, and Judex freed himself of their weight. The chain around his legs and the base of the cross, however, he kept. It still had the lock hanging from it. As he moved, he grinned. The creature, in all its hubris, had left Judex with weapons.

Maciste and Gouroull stood chest-to-chest, hands clasped in a test of strength. The earlier poison had done its work well, and Maciste felt himself slipping back. The jagged teeth of the creature snapped in his face, and he fought to keep from flinching.

There was a whistling sound, and a meaty whack, and for a moment the creature's strength faltered. Maciste chanced a look past, and saw Judex whirling a chain over his head. The black-clad figure swung again, and the heavy lock thudded a second time into Gouroull's left knee.

The creature yelled its frustration, and Maciste drove his knee upwards into its midsection. He felt at least one of the creature's ribs bend and break.

"Duck," Judex said softly.

Maciste tucked his head down, and the next second, the lock smashed into G—————'s ear. The creature howled again and released Maciste's hands. Black, sludgy liquid oozed from the creature's ear, and it wobbled on its feet, equilibrium lost.

Laughing, Maciste dove forward and grabbed both of Gourould's legs behind the knees, driving his head into the creature's unprotected midsection. Like a felled tree, the monster went straight back, cracking its head against the tiled floor. Maciste struggled, keeping the creature's arms down.

"Now!" he yelled. "If you're going to do something, do—"

He was cut off by a tremendous crash as a marble baptismal fount came smashing down onto the creature's head. The creature went still, and Judex sagged against the fount.

Maciste pushed himself to his feet. He pointed a shaky finger at Judex. "You are good."

He lumbered away, grabbing a pair of candelabras and shaking the candles off them. He rolled the creature over and twisted the ornate ironwork into improvised handcuffs. He went away and came back with two more, wrapping these around the creature's lower half, binding its legs together.

"What do you think?" he asked Judex, who only smiled and gave him an appreciative nod.

"Wake up!" Maciste shouted into the Magistrate's window. "We have a special delivery for you!"

Smoothing down his mustache, Buratti came outside, his eyes wide at the sight that greeted them. Maciste stood there, with the giant Gourould across his shoulders. A man in black stood behind them, leaning against a great, sleek black car. The Magistrate thought he could make out the shape of a woman in the front seat.

"What... what... ?"

Maciste dumped the creature at the Magistrate's feet like a sack of corn. "Your killer. Does he not match the description I gave you?"

While Buratti did his best impression of a goldfish, the man in black stepped away from the car. "He is Gourould, and you would be best served if you wrapped him in chains, weighted him down, and dropped him in the deepest part of the Mediterranean." He clapped the Magistrate on the shoulder. "Rest easier now, *Signore*. There will be no more of these horrific murders. And you don't have to embarrass yourself trying to execute this one."

Maciste laughed heartily, slapping the Magistrate on the other shoulder, bowling the man over completely.

When the Magistrate got back to his feet, the man in black was in the car already. "Who are you?" he shouted, but the engine was revving, and then the car was off like a shot.

"Who was that?" he asked Maciste.

The big man only shrugged. "I don't know. Now... about the charges against me... "

"Where will we go now?" the woman asked. She looked at her hands, her treacherous hands. From the short conversation she'd already had with Judex, she understood it was over a hundred years since her time. And she understood how she'd come to be again; the means, if not the method. The monster had rec-reated the shrub that had once been inexorably linked to the life of Rappaccini's daughter. He had nourished it with the blood, the living tissues of the murdered girls, and it had some been able to regrow her. Somehow, the spirits of the murdered girls had called her back.

She shuddered.

"Beatrice," Judex said, "you can't stay here in Italy. Not now. Will you come with me to France? I know scientists, men who will give their all to help you."

Beatrice's eyes welled with tears. "I beg your pardon, but someone tried that once, already." She sniffed, looking down at her hands again. "I am what I am."

Judex patted her hands with his gloved one. "But that's not what you have to be. We'll find a way." He smiled, the most brilliant and genuine smile she'd ever seen.

"We'll find a way," he repeated.

The car sped into the night.

1919. The following story pits Judex against perhaps the most fearsome foe of all, with the background of the search for immortality. As we stated in our introduction, Judex appears timeless and his adventures extend well beyond that of an ordinary man's lifespan. Whatever his secret, we can, however, be certain that he did not choose the dark path taken by real-life actress, dancer and singer Gabrielle Deslys in this tale...

Christofer Nigro: *The Ultimate Prize*

Actress Gabrielle Deslys found herself surprisingly calm when she entered the hotel room of the Grand Hotel, despite being in the company of a man she had just met hours earlier at the after-show party. Nevertheless, she found herself quite charmed by the Count, and his striking, almost hypnotic, eyes had truly captivated her. Despite his suave demeanor, there was a sense of power about him that she could scarcely describe. She felt this attribute was well befitting of a man of his position in his native Carpathians, however, and she found herself thoroughly flattered that he had traveled all the way from that part of Europe to see her perform on stage. She was still initially surprised that he had been given entry to the after-show party on such short notice, but she had since come to realize that a man like the Count doubtless had ways of convincing even the most stubborn members of her Marseilles entourage who acted as door sentries to give him a free pass.

As Gabrielle looked about the elegant décor of the suite, the Count offered her a glass of wine.

"May I offer such a beautiful young woman a glass of this city's finest wine?" he asked her as he uncorked the bottle. "It has reached a fine age. You may have as much as you wish, for I do not drink...wine."

"Are you trying to get me in a state of inebriation, Count?" the 38-year-old actress asked her regal escort with a wry tone.

The Count laughed lightly. "It is only my desire to see to your pleasure, Madame. For your pleasure equals mine."

"Very generous of you, my dear Count. But I must say, in all seriousness, you flatter me by calling me 'young.' And I cannot help but wonder if your remark about something older—like the wine—always amounting to better is accurate. When an actress reaches my age, these things are no longer the truth. That is why I find myself all the more flattered that you still find me worthy of this type of admiration."

"You have no cause to doubt the extent of that admiration, Mademoiselle! Your loveliness is as profound as it ever was, I can assure you of that."

"But even if I retain a great degree of that which was instrumental in the success of my career, this will not be true for much longer. Aging is the bane of humanity, and even more so to those who belong to a vocation where the beauty of youth and the continued limberness of the body are so essential. And please remember that I'm a dancer as well as an actress. How long will I be palatable to either of these professions? How long will it be before all that I have built vanishes, and gentlemen like you no longer seek my company?"

The Count grinned upon hearing those words, exuding the mien of a schemer. It made Gabrielle quite uncomfortable, but it was also clear his thoughts would lead to words that would actually suggest a viable solution.

"What you have said about humanity and the curse of aging are quite astute, my dear lady. And what's worse, the brevity of youth and how little can be accomplished under such a short span of time makes its passing all the more tragic. But it need not be that way for everyone."

"How can you say that, Count? No human being is spared the physical deterioration that comes with age. It is a universal curse among our species."

"*Your* species, perhaps, beautiful Gabrielle, but not all who look and walk like men belong to that inferior race. And those of us who do not need not fear the passage of time and the grief it brings."

A look of profound shock befell Gabrielle's lovely visage, as the Count's tone was in no way flippant. But her inclination to be terrified was soon overwhelmed by her curiosity.

"What exactly, do you mean by that, Count?"

"What I mean, my dear Gabrielle, is that despite the alias that I used to gain entrance to your party, my real identity is that of Dracula, Son of the Dragon."

To prove his boast, the Count opened his mouth and extended the two large fangs that he and others of his kind used to puncture the throats of mortals to procure their required sustenance. His glaring eyes took on a bright reddish hue, almost glowing despite the illumination of the suite's electric lights.

Forcing herself to speak despite being near-paralyzed with shock, Gabrielle managed to utter:

"Dear God, you're...you're actually..."

"If you're trying to acknowledge the whispered rumors of more than two decades, then you are quite correct, my dear lady."

"But this... this is impossible..."

"While a mouth can lie, the eyes cannot, Gabrielle. And I would like to think my offer to you is quite clear. I have long admired you and your illustrious career, and have hoped you could share some of that life with me. May I grant you the ultimate prize, so you will need never again fear the ravages of time?"

Gabrielle choked out a response. "You want to make me into a vampire? But then, I could no longer walk about in daylight. And I would have to... feed upon other people to survive. Count, I am not an evil woman! I have never harmed others! I cannot live like that..."

"Yes, elevating yourself to one of the Undead does come with certain... inconveniences and requirements which may seem unpleasant, even vile, to the standards by which mortals are typically raised. But consider...

"For one thing, I soon learned after my ascension that the ability to walk in daylight is vastly overrated. The more interesting facets of existence tend to occur at night—including all of your performances. And for another, mortals are quite the hypocrites. They boast of concepts such as justice and peace to put their conscience at ease, yet they annihilate large numbers of themselves over trivialities such as money and land. The Great War that just ended was wrought by *your* species, not mine. Note how those amongst the mortals with the most wealth consider themselves higher forms of life, above the majority who lack such privileges. Look at how they exploit their 'lessers,' treating them as lap-dogs, using them to increase their own power. Do they not create horrific weapons to wreak destruction upon each other? I did the same when I ruled Wallachia during my years as a mortal, and I have done so in Transylvania since my ascension; but never have I apologized because of silly notions of morality. Vampires do not do to each other what humans regularly inflict upon their own kind."

Gabrielle turned her gaze from Dracula. "But it's not like that. I would be killing other humans for their blood, making me no different than..."

"Do you mean, just as humans kill lesser animals for their meat and hides? You wouldn't be doing it to acquire anything as puerile and meaningless as money. You would be doing it to survive—and you would kill far fewer humans over the course of an indefinite lifespan than the multitudes of humans typically killed by their own kind over a mere week by the weapons they create. Or even those peasants who kill each other while committing petty crimes.

"Moreover, dear Gabrielle, once I help you ascend, you would be human no longer. You would be as above the mortal rabble as they are above the pig or the goat. You would be taking nothing more from them to survive than they routinely take from scores of animals for the same reasons every year since time immemorial."

A look of abject turmoil continued to mar Gabrielle's exquisite features. "Dear Lord, I just want to continue to practice my craft, and to retain a life of quality while doing so. I don't want to become a predator for countless years. Why did you place this choice before me, God? *Why?*"

"I assure you that the God you worship has nothing to do with this, Gabrielle. The choice is offered by me and *me alone*. You worry about becoming a predator, yet you ignore the predatory nature of those who oversee the very vocation you value so highly. You know how quickly they will cast you aside once your beauty and nimbleness have passed. And you know how soon those days are coming. You are aware how equally pernicious are those who control this fledgling moving picture industry, in which you have managed to make some inroads; you can readily guess how much more so they will become should its popularity expand in the future.

"You saw how the appearance of those elderly mortal women who stood amongst us at the party. You see how decrepit you will become in just a few years. Just imagine slowly dying of a wasting illness, like cancer or tuberculosis, while being unable to control your own bodily emissions in a hospital bed, forced to suffer the indignity of having to be cleaned by others. Imagine senility overcoming you, taking away your mental faculties, the last thing of value you would have during that period of decline..."

"Please, Count, stop talking about these things!"

"Even if I were to stop, you would be unable to cease *thinking* of them, lovely Gabrielle. The seed has been planted, the die has been cast, and a decision must now be made."

"No! I will not..."

"*Think*, my dear lady. Think of what you could accomplish in your chosen vocation with an endless number of years at your disposal. You would be able to helm masterpieces that surpass those currently playing in the picture theaters! You could do what I have often done: change identities after enough time has passed, and operate under the guise of a younger relative to whom you would have bequeathed your fortune. This ruse could forever keep the secret of your true nature from the unbelieving masses. Granted, there are troublesome fools, like the Van Helsings to contend with, but they can be evaded or dealt with, especially with one such as me at your side.

"Further, you could have many lovers amongst both male and female mortals in addition to myself, to love for eternity. You will be the one discarding them when they are no longer needed, rather than the reverse, as you now have reason to fear."

Gabrielle shed tears, covering her face in anxiety over the thoughts flashing through her psyche like the fast-moving images on the picture screens.

"No... no..."

"Make your decision at once, Gabrielle! You have but seconds! After that, I shall leave this place and walk out of your life forever, and you can slowly deteriorate as do all mortals!"

"Very well, damn you! I won't let that happen to me! Do it, Dracula. Do it *now*!"

As tears continued to roll down her face, she tilted her head and bore the fair skin of her neck to the nefarious Count. Smiling in triumph and anticipation, Dracula opened his mouth and greedily sunk his fangs into Gabrielle's jugular. She first winced in pain at the twin lacerations, but, within moments, the physical pain was replaced by a strangely euphoric sensation that reminded her of an intense orgasm.

Her look of pain and tumult was slowly replaced by a hesitant smile as Dracula drank her life's blood and simultaneously injected her with physiology-altering enzymes...

A few months later, Jacques de Trémeuse sat on a large comfortable *canapé* in his headquarters deep below Château-Rouge. His old friend Prosper Cocantin was there. A beam of delight crossed the detective's beak-nosed visage as a cup of the herbal tea he loved so much was handed to him. He eagerly took a few sips.

"Is it to your liking, my friend?" Jacques asked his guest.

"*Pas mal*, as always!" Cocantin replied with a great look of satisfaction. "The English truly have nothing on you when it comes to tea."

"I'm glad you are pleased. But now onto business... How are things in Paris?"

"I'm afraid the business at hand is most serious."

"Have you found a pattern to the disappearances?"

"Some of the finest minds are looking into the matter, including Inspector Maigret, but whoever is involved appears to be quite crafty. All the reports indicate that each disappearance—mostly men—have been individuals amongst the entertainment vocation. Among their number have been a well-known playwright and the respected owner of a theater."

"That sounds like a worthy lead. Whoever is behind these disappearances, it must be someone of high profile who walks in those circles."

"I agree, otherwise the culprit would not be trusted by these people of influence."

"Have there been any ransom demands? Or signs of a struggle at any of the last places the victims were known to frequent?"

"Nothing of the sort. This makes me believe that none of them detected an imminent danger, because they allowed the perpetrator to remain alone with them. He or she must not appear menacing. Everyone who has investigated the matter agrees that these are not simple cases of moguls taking impromptu vacations without telling their staff. Some of the victims had important engagements, and it's totally out of character for them to evade such responsibilities. I am telling you, my friend, there is foul play at hand here."

"I concur. However, I've read in the press that in one case, a suicide note was found, and in another, the pay stub of a one-way cruise to the Greek Islands."

"*C'est vrai*. But in both cases, that was still utterly uncharacteristic of the victims' normal behavior. Their reputations preclude such abrupt, irresponsible actions. Besides, for so many incidents to have occurred in rapid succession over only three months..."

"Indeed. I suspect that the perpetrator created bogus excuses to cover the fact that his victims will never be seen again. Much care was taken to hide the bodies so that the cause of death will never be known. And yet, no ransom notes... That is strange..."

"It led me to think that the presumed murders—let's call them that—are part of a calculated revenge spree. People of great power in the entertainment world are known for leaving many disgruntled thespians, writers and others behind due to their whims and rapacious business decisions."

"No doubt. Let's conjecture that the perpetrator is among those who work for the elite, but not actually one of them. Someone who has means as well as inroads into the private world of these individuals, but not the clout, financial or otherwise, to effect retribution via a boardroom or a bank. Hence, they had to use means outside the system to dispense their reckoning."

"That, my friend, is surely something you can relate to, *non*?"

"You slight me by making such a comparison, Cocantin. You know that I dispense justice to the guilty whom the system fails to punish. My actions are never based on petty selfishness."

"No need to take what I said the wrong way, Jacques. But let us be honest about a certain similarity between what you do and..."

The large-nosed detective's spiel was cut off by a much younger voice emanating from behind them on the threshold.

"Aw, please not another fight over this again," said the Licorice Kid, a youthful informant of Judex, and now Cocantin's ward. "Let's clobber the bad guys, and not each other, *d'accord*?"

"What are you doing here, my lad?" his surrogate father asked him.

"Got bored at home, and jus' wanted to help out like I always do," the adolescent boy replied as he adjusted his distinctive hat and overly large suspenders. "Do ya got any more of that tea or maybe a cigar or somethin', Uncle Jacques?"

"Ask Uncle Roger," Jacques replied, rather brusquely. "Right now, we're in the midst of studying the patterns surrounding the disappearances of..."

"Oh, do ya mean those rich theater people?" the Kid queried. "I been followin' that whole story in both the paper and on the streets. I'm a tradesman by nature, and gettin' and givin' info is what I do, ya know? I was hangin' 'round the theater after sneakin' in to see the late special showin' of *Bouclette* an' after that, I saw the star walk out with the producer who dis'peared. Wow, was she ever a looker!"

"No one reported seeing that, my boy," Cocantin retorted.

"Yeah, well, that's 'cause they don't know 'bout the secret back door of the theater that the stars use sometimes to sneak out so no one knows if someone is leavin' wit' someone else that they don't want everyone to know 'bout. But I know 'bout it 'cause I'm no dummy and I always use that door to sneak in. Ha!"

Cocantin's face suddenly turned red. "You mean to tell me, you've been sneaking into the theater all this time without purchasing a ticket, young man!"

"Don't be too harsh on him, my friend," Jacques said. "His illicit entries may have given us the important clue that will enable us to solve these crimes. Justice will be dispensed, and as always, I shall be its conduit!"

Sequestered in her hotel room at the Grand Hotel shortly after her latest feeding, Gabrielle looked into a mirror in anguish over her inability to see her reflection.

"Damn it all!" she shouted. "This suite would have to be fitted with one of those mirrors backed with a silver coating that cancel out a vampire's reflection! How can I enjoy my eternal beauty if I cannot admire it in the great majority of available mirrors!"

Gabrielle's impassioned fit was interrupted when the lock on the door was suddenly forced open. Entering the room was a different tall, dark-clad man with a flowing black cape—but this one had a slouch hat atop his head, partially obscuring his features. In each hand he held two high-caliber revolvers of a design she did not recognize.

"*Qui diable êtes-vous?*" she yelled.

"*Bonjour*, Mademoiselle Deslys," Judex said in his icy voice. "Would you care to explain your motives for taking the lives of those people you murdered before I mete out justice for your actions?"

Gabrielle grinned at the sight of the imposing vigilante before her, making no attempt to conceal her extended fangs.

"So, you are the infamous vigilante Judex, *non*?"

"*Oui*, Mademoiselle. And I see by your oral characteristics and curious lack of fear at the sight of me that you can no longer be categorized as human. I believe that may explain everything."

"See fit to judge me if it pleases you, vigilante. I did what I had to do to secure my career, and to avoid the curse that degrades and eventually claims all human beings. You would have made the same choice if offered the ultimate prize—as I was."

"So you took this state of being of your own volition? That means that you are especially deserving of justice. Though I sympathize with your fear, taking a gift that requires the continual sacrifice of innocent lives is ignoble and unforgivable, despite the power of that fear. A truly good person—as you always purported to be with your expressed sympathy for the underprivileged—would have faced such an unpleasant fate over bringing harm to innocents."

"There are no true innocents in this world, vigilante. You of all mortals should know that. Everyone makes choices at some point for self benefit that are to the detriment of others. The entire system under which we live is predicated upon such actions."

"Even if there were ten billion people in this world, all committed to such actions on a daily basis, it wouldn't make them *right*. It wouldn't justify not trying to find another way to acquire such benefits, even if it took much more work and much longer to achieve. You deliberately chose to become a predator of humans for personal gain, and for that, justice will be carried out. But first, who did you obtain this pernicious 'gift' from?"

"From me, you insipid fool," came a voice with a noticeable accent from the other side of the room.

As incredibly swift as Judex was when he turned to face the source of the voice, the arm that suddenly extended and grabbed his throat in a crushing grip was faster still.

The powerful arm then hurled the vigilante against the wall on the far side of the room as if his 225 pound frame weighed no more than ten. Regaining his senses with impressive speed, Judex turned to look at the individual many feet distant who had had the temerity and power to hurl him so effortlessly.

Standing before him, appearing to fully materialize within a cloud of mist, was a man of equal height to his own, also dressed in a black garment and cape, but with hellish red eyes and protruding fangs.

"Welcome to your doom, Judex," the stranger told him. "For never before have you faced a foe like Dracula."

My God, so the rumors are true, the vigilante thought. *This is going to be incredibly difficult; but for the sake of justice, I must prevail.*

Expertly somersaulting across the floor, and retrieving his revolvers from where they lay on the rug, Judex opened fire on the Vampire Lord. Dracula simply stood there impassively as the lead bullets seared through his body with negligible effect.

"I see you have failed to come prepared," the Prince of Darkness observed. "You're a poor excuse for a creature of the night, and you know that my opinion in that regard is quite well informed."

"You have escaped justice for too long, Dracula," Judex said with no emotion save for a hint of anger. "Prepare to pay your debt to Her at long last!"

Dracula simply laughed. "Let us see you attempt to collect that debt, dark one. I wager the power you fight for will be sorely disappointed this night."

"We shall see."

Realizing that his revolvers would be next to useless against a vampire, Judex swiftly holstered them and seized a long, razor-sharp blade from a slot in his boot. He had read enough reports and folklore accounts to know that vampires could be slain if their head was severed; he would make a strong attempt to decapitate the Lord of Vampires, or die trying.

Rushing at Dracula with impressive speed, Judex slashed the knife towards his opponent's neck with a powerful stroke, hoping to at least halfway severe it with this initial swipe. But Dracula's preternatural speed proved superior, and the Vampire Lord caught the dark avenger's wrist on the downswing.

Determined to escape the vice-like grip and carry out his gruesome intent, Judex initiated a palm heel strike to Dracula's chin, hoping to stun him into releasing his hold. Though startled by the unexpected force of the blow, the Prince of Darkness barely lessened the strength of his grip, and his quickly executed backhand blow would have shattered the vigilante's jaw if not for Judex's skill at rolling with such cracks.

Nevertheless, the dark-clad crusader was knocked senseless by Dracula's strike. The vampire then effortlessly lifted Judex off the ground and smashed him into the wall. Though badly stunned, Judex's tolerance for pain and will to overcome were formidable, and he managed to deliver two strong reverse punches to Dracula's face, followed by a brutal forward kick to the vampire's solar plexus.

The unexpected nature of these blows succeeded in knocking the Vampire Lord back a few feet, and Judex successfully pulled out of his grip.

The caped crime fighter then leaped to the ground to recover his blade, only to have Dracula crunch his arm under his the heel of his shoe before he could grab the weapon. Judex forced himself not to shout in pain as his deltoid bone cracked. Before he could carry out his plan to pull Dracula's leg out from under him, the Vampire Lord again lifted him with minimal effort and tossed him several meters across the room. This time, the vigilante struck the dresser holding the mirror, shattering the glass to pieces and landing on the ground, broken and stunned nearly to unconsciousness.

"I grow weary of this foolishness," Dracula said with annoyance. "You have proved an irritant, and your attempt to take what I have given to my new paramour angers me. I shall end this now. I believe that you would make a grand lackey of mine were I to change you into a *true* creature of the night...."

"He doesn't understand!" Gabrielle shouted from her vantage point across the room, wondering if she should assist her benefactor and lover. "Make him into one of us, so that he understands! He will be grateful, as I am, and only by ascending will he come to know the delight of eternal youth!"

"That is my intent, dear Gabrielle," Dracula assured his lady love as he approached the fallen hero.

With a sudden heave, Dracula hoisted Judex to his feet, pushed him against the wall, and twisted his head back with the intention of sinking his fangs into the vigilante's jugular. The adventurer struggled with all his might, but his lesser level of strength and the extent of his injuries made his valiant efforts seemingly futile.

"You will... not escape... justice... no matter what you do to me... vampire," Judex choked as loudly and defiantly as he could.

"Justice isn't a major factor in this world, my soon-to-be-soldier-of-the-night," Dracula told the struggling hero in his grip. "Only *power* matters, as you shall soon see."

Just as Dracula was about to make an attempt to sink his fangs into Judex's flesh, his keen hearing picked up slight footsteps behind him.

He turned to see the diminutive figure of the Licorice Kid, holding a small, metallic squirt pistol.

"*Bonjour*, Monsieur Dracula," the boy said as he pointed the pistol at him. "I snuck in the church before comin' here, an' guess what I filled this up with?"

The boy then squirted a thin stream of holy water at the Count's eyes, burning them severely.

The Vampire Lord bellowed in agony and fell back against the wall, releasing Judex from his grip in the process.

"Hurry an' get 'im, Monsieur Judex!" the boy shouted. "My squirter gets only one shot!"

"You're a fool to admit that, little boy!" Gabrielle exclaimed. "Now I will spank you until you bleed!"

As she moved towards him, the Licorice Kid astounded her by pulling a small cross attached to a string of rosary beads out of his pocket.

"Oh, yeah? Well, look what else I took from the church. I'm no dummy, ya know!"

Gabrielle hissed violently at the sight of the hated icon, and then recoiled from it, helpless to proceed with her attack.

This gave Judex enough time to get back to his feet, despite how unsteady he was.

"Kid, I told you to stay behind!"

"Yeah, I know. Aint'cha glad I didn't listen?"

Dracula suddenly turned back towards Judex, the flesh around his eyes terribly scarred, but already partially healed. Once again moving almost faster than the eye could follow, the Vampire Lord seized the vigilante by the throat, holding him against the wall and choking him with monstrous strength.

"Uh-oh..." the Licorice Kid said aloud.

"I'll rip your throat out for this!" the Vampire Lord howled with extreme fury.

"Not if I rip yours out first," Judex replied, quickly grabbing a large shard of silver-coated glass from the shattered mirror that lay on the dresser and slashing Dracula across his throat.

Remembering that silver is a major weakness for some vampires, Judex managed to inflict a grievous injury upon his opponent. The Vampire Lord again released his grip and backed against the wall as smoldering blood streamed from the horrific gash torn across his larynx.

Acting without delay, Judex grabbed another, larger shard of the silver-coated glass and shoved it into the left side of Dracula's chest, skewering his heart. The vampire attempted to wrest it from his torso, but only succeeded in painfully slicing up his fingers from further exposure to the sharpened silver.

"There... will be... another time..." Dracula managed to sputter as he fell to the ground, his flesh bubbling from his bones and leaving nothing but a bare skeleton behind.

"Wow, major case of heartburn!" the Licorice Kid yelled with a triumphant thrust of his fist.

Not reacting to the comment, Judex turned towards Gabrielle, now holding another large shard of the glass in his hand.

"Are you ready to receive justice, like your inhuman lover just did?" he asked her.

A look of anguish overtook her features, as if her mind was torn in contemplative indecision.

"No!" she finally hollered in a tormented voice. "Please don't make me give up the ultimate prize! I'm not evil, I just don't want to lose it all!"

"You already lost it all the moment you took Dracula's offer," the hero said. "You sacrificed others for your own benefit. If any spark of goodness remains within you, Madame Deslys, then do the right thing. Submit to justice, and meet your fate with some honor."

"No…" was her only, barely audible response while she stood shuddering, as if something within her were struggling against her strong desire to take bat form and escape through the open window.

Determined to make certain that one of the two equally potent urges didn't lose to the other, Judex hurled the shard of silver-coated glass with expert aim at Gabrielle's chest. It penetrated enough for the silver to cause her debilitating agony. He then rushed forward, pulled out the shard as she dropped to the floor, and brought it down on her throat with all of his might, severing her head and ending her undead existence.

Judex then turned to the Licorice Kid as he forced himself to remain on his feet despite the injuries he received.

"Thank you for the assistance, Kid. How did you know I was going up against vampires when I wasn't aware of it before breaking into this room?"

"Well, I saw Madame Deslys walkin' out that back door at the theater with Dracula once or twice, and I kinda thought he dressed a lot like the actor who pretended to be him in that play I used to sneak into the theater every other night to see. And when I heard you connected the disappeared people to her, then, well, I just kinda figured the guy I saw her with might be the *real* Dracula. An' so I stopped at the church while I followed ya here, and ya know the rest. Like I always say, I'm no dummy!"

Judex couldn't help but smile that time, something he very rarely did while in vigilante mode. He never ceased to be impressed with this young man whose resourcefulness and bravery had so often been an asset to him.

Looking at the bloody scene before him, the streetwise Licorice lamented, "I kinda can't help but feel sorry for the lady a bit. She only wanted to stop gettin' older, and…"

"I feel sorry for her too," Judex interrupted. "But not too much. She made a bad choice with horrid consequences for both other people and her own soul. Justice had to prevail."

Upon hearing that the late Gabrielle Deslys' final will and testament, which she penned before becoming a vampire, had left her ample estate and entire sizable earnings to the poor of Marseilles, Judex's sympathy for her increased. He began wondering if, perhaps, he should have trusted her enough to give her the opportunity to make the right decision at the last moment, rather than taking it out of her hands.

In the end, however, he believed that the triumph of justice was more important than the possible victory of her soul. Hence, he would live with himself for his decision, whether it was made in haste or not.

Nevertheless, seeing that she was a good and generous soul at heart, and had simply been led down the dark path due to desperation—a very human foible he could well relate to—he used his resources as Jacques de Trémeuse to collaborate with her own agent and publicist to feed a plausible but false story to the press to explain her death in a non-sinister fashion.

It read that she developed a severe throat infection due to a case of influenza, and that, despite several surgeries in an attempt to cure her, she refused to let the surgeons do all that was required out of fear of leaving large, permanent scars on her neck. He felt the irony of the bogus story for the press regarding wounds to her throat was a form of poetic justice considering the far less believable truth.

And justice in all its myriad forms were of great interest to the man called Judex.

1925. As the years go by, Judex—who is now in his early 40s—slowly turns into a legend, but nevertheless remains the nemesis of corrupt financiers everywhere. In the following story, a young "man of bronze," fresh out of medical school, ably assisted by Inspector Ménardier, last seen in Belphegor, *faces a terrible conspiracy. Judex plays a peripheral, yet determining role, in unraveling...*

Vincent Jounieaux: *The Dreadful Conspiracy*

Inspector Ménardier wrinkled his nose when he stepped into the interview room at the Quai des Orfèvres. A strong smell of mildew permeated the small room because of its peeling wall paper. On the ceiling, only two bulbs out of four were working.

It seems President Doumergue is still powerless to change the mind of the Banque de France, he thought. *Times are tough for public services. I think we'll still have a long wait before they fix the ventilation or replace the lights...*

He sat down in front of a metal table, across from the empty seat that would soon welcome his suspect. Ménardier thought that the modern psychological theories that encouraged the police to put the perpetrator in a position of inferiority were absurd; he didn't care in which chair the suspect sat. He glanced at the one-way mirror, behind which stood one of the faceless minions of the Préfecture de Police. The interview would be recorded for later analysis.

"Bring him in."

Someone heard his command and the door creaked open. A tall, young man with a light bronze complexion was ushered into the room. His hands were cuffed behind his back. Because of his size, he had to bend a little to cross the threshold. His powerful muscles stood out under his khaki-colored shirt.

"You may leave us," Antoine said to the policeman who was escorting the suspect.

The man gave a brief salute, complied, and closed the door on the two men. The inspector began the interrogation:

"Are you Monsieur Francis Ardan? Or do you prefer to be called Clark Savage Jr.?"

"I'm the only one here, am I not?" replied the young man, still standing up. He eyed the policeman suspiciously, hostility burning deep inside his golden eyes.

"Whom have I the honor of addressing?" he then asked.

"I'm Inspector Ménardier of the Police Judiciaire."

"I wish I could say I was pleased to meet you, Inspector, but I'm not."

"I'm sorry to hear that, Monsieur Ardan. I know it's always painful to be brought before the police..."

"Only if you've done something wrong—which I didn't."

"That is for me to determine."

"I fear that this conversation is starting out on the wrong track, Inspector. As an American citizen, I have rights. I demand that you contact my attorney, Mr. Theodore Marley Brooks of New York."

"Calm down, Monsieur Ardan. You're not in America here! You're in Paris, at the Quai des Orfèvres. Right now, the only person who can say what rights you have is me, and I'm telling you to sit down!"

"For a policeman, you seem to be singularly disrespectful of the Law."

"And for a student of medicine, you look like a fairground Hercules."

Ardan ignored the sarcasm but, under Ménardier's astonished eyes, he flexed his biceps; the veins of his arm swelled and the muscles tore the seams of his sleeves. There was a loud snap and the handcuffs fell to the ground. The man of bronze leaned forward, pressing his fists on the table. The inspector remained impassive, with only a discreet smile on his lips.

"Monsieur Ardan, do not aggravate your situation!"

"What am I accused of?"

"You are accused of the murders of Baron Hampain, Ferdinand Finalit, Horace Dasseaux and Serge Bouriet, all punishable by the death penalty under Article 295-298 of the French penal code."

Ardan clenched his fists; his knuckles turned white.

"And why would have I done that?"

"For the money, of course! They were four of the largest fortunes in France..."

"Ridiculous! I have more wealth that I could ever spend in a lifetime."

"Ah, yes! I forgot! Your father's Central American gold mines!"

"Indeed. And the income generated by the Hidalgo Trading Company which guarantees me a very comfortable standard of living..."

"While it is true that my meager pay does not allow me to look at this business with complete impartiality, it seems to me that wealth always creates a desire for more of the same. The thirst for it is insatiable..."

"Let me call my lawyer. Ham will soon get to the bottom of this."

"Unfortunately, we have too much evidence against you. I am forced to incarcerate you at La Santé prison."

"You're making a terrible mistake..."

"I don't think so. Unless I'm in error, you are soon scheduled to present your doctorate thesis at the Medical School of La Sorbonne, is that right?"

"Yes, but I don't see the connection..."

"And your research is about...?"

"I doubt that you're educated enough to grasp it."

"Let me be the judge of that, please."

"Well, my thesis deals with the after-effects of partial lobotomy on human behavior."

"Good. We're making progress! Now, let me introduce you to some of the evidence against you. First, all four victims suffered from some odd brain surgery only a few weeks before they were killed; second, they all developed abnormal behavior and emptied their bank accounts in a totally irrational fashion before their alleged suicides; third, we found your student card under the sofa at the home of the banker, Serge Bouriet—the last victim! You see, Monsieur Ardan, we know a lot about you..."

"You know nothing! Someone is obviously trying to frame me for this."

"Really? What about the billions of francs that Bouriet transferred to your bank account before he died? I'm referring to the account held in your name at the Depository Bank of Zurich. It belongs to you, doesn't it?"

"..."

"I see that I've managed to surprise you at last... You see, even a lowly French official with a questionable level of education might know a thing or two about tax havens. Finding your trail was difficult but not impossible... I wish you good night now, Monsieur Ardan. I hope your bed at La Santé won't be too hard!"

Winter was rapidly approaching; the days were shortening; the weather had turned cold and damp. On the Rue de Turenne, under the wan light of the street lamps, the passers-by were raising the collars of their coats and burying their hands in their pockets.

The offices of the banker, Berthelaux, occupied a building at the corner of an upscale street in Le Marais district.

"Vallières! You're still here? Excellent! Bring me the file on the Industrial Bank of China. It's in the safe in my room. I left it open... Stop dilly-dallying and hurry up!"

Silently, Berthelaux's personal secretary obeyed the order. The early night had surprised Berthelaux at work. After Vallières had left the office, the banker stretched in his chair and looked at his books filled with carefully calligraphied figures in black ink. His bronze art deco desk lamp cast a shadow on his worried face. With his fingertips, he prodded at the back of his neck... What had happened to him? That morning, he had to twist in front of the mirror to catch a glimpse of a thin, white scar. His hair had been cut there but was already regrowing. Someone had performed some kind of surgery on him, maybe a week or ten days before, judging from the hair, but he had no memory of it...

"I've got it, Monsieur."

Berthelaux was startled; he had not heard Vallières return. The old secretary stood at the door, file in hand.

"Damn! You scared me! Next time, knock on the door will you? Leave the file here. I'll look at it alone. See you tomorrow, Vallières. Be on time."

"Yes, Monsieur. Certainly, Monsieur."

173

With the corner of his eye, Berthelaux stared at the departing secretary. The man was tall, seemingly alert, but his temples were covered with pure white hair. He couldn't tell his age... Forty? Fifty? Older? The secretary hadn't seemed to notice the banker's concerns, which suited Berthelaux well. Vallières' absolute discretion was, on occasion, verging on naiveté. Berthelaux never had to complain about the man's professional behavior. Vallières was an ideal employee, hard-working, effective, even-tempered and loyal to the point of stupidity. Even today, the secretary had not questioned any of Berthelaux's unexplained absences.

I should give him a raise, he thought before returning to his main subject of preoccupation.

His inexplicable amnesia worried him. There was no way he could tell the police. With all the evidence of his financial wrongdoings lying around, he would be the one to find himself behind bars! He could consult his physician, but the strange scar night trigger a cascade of investigations and interrogations... Who had kidnapped him? For what reason?

The problem haunted him and disturbed his thoughts. He did not remember anything... Simply waking up one morning fully dressed with a raging migraine. Panic had overwhelmed him, prompting him to burn his accounting books and destroy all incriminating documents. But he had saved the file on the Industrial Bank of China because it was his highest concern. He, Hampain, Finalit, Dasseaux and Bouriet had started it, supposedly to finance French industrial expansion in the Far East. In reality, the bank allowed them to siphon away the savings of small French investors and divert investment from the Chinese government... The scandal had broken in 1921, but it had been quickly stifled and Berthelaux had been sentenced to only a ten year loss of his civil rights—a trifle!

Today, the newspapers had reported the death of his fourth partner! What a strange coincidence—or was it? This series of murders may have been committed by one of the many French investors ruined by the scam. Could someone have decided to wait four years before taking his revenge? Was he next? He glanced at the file labeled BIC and threw it into the fireplace. Then, he lit a match after dousing it with rubbing alcohol and watched it burn.

"All the evidence is going up in smoke!" he said to himself.

Vallières slammed the outside door when he left the house. The aged secretary, his hands in his pockets, plunged into the Parisian night. At the end of the street, he glanced back. One could see Berthelaux's shadow illuminated by bursts of light from the fireplace, on the curtains of the first floor windows.

"Damn you, Berthelaux!" muttered Vallières. "Your time has come, villain... I see that fear is driving you to try to destroy the evidence against you... But you'll soon discover how useless it is..."

Berthelaux was his mortal enemy! The man had set up shop again, but his public notoriety was merely a front; behind it hid one of the worst villains of the world of finance. Not just any crook to Vallières, but one of the men who had conspired to ruin his father, the Comte de Trémeuse. Buried under his debts, and the schemes of the bankers, the unhappy nobleman had committed suicide. It all dated back to before the Great War, when he was but a child. Over the years, he had grown into a fearsome crime-fighter called Judex, who had succeeded in avenging his father and was now going after the criminals of high finance who destroyed the lives of their victims, but were rarely pursued by the Law. For the identity of Vallières was but a mask, a disguise useful to infiltrate the privacy of the scoundrels he hunted.

An odd couple was strolling through the streets of Paris. One was a dapper dandy, carrying a thin black cane; his companion looked more like a gorilla than a man. The dandy was the lawyer Theodore Marley Brooks, a.k.a. Ham; his burly friend was Andrew Blodgett Mayfair a.k.a. Monk. They always seemed ready to jump at each other's throats and neither missed an opportunity to hurl insults at the other. Yet, Ham had often risked his life to save Monk, and vice versa. The lawyer, used to the square grid of New York streets, felt lost in the maze of the French capital and blindly followed his friend. Monk, his bushy eyebrows furrowed, studied a map of Paris.

"Right, then right again, then left" he announced. "It isn't very far! Here, look: a café! I would love to have a *petit blanc*, as they say around here... What do you think, Ham? It would do us a world of good before we have to wrestle with that undertaker!"

"God, no! Not on an empty stomach! Besides, we don't have time. Sorry Monk, it'll have to be another time!"

"That's fine, I can wait until tonight. How about we go and listen to our compatriot at the Dome?"

"What on Earth are you talking about?"

"Josephine Baker! The singer, you idiot! The one who walks in the streets of Paris with a Panther on a leash! They call her the Queen of Montmartre!"

"The name does ring a bell," the lawyer admitted.

"I have two *amooouuurs...*" Monk began to sing.

"With your face, just one would be a miracle."

Monk growled, baring his fangs and gave his friend a small blow to the solar plexus. The young lawyer, breathless, was forced to listen to the entire song...

The telegram reporting the arrest of Francis Ardan had been delivered to the Empire State Building the day before. It had been received by Colonel John Renwick a.k.a. Renny, who had immediately notified his two associates Thomas J. Roberts, a.k.a. Long Tom, and William Harper Littlejohn, a.k.a. Johnny. All three were ready to travel to France, but the Atlantic crossing proved impossible! Traveling by boat would have taken too much time, and the test flight of the dirigible *Graf Zeppelin XI* between New York and Cherbourg wasn't scheduled for another few weeks.

Monk and Ham, however, were already in England, each attending professional conferences, Ham on International Law in Cambridge and Monk on chemistry in Oxford. It was child's play for them to take the first ferry from Dover to Calais. Meanwhile, Long Tom, Johnny and Renny had set up a hotline at the Empire State, in case their help became necessary.

Ham had a lot of professional contacts around the world and knew Mr. Ferval, the Director of the Police Judiciaire. The two had met at Harvard the year before and had immediately hit it off. At the time, Ferval had been in Boston to acquaint himself with the modern methods of American policing. His support would be invaluable in helping Ardan prove his innocence.

Ham and Monk had arrived in Paris the day after the arrest of their friend. A telegram from Johnny was already waiting for them at their hotel. They were to proceed at once to the hospital of La Pitié-Salpêtrière where the autopsy of the latest victim, Serge Bouriet, was being conducted. Then, a meeting at the prison of La Santé with Ardan, Ferval and the arresting officer, Inspector Ménardier, had been arranged.

Once the two Americans reached the Boulevard Saint-Marcel, they looked at the map and quickly located La Pitié-Salpêtrière. There, the receptionist gave them directions to the pathology department where the Morgue was located. They introduced themselves to an orderly and sat patiently in the waiting room.

"I hate the smell of hospitals," muttered Monk, wiping the sweat beading on his forehead with one of his paw-like hands.

"You mean that irresistible fragrance of ether and excrement?"

"Yes! With a touch of mycosis."

"Stop being such a girl."

"And if you keep making fun of me, I'm leaving you here alone here to deal with the Frenchies!"

Monk was pretending to leave when a door opened and a voice called out:

"Mr. Brooks? Mr. Mayfair? The Doctor will see you now."

A thin, lanky, orderly, reeking of formaldehyde, invited them to follow him.

"Doctor de Grandin apologizes for the delay," he added. "He just finished the autopsy and immediately sent me to fetch you."

"Excellent," said Ham. "It is very kind of Doctor de Grandin to see us so quickly. This is a matter of grave urgency. The clock is ticking!"

The orderly looked at him, a little shocked by his bluntness... He took the two Americans into a room filled rows of gleaming stainless steel tables, upon which were cadavers. Some were wrapped in a black plastic sheath, but the vast majority were naked, some as pale as snow, others mottled with cyanosis. Monk

176

almost had a heart attack when he saw the grisly scene. At the end of the room was a doctor in a white coat, mask, gloves and goggles.

"Come in, gentlemen!" he shouted to the newcomers. "I've just finished the autopsy of our 'client.' Step right up! I think some my findings are bound to be of interest to you...

The remains of Serge Bouriet rested on the autopsy table, his skull opened and his thorax ajar. Various bloody bodily fluids had collected in the metal gutters. Monk turned green at the sight of the dismembered corpse.

Doctor Jules de Grandin, of the Ecole de Médecine of the University of Paris, was a small blond man with a beautiful waxed mustache and extraordinarily piercing blue eyes He appeared perfectly at ease as he completed his gruesome task. He told the two Americans that Bouriet had died of asphyxiation by hanging, as evidenced by a pulmonary edema and a tracheal cartilage fracture. But a strange scar on his neck had captured the doctor's attention.

"You see, right there!" he said, animatedly. "This scar is relatively recent, less than four weeks-old. It is clean; the work of a surgeon, made by a scalpel and professionally stitched. I'm still trying to figure out its purpose... As you can see, the left trapezius and complexus muscles were cut and then stitched back together. There is a small swelling right here..." added the doctor, inserting a gloved finger inside the body/ "Ha-ha! I feel something!"

"Have you found something?" asked Ham.

Monk, his mouth half open, stood speechless, unable to tear his eyes away from the opened skull.

"Yes! *Par la barbe d'un bouc vert!* It's something small—and metallic! I'm going to pull it out..."

Making a careful excision took some time, but de Grandin finally extracted a small, black, metallic sphere, the size of an olive, with very fine, silver filaments hanging from its ends.

De Grandin deposited the object in a basin and, adjusting magnifying lenses over his glasses, returned to his study of the dead man's brain.

"I'm cutting through the ligaments to study the lower segment of the medulla oblongata. *Parbleu!* The columns of Goll and Burdach are riddled with microscopic holes..." De Grandin adjusted his magnifying glasses. "The holes are pointing towards the cerebral protuberance. It's impossible... How could this man have endured such an intervention? It's..."

The rest of his words became lost in incomprehensible medical jargon. Ham suddenly felt a nagging doubt. Ardan had come to France to complete his medical studies and benefit from the teaching of Clovis Vincent, the famous neurosurgeon. Could this be their friend's work? No! He couldn't believe it! Maybe the analysis of the strange metallic "olive" would provide a clue towards the solution of this puzzle?

Suddenly, a loud thud interrupted his thoughts: Monk had just fainted.

Monk quickly recovered from his shock and the duo soon joined Monsieur Ferval and Inspector Ménardier at the prison of La Santé. The meeting between Ham and the Director of the Police was enthusiastic, and the smartly-dressed lawyer even allowed the Frenchman to hug him.

Ferval used his position to take them inside the prison without the usual searches, etc. They expected to find their friend laid low by this terrible trial. But that would have been a mistake! Instead, Ardan welcomed them with good spirits and open arms and only the short stubble on his cheeks testified to his incarceration...

He had taken advantage of his day behind bars to continue writing his thesis, between his usual tough training sessions. His incredible skills were not the result of magic, but of great physical and mental discipline. His perfectly proportioned body and vast intellectual abilities were the result of intensive training, scientifically designed by his father, who had begun to work with his son in the cradle...

Ardan thanked his friends for coming so quickly. Ham introduced him to Monsieur Ferval and the two men bowed to each other. In the prison's parlor, they quickly reviewed the situation. Ferval had asked Ménardier for a copy of the file in order to form his own opinion. It appeared that the four victims had several things in common: they were all involved in the scandal of the International Bank of China, they all had undergone some strange surgery during which a mysterious artificial implant had been connected to their brains, and finally, they all had emptied their bank accounts before committing suicide.

The first three men had transferred their assets to banks located in the Far East, but the latest victim, Serge Bouriet, had transferred his money to an account in Switzerland in the name of Francis Ardan...

That, in addition to his student card, unexpectedly found at the crime scene, seemed to incriminate him; but Ferval was suspicious. Ardan explained that he had no recollection of when the card had disappeared from his wallet.

The only lead left to the police was to interview the last surviving founding member of the International Bank of China. The man's name was Berthelaux. Ferval asked Ménardier to call on him and place him under police protection as soon as possible.

Ardan asked to attend, or even participate in, the analysis of the strange olive-shaped implant that was to be performed by Doctor de Grandin that same night. Ferval was, at first, reluctant to authorize it, but Ham suggested that, if his friend was accompanied by a police escort, gave his word of honor not to attempt to escape, and deposited a large sum of money with the Caisse des Depôts & Consignations, then bail was possible.

"But you need to obtain authorization from the Investigating Magistrate," said Ferval, still hesitating.

"You mean, this kind of authorization?" said Ham, smiling, producing a letter signed by Judge Coméliau, whom he had met before they even got to La Pitié-Salpêtrière Hospital.

Ferval smiled. Certainly, his friend from Harvard had not usurped his reputation as one of the finest legal eagles of the bar!

It was five o'clock when Judex / Vallières heard a Talbot turn into the Rue de Turenne accompanied by a howl of screeching tires. He drew aside the curtain of the first floor window and saw two men jump out of the car and walk at a brisk pace towards the Berthelaux house, They were followed by the well-known figure of Inspector Ménardier.

The police!

The net is closing, thought Judex. *I do not know what you did during your unexplained absence, Berthelaux, but the police are on to you. You can't escape me though... You belong to me!*

He let the curtain fall, as he heard the police ring the doorbell several times.

"Monsieur Berthelaux?"

"This is he."

"I'm Inspector Ménardier of the Police Judiciaire. May I come in?"

"May I see your badge?"

The badge flashed, revealing a quick glimpse of the service pistol under the inspector's jacket.

"Fine, Inspector! What can I do for you?"

"Let me introduce you to my two friends: this is Mr. Brooks of the New York bar, and Mr. Mayfair, also an American. I'm sorry to burst in on you like this, but we have evidence that leads us to believe that you're in great danger."

"That's ridiculous! I'm an honest businessman. Who on Earth could want to hurt me?"

"It's about the International Bank of China."

"Sorry, Inspector, but that's all in the past. However, since you've come all the way here on my behalf, you might as well follow me into the library..."

The three men accompanied the banker to the other side of the house. The library was a sumptuously decorated room, filled with ivory carvings, and a collection of small *objets d'art* made of wood or terracotta lining the shelves.

Berthelaux sat in an impressive armchair in a corner and silently invited his "guests" to take the remaining seats.

"As I said," began Ménardier, "we're convinced that four of the founders of this bank, Baron Hampain, Finalit, Dasseaux and Bouriet, were murdered. You are the last surviving member of that group. But don't worry, reinforcements are on their way. You've got no reasons to be concerned..."

"Tell that to my dead colleagues!" said Berthelaux bitterly.

"Is it possible," interjected Ham, "that the problems at the International Bank of China might have injured a Chinese tong? Two years ago, a colleague of our friend Ardan, Dr. Lyndon Parker, faced such an organization called 'Si-Fan.' Could the same thing have happened here, and it is that organization which is now seeking revenge on those it holds responsible for their losses?"

Berthelaux thought for a moment, then said:

"Well, now that you mention it, one of our most important Chinese depositors, who, of course, lost all their money in the bankruptcy, was called Ming Tsai Tsu. He was the head of a consortium known as the Shin Tan..."

"The Shin Tan?" exclaimed Ménardier. "Over the years, I've had to investigate matters relating to Orientals. It is a little known fact, but there are many Far Eastern secret societies operating in France. They are extremely powerful and have branches throughout the world... The Shin Tan is one of them. Their Master is said to be a Mongol 'demon' known only by the nickname: the 'Yellow Shadow.' The few informants who told us about him died suddenly—and not from old age. They all perished from unexplained causes."

"If this Ming character was hurt by the collapse of the International Bank of China, it isn't surprising that he seeks revenge," Ham said. Turning to the banker, he added: "I'm afraid that your financial shenanigans, Monsieur Berthelaux, have had unhappy and unforeseen consequences!"

"Or perhaps," said Monk, "it's a reprisal against the French government's involvement in the death of 52 demonstrators in Canton last June?"[7]

"In any event," said Ham, "this cannot but stir the ardor of the defenders of the Treaty of Versailles and ruin the Franco-German *rapprochement* advocated by your President, Monsieur Heriot, and President Von Hindenburg."

"One thing is certain," concluded Ménardier, "all trails lead to you, Monsieur Berthelaux!

That night, at the laboratory at the Sorbonne, Doctor Jules de Grandin, assisted by young Francis Ardan, examined the microscopic metallic olive found in the victim's skull.

The analysis revealed a very advanced technology, well beyond the capacities of either France or the United States.

De Grandin consulted some old books and various documents that he kept locked in a safe. Then, after carefully putting them back, he said:

"In 1901, a man known by the pseudonym of Anton Zarnak spent twenty years in Tibet studying the occult with those he called the 'Masters of A'alshirie.' I had access to some documents kept secret by Zarnak, and the

---

[7] On 23 June 1925 in Canton, British and French troops opened fire with machine guns on Chinese demonstrators, killing 52 people and injuring over 100.

components of this 'olive' appear identical to their technology. I do not pretend to understand it, but I know that its power can affect the mind."

"What if the bankers were remotely mind-controlled?" said Ardan. "That 'olive' turned them into human robots, subject to the will of another—the inventor of this devilish device—who forced them to empty their bank accounts, and then to commit suicide!"

"It is indeed quite possible," nodded de Grandin, stroking his mustache. "Anyway, my young friend," he added, with a friendly tap to Ardan's shoulder, "that's what I intend to write in my report. *Par la barbe d'un bouc vert!* You will not spend another night in our jail at the French taxpayer's expense!

As Ménardier had said, the Police Judiciaire's archives contained very little information about the Shin Tan. There were some extremely sketchy reports from informers, and a document written by the "King of the detectives," the great Chantecoq himself. He had identified one of the few French agents employed by the Shin Tan, a man named Leclerc, who served as a cover for the organization when conducting a number of secret transactions with the French underworld, whose well-known patriotic fervor would not have easily accommodated the notion of dealing with Oriental heathens.

Leclerc's family, according to a report from the last century, written by none other than Chevalier Dupin, had served the Shin Tan for several generations. Leclerc himself met his masters every week at six a.m. at the Notre-Dame Cathedral. Ménardier and his men had only a few hours to get ready.

Ménardier was hiding inside the Saint Denis portal. He was on the lookout in the shadow of the cathedral, his eyes piercing the darkness broken only by the feeble light of candles.

The four bells of the north tower, the Benjamines, struck six o'clock. The Inspector pulled up his overcoat and, by reflex, checked the time on his pocket watch. Leclerc had entered the empty cathedral by the north transept five minutes earlier. The police, as a precaution, had evacuated the church personnel and the few church goers, replacing them with officers in disguise. The man had stood for a moment on the porch, scanning his surroundings. Apparently reassured, Leclerc had then crossed the cathedral without noticing the presence of the police, and gone towards a confessional. Still lurking in the corner of the chapel, Ménardier had seen him enter the booth and sit at the place normally occupied by the priest.

Now, the wait was on...

Ménardier had begun to doubt the arrival of the minions of the Yellow Shadow when, suddenly, an electric torch was lit several times on the other side of the nave. The signal came from Brooks, lurking on the other side of the cathedral.

Ménardier looked up at the side entrance. *Here we go*, he thought, checking his 9 mm Luger. *Si vis pacem, para bellum*, he added, because he hardly knew what to expect from the Shin Tan...

With an undulating walk, a Eurasian woman had suddenly appeared and slowly approached the confessional. Tall, beautiful, she wore a black silk dress that molded her beautiful, slim body. The top of her dress did nothing to hide her voluptuous chest. A long string of pearls hung around her neck. Her proud bearing and extreme sensuality clashed with the austerity of the cathedral.

The young woman slipped under the short curtain of the confessional and knelt with a grace so full of lust that the Saints themselves would have sighed in despair. Ménardier twitched when she rummaged in her bag, but she only pulled out a wad of bank notes, which she handed to Leclerc. The latter began to count them feverishly. Then, quietly, the woman got up and left the confessional.

This was the moment that Ménardier chose to leap from his hiding place and shout:

"Police! Nobody move!"

The door of the confessional suddenly burst open and Leclerc rushed into the nave. Ménardier aimed his gun at the villain, but, faster than lightning, the man had already vanished in the darkness between the stone pillars.

The Eurasian woman took advantage of the moment of uncertainty to scamper towards the choir. Ménardier turned his gun on her. He did not intend to kill her, just to stop her with a bullet in the thigh. He was going to fire when Monk broke into the cathedral, blocking his aim. The Inspector lowered his gun, afraid of harming the American who was now in his line of fire.

Monk, spreading his arms, prepared to intercept the Eurasian woman, but she executed a perfect roll that placed her directly between the legs of her adversary. There, she struck him a hard blow to the groin. The gorilla-like Monk bent under the pain of the blow, but riposted immediately. His left fist described a curve, but encountered only emptiness. However, it had been but a feint. He followed it immediately with a right hook that the Eurasian could not avoid.

The woman uttered a sharp cry of pain. Monk thought he had won, but as he was preparing to grab her, the Eurasian dealt him a violent karate chop to the larynx.

Monk let out a rumbling noise and collapsed, nearly asphyxiated. Bug-eyed, helpless, he saw the woman step over him and fade away into the night.

Meanwhile, Ham. who had observed the whole scene, had rushed out in pursuit of Leclerc, whose stocky body zigzagged between the pillars of the cathedral. The lawyer was gaining ground on his prey, and was about to tackle him to the ground, when the villain suddenly collapsed to the ground, uttering a horrible groan.

Ham looked at Leclerc whose face was becoming swollen.

"The Yellow Shadow... lachrymatory..." the man had time to whisper before he died with a gasp.

His head rolled to one side. His black tongue, abnormally large, jutted from his open mouth like a tumor.

"He's been poisoned," said Ménardier who knelt beside the lawyer.

"Look! The bank notes!" exclaimed Ham.

In the white circle reserved for the watermark in the center of the notes from the Banque de France, which normally depicted a blacksmith and a pretty girl in a toga, a grinning Tibetan demon mask had just appeared!

The mark of the Yellow Shadow!

"He poisoned himself by licking his fingers while counting the money," said Ménardier. "I saw him do it. It's diabolical!"

They were then joined by Monk, who muttered in a hoarse voice:

"That devil woman is gone!" Massaging his sore neck, the 'gorilla' added: "Right now, a shot of bourbon would do me the greatest good..."

Ham smiled, pleased that his friend had recovered his usual banter.

"I just searched the victim," said Ménardier, "and I haven't found any papers on him. Unless the post-mortem turns up something..."

"Shit!" growled Monk. "Another dead end!"

"Not necessarily," said Ham. "I carefully memorized his last words... It's amazing how death loosens tongues!"

The Paris catacombs were spread before them, like a deadly maze winding through the darkness.

Ménardier, Ham and Monk were marching in a line, their crepe soles stifling the sound of their steps. On each side of them, piles of human bones and friezes of skulls shone softly under the light of their electric torches.

Ham shuddered. He had not taken the time to dress himself warmly and the stress only added to the chill generated by the ambient 57 degrees F. He had drawn his sword from the scabbard of his cane and followed Ménardier and Monk, who were both armed with crossbows. Behind them came a small squad of policemen, armed with Thomson submachine guns, dispatched by Commissaire Valentin of the notorious *Brigades du Tigre*.[8]

Meanwhile, several elite policemen stood guard at the home of Berthelaux, which had been converted into an impregnable citadel. Ferval believed firmly that the banker would be the next target of the mysterious Mr. Ming...

As for Francis Ardan, the file requesting his release was now on Judge Coméliau's desk. There was no doubt that he would soon sign it, and that the

---

[8] The so-called "Tiger's Brigade" were created in 1907 by President Georges Clemenceau, whose nickname was the "Tiger," hence their name, to serve as the first, modern crime fighting unit, not unlike London's Flying Squad created in 1919. They formed the basis of a popular French television series which ran from 1974 to 1983, referenced here.

young man would be free before the end of the day. However, Ménardier had not seen fit to wait for Ardan's release to launch his offensive.

Leclerc's last words seemed to indicate that the Parisian lair of the enigmatic Mongol—whom no one doubted was behind the mysterious "olives" implanted in the villainous bankers' brains—was located near the lachrymatory, one of the famous tombs located in the Paris catacombs. Ferval orders were clear: to protect Berthelaux on the one hand, and to invade the ossuary.

Around noon, the task force sent by Valentin quietly joined the trio at the entrance of the catacombs. Silently, the dozen men made their way into the depths of the capital. Like an army of ghosts, in absolute silence, they rushed down through an endless succession of aqueducts and winding quarry tunnels.

When they reached the ossuary, the access of which was blocked by a heavy metal door, Ham shuddered at reading the words carved on the lintel: "*Stop! Here begins the realm of Death...*" The curator of the Carnavalet museum had handed him a key and Ménardier used it to unlock the enormous metal bolt as discreetly as he could.

The expedition resumed its macabre progression, heading for the crypt of the lachrymatory. Suddenly, Inspector Pujol, one of Valentin's men who had gone ahead as a scout, warned them of the presence of guards preventing access to the tomb. Ménardier asked the men to extinguish their torches and they continued their advance in the most complete darkness, walking silently in single file. Ham shuddered again.

Soon, they reached the crossroad where Pujol waited. With a gesture, he showed them the tenuous glow of torches shining at the end of a gallery leading to the tomb.

They tip-toed forward, hugging the damp walls. As they reached a column of bleached bones, Ménardier beckoned Ham to join him. The lawyer walked silently and cast a wary eye behind the pillar.

Two figures stood there, motionless. There were two *dacoits* with long hair and dead eyes, armed with large knives, guarding the crypt. Ham turned around and ran his thumb across his throat. The message was clear! Monk and Ménardier took aim with their crossbows in perfect synchronicity and shot. Whistling through the air, the bolts pierced the necks of the sentinels, who barely had time to cough up some blood before expiring. Their bodies had not even touched the ground when they were picked up and removed by the policemen.

In the center of the darkened hall stood the lachrymatory, the famous tomb of the poet Nicolas Gilbert, bearing the famous inscription: *Au banquet de la vie, infortuné convive, j'apparus un jour et je meurs...* [9]There was no sign of life, or activity. The echo of the removal of the dacoits had not raised any alarms...

Pujol and his colleague Inspector Terrasson went to check the neighboring tunnels and quickly returned, gesturing to certify that the premises were secure.

---

[9] At the banquet of life, unfortunate guest, I came one day, then died.

The squad then began to conceal themselves around the tomb, and the interminable wait amongst the remains of six million dead began. The strangeness of the place, the threat of the Shin Tan, the ominous Mr. Ming, all these things worried Ham. To add to his torment, Monk taunted him by making constant, apelike grimaces at him.

At about six o'clock in the evening, they heard a creaking sound echoing through the tomb; a stone rubbing against another stone. Ham, shivering with cold, stood up. Around the room, the policemen, alert, stood up quietly, ready for action.

A sliver of light appeared on the wall behind the tomb, then widened to reveal a secret passage from which emerged a silhouette. It crept cautiously into the tomb. Monk immediately recognized the Eurasian woman whom he had fought at the cathedral. Her right arm was in a sling. She emerged from the shadows. She was just as stunning as she had been at Notre-Dame; this time, she wore a short dress made of silver *lamé*. She inspected the tomb with a flashlight, but did not detect any danger.

The Eurasian woman then went to the sarcophagus and touched a secret mechanism, which revealed another secret passage. The sarcophagus opened over a narrow stone staircase which the woman took, hurrying down. Already, the sarcophagus was about to close when Ménardier, rushing forward, slid his crossbow inside to prevent the mechanism from shutting down. The weapon bent, the wood groaning under the strain, but the opening remained ajar...

The Inspector quietly slipped through the passage, immediately followed by Monk, Ham, and the men of the *Brigades du Tigre*. The spiral staircase curved through countless strata of bones carved with runes and ended up in a narrow gallery. Below it was a vast cavern, carved out of the stone, illuminated by a pulsed light accompanied by a low hum.

The policemen, holding their guns at the ready, looked into the cavern, which was filled with banks of scientific-looking machinery. At the center of the room was the Eurasian woman. She stood in front of a human-sized glass jar; inside which was a dark, motionless humanoid form. It was a bald man with amber-colored eyes, wide open, in an olive face, dressed as a clergyman, seated in an armchair, the high back of which was carved with dragons and chimeras. His head was under a transparent helmet bristling with coils, conductors, and resistors.

The dreaded Mongol was bathed in the same murky light that seemed to come from nowhere.

"The Yellow Shadow," whispered Ménardier.

Suddenly, Ming seemed to awaken from his trance. With a gesture, he removed the helmet to which he had been attached. Then a mechanism caused the glass jar to lift upwards.

Ming rose.

"Ivana," he said, addressing the Eurasian woman, "have you accomplished your mission?"

"Yes, brother," she replied. "Leclerc will never speak again. But the police are on our track. I'm afraid..."

"I know her, now," Ménardier murmured. "She is Ivana Orloff, a Russian princess related to the Counts Boehm of Germany. Much was made of her in the press recently when she arrived in Paris..."

"Drop your weapons!" said a heavily accented voice.

Ménardier, Ham and Monk turned around and discovered a horde of dacoits, each more sinister than the other, pointing the barrels of their guns at them. They all wore strange dark glasses. Rather than comply, the police went on the attack and opened fire on the dacoits.

Taking advantage of the melee, Ming took a small crystal ball filled with a greenish liquid, which had been resting on a work table, and smashed it on the ground. Immediately a ray of blinding white light flooded the room. The brightness of the rays burned the eyes of the police. Ham howled in pain. He understood the reason for the strange glasses worn by the dacoits: they shielded their eyes from effects of the weapon used by their master!

He heard hurried steps, then words spewed in a dialect unknown to him. The lawyer dropped his sword for fear of hurting his friends. A pair of arms seized him. He delivered a series of blows to defend himself, feeling jaws crunching under his fists. But a hard object hit his head, making him see a thousand stars in the bright afterglow. Ham fell to his knees. His tongue welded to the palate of his mouth, he could not call for help. His legs and arms hurt... The second blow mercifully rendered him unconscious...

When Ham came to, he felt as if two red-hot pincers were crushing his skull. He saw Ming look at him:

"Are you in pain, Mister Brooks? Good—but try not to die... You think you may have won the war, but you have won but a single battle! Tell your friend Ardan that I shall ruin his plans for peace! You Americans, you only want to get rich on the backs of the less advantaged... You wish to forget that there are wars and revolutions, but I'm here to remind you... I will foster a future darker than your worst nightmares!"

Ming laughed a long and cruel laugh, like the growl of a tiger.

Before passing out again, Ham saw him smile and disappear with his sister, Ivana Orloff in tow. Then he sank back into unconsciousness and a mindscape of fragmented arabesques...

A policeman lifted his eyelid and shouted something that Ham did not understand.

The man turned him on his stomach and he felt the blade of a knife sliding between his wrists, cutting the ropes that had hindered him, freeing his hands from behind his back.

Ham huddled on the cold ground, wet, dazed, vaguely discerning Monk at his side.

Acrid smoke filled the cavern. He heard a series of explosions and chunks of ceiling crashed near him. The lawyer didn't care. The only thing that existed for him was his violent headache. He could barely move. The bitter taste of bile was in his mouth... *Above all, don't move*, he said to himself.

He saw Ménardier haranguing his troops... So the Brigades du Tigre had won the battle after all!

Then, he saw the familiar figure of Francis Ardan, accompanied by Doctor de Grandin, who was busy dismantling Ming's diabolical machines. Naked filaments hurled showers of sparks in the air.

We have to get out of here asap, Ham thought in a flash of lucidity. *Everything must be booby-trapped. The Yellow Shadow wouldn't want anyone unlocking his secrets...*

There was another blast, followed by another blackout. Time stretched endlessly. Someone tried to lift him.

"No! I beg you... Evacuate the room!" urged the lawyer.

He hardly recognized the man built like a gorilla, his face bloodied, who grabbed him under the arms and carried him to safety.

A pale sun rose over the rooftops of Paris, dissipating the opalescent dawn.

Ménardier had been pacing the sidewalk for five minutes when the automobile appeared at the corner of the Rue de Turenne. The Inspector saw the tall figure of Ardan, followed by the massive one of Monk, get out of the vehicle, not without some difficulty.

"I've been waiting for you," he grumbled.

"Sorry," said Ardan. "We had to go to the emergency room of the Hotel-Dieu to check on Ham and take care of Monk's head..."

Monk's flat forehead was bandaged, and the left side of his face showed numerous scratches. His clothes were spotted with blackened blood stains. Ménardier, turning to Ardan, asked:

"How is Mr. Brooks?"

"A skull fracture. He was being taken into the operating room when we left... But I'm assured that his life is not in danger."

"Thanks for arriving at the last minute with those reinforcements Ardan. Without you..." The Inspector shuddered at the thought of the gruesome fate that the Mongol could have inflicted on them.

"All the credit should go to Doctor de Grandin," said Ardan. "It was he who designed a machine capable of tracing the source of that mysterious 'Mega Wave' used by Ming to enslave his victims, allowing us to arrive just in time to lend you a helping hand. De Grandin drew on the work of an English physician, Doctor Septimus, whose book on the subject was published in 1922, but..."

But Ménardier wasn't listening anymore; the Inspector had turned around and was heading toward the steps of Berthelaux's home.

The curtain was about to fall!

Some police officers stood on guard in the lobby, searching the visitors. In an adjacent room, they saw more policemen and de Grandin seated before his electronic equipment. A small parabolic dish on top of it turned slowly, while the round, grey screen showed a tiny, erratic sinusoid green line.

Ménardier observed the light patterns without understanding. This modern technology was beyond his comprehension...

"Still nothing to report, doctor?" he inquired.

"Nothing," replied de Grandin; his eyes were underlined with dark circles due to the lack of sleep from the night before.

He was trying to modulate the reception of the signal when Berthelaux appeared in his dressing gown, walking down the stairs leading to his living room.

"What's all this fuss?"

Ardan, who had hitherto remained silent, jumped on the banker and seized him by the throat, lifting him up off the ground. Berthelaux, his neck caught in that giant grip, kicked at the air with his legs.

"Help!" he cried. "Who is this madman? I'll ruin your career, Inspector! I have friends in high places!"

The man of bronze man forcibly turned the banker's head, revealing the short white scar on the occipital bone on the back of his head. He then said coldly:

"Just as I feared, we're too late. This man has already undergone Ming's operation. He's under the control of the Yellow Shadow. It is through this abominable scheme that Ming grabbed the fortunes of the first three bankers who'd robbed him, and tried to frame me for the death of the fourth..."

Ardan dropped Berthelaux, who fell heavily into a chair, coughed, gasped, struggling to catch his breath. Ardan went on:

"But now, we're on to you, Ming! We know the directional nature of the Mega Wave and Doctor de Grandin's equipment will find you, wherever you are!"

Berthelaux continued to squirm in his seat, uncomfortable. Ménardier turned towards him.

"What do you say to that, Monsieur Berthelaux?"

"Inspector, I have no idea what this man is talking about! I know nothing about a Mega Wave or anything else, I swear... It's true, I woke up two days ago with that scar, and I can't remember how I got it. I must have been kidnapped and drugged, but I don't remember anything!"

"Of course, you didn't see fit to call the police..."

"I was going to, but I was scared! You understand... A man in my position! I thought that it may have been someone upset with his investments... But my intention was always to contact you and help you with your inquiry..."

"Nonsense, Ming!" interrupted Ardan. "Your plan is subtle, but we now know that you're in control of Berthelaux through that olive implanted in his skull. I want to know what you real goals are!"

"You're crazy! I may have that thing inside me, but right now, I am the banker Berthelaux! I demand a lawyer! Inspector, I order you to take me to a hospital in order to have that thing removed..."

Suddenly, a bell rang.

"8:59 sharp!" said the banker. "No one is more punctual than my good man Vallières..."

Soon, Vallières entered the room, carrying a tray with tea and coffee which exuded a powerful aroma and another, more subtle smell, undetectable by all, except for Ardan's olfactory sense, trained since birth to uncover traps of all kinds.

"No!" yelled Ardan, realizing what was happening. "It's Ming! You mustn't ..."

Then, he lapsed into unconsciousness, joining Monk and the police already asleep from the effects of the soporific gas made from a rare species of mushroom of which only Judex knew the secret.

"Justice is done," murmured the avenger, carrying the body of Berthelaux and disappearing towards the roof.

When the police came to, Ménardier rushed into the lobby. Short of breath, his eyes still tearing, he asked the policemen on guard:

"Tell me that you saw something...?"

"Nothing, Inspector! We saw nothing at all!"

Ménardier was about to unleash a volley of oaths when Ardan pointed to something white fluttering through the room. It was a dove, which, cooing, landed on Berthelaux's desk, then flew away and disappeared through an open window in the morning sky of Paris.

"Shit!" swore Ménardier, his face crimson. "It's Judex! He's got Berthelaux!"

"Judex?" asked Ardan.

"A vigilante who goes after crooked businessmen and crazy industrialists... There's a good chance that we'll never see Berthelaux again..."

"The only victim of Judex that we've ever identified," added Jules de Grandin "and that was purely by accident, was located by Chantecoq. It was Gontran, a billionaire and a madman. Judex had performed plastic surgery on him, making him completely unrecognizable. He had also undergone some kind of lobotomy that had left him a wreck. He lived like a bum under a bridge in

Paris... He was interned. What a mess... If only this man used his talents to rehabilitate criminals, instead of punishing them..."

The expression on Ardan's face became pensive.

"Rehabilitating... Yes, that's a thought," he murmured.

"What will you do with Bouriet's fortune, which you now own, albeit unintentionally?"

"First, I'll compensate all the victims, of course. Then, I think I'll set up a fund to support Aristide Briand. I believe in him. He advocates reconciliation between France and Germany... Because I fear that the Yellow Shadow may already be fomenting a new war..."

(translation by J.-M. & Randy Lofficier)

1925. The dregs of the Great War have barely settled as another conflict already looms over the horizon. Judex, trying to stop a new blood bath, tangles again with the supernatural, this time with the assistance of a young and promising American archeologist...

Nicholas Boving: *The Talisman*

"Mr. Jones?"

The young man looked up. The table he sat at was covered with scattered paper. He seemed annoyed at the interruption.

"Who wants to know?"

"Mr. Henry Jones?"

"That's what my mother called me."

"My name is Jacques de Trémeuse."

Jones threw down his pencil and sat back. He looked up at the man who had introduced himself. He was tall, dressed in a long black cloak and a black, wide-brimmed hat. He looked dramatic. "And that's supposed to mean something to me?"

Trémeuse pointed at the chair next to Jones. "May I?"

Jones shrugged. "It's a public library."

Trémeuse slid the dark cloak from his shoulders, folded it and laid it carefully over the back of a chair. He sat down.

"You are very young to have such a reputation, Mr. Jones."

Jones' steady blue eyes gave nothing away. "Oh. And what are they saying about me?"

Trémeuse smiled slightly. "That you have a certain, shall I say, capacity for finding that which should not exist."

A church clock outside the library cleared its throat and solemnly announced that it was midday. Jones collected his papers, slid them into a leather folder and then into an attaché case on the floor at his side. He got up.

"I usually have a beer at about this time. It kinda helps my digestion. Care to join me?"

Trémeuse inclined his head. "Lead the way."

Jones put his glass carefully down on the table and wiped froth from his upper lip. "And what can I do for you Monsieur de Trémeuse?"

The Frenchman flipped a finger at the menu. "Perhaps we should also eat." He glanced at the typed sheet. "It appears adequate, provided one is not too fussy." He glanced at Jones. "Are you fussy, Mr. Jones?"

Jones shrugged. "Depends. Right now I want to know who you are and why I should be having a beer with you."

There was a pause while the other man seemed to make up his mind. He looked at Jones, staring hard into his eyes as if trying to penetrate the truth.

"Does the name *Judex* mean anything?"

"Latin for judge. Otherwise…"

Trémeuse gave a ghost of a smile. "I think maybe it means more."

Jones shrugged. "And if it does?"

"Then, maybe you will know why I seek your help in finding the Baroness Hilda von Einem?"

It was the young American's turn to smile.

"You're barking up the wrong tree. Von Einem got killed by a Russian shell somewhere in Turkey."

Trémeuse shook his head. "As they say, rumors of her demise have been greatly exaggerated. She was wounded, but escaped with her life."

Jones shook his head. "Well, in that case there's a lady I'd run a mile from. I guess half the free world must have a warrant out for her arrest."

Trémeuse nodded. "Yes, she has gained some notoriety. However, it is not in her past and well known misdemeanors that I am interested. She acquired a certain object which has, shall I say, great value to me: an *objet de magie noire.*"

"So get it back."

Trémeuse sighed. "Unfortunately, she has secreted it."

Jones gave a lop-sided grin. "And Judex can't find it?"

The Frenchman chuckled. "Ah, so my secret is out. Now I know you are the man I need."

Jones finished his beer and raised a finger at a passing waiter. "Monsieur, it was never in."

"So you will help?"

"Depends. The American Delegation doesn't pay translators too well."

"Find this item, and you can name your price."

The waiter brought a beer. Jones took a pull at it and picked up the menu. "I was going to."

As meals go, that one left much to be desired, but as a meeting it was successful. Jones was told what Jacques de Trémeuse wanted. He named his price. Trémeuse didn't so much as blink. It was all very satisfactory, up to that point. They shook hands and parted, with a rendezvous at Gare de l'Est the following evening. Jones approved. He was a young man with little money, but it seemed the Frenchman did things in style. And the Orient-Express did indeed signal style.

On his way back to his rooms that night, after a long afternoon in the library, Jones was attacked by Apaches. It was the *coup du Père François*, a tactic by which a victim was stalked by several Apaches before being garroted from behind and robbed. At least, that seemed to be their plan. There were three of them. But they had made a mistake. Henry Jones was a large, young man, very strong, and knew how to look after himself. He objected strongly to being mugged.

The result was a broken arm, a dislocated kneecap, and Jones ended up holding the dropped Apache pistol to the temple of the third man and making a savage demand to know who had sent them. All he got was the assertion that *she* would kill them if they said anything. Jones countered by saying that he'd kill them if they didn't; but it seemed the man was more afraid of her than of him.

So he let them go. He could have marched them slowly and painfully to the nearest police station, but it would have meant endless questions and statements, and he was tired.

As he made his way back to his somewhat squalid hotel, he wondered who *she* was. The name Hilda von Einem kept popping into his mind, and that meant she was a very resourceful lady, who had been keeping tabs on Judex.

Jones wondered if Judex knew. He decided the Frenchman probably did. He also decided that there was the real possibility of an adventure in the offing, and that filled him with warm thoughts. Translating for the Delegation was all very well, and meant he could stay in Paris, but it didn't exactly get his blood racing, and Henry Jones, Jr. was ripe for a bit of adventure. He just hoped it wouldn't involve any snakes.

The cream and chocolate carriages of the Orient-Express run by the Companie Internationale des Wagon-Lits stood invitingly and somewhat mysteriously at the platform at the Gare de l'Est. It was scheduled for the Vienna, Bucharest route, ending, as always, in Istanbul. Jones was a romantic at heart and the names did something to him as he arrived at the ticket office to wait for Jacques de Trémeuse. He glanced at the big overhead clock. He was on time. He turned as he heard a voice at his shoulder.

"It is so nice to know you are punctual, Mr. Jones; something so seldom found in the young these days." The Frenchman patted Jones' shoulder. "Come, let us on board."

Jones hitched up his leather carryall. "The only thing I plan on being late for is my funeral."

Trémeuse chuckled and pointed at the train with its engine huffing and hissing like a dragon waiting to race. "Shall we go? I have engaged two sleeper cabins. I so dislike being uncomfortable."

As they boarded, the cabin steward hurried to join them and explained with many apologies that the cabin booked in Mr. Jones' name had been inadvertently given to another gentleman. Mr. Jones had therefore been assigned to another cabin, but of the same exacting standards.

Mr. Jones replied that so long as he got a place to lay his head, he didn't much give a damn.

When they had been shown to their cabins, Trémeuse announced that he intended to change and would then repair to the dining-car for dinner. Would

Jones like to join him? Jones decided that he would and, slinging his bag on the rack, asked which way the diner was. Trémeuse raised an eyebrow.

"Surely, you cannot mean to dine wearing that?"

Jones looked down at his leather jacket and khaki pants. "What's wrong with it?"

"A dinner jacket, Mr. Jones. One changes for dinner at all times."

Jones gave a slightly twisted smile. "I'll put on a clean shirt, but I don't even own a tie."

Trémeuse smiled inside. He knew he had the right man for the job.

The waiter looked down his nose. Jones gave him a withering look that dared him to keep it up. The waiter, thinking of his tip, sensibly backed down and stood, a false smile pasted on his face, waiting for their orders.

Moments later the train roared through a tunnel, making conversation impossible. Jones looked at his face reflected in the window and wondered what was in store. He thought that, whatever it was, it had to be better than sitting at a table translating tedious documents.

And then the train flashed out of the tunnel and the lights of a small town blossomed, they rattled over points and a station came and went almost before he was aware of it or the name.

The dart appeared as if by magic, sticking into the seat back six inches from Jones' head. If it hadn't been for a momentary jolt over the track points, the outcome would have been very different. Jones plucked the dart gingerly from the seat and examined it. The point had a brown sticky substance on it. He didn't need the new forensic science to tell him it was curare.

Jones scrambled to his feet, knocking over a water glass, and scanned the other diners. The waiter hurried to them to mop up the spill but got shooed away. Funny thing was, no one was looking at him, there wasn't a hint of suspicious behavior, there was no obvious assassin, and anyway the high backs of the banquettes precluded all but a few people from being shooters, and they were busily engaged in eating or conversation. The only possibility was a smooth haired, dark man of perhaps eastern origin who was sitting alone and engrossed in a newspaper, but he had his back to him. Jones sat down, mystified.

Trémeuse leaned forward, his face intent and angry. "Is that what I think it is?"

Jones nodded. "That's the second time. Let's hope it's not third time lucky."

"There was another attempt? You did not tell me."

Jones shrugged. "Just a couple of apaches; but one of them seemed worried about a woman." He smiled lopsidedly. "But then all women worry me."

"A pre-emptive strike?"

"Maybe this von Einem wants to eliminate the Judge before he can deliver a verdict."

Trémeuse reached across the table to grasp the young man's wrist. "Are you still game?"

"Hell, yes! This has gotten personal."

The Frenchman nodded his satisfaction. "The verdict has already been handed down. What remains is to carry out the sentence."

An hour later when the debris of their meal had been cleared away, coffee and brandy had been dispensed, and both men had lit cigars, Jones flicked his finger against the feathered dart.

"So, Monsieur de Trémeuse, or perhaps we should cut the crap and call you who you are—Judex." He held up his hand as the Frenchman seemed about to protest. "I've known who you were all along, so don't try to pull the wool over my eyes. Let's cut to the chase." He tapped the dart again. "This gives me rights, and those rights say you're going to tell me what the hell is going on, all of it. Also, why just me when you've got your own organization?"

Judex gave the young American a searching look. He was momentarily concerned that his identity was known; but then, he realized that it was exactly the ability to ferret out mysteries that had made him seek Jones out in the first place. He shrugged.

"My men have their uses, many of them, but none has your nose for this kind of thing. And anyway, this is not a task for a gang, but a very select team —just me and you."

There was a long pause during which the Frenchman made up his mind. He shrugged. "*Eh bien.* You deserve the truth. But I warn you: though it beggars belief, it is nevertheless the unvarnished truth."

Jones blew a stream of smoke at the roof and sat back, relaxed as the rhythm of the wheels on the rails lulled him back down from the moment of high tension. Judex continued.

"There is an object, a talisman, that was stolen from me." He shook his head. "Not by von Einem herself, but she commissioned the theft."

Jones tried a little coffee, and then a sip of brandy. Both were very good; better than he could have afforded. Come to think of it, his sleeper on the wagon lit was better than his atelier. He cocked an eye at Judex.

"Must be one hell of a talisman."

Judex laughed, a small bark of sound. "You do not know how apt that word is." He laid a length of ash from his cigar onto the china ashtray. "The Talisman of Seth was assumed to be mythical, a kind of philosopher's stone of magic until its discovery in Egypt thirty years ago. Even then, no one really believed it until the Great War was set in motion by those with huge vested interests and the knowledge to use what they had acquired."

Jones snorted indelicately. "Sounds like a load of hogwash to me."

Judex shrugged. "And yet, it is not, my young friend. It is very real, and, in the right hands, could become a thing of awesome power and frightful evil."

195

The young American felt icy fingers of unease crawling up his spine. "Are you talking about black magic, 'cos if you are, I'm getting off at the next stop and taking the first train back to Paris. I won't have anything to do with that kind of filth."

Judex stared at him until he felt uncomfortable. "And yet, you will not, because together we must find it and rid the world of what is, as you say, filth, and also a very great evil."

Jones' suspicion was strongly evident in his face. "How did you get hold of this talisman?"

Judex was quite open. "I, er, obtained it, from a man who failed to realize its true value."

"You mean you stole it."

Judex shrugged as if such behavior was of no importance. "I intended to destroy it so it could never be used again."

"Why didn't you?"

The Frenchman shrugged expressively. "I was, shall we say, otherwise engaged. And when I returned to Paris, it was to discover my safe open and the talisman gone."

"How come you know this von Einem woman has it?"

"She was seen in Paris the following day. In itself that was nothing remarkable. What was remarkable was the man whose company she kept. He is called Pius Augustus; a renegade priest and now goes under the name of Mocata. Augustus, or Mocata, is an adept of the highest order in the ranks of black magicians. He is a man of considerable power—oh yes, it is real—and it took very little deduction on my part to come up with the requisite addition."

"So why Istanbul?"

"Because Turkey is where Hilda von Einem lives, and anyway, she was seen boarding a train to Vienna a few days ago."

"What's she going to do with this—thing?"

"She has an obsession that was thwarted during the Great War." His eyes bored into Jones. "Does the name *Greenmantle* mean anything?"

Jones frowned. "I vaguely remember hearing the name. Some prophet or other, wasn't he?"

"Indeed."

"What's this obsession?"

Judex smiled. "You will find it amusing, and yet believe me it is not. Hilda von Einem passionately wants the reunification of the Ottoman Empire."

"And this talisman thing is going to help in some way? Oh crap, she's nuts."

The look in the Frenchman's eyes told Jones his assessment was way off base. He touched the dart again. "I guess two goes at getting rid of me makes it serious."

Judex pointed to the small feathered weapon. "Have you considered that may have been meant for me?"

Jones snorted. "Then he's a lousy shot."

"Also very good at disguising what just happened."

Judex finished his brandy and got up. "Tomorrow will be a long day with little to do but watch the passing scenery. I shall retire."

Henry Jones Junior, Indiana Jones thanks to a dog and a dislike of the tag junior, stayed in the dining car. He ordered another brandy and sat watching the nighttime country slide past his reflected face. He thought life was a funny old thing, and got you into some funny situations. He grinned at his reflection and felt a small surge of excitement that tightened his gut. He also thought life was what you made of it, and even at his age he'd done a couple of things others only dreamed of.

He glanced down at the small feathered dart, was about to slide the window open and throw it into the darkness when something prompted him to slip it into his wallet. Then he finished his drink and left the dining car.

The man standing gazing out of the window in the corridor of the sleeping car was fairly short, balding, immaculately dressed, in his thirties and had waxed moustaches turned up at the tip. Jones thought he looked a typical Parisian boulevardier and a dandy; the kind he'd go a long day's march to avoid. The man squeezed against the carriage wall to let him pass and smiled, but it was a mere twitch of recognition and politeness rather than pleasure at seeing a fellow traveler. Jones answering smile was equally meaningless.

He went into his cabin. Ten minutes later he was asleep.

He came to with every sense telling him that something was wrong. For a couple of seconds he listened, half in and out of sleep, still lulled by the clickety-clack of the carriage wheels over rail joints. And then he distinctly heard voices, emotionally charged but suppressed to harsh whispers. He slid out of bed and cracked the door.

There were four men in the passage. The conductor, the steward, Judex and the well-dressed stranger who now sported an embroidered silk dressing gown. There was an argument going on of considerable intensity. Jones pushed into the passage and joined them.

"What in hell's name's going on? Can't a guy get any sleep around here?"

Judex took him by the arm. "A man has been murdered."

"Who, where, how?"

The little man smiled. "Admirably put." His accent was French. He held out his hand. "Permit me to introduce myself. I am Hercule Poirot. And you are?"

"Jones. Henry Jones."

Judex cut in. "Mr. Jones is traveling with me."

"Ah." The little man seemed to pack a wealth of meaning into such a simple syllable.

Judex went on. "Monsieur Poirot is a detective of considerable renown. It is fortunate he is traveling with us."

"Fortunate for whom?"

Judex frowned. Jones felt he hadn't considered the implications. He shrugged. "For the police, one assumes. By the time the train reaches the next station Monsieur Poirot will have solved the mystery."

"Where's the dead guy?"

Judex pointed to a slightly open cabin door. Jones pushed it further open and looked in. A man lay on the floor. There was a silver handled knife sticking out of his throat and he lay in a pool of blood. Jones recognized him from the dining car. He had been talking animatedly to a woman wearing fur and too many jewels.

"Robbery?"

Poirot appeared at his elbow. "Non, Monsieur, I think not. The room, it is tidy, the search, it has not been made, and yet a man lies dead. Poirot's grey cells tell him this was murder for its own sake. The question is why, and of course, by whom."

Jones backed out of the doorway. There were cold ants crawling up his spine and he didn't like it. He glanced down at the detective.

"I don't know who, but I know why."

Poirot's eyebrows rose quickly. "*Ah oui?*"

"Mistaken identity. The guy, whoever he was, got the wrong room." He pointed at the corpse. "That should have been me."

Poirot continued to show surprise. "And you know this how, Monsieur?"

Jones explained the mix-up with cabin bookings. Poirot glanced from him to Judex and back again. His moustache tips seemed to quiver with excitement.

"*Certainement*, this is, how you say, a matter most grave. The police must be made aware of this."

Judex placed a firm hand on Poirot's arm. "Monsieur Poirot, with great respect, the case of mistaken identity cannot be allowed to come out, at least, not yet." He eased the detective a few meters down the corridor out of earshot of the conductor and steward. His tone dropped melodramatically. "You understand that this is a matter of national security; an operation jointly being conducted by the French and American governments."

Jones was amused to see the frantic tussle in the detective's face: a fight between his desire to solve the case and respect for national security. In the end, he shrugged his agreement.

"This is most irregular, you understand. I have the reputation. Poirot cannot be seen to turn the blind eye to such a crime."

"And yet you will, Monsieur. Also, rest assured that on my return to Paris, your cooperation will be made known to those who have the necessary influence."

Poirot's final smile was a little crooked. "You are most agreeable, Monsieur; however, I am not French, but Belgian."

Judex' reply was smooth as silk. "Then the matter of your cooperation will be passed on to Brussels."

Poirot nodded, and then his face brightened. "There can, however, be no objection to Poirot conducting a little investigation. It may be that I shall discover much, and knowledge is a useful tool when dealing with the police in any foreign country."

Judex nodded and consulted his watch. "We should reach Vienna in six hours. You have until then Monsieur."

Henry "Indiana" Jones declined Judex' offer of company and returned to his cabin in a thoughtful mood. He thought the old adage of third time lucky and should be amended to four. He wondered why someone, presumably the von Einem woman, had singled him out for special attention when she could just as well have gone after Judex, whom she obviously knew. He decided that he must be getting a reputation for being a nosy customer.

Vienna was unremarkable. There was a slight delay to the schedule, but once the police had been made aware of Poirot's availability, a senior *Gruppeninspektor* appeared amid a lot of bustle, the body was removed and Poirot bade his adieus to Judex and Jones.

"It seems Poirot's little grey cells are needed." He gave a knowing little smile and touched his forefinger to his lips. "*À bientôt*, Monsieur Judex." And with that he stepped onto the platform, leaving Judex puzzled and slightly annoyed. It seemed his identity was not as covert as he might wish.

By late afternoon, the Orient Express pulled into Sirkeci railway terminal in Instanbul. Half an hour later, Jones and his employer were in their rooms at the Ritz-Carlton. Jones threw his one battered bag on the bed and going to the window, opened it and leaned out. He had to admit that the view over the Bosphorus was just the other side of astounding, and the familiar feeling of excitement started to creep through him as he thought of the incredible history that had been, and the thought of what looked like might happen. He had a future mapped out that didn't include spending his days sitting behind a desk. Adventure had called and he'd heard that call loud and clear.

"So what's the plan of action?" Jones forked a meatball from his *Köfte* and popped it in his mouth. Judex speared an oyster before answering.

"Tomorrow I must make some inquiries. There are certain people who know things, you understand, things not readily available."

"Such as where this von Einem dame hangs out. I'm surprised you don't already know that." A second meatball followed. Judex smiled.

"Hilda von Einem is, shall we say, reluctant to disclose her whereabouts. But there are ways, and the gateway to the Orient is also the gateway to knowledge if one has the right key."

"Which you have."

Judex glanced around before answering. "There is a teahouse, frequented only by those with good reason to visit. There is a certain brotherhood of wanderers who perform occasionally. They will be there tomorrow evening. I wish to speak with their leader."

Jones vainly looked for more meatballs, and then reluctantly pushed his plate away. "The mysterious Orient is about right. And if this performer guy tells you what you want, then we get going?"

"You are an impatient young man. This is the East. Things move more slowly here."

Jones grunted and signaled the waiter for the menu. "I got the idea that this Talisman thing was kinda urgent."

Judex smiled at his impatience. "We shall have coffee, a brandy, and then pay our respects at the great mosque of Aya Sophya." He snapped his fingers at the waiter. "After that, we shall make our way to the tea house, and see what we shall see."

The Garden-house of Suliman the Red didn't fill Jones with any feelings of excitement. At first glance, it looked cheap and tawdry, filled with people sitting at small tables drinking coffee and smoking *litakia*.

A fat looking waiter ushered them to a table, but Judex chose one in a far corner. He ordered in Turkish, which surprised the young American. But then, since arriving in Istanbul he had noticed a change in the Frenchman; a tightening of emotions, a firming of the jaw and a coldness in his eyes that belied his occasional humorous banter.

He glanced across the table. The man hadn't removed his hat or cloak, and seemed to be waiting for something, or someone.

The waiter came with coffee and two glasses of *raki*, and then they sat until Jones was just about to ask why they were wasting their time in a dump like that, and the atmosphere changed and the hairs on his neck stirred.

A man in ragged robes strode into the open space that doubled as a dance floor for the afternoon *thé dansant*. He was closely followed by a half dozen similarly ragged and fierce figures. For the space of a dozen heart beats they stood, a wild tableau; and then they began to dance, accompanied by eerily unseen pipes and tam-tams.

Never in his life had Jones witnessed anything like it. The men leapt like Nijinski, seemingly suspending the law of gravity, and the next moment they were whirling dervishes, eyes flashing, promising unknown horrors to those that disobeyed them. And the light in that second rate café changed from dreary winter afternoon daylight, to a soft rose color he couldn't lay a name to.

How long it went on, he never could really remember, but, suddenly and without any kind of coda, the performance stopped and, as if by magic the dancers left. The audience of patrons made not a sound, not a single clap of appreciation: they simply sat, stunned, although Jones knew they must have seen it before.

And then the conversation resumed, the waiters carried on taking and delivering orders, and the magical returned to the banal. Judex stood up.

"*Les Compagnons des heures roses.* Come. We must hurry. The leader has a message for us."

Jones scrambled to his feet, wondering who the hell the Companions of the Rosy Hours were. As an afterthought he snatched up his glass of *raki*, down it in one and did the same for Judex' untouched glass. He felt he might need a bit of moral strengthening. He strode after Judex' swirling cloak.

There was an alleyway at the back of the garden-house with a view down a street to the Ratchik ferry. Judex and the leader of the companions were standing close, heads together in urgent conversation. There was no sign of the others.

As Jones reached them, the two men reached out and clasped each other, forearm to forearm. Then the leader snapped a word, made a sign that might have been a blessing or a curse, and vanished around a corner.

Jones skidded to a stop. "What the hell was all that about?"

For a few seconds Judex appeared to not hear him, then he turned and there was a smile of triumph on his face.

"We have the Baroness's whereabouts."

"Who were those men?"

Judex touched his arm. "Did you not hear? I know where von Einem can be found."

Jones wasn't that impressed. He still wanted to know about the wild and weird dancers. Judex shrugged.

"They are known as the Companions of the Rosy Hours. They come, they go, and they are to be more feared than the Devil, if you are their enemy. Fortunately I am their friend, having been able to lend some small assistance at one time."

"But..."

Judex face hardened. "No more questions about the Companions. Accept what they have given and leave it at that." He looked around. It was not a prepossessing area of Istanbul. "First, we must return to the hotel and arrange for the hire of an automobile, after that we shall have them make up a basket of provisions, and we will be on our way."

Jones didn't move. "Not a goddamned step," he said mulishly. "I guess I'm OK about those fellas if you insist, but not until you've told me where we're going."

"The Villa Lanet, my young friend. We are going to the Villa of the Damned."

As he said it, a soft persistent rain began to fall and Jones knew the chill he felt wasn't just on account of the weather.

"Sounds appropriate," Jones said sourly. "And von Einem and this Mocata are there?"

Judex nodded. "According to—the Companion."

"And of course you know exactly where it is."

"I have some small knowledge of the area. It is close to the border with Greece."

"I'll just bet. But, if you already know, remind me why I'm traipsing across Europe."

Judex managed a smile. "The villa is where we shall find von Einem. The talisman? Who knows? That is where your expertise comes in." He patted Jones' shoulder. "Each to his own, my young friend. I find them, you find it." He wrapped his cloak around him, half covering his face, and together with the wide brimmed black hat pulled low it made him seem deeply mysterious. "Go back to the hotel, Henry, and make arrangements for the automobile. There are some items I must collect. I will join you in one hour."

Judex turned the Delage CO2 Grand Sport onto the coastal road. It was painted bright yellow. The hotel management had been most helpful in obtaining it, but Jones thought it couldn't have been more conspicuous if they'd hired a marching band to advertise their arrival. Judex seemed unconcerned as he pressed the accelerator and the 4.5 liter engine drove their speed up to nearly sixty miles an hour.

For the next one hundred and fifty miles as they roared through Silivri, Tekirdağ and then turned inland towards Keşan, he just hung on as the execrable roads slammed and shook the big car until he thought it just damned well had to fall to pieces. Twice they passed through drizzling rain that made life miserable, and once a bitter blast of sleet that nearly stripped the skin from their faces and made visibility so bad Judex almost put them in a ditch.

Twice they stopped for gasoline and once Judex pulled off the road under a grove of olives where, hunched under a blanket they ate their *al fresco* dinner, and then with headlights blazing they thundered on into the gathering dark.

The cloud parted as they ran out of the bad weather and the moon washed the surrounding country in a blue eerie light when Judex stopped once more, consulted the map, grunted with satisfaction and, a couple of miles later turned the Delage onto a side road that wound up into a range of low hills. He pulled

202

into the shelter of another grove of olives and shut off the engine. Jones silently thanked his gods and got out, bending and stretching to ease cramped muscles. The only sound was the gentle sough of wind in the branches overhead, and the tick of cooling metal.

"What now?"

Judex took the picnic hamper off the back seat, sat on a fallen log and took out a bottle of wine and two glasses.

"Now we wait until it is dark. The Moon will set in another three hours. Until then, we eat and rest."

After they had eaten, they returned to the car, raised the passenger hood and settled to try and sleep.

Jones came to with a start to find Judex crouched before a small fire. The aroma of coffee wafted towards him with all the allure of a siren call. He threw off the blanket and stumbled out of the back seat, bleary-eyed. Judex handed him a chased silver traveling glass.

"From now on, my young friend, we must exercise great caution."

Jones sipped the hot nectar and sighed. "I guess that means we're on foot from here on."

"Indeed. But there are certain precautions we must take. From what I know of him, Mocata is a magician of considerable power, being an Adept of the tenth grade."

Jones' attention was still focused on the coffee. "You just lost me."

Judex made a dismissive gesture. "Suffice to say that he may well be able to perform a conjuration that will tell him of our approach."

The coffee lost a bit of its allure as chilly ant's feet trotted down Jones' spine again. He was used to a bit of adventure, and a bit of rough and tumble didn't much bother him; but this talk of Adepts and magic didn't sit too well with his New Jersey upbringing.

"And if he does, find us I mean?"

Judex topped up his glass. "Then we are prepared. There are certain items... but we may have no use for them."

Jones wasn't all that convinced. "But this von Einem dame knows we're coming, right?"

The Frenchman shrugged. "I fear that is inevitable."

Jones looked out into the darkness. He pointed with his chin. "This villa: it's that way, right?"

"About two miles as the crow flies."

"And the talisman thing will be there."

Judex frowned. "I doubt it." Then he smiled. "But, as I said, that is where you come in. My sources tell me that there is a ruined monastery in the vicinity. It is exactly the kind of place a man like Mocata would use for his rites."

The Baroness Hilda von Einem was furious. She held a slip of paper in a shaking hand and thrust it towards the other occupant of the room, a stoutly-built man in his forties whose sole remarkable feature was his dark, piercing eyes.

She inserted a cigarette into a long holder and lit it with a taper from a candle. She blew smoke at the ceiling the leant against the mantelpiece.

"How? How did he find me?" She crumpled the paper, a telegraph form, and angrily threw it into the flames.

The man, Mocata, shrugged. "Judex is a resourceful and intelligent man."

"But so quickly? I had thought him to be casting about for clues, by which time our work would be done and he would have been too late."

"He had help."

Von Einem glared at him. "Spare me the obvious. The question is who." She drew heavily on her cigarette. "No matter. The damage is done." She straightened, went to a table on which an assortment of bottles stood, and poured herself a brandy. She swung back to Mocata.

"Can you send an entity to destroy him?"

Mocata's face hardened. "Assuredly. But I will not."

Von Einem sneered. "And I thought you were a high-ranking adept."

Mocata sighed. "To send an entity is exceedingly dangerous, for the one who sends it as well as those at whom it is aimed. Should it be blocked, or fail to find its mark it will return to seek another victim." He paused. "I always use an intermediary, a medium. That way, I am safe." His full lips curved in an evil smile. "Perhaps you, my Lady, would care to be that medium?"

Hilda von Einem quivered as if struck. "Do not even suggest such a thing."

"Then what?"

"For the time being, keep a psychic watch on them. I wish to know the moment they are, as it were, at the gates." She paused. "You mentioned before being able to send an astral projection, a creature to cast terror."

Mocata inclined his head. "When they are at the gates, it shall be done. But Judex is a man of many skills and much knowledge. It is possible he has fore-armed himself as he knows I am involved."

The Baroness nodded. "Do whatever it takes. The rites must be concluded tomorrow night. There can be no delay or we will have to wait another year and then… who knows what obstacles may be in our path. Judex is close. We are forewarned and must be prepared."

"He is not alone. And if I know Judex, he will not have come unprepared. It would be a mistake to underestimate him."

Von Einem shook her head. "Just keep a psychic watch on them. I wish to know the moment they are, as it were, at the gates."

Mocata looked at the tall, dark, beautiful woman and brushed a fleck of dust from his elegantly creased trousers. He seemed unimpressed. "It would also be a mistake to underestimate my powers."

Von Einem's reply was excessively silky. "I would also be a mistake to underestimate me, my dear Mocata."

The Ormolu carriage clock on the mantle struck midnight. Von Einem removed her cigarette and tossed it into the fire. "I shall rest for a few hours. Keep watch, and make sure the servants stay alert."

And with that she swept dramatically from the room. Mocata watched her leave with the feeling that all was not quite as it should be between allies. He would keep a close eye on her. And after the rite, he would keep the Talisman and thus have more power than any Adept of the Black Arts in history. Of course, the woman knew nothing of his intentions, but she would find out that when supping with the Devil, it was best to have a long spoon.

He got up and went to a crystal orb that sat on an ivory inlaid teak table. The inlay was of a pentagram encircled with the signs of the Zodiac. He passed his hand over it in a sweeping gesture and peered into the swirling mistiness that had appeared. The mist cleared and the figures of Judex and Jones appeared, sitting before the small fire.

Mocata smiled, swept his hand across the crystal again, and the image vanished. He left the room.

Judex retrieved a cloth sack from the Delage. He brought it to the fire and took out several items. Jones watched with interest as they were laid in a row on the ground.

"Garlic, asafetida grass, holy water, crucifixes and, lastly but not least, a couple of serviceable revolvers with spare ammunition."

Jones was doubtful. "Looks like the makings for a stew."

Judex was not amused. "This is deadly serious my young friend. Von Einem may be just a woman with delusions, but know this, Mocata is more dangerous than any man you have met, or even heard of. His powers are genuine and to be feared greatly."

Jones thought about that for a couple of minutes. Judex he knew about: a man with a fearsome reputation for justice and revenge, but he also had a reputation for being careless with the law. He wondered if his desire to get back the talisman was indeed to destroy it, or perhaps to use it for his own ends. He decided that right then it didn't much matter as the first thing was to ensure the woman and Mocata could not use it.

He smiled at the thought of von Einem's plan to perform some magical rite and then rule the Middle East. He thought that when he got back he'd write to his friend Lawrence and ask him what he reckoned.

Judex cocked his head and eyed the American speculatively. "You do not completely believe, but it would be better if you did. When I said this man is dangerous, I meant it in all sincerity." He handed Jones a garlic bulb and the grass. "Place the garlic in your left pocket and make a loop of the grass around your wrist." He waited till Jones had done as asked, then handed him a vial of water. "This is Holy Water. Mocata may send an Astral Projection to frighten us. With this we can defeat it. Put it in your right pocket, and if such a manifestation attacks us, throw it at it."

"How come you know all this stuff? I mean, it's not exactly the kind of thing you can pick up at the library."

Judex shrugged. "When you fight crime with crime it is as well to have knowledge of many weapons." He stood up. The Moon was half obscured by the range of hills. "The time has come."

The stony track wound uphill through a maze of twisted, ancient olive trees. Judex led, careful to stay in the darker shadows when the sharp outlines of the villa roof came into view. He paused, took Jones' arm and whispered.

"From now on, be vigilant for anything out of the ordinary."

Jones didn't like the sound of that. "By that what d'you mean?"

"Lights, patches of colored brightness, dark shapes moving."

Jones looked over his shoulder. His voice came out as a hoarse whisper. "Like that?"

Judex whirled and swore. "*Sacrebleu! Exactement!*" His grip on Jones' arm tightened. "Do exactly as I say."

"Which is?"

"Don not run. Control your fear. Think of the color blue. And repeat the words of the twenty-third psalm. You do know the words, hein?"

"Yea, *though I walk through the valley of the shadow of death, I will fear no evil?*"

Judex managed a grim smile as he reached into his pocket for the crucifix and the vial of holy water. He walked firmly towards what appeared to be a ball of deep, pulsating violet and began to intone a chant.

"Father, mother, Masters of the Light, hear my prayer and protect us."

Then he switched into a language Jones didn't recognize but was dimly aware must be incredibly ancient. And still he strode forward, and still the ball of light increased in intensity until it started to take on shape and form that was vaguely humanoid. He hissed a warning.

"See. It is an astral entity. Mocata has called this abomination from the pit of Hell."

Jones needed no prompting and increased the volume of the psalm, trying as he did so to conjure up a mental image of something intensely blue. He got as far as his sister's eyes and the cornflowers in some field he'd once seen, and then the entity solidified into a crouching, fanged horror, and he felt an almost irresistible desire to turn tail and get the hell out. Judex called out.

"It cannot hurt you. It is not real."

"Looks goddamned real to me," Jones snarled.

"It is energy. It is not solid. But whatever you do, do not look into its eyes. At all costs, do not look at its eyes."

Which advice was nicely calculated to make Jones want to do exactly that. But he managed to tear his gaze away.

"What now?"

"Your crucifix. Hold it up. Thrust it forward. Repeat the words of the psalm, and when I shout, hurl your vial of holy water straight at it."

Now that was one thing Jones knew he was good at. Hurling things with force and accuracy was a natural to a young man who'd spent his summers pitching baseballs.

He gritted his teeth. "Just say the word." He punched the crucifix forward and started to grate out the words of the psalm."

He'd just got to, "*I will fear no evil...*" When Judex shouted, "Now!"

Jones vial of water took off like a rocket. The result was dramatic. The entity gave a scream of mingled rage and pain. It took a step forward, great, clawed hands outstretched and grasping. Jones had never seen such a terrifying thing and hoped to God he never would again.

And then, the entity, demon, astral projection, whatever it was, started to shrink. The purple ball of pulsating light grew dimmer until it was no more than a glowing aura around the still diminishing thing at its center.

Finally, with a shriek that was no louder than a distant eagle's cry, there was a pop like a balloon bursting and the projection vanished, leaving only a foul, sulfurous smell.

Jones leaned against a twisted olive trunk. He was sweating and his heart going a mile a minute. He looked across at Judex. The man seemed as cool as ice as he tucked his astral weapons back in his pockets. Jones unhitched himself from the tree.

"Well, at least we know he knows we're coming. What now?"

"There will be a time table. Some confluence of events that is most favorable."

"Like a full Moon. Like tomorrow night's full Moon?"

Judex smiled grimly. "I knew there was a good reason for bringing you all this way."

Jones was not amused. "Then we've got to find this talisman thing and get rid of it. Seems easy when you put it like that, but I guess this Mocata and von Einem aren't going to make this exactly a cake walk."

"Mocata will use every power he possesses to stop us."

"And I'm guessing that astral thing was just a free sample."

Judex pulled his cloak tightly around himself as a thin, sneaky wind rose and probed with icy fingers.

"You said there's an old monastery."

Judex pointed. "It will be beyond the villa, further up the hills."

The two armed guards appeared out of the darkness as silently as ghosts. For a split second Jones thought they were more of Mocata's apparitions, but then he didn't reckon apparitions went around waving serviceable shotguns.

Language wasn't a problem. The directions were clear. Get up to the villa or get shot, and no funny business.

"It would seem prudent to obey," Judex said quietly.

Baroness Hilda von Einem seemed glad to see them. There was a smugness in her face that shouted superiority.

"Judex, and Mr. Henry Jones. Please come in. I was expecting you."

One of the armed guards coughed meaningfully. They accepted the invitation. They entered the sumptuous room with a curious mixture of western and oriental furnishings, lit only by oil lamps suspended from the ceiling by chains. A log fire burned brightly in the huge grate. Von Einem lit a cigarette with deliberate slowness and then continued.

"Unfortunately for you, your intentions have now been thwarted. You will be imprisoned in the cellars of this house, and in a couple of days, we shall leave, never to return. I regret I am unable to provide you with either food or water."

Jones wasn't much amused. He strode to the fire, ignoring the shotguns, and held his hands to the blaze. "If your arrangements are as good as your pathetic attempts on my life, you may as well just leave us the keys."

Hilda von Einem was not amused. Her eyes narrowed angrily as she snapped orders to the guards. The shotguns were brought into play again and they were pushed towards the door. Judex stopped and turned.

"Where is Mocata?"

Von Einem's blew a streamer of smoke. "He is, shall we say, otherwise engaged."

The cellar door banged behind them with a heavy finality that told Jones it was very solid. The grating sound of the massive bolt added to the unlikelihood of it being a way out.

"I think we have a bit of a problem," he said. "What do we do now?"

"We think." Judex walked slowly around the cellar, touching, probing, examining. "There is no such thing as an escape-proof prison," he said at last.

"Provided you have ten years to work at it. We've got till tomorrow night. Correction tonight." Jones answered. "I suppose this talisman thing really does work. I mean, the lovely Hilda isn't having a pipe dream."

Judex shook his head. "Would that it were so."

"And the cavalry isn't coming."

"No, my young friend. We must rely on our own resources." He wrapped his cloak firmly around himself and sat down on the stone floor, cross legged.

"It is time to call on those powers beyond our understanding. It may be that the Masters of the Light will hear our prayers."

Indiana Jones lost track of time. For a while he simply watched Judex as he sat intoning a continuous mantra, and then a night without sleep caught up with him, his eyes drooped and he slept.

He woke from a dream of chaos with a shout of alarm and shot to his feet, to be immediately dashed to one side. He felt as if he was on some fairground ride in which the floor shook.

"What the Hell...?" But even as the words came out he knew what it was.

Judex shouted. "An earthquake. Cover yourself."

Jones staggered to the wall, arms over his head, but a slab of stone fell, hitting him on the head. There was a split second of pain and darkness fell.

He came to consciousness, to find himself lying on his back with a cold breeze blowing and a wheel of diamond bright stars above his head. He tried to struggle up, but a firm hand held him down.

"What happened?" he said.

Judex chuckled. "It seems the Masters of the Light heard our pleas and have acted. There was an earthquake. The villa is badly damaged and the roof of the cellar split."

That time Jones did get up, a bit groggy, but ready to go. "How long...?

"No more than fifteen minutes."

Jones spat out some dust and wiped his sleeve across his face. "Then let's find that goddamned monastery and put a stop to this. I don't know about you, but I had about enough of this dame."

Judex smiled at the young American. "Your spirit is to be admired. You are sure you are unhurt?"

"The monastery. Which way?"

The looming ancient walls of the abandoned building towered above them, ivy clinging to the walls and rank grasses sprouting. Judex grasped Jones' arm.

"From now on we must be very careful. This is the only chance they will have for this year. If Mocata feels threatened he may well summon and entity from the pit of hell."

Jones wasn't impressed. "We dealt easily enough with the last one."

"That was an astral projection. What may come will be very real and horribly dangerous." An owl hooted. Jones thought all they needed was a couple of bats. Judex continued. "But that is my worry. It may be that I can protect us, if the Masters are willing again. "Finding the Talisman is your job."

"Think blue, huh? Twenty-third psalm again?"

Judex shook his head. "It will help. But this time more, much more."

Jones didn't much like the sound of that. But he shook the images away and started thinking about ancient ecclesiastical buildings. What did they have that was special? Tombs, crypts, holy of holies, a Christian community in the Middle Ages might well have had hidden rooms against marauders. He needed to focus.

"Only one way to find out," he said. "Get in and look around." He managed a grin. "Find this talisman and then get the hell out."

Judex smiled tolerantly. "You make it sound simple."

"That's because it is. Things usually are: people make things complicated." He scrambled to his feet. "Those old monks were canny fellas. We look for the back door."

The small door was hidden behind a fall of ivy. They nearly missed it, and it took their combined strength and a bit of rock clearing to open it wide enough to slip through. Once inside they were confronted with a square block with arrow slit and tall church windows. From one of the arrow slits a stream of yellow lamplight shone onto a gnarled olive.

"Is there another back door?" Judex whispered.

Jones pointed. "The roof. The door'll be covered." He smiled. "I like ivy, don't you?" And with that comment he ran lightly forward, grasped a thick stem, and began climbing with the agility of a monkey. Judex shrugged and started after him.

It was as Jones had said. The flat roof was partially caved in, the rotting beams traps for a careless foot. But in the far corner was the top of a stone staircase.

With only the starlight to guide their feet away from traps, they crept across the open roof like burglars. Once, an ancient beam creaked and they froze, but as it raised no alarm; they made it to the stairs. Jones signaled that he was going first.

Half way down the open staircase that clung to the side of the outer wall, he found the source of the lamplight. There was a recess at the east end, the apse beyond which stood a stone altar made of a huge slab on four pillars. In front of it stood Mocata, dressed in a long red hooded robe embroidered with cabalistic designs. He was intoning what might have been an invocation or a prayer: it meant nothing to Jones.

To his left, also in a long robe, but of pure white silk edged with gold, sat Hilda von Einem, her hands clasped and a look in her eyes that approached ecstasy.

But what held both men's attention was the ivory casket inlaid with gold and chalcedony that lay on the altar. There was no doubt. Inside it had to be the Talisman of Seth: a simple piece of withered and mummified flesh that by all accounts was the source of unimaginable power and evil.

210

It seemed too easy. All two strong and agile men had to do was run down a flight of stairs, overpower a middle aged effete man and a slender woman, grab the box and hightail it to the nearest bonfire.

And like all things that seem too easy, it was.

Mocata, alerted by whatever magical power he possessed, stopped chanting and whirled with a snarl of fury on his face. Von Einem, puzzled for a second, also saw the danger, rose from her chair and pointed one long, red-tipped finger.

"Seize them. Kill them." She didn't seem to much care what the final outcome was. Mocata lifted his head and spread his arms, fingers clawed into talons as he spat a sentence. The words meant nothing to Jones, but Judex shouted a warning.

"Get down. On your face. Make yourself small. And for God's sake don't look until I tell you."

Jones groaned. "Oh Christ. Not another one."

Judex' answer was a string of words in another language dead before recorded history. Vaguely Jones wondered where he'd learned it, and then his attention was caught by a shimmering outline appearing behind the altar. Again Judex shouted.

"Don't look at it. Whatever you do, don't look at it."

Jones tore his eyes away from the outline that was taking the shape of something he very much didn't want to see and, because it was the only thing he could think of, he started on the words of the psalm, but it got mixed with Judex' mantra of the Mother and Father, and something about the Masters of Light.

And then he was alone on the stair feeling very exposed. And below in the apse before the altar, it sounded as if a battle royal was going on.

Fear, curiosity, a desperate need to know what was going on compelled Jones look down onto what had become an arena of titans. Mocata stood before the altar, throwing his hands at Judex as if hurling spears. And even as he did so the outline of whatever Mocata had summoned took shape and form, morphing into the sum of all Jones' worst terrors. He saw, standing at ten feet to the top of its ghastly scaled and fanged head, the living embodiment of a creature he had seen recreated in the Natural History Museum. Indiana Jones saw a velociraptor, but like none that had ever roamed the Earth in the Cretaceous era of the distant past.

Blazing eyes, foul slime dripping from its bloody fangs, and a stench of rottenness and death; it was the stuff of nightmares. And as he watched it leaped onto the altar slab and roared a challenge.

Jones saw Judex back away, and though he could not see, he knew the man's eyes would show fear. Holy water and garlic might indeed be good in a stew, but even with the crucifix he clutched in his hand the outcome was without doubt. Judex had met his match and was staring into the open mouth of the pit of Hell.

Mocata's snarled with a bare-toothed grimace. He raised his arms in a gesture of triumph. And then, a bolt of blue flooded through the window above the altar, swirled through the ancient church and found its mark in Judex, circling him in a protective aura. Jones knew that the Masters of the Light had once more answered the call of a soul in mortal danger.

There was a period, Jones never knew how long, when the arrow of time stood still. And then the lock was broken and with a roar of fury the entity, cheated of its prey, did the only thing it was capable of: it turned back for revenge on the one who had summoned it.

Mocata knew, and there was nothing he could do to stop it. His scream of fear echoed through the church. And he ran. But it was useless. He had not gone ten paces when the entity was on him. It picked him up, its terrible jaws closed around his shoulder. He screamed again, a terrible cry of pain and horror. It shook him like a terrier shakes a rat, and then hurled him along the aisle. He slid, leaving a bright smear of blood on the ancient stones.

The creature was about to take off after its prey when the blue light swirled away from Judex, hurled itself against the entity like a bolt of lightning. It gave a scream of agony and fury, twisting as if caught in the fires of its own hell. Scream after scream of rage and pain came from the awful long-fanged mouth as the light circled it.

It began to shrink, still screaming, until it was no bigger than a wolf hound. And then…

It vanished.

Mocata, whimpering with pain hauled his bleeding, broken body till he was partly hidden behind a pillar, and collapsed.

There was silence. The blue light circled the church once again and flew back through the window as it had come.

Jones watched open mouthed, hardly able to believe what he'd seen, knowing only that the thing, whatever it was, had been hurled back into the pit it came from. He ran down the stairs to where Judex had fallen to his knees in total exhaustion.

"What the hell just happened?"

Judex raised his head. "Indeed. Hell is what happened."

"But the blue light, the Masters?"

Judex nodded. "Answered our call."

There was a sound of scrabbling feet. Jones whirled to see Hilda von Einem emerge from the side of the altar where she had been cowering. He saw her stretch out an arm towards the casket and, in a reflex action he whipped his wallet from his pocket, took out the dart and threw it at her. It struck her on her exposed shoulder and hung like a black, feathered growth. She gave a yell of pain, snatched it out of her skin, looked at it, and with a snarl of anger dropped to her knees.

She glared across at Judex and hissed through clenched teeth. "Damn you. Damn you." And then she choked, coughed blood, gave a series of juddering spasms and fell to the stone floor, dead.

Jones let out a great woof of breath. "Well, she won't get away with it this time." He pointed down the aisle. "What about him? What about Mocata?"

Judex struggled to his feet. "What about him?"

"He'll get away?

Judex laughed, a horrible sound. "Let the Devil look after his own." He swayed and nearly fell again, then caught himself and went to the altar. He scooped up the casket. "Come," he shouted. "Let's get out of here before…?"

Jones didn't need the rest of the sentence. They made a stumbling, tripping, headlong dash back to the Delage and threw themselves into it. Judex jabbed the started and passed the casket to Jones.

"I will dispose of this in the proper manner."

"Just stamp the damned thing under you boot, or better still burn it."

Judex shook his head. "It must be destroyed according to ritual by those who understand these things."

"And you don't?"

"No. But I know one who does. Sâr Dubnotal. He is an Ipsissimus of the Right Hand Path."

Jones tucked a rug around his shoulders. "You get any more bright ideas like that one, call someone else."

It was nearly a week later when a taxi pulled up outside Judex' apartment. He got out. He was carrying a cloth-wrapped bundle. He glanced up at the evening sky, smiled secretively and went inside.

In his study, he laid the bundle on his desk, took a panatela cigar from a silver humidor, lit it and unwrapped the bundle. It was the ivory casket.

He opened the lid, looked long and hard at what it contained, then, shutting the lid he carried the casket to his safe and locked it inside.

He drew on his cigar, inspected the ash and, going to his desk sat down and leaned back.

"Waste not want not," he murmured.

213

1927. The tide of history proves nearly unstoppable when Judex tries to stop Germany from using the awesome power of an artifact which was once one of the prized Four Treasures of the French Crown, later collected by Arsène Lupin. This adventure can, in fact, be read as a sequel of sorts to The Secret of Sarek, *one of the gentleman-thief's most harrowing sagas...*

Matthew Dennion: *Training Day*

Inside the Institut de Recherches Scientifiques Perenna, located on the Left Bank of Paris in the opulent 16th Arrondissement, Professor George Edward Challenger scratched the chin under his long beard as he jotted down notes from his latest experiment.

The enigmatic professor had recently been asked to come and lend his expertise in the study of the so called God-Stone of Sarek. Challenger's research had confirmed his suspicions that the stone's radioactivity had the potential to become a tremendous source of energy. While these initial findings intrigued him, his research had also suggested that the energy from the God-Stone could be used to create a weapon of unimaginable destructive capabilities.

Challenger's previous experiences had taught him the value of balancing the potential dangers of new discoveries against their benefits.

The Professor had just finished writing his notes when the doors to the laboratory were smashed off of their hinges. On the threshold stood a massive being whose appearance was more akin to that of a Neanderthal than an ordinary human being.

"Professor Challenger, allow me to introduce myself," he said, stepping forward. "My name is Grun. I am here for the God-Stone, your research, and your life."

The German charged the Professor. Challenger responded with a primal scream which belied his intellect and ran toward his attacker. From the skylight above, unnoticed, a shadowy figure watched as the two combatants collided.

Grun threw a punch which Challenger ducked. Then, in one fluid motion, Challenger wrapped his arms around his opponent's leg and, with the strength of a small Hercules, lifted him into the air, then slammed him to the ground. The Professor pounced on his opponent, using his barrel chest to hold Grun down. He delivered a series of blows to the German's face.

"Apparently you were unaware of my days as a collegiate wrestling champion!" he bragged.

Challenger was still pummeling his attacker into submission when a shot rang out over his head. On the threshold now stood Challenger's lab assistant and several other men. A puzzled look ran across the Professor's face as he saw his assistant brandishing a pistol.

"Prunesti? What's the meaning of this?" the scientist inquired.

Lorenzo Prunesti gestured for his men to surround Challenger.

"Please release my associate, Professor. I am afraid that your services are no longer required here. You have uncovered a great many secrets of the God-Stone. However, it is now time for it to return to the Fatherland where I and other German scientists will uncover the destructive power you have stumbled upon. Don't bother denying it, Professor. I played the simple errand boy, but I am quite aware of your recent findings." Prunesti lowered his gun on the Professor's head. "Goodbye, Professor. Germany thanks you for your work on her behalf..."

Before Prunesti could pull the trigger, a loud crash echoed through the laboratory. Shards of glass rained down on those below. Prunesti saw a cloaked figure fall from the sky and land on two of his men, knocking them unconscious.

Judex spun and delivered a backhanded fist to one of the men standing near him. Grun rushed to attack the vigilante, but was stopped in his tracks when Challenger punched him in the stomach, following it with an uppercut to the jaw.

Judex dashed across the room, grabbed the Professor, and dived behind one of the tables. Bullets tore into it as the crime-fighter handed Challenger one of his pistols. The two men fired at their assailants but remained pinned down. In the midst of the battle, Prunesti yelled:

"Forget them. We came for the Stone. Grab it and leave!"

One of the men grabbed the God-Stone while the others rushed out of the lab. Grun was the last man through the door. As he exited, he punched the door frame, smashing the supporting beams underneath. The wall collapsed preventing Judex and Challenger from going after the spies.

Judex helped Challenger to his feet.

"I am sorry I could not intervene earlier. I had to wait until they were in a position where I could take several of them out quickly."

Challenger shook his head.

"We need to retrieve that stone. If the Germans discover its true power, the consequences for the rest of the world will be cataclysmic."

"I agree," said Judex. "I will do my utmost to stop them."

"There are quite a few of them," sighed the Professor. "Let me contact the owner of the stone. He may be able to help you."

The Island of Sarek, where the God-Stone had once lain dormant for centuries, had been abandoned since the massacre which occurred there nearly a decade prior. Arsène Lupin had assumed control of it, and was now using its isolation to assist an old friend.

Lupin had long ago studied martial arts under the tutelage of the great Huo Yuanjia. During his training, he had become friends with Yuanjia's most prized pupil, Chen Zhen. Yuanjia had been murdered shortly after Lupin had left the school, and it was Zhen who had tracked down their master's murderer and exacted revenge, nearly dying in the process. Lupin's considerable resources had saved his life. When Zhen's health had returned, he assumed their former master's role as head instructor at the school. Their friendship aside, Lupin always felt that he owed Zhen a debt of honor for avenging the murder of their teacher.

With this in mind, when Zhen reached out to Lupin for assistance, the Frenchman could not refuse. Zhen's school had become involved in a feud with another martial arts school. Zhen did not offer to explain the nature of the feud and, out of respect, Lupin never questioned him on the topic. Looking to avoid the bloodshed of an all out war between the two schools, Zhen had offered to face the master of the rival school in single combat to settle the matter. All that remained was to find a neutral location to host the battle.

When Zhen had consulted Lupin on the matter, the Frenchman suggested moving the battle out of China entirely and offered to host it on the legendary Island of Sarek. Given that it was a neutral location, with an aura of mysticism surrounding it, both parties agreed that it would be an ideal location for the epic confrontation, and opted to make the long journey.

Large numbers of members from both schools had descended upon the island to see the two masters settle the matter of honor. When the time of the battle was at hand, Lupin stood in as the second for his long-time friend. The man that Zhen was facing was known as Pai Mei, a master of the Bak Mei form of Kung Fu.

The two masters walked to the center of the arena, bowed, and then the battle began. The gathered schools watched in awe as the two masters exchanged blows, kicks, and defensive postures. After a long and difficult fight, Zhen finally defeated his opponent. The two men bowed to each other and left the arena. The feud had been settled.

Zhen no sooner returned to his friend than a man came sprinting up from the beach toward the gathered crowd. He approached Lupin and addressed him, using his then-current alias of "Don Luis Perenna":

"I beg your pardon, Don Luis, but this urgent telegraph arrived for you."

Lupin quickly reviewed Challenger's message detailing the events relating to the God-Stone. He had to wonder if it was a mere coincidence that it had been stolen on the very same day that he had reopened the island, as if some higher power was controlling the situation.

Lupin relayed the contents of the telegraph to Zhen and begged his forgiveness for having to leave so soon after the battle. Zhen bowed to his friend and replied, addressing him with the name Lupin had used when he was a young man:

"Raoul, if what you have told me of this stone is true, you must not waste time returning to Paris. A train will take too long to get you there. Come with me; one of my students may be able to help you."

The two men walked to the beach where stood a young man and a boy, training at the water's edge. Both were Caucasian and dressed in black outfits.

The man had piercing eyes which sat above a hawk-like nose. The boy was a handsome young man, whose face bore a grim look of focus and determination. Zhen approached the two.

"Excuse me, Mr. Allard," he said to the older man, "I need to speak to you for a moment." He turned to the young boy and added: "Bruce, please continue your exercises while I speak to your mentor. Monsieur Lupin, may I introduce Kent Allard? Mr. Allard is my most highly-prized pupil. He is also an excellent aviator. During The Great War, he flew for your country under the name of The Black Eagle. His training with me is complete. You may use my plane, and I am confident that no pilot will return you to Paris faster than him. Furthermore, he is also a skilled and fearless fighter. I feel he will be of assistance to you in your quest to regain the God-Stone. I also suspect that, given Mr. Allard's ultimate goal, he may be able to learn something from you as well."

Allard bowed.

"Master, of course I will go where you ask me to—but what about my pu-pil?"

Zhen smiled.

"Ah', yes, young Bruce. He is a most promising student…"

Allard breathed deeply,

"Master, I fear I am responsible for the boy. Not only is he my pupil, but I was acquainted with his mother prior to her death. I feel that in leaving him, I may dishonor her memory."

Zhen put his hand on Allard's shoulder.

"Kent, you are my best student. If what you have told me of your goals is true, you must leave all sense of attachment to others behind. Go with Monsieur Lupin, learn from him, and continue progressing toward your objective. You can fly through the air like an eagle; he can teach you to move through the darkness as a Black Shadow. Fear not for your protégé. I personally will train the boy. We have much in common. He feels the same need for justice over the murder of his parents that I did for my teacher. I will treat him as my own son."

Allard bowed once more.

"Thank you master."

Lupin bowed to Zhen as well.

"Thank you, *mon ami*."

With that the two men headed for the small plane parked on the beach nearby.

When Allard and Lupin returned to the Institute, they found a police in-spector named Maigret still investigating the site.

Lupin introduced himself as Don Luis Perenna, founder and owner of the institute. As the two discussed the events of the previous night, Allard studied the master thief. He was amazed at how easily the man changed from one identi-ty to the next. The transition from Lupin to Perenna had been instantaneous and complete. Lupin applied no manner of disguise, but rather changed his very mannerisms, expressions, speech, and posture. Allard thought that had he not walked into the Institute with the man, he would have a difficult time believing Arsène Lupin and Don Luis Perenna were one and the same. Allard committed to memory the effectiveness of switching identities as well as the methods Lupin used to transform himself. He was sure that he could apply the same techniques himself if and when he needed to.

While Lupin listened to Maigret, his attention seemed to be elsewhere, as if he was looking at something in the distance. Eventually, he thanked the inspector and returned to talk to Allard.

"The police have sealed off most routes out of the city, so it would seem unlikely that the Germans escaped. Otherwise, the information the inspector supplied me with was the same as in Challenger's message. It seems, however, that the good Professor neglected to inform the police that a third party was involved in last night's activities. Let us discover what he can tell us."

Judex was crouched on the rooftop of the church Notre Dame de Grâce de Passy. From this vantage point, he had watched the entire interaction between Don Luis and Maigret from a distance. Then, he lost sight of Perenna and his companion when they stepped around a corner and seemed to disappear. The crime-fighter headed down the stairs of the church, but when he reached the main floor, he found Perenna and his companion seated in the pews, waiting for him.

"Judex, is it not?" said Lupin, smiling. "We have not been introduced, I am Don Luis Perenna…"

Judex cut him off.

"I know who you are. You are the thief commonly known as Arsène Lupin! I also recognize your companion. I am not surprised to find Mr. Allard in your company. The last time I spoke to him, he was behind bars."

"I take it that the vigilante does not approve of the thief?" grinned Lupin.

"No," replied Judex, sternly. "I punish all those who hurt the innocent, but I have never sought to enrich myself…"

"You don't need to, having the Trémeuse fortune at your disposal. Not everyone is so lucky," said Lupin, with a disarming smile.

Judex nodded, as if to acknowledge that his opponent had won this bout.

"True," he said. "I have looked closely at your escapades, Monsieur Lupin. Those you steal from are far worse criminals than yourself. You and I are cut from the same cloth, after all. We both understand the need to operate on the wrong side of the law to see justice done."

"Indeed, and since we are reviewing each other's resumes, may I congratulate you on the methods which you used to handle that despicable banker. Now, we should attend to the business at hand. What can you tell us about the theft of the God-Stone? I assume that you have been keeping tabs on the German spies who stole it."

Judex took a moment to compose his thoughts.

"Yes. They appear to be affiliated with a growing political movement in Germany called the National-Socialist party. There were seven men who broke into the institute; two were arrested by the police after the battle. The remaining five met up with five more accomplices after the raid and fled into the sewers. They are trying to avoid police detection as they make their way to the Canal Saint-Martin and, from there, out of Paris. They are led by a man who passed himself off as Professor Challenger's lab assistant. His name is Lorenzo Prunesti. He is a brilliant scientist in his own right and a ruthless gangster as well. They are accompanied by a man-mountain named Herr Grun, about whom I have little information."

"I know of him," said Allard. "I've had several runs in with him while flying missions with G-8 during the War. He has amazing physical attributes, including immense strength and incredible durability. I once saw him stuck by three bullets during a battle. Despite his wounds, he kept fighting as if he had merely been bitten by a mosquito."

Lupin turned towards Judex.

"I take it that you have not alerted the Police as to the whereabouts of the spies?"

"No," Judex replied, shaking his head. "Sending them into the sewers would only get them killed. They would move through the tunnels without cover, and the Germans would gun them down without mercy. Besides, to them, a simple robbery would not be worth such a massive effort. Whereas I assume that you, on the other hand, are well aware of the potential destructive power of the God-Stone. When I realized the true identity of Don Luis Perenna, I thought that you and I would be better suited to apprehend these Germans without the intervention of the police. Mr. Allard is a welcome addition to our small force."

Lupin paced the floor of the church as he ran over the details of the task before them,

"In short, we are outmanned, outgunned, and outmuscled. We are also looking at engaging this superior force in a dark, confined area. Judex, do you have an idea where in the sewers can we find these spies?"

Judex removed a map of the Paris sewer system from under his cloak.

"There are several main tunnels that would be large enough for a group of men that size to move through. Only a few lead to the Canal, where they will surely attempt to rendezvous with a boat to carry them out of Paris. Currently, the Seine is at high tide, and most tunnels will be flooded. Therefore, the Germans can only be here," he said, pointing at a spot on the map, "waiting for the tides to change in the next three hours. When the tide goes out, they will make their move for the Canal. Attacking them at the intersection will be difficult with their numbers. They can defend themselves from all sides."

"Yes, a frontal attack would be suicide," said Lupin running his hand across his chin. "Instead, let's make them come to us..." He shifted his gaze between Judex and Allard. "Our advantages are our wits and the element of surprise." Lupin walked up to Judex and grabbed his cloak. "The cloak, hat, overcoat, all of these things are designed not only to make you appear larger, but serve to scare and confuse your opponent when they look at you?" Judex silently nodded, as Lupin continued: "A wise use of theatrics. Thugs such as those we are facing tend to be a cowardly and superstitious lot. I see that you and Mr. Allard are roughly the same height and build. Do you by any chance have a spare outfit to match this one?"

"I have one nearby in one of my hideaways," said Judex, looking at Allard. "It's identical to the one I am wearing, with the exception that it is entirely black."

"That will do fine, especially in the sewer system. Well, Mr. Allard, what was it that Chen said I would turn you into, a Black Shadow? Yes, I think that description will fit perfectly. Judex, do you know of a few men with strong backs and who won't ask questions that would be willing to do a couple hours' worth of work?"

"There are several men whom I have assisted over the years who would be more than willing to help me."

"Excellent! Mr. Allard, there is one more thing I will need from you. It occurs to me that you have a rather ominous voice. I think that can be useful to us."

Allard sat and took in every word that the two men spoke. He had learned more in the past few moments about fighting crime than he could have in a decade on his own. He once believed that being a powerful fighter was all he would need to wage a war on criminals. These men used psychological ploys against their enemies, and incorporated a network of assistants to help at a moment's notice. He committed all that he had learned to memory for use in his forthcoming endeavors.

Three hours later, in the sewers of Paris, Prunesti and his men prepared to make their way to the Canal Saint-Martin and meet the boat that would take them back to Germany. Prunesti felt that delivering the God-Stone to the new leader of the Party would assure him a high-ranking office in the coming regime. He could see the party taking over Germany, and then the rest of the world, with him answering only to the leader himself.

The group walked through the tunnels with Prunesti and Grun flanked by men both in front of and behind them.

"Soon, Herr Grun!" said Prunesti. "Soon, we will unlock the secrets of the God-Stone, and the Party shall rise to power. You and I will be hailed as the heroes who made the ascension possible."

Before Grun could respond, a blood chilling laugh echoed through the tunnels, causing the group to stop in their tracks. As they scanned their surroundings, the sound of gunfire ripped through the darkness and the man in the front fell backwards into the dirty water, dead from a bullet to the heart.

When the gun flashed, the Germans saw a cloaked figure with a slouched hat in front of them.

"The man from the Institute! Kill him!" screamed Prunesti.

The cloaked figure jumped down a side tunnel as gunfire exploded again. After a few seconds, the Germans stopped firing. There was silence for a second, and then the ominous laugh once more echoed through the darkness.

The Germans were staring in front of them when, suddenly, two men at the rear of the group fell dead from gunshots to the head. They spun around and fired as the blood of their comrades flowed over their feet. As they shot, once more the laugh echoed, and yet another shot rang out, from the front, causing another spy to fall dead in the water.

One of the remaining men screamed that they were under attack from a ghost. With the thought of a supernatural enemy in mind, the Germans began firing wildly, in every direction. From the small cover provided by adjacent tunnels, the two cloaked figures continued to fire on the group of terrified spies from both sides with deadly accuracy. Within ten minutes, all that remained of their group were Prunesti and Grun.

Judex fired his last bullet and grazed the massive Grun across the shoulder. He heard a scream of pain, but no further shots followed. The crime-fighter realized that Allard—the Black Shadow—must also have been out of bullets. But the meaning of the lack of gunfire had dawned on Prunesti too.

"Quickly, they're out of ammunition," he shouted to Grun. "We must make a run for the Canal."

The two dashed down the tunnel in which Judex was hiding. The vigilante jumped in the path of the two Nazis. Prunesti shrieked.

"Grun, kill him! I must get the God-Stone to the boat!"

The giant lumbered toward Judex while Prunesti ran down the second tunnel leading out of the sewer system.

Judex sprang forward and landed a sidekick to Grun's chin. The blow had no effect. Grun simply smiled at Judex and reached out to grab him. Before his massive hands could reach the vigilante, the Black Shadow leaped onto Grun's back, wrapping his arms around the gargantuan neck.

Grun snarled and threw himself into the wall, crushing the Black Shadow between him and the unforgiving stones. The Black Shadow slid off of Grun's back as the air was forcibly expelled from his lungs.

Once more Judex attacked, delivering a series of punches and kicks to Grun's midsection. The giant simply continued to walk forward as if he was battling a child rather than one of the most dangerous men in the world. Judex jumped backwards as Grun reached for him. His speed and agility were his only physical advantages over the brute. As the battle continued down the tunnel, the Black Shadow crept up behind Grun and delivered a powerful roundhouse kick to his ribs. Grun spun around and threw a back-handed strike which missed Allard's head by inches and buried itself in the wall.

The Black Shadow sprinted past Grun and stood side-by-side with Judex, appearing as if he were a dark reflection of the vigilante. Grun laughed.

"You fools can't defeat me. All you can do is annoy me and continue to leap out of my range, but now you both have your backs to the Canal. It's only a matter of time until I catch you—or drown you!"

Prunesti, still clutching the God-Stone, could smell the fresh air of the Canal in front of him as he continued down the tunnel. Through the opening at the end, he could even see a small patch of night sky. As he approached the end of the tunnel, a shape started to come into view. From the distance, Prunesti could see what appeared to be a man standing just in front of him. The German drew his gun. When he was a few meters away, he recognized the man. They both had their guns pointed at each other.

"Don Luis Perenna," said Prunesti. "I must admit, I am amazed that you were able to find me here."

"Your amazement at me finding you may be diminished if I give you my real name. I am Arsène Lupin!"

Prunesti's eyes widened at the revelation and his jaw slacked. Lupin took a bow and continued:

"Now that we know where we stand, I must commend you as well. Few people have ever attempted to steal from me, and none have yet succeeded, but you have come close. I will ask you once to return the God-Stone to me, and please, know that I am fully aware of the discoveries Professor Challenger has made with respect to its destructive powers. With this knowledge in mind, I cannot, in good conscience, ever let it reach its destructive potential."

Prunesti spat into the water.

"You speak as if the French Government would not use the God-Stone to create their own ultimate weapon! The Nazis are the rightful rulers of this planet, and this stone shall be the instrument of our ascension!"

Prunesti lifted his pistol and fired. Lupin threw his body to the left, causing the bullet to miss him by mere inches. As he fell, he also fired. His shot hit the God-Stone and shattered it into a fine radioactive powder, which flew into Prunesti's face.

The German fell to the ground, clutching his face and screaming in agony. As he writhed in the tunnel, Lupin walked over to him.

"You misunderstood me, Mr. Prunesti. When I said that I could not allow the God-Stone to reach its destructive potential, that statement applied to *all* governments. Once I was made aware of Challenger's findings, I always intended to destroy the stone. The only question was whether you would surrender it to me, or I would be forced to destroy it in your hands. The boat you are searching for is waiting for you at the Bastille. If you can still walk there, you are free to go. I have seen what direct exposure to the God-Stone can do to a man. The pain and disfigurement you are likely to suffer will be a far worse punishment than delivering you to the authorities. Now, if you will excuse me, I need to see how my allies are faring with your beastly accomplice."

Judex punched Grun across the face while the Black Shadow simultaneously kicked the man-monster in his knee. After their attack, the two heroes leapt backwards to avoid Grun's reach.

"We've almost reached the end of the tunnel," the brute snarled. "There's no more room for you to jump away."

Grun charged and the twin warriors ran to the edge of the tunnel. When they reached the opening of the tunnel, the two warriors each jumped out the tunnel at sharp right angles in opposite directions both landing on the slim shoreline of low tide. Grun lumbered out of the tunnel, as his feet landed on the ground directly underneath the tunnel opening, he immediately sank up to his knees in mud. The brute growled and attempted to pull himself free only to sink deeper into the muddy bank of the river.

The Black Shadow stood to the left of Grun, and now, to his right, were Judex and Lupin. Lupin walked close enough to Grun to be just out of the reach of his powerful hands.

"You know, Herr Grun, that today, many paleontologists find the remains of massive beasts from prehistory at the bottom of tar pits. While these beasts possessed immense strength, they were not gifted with intelligence. Often these animals would simply move forward without thought. Sometimes, they would walk directly into one of these tar pits. The soft nature of the pit would turn their size and strength against them. The more they struggled, the deeper they sank into the tar." Lupin knelt down so that he was at eye level with Grun. "Given your limited intelligence, I feel obligated to point out the relevance of this lesson to your current situation. Much like those great beasts of the past, we guessed that, if you were angered, you too would simply rush forward without stopping to examine your surroundings. With this in mind, we set a trap for you.

"Several of Judex's allies agreed to dig a pit at the end of this tunnel. To their credit, they worked in knee-deep water. The pit they dug did not remain an open hole, but rather the sewers filled quickly filled it with soft mud and other materials less worthy of being mentioned, creating an effect similar to that of the tar pits that I have just described. My two associates then enraged you to the point of charging headlong into said trap. Now, let me enlighten as to what options are available to you now. First, you should know that I have destroyed the God-Stone, so your mission is a failure. Now, I want you to take a look over there… Do you see that man climbing onto that boat? That man is your comrade, Herr Prunesti, and the boat is the vessel that was supposed to transport you and your men safely back to Germany. Let us take a minute to see what they do next…"

They watched as Prunesti was pulled aboard and then, they saw the boat slowly move away on the Canal towards the North.

"Sadly, Herr Grun," Lupin continued, "it seems as if your comrade has abandoned you. Since you will not be receiving any assistance, here are the options still available to you. Your first option is to let us contact the police and they will come and free you from the mud. No doubt, you shall eventually be tried and convicted for the crimes you committed. I've heard the weather on Devil's Island can be very slimming. Your second option is to be uncooperative, in which case you will not succeed in freeing yourself from mud pit in which you are currently trapped, and no one will come to your rescue. The good news is that I doubt you will sink much further; however, the tide will eventually come back in. Let me ask you, Herr Grun, exactly how long can you hold your breath?"

Grun mumbled that he would allow the authorities to arrest him.

"Gentlemen, it has been both a pleasure and honor to work with the two of you," said Lupin, bowing to his two associates. "Now, if you will excuse me, I shall contact Monsieur Maigret and alert him to Herr Grun's current predicament."

Lupin climbed out of the tunnel and disappeared into the city streets. The Black Shadow and Judex stood on the Canal's bank, looking at Grun.

"Judex, I have seen the methods you employ in your war on crime," said Allard. "I, too, wish to battle crime, but I still have much to learn. You have seen the skills I possess. Please allow me to work with you for a few months and study your methods so that I may apply them myself when I return to New York."

Judex took a long look over the water prior to answering:

"I will agree to teach you my methods. May I make one suggestion already? 'The Black Shadow' is a bit burdensome. You will need to establish a reputation. Your name will spread more quickly if you shorten it to one word."

A smile crept across Allard's face, and for the first time, the laugh of the Shadow echoed through the night sky.

1929. Dennis Power's novella was originally published as a piece of fan fiction on the official Wold Newton's website, devoted to Philip José Farmer's wonderful amalgam universe of popular literature. Because of its thrills, its scope, and its connection to the Judex, we chose to republish it here in a new, edited and revised version. Both Rick Lai and Emmanuel Gorlier have hinted previously at the mystery of Judex's origins; Dennis Power here takes us on a journey that will stretch to the very dawn of Time...

Dennis E. Power: *The Judex Codex*

1. The Treasure Trove
(Guatemala, 1929)

Elegant fingers softly but deftly stroked.

Raymond Mystère watched this strong, feminine hand with admiration and, with all due honesty, amorous fascination as it moved up and down, holding the shaft in a firm, yet tender grip.

Henrietta de Marigny, a petite, raven-haired beauty was a sorceress, bewitching and enchanting. Raymond thought she worked wonders with the wand in her hand.

Raymond and Henrietta shared a smile as she wove her magic.

"*Bon sang!*" she exclaimed as the shaft in her hand quivered and slipped from her grasp sending a spray into her face.

Henrietta wiped off her lips and nose and with a satisfied smile surveyed her handiwork.

Her expert strokes had thoroughly cleaned the dust and grime from the petroglyph in the tunnel wall, cleanly exposing a line of Mayan pictoglyphs. Yet the brush had caught in an unexpected crack in the wall and spun from her grasp.

Raymond handed Henrietta back her brush with a smile and a bow. She paused as their hands momentarily brushed up against one another. Her blue eyes twinkled as she met his gaze.

Once the brush was in her hand however, she returned to her work with renewed vigor. Upon cleaning out the crack further, she soon realized that it was not a crack at all, but rather a masoned edge. Concentrating her efforts on this edge, rather than on the interior of the petroglyph, she uncovered a rectangular outline punctuated by five circular openings.

This was not an ordinary petroglyph, but a tablet, which had been set into a niche in the tunnel wall. Henrietta was prudent enough not to insert her finger into the round holes, so she reversed her brush and pushed the wooden part into one of the holes. She heard a small click and quickly pressed the brush end into each of the five openings.

Raymond watched this operation with interest, yet kept alert. Feeling a slight gust of wind and a tiny rumble behind him, he leapt forward and pulled Henrietta to the ground, shielding her from harm by lying atop of her.

As he hugged Henrietta, he heard several small objects ping off the stone wall above him.

After the immediate danger had passed, he became all too aware of the full and supple body of the woman beneath him. The unconventional Henrietta had foresworn wearing stifling women's undergarments in the tropical heat, so even through the oversize cotton work shirt and baggy workpants, he felt more than was proper. Not that he was going to complain.

Her luminous blue eyes gleamed with excitement and amusement.

"While I'd like to believe that you swept me off my feet because you were overcome with passion and could no longer withstand my charms, I'm certain that there's another reason."

Raymond chuckled.

"While it's true, I've been struggling not to grab you, I noticed several tiny chips in the stone walls. You triggered a death trap when you pressed the brush into the holes. Apparently, there is a sequence to opening the keystones."

Henrietta raised her head up from the floor and looked over his shoulder at the opposite wall, suddenly noticing that it was pocked with dozens of pinholes.

"Do you think that it would be safe to try and find the combination?"

Raymond shrugged.

"I cannot be certain. It seems that it would, the trap was sprung and needs to be reset."

"Then as pleasant as this may be, we should get back to work."

As Raymond rose from the floor, Henrietta's arms encircled his neck so that as he stood up, he also pulled her to her feet. She kept her arms around his neck after they were upright With a mischievous smile and sparkling eyes she said:

"First, however, my hero deserves a reward."

She covered his lips with hers and crushed her body against his. She kissed him passionately and, when he was quite dizzy, she released him and pushed away from him softly. Smiling playfully, she turned back to the wall.

Her smile faltered a bit when she noticed that the floor beneath the tablet was littered with dozens of feathered darts.

Henrietta de Marigny and Raymond Mystère spent the next couple of hours running through combinations of sequences for the five holes.

As they worked, Raymond wondered if Henrietta knew it truly was a constant struggle for him not to give into the impulse to take her into his arms and smother her with kisses.

Raymond had met Henrietta at the University of the Sorbonne when they were both first classmen. At first, they had not gotten on well together. Despite Henrietta's great beauty, Raymond had considered her too outspoken, too flippant, too saucy and, to be honest, a bit of a tramp. It seemed as though she was continually enamored of visiting professors, such as Henry Jones, Thomas Swift and John Kenton. Although she never seemed to be serious about it, she had flirted with them outrageously.

Later, Henrietta told Raymond that she thought he was aloof, self-centered and humorless.

Gradually, Raymond had realized that the basis for his dislike of Henrietta was jealousy. He was, first and foremost, jealous of her brilliance. It angered him that he had to work much harder than she to keep up his grades. Once he had come to terms with the knowledge that she was more brilliant than he, Raymond also realized that his dislike of her was a denial of his true feelings. He liked her all too much. Her many flirtations bothered him deeply because they had never been directed at him. Raymond realized that he had fallen for Henrietta the first time he had ever seen her. The first day of the semester she had walked into Professor Metraux's lecture when it was half over. He had been angered the Professor had asked her to come down and finish lecturing to the class about the discovery of the Neanderthal. Without missing a beat, Henrietta had taken over the class and even answered questions.

Yet, she seemed oblivious to his interest in her. When it was announced that Henrietta would be graduating top of their class, he had sent her a bouquet of a dozen red and white roses. He congratulated her and told her that he regretted that their relationship had been so adversarial.

After graduation, Henrietta and Raymond were among two doctoral candidates chosen to study under the great Professor Pierre Montet. They had worked together on several archaeological projects. Their earlier rivalry evaporated and they became close friends. It was Raymond to whom Henrietta had turned to for comfort when she received news that her brother had vanished.

Etienne-Laurent de Marigny was also an archaeologist, although he specialized in what could be called arcane archaeology. His friend, Pierre d'Artois, had cultivated Etienne's interest in this aspect of archaeology. Henrietta was not so fond of Pierre d'Artois, even though he had saved her life once. A madman named Don Jose had kidnapped her to sacrifice to some dark god. Don Jose had previously abducted and killed Henrietta's twin sister, Louise, but his god had not been satisfied and so he had later gone after Henrietta. She believed that it was their father's acquaintance with Pierre d'Artois, combined with the latter's occult fascination, that had contributed to her sister's death and her brother Henri's disappearance. While Henrietta had cut ties with Pierre d'Artois, Etienne-Laurent's had become something of a protégé to him.

It was through Pierre d'Artois' influence that Etienne-Laurent had attended and earned his degree at the prestigious Miskatonic University in the United

States. Etienne had dropped out of sight in 1926 while investigating some ruins in the swamps of Louisiana. He believed that the inhabitants were a remnant of a Tcho-Tcho group that had come to North America during the Asian Migration. His disappearance had worried his friends and family; yet, Etienne-Laurent had turned up a few weeks later, none the worse for the wear—physically at least. However he had been emotionally and psychologically distraught. Etienne had investigated a group of people who claimed to be Cajuns, but whom he believed were descendents of the Tcho-Tcho. They had not taken a liking to his claims and locked him away in a cage near an alligator pen until he recanted. After this incident, Etienne-Laurent put his talents towards collecting, authenticating and selling artifacts, opening up a shop in New Orleans for this purpose.

During the period that Etienne was missing, the friendship between Henrietta and Raymond had deepened.

On this latest trip to Central America, their friendship had become something of a romance. Raymond used propriety as his excuse not to initiate a full-blown affair with Henrietta. It would not be seemly for them to become involved while on a dig. Yet, he knew it was simply cowardice. Raymond thought that Henrietta felt the same way about him as he did about her, but was afraid to find out. He once had faced down a group of gun-toting angry villagers who believed he was pilfering their sacred burial grounds; yet, he was afraid of the pain that this petite woman's words could very well cause him.

However, he found it harder and harder to keep thoughts of love at bay. Even now, as Henrietta bent over and pushed the end of the brush into the chiseled holes, his eyes lingered on her rather than the work. How kissable her lips seemed, pouted in concentration; how her shimmering black hair beckoned to be stroked; how her work clothes grew taut in the most delectable manner...

Several clicks and a rumbling behind the stone tablet broke his daydreaming. With a grating of stone on stone, the tablet was pushed forward from the wall. The tablet was two and a half-feet long and one and a half foot wide. It was much lighter than Raymond thought, weighing perhaps ten pounds.

Before they stepped away from the area near the tablet, Raymond told Henrietta:

"I don't know if our first incorrect combination triggered any other death traps, so be alert. Be careful and expect anything to happen."

"Anything?" she asked, wagging her eyebrows and giggling. At his exasperated look, she lightly slapped his arm. "Don't be so grumpy, I'll be careful."

Raymond carried the tablet under one arm. His other hand was grasped by Henrietta, who carried a lantern in her other hand. Slowly and cautiously, they made their way through the tunnels leading out of the Mayan temple.

When they had traveled approximately five yards, Henrietta suddenly stopped short. Pausing for a second, she jerked Raymond forward as hard as she could. There was a blast of air behind him accompanied by a stinging sensation in the back of his thighs.

A large flat stone disc attached to a pendulum swung in the tunnel behind him. The disc was made of razor sharp flint.

Five yards later, it was Raymond who suddenly dropped Henrietta's hand, grabbed her waist and jumped backwards. Several obsidian tipped stakes jutted up from the floor where she had been standing.

Gingerly, they threaded their way through the ankle-high stakes. They entered a mysterious dip in the tunnel that no one had been able to explain with any degree of certainty. The tunnel abruptly narrowed and then slanted downwards, exiting in a concave room. At the other end of the room was a tunnel that abruptly slanted upwards.

Raymond heard the distant trickling of water. When they reached the concave room, the floor was covered with a liquid that poured from a hole in the ceiling. The liquid was mineral oil, Raymond had the thought to pause but Henrietta strode rapidly into the concave room as if trying to get through it before the level of the liquid rose. Grinding crashes came from in front and in back of them. They retraced their steps to find that they could no longer exit the room the way they had entered. A stone slab covered the tunnel mouth. Henrietta and he hurried forward sloshing through the ankle deep liquid towards the other exit only to discover that another stone slab had slid down to block that outlet.

They examined the room for any means of escape, but could find none. It was smooth and round.

As mineral oil continued to pour into the room, Raymond blew out the lantern.

The only way out of the room was through the hole in the ceiling where the mineral oil poured in. The ceiling was about eleven feet above them.

The mineral oil finally stopped pouring into the room when the oil was waist-high to Raymond and nearly covered Henrietta's impressive chest.

"You'll have to climb up the hole in the ceiling and either send a rope down or go get help."

"And leave you here to perhaps drown. Because you are the man and I the woman, I must be the first to be saved? No, we're in this together." Hands on hips she glared at him, as if incensed for even suggesting she leave him alone.

"It's not because of chivalry but simple pragmatism, I can't reach the hole and you can't lift me high enough but I can lift you high enough"

Henrietta's eyes darted to the hole, to Raymond and to the lake of oil. The war between emotion and reasoning played across her face. As she calculated their odds of escape, her eyes glimmered with frustration and a hint of fear as her gaze rested upon his face. He realized that her fear was not about anything that might happen to her, but rather for him. Raymond knew, without a doubt at that moment, that Henrietta loved him, for what she feared most was losing him.

She gave a prodigious sigh that momentarily distracted Ramon from their dire situation. Henrietta bit her lip and blinked back tears as she pushed her emotions aside letting her rational mind take control. With a firm jaw, she said:

"You're right. Lift me up. If possible I'll find a place to cache the tablet, then return to throw the rope down to you. As a last resort I'll return to camp and get more rope and help."

Raymond squatted so Henrietta could climb onto his shoulders. With her feet on his broad shoulders, her finger tips reached the lip of the opening in the ceiling. When she was steady, he grasped her legs and lifted her up an additional six inches. Now able to reach her arms up to her elbows, Henrietta pulled herself inside and looked around.

"Raymond, the hole is a tunnel about three feet wide, however it seems to run vertically with a slight slant, so there's no place to cache the supplies or to tie a rope. I'm coming back down."

Raymond caught Henrietta in his arms as she dropped down. Any other time she would have made some flirtatious remark, but now she was all business and jumped from his arms back into the mineral oil pond. He emptied their rucksack and pulled out the eight-foot length rope that they had brought with them. Henrietta tied one end of the rope around her waist and wrapped most of its length around her; Raymond tied one end of the rope around the tablet and cinched it to her waist. As he lifted her once more, she grabbed his head and gave him a kiss so passionate that he felt fortunate that the oil surrounding them did not ignite.

Henrietta pulled herself into the tunnel and slowly climbed it by bracing her arms, legs and back against the walls of the small tunnel, finding slight purchases in the cracks between the stones.

Shortly after Henrietta had entered the ceiling tunnel, Raymond heard pebbles falling from the ceiling near the blocked exits. He saw a pebble shoot out of a finger sized hole. It flew with sufficient velocity to strike the other wall. He looked about the room and counted nineteen such holes.

He wondered about this new torture. Were the pebbles to fall in sufficient quantities to gradually raise the level of oil and slowly drown the victim? If so, Raymond believed he had little to fear on that account, his six-foot frame was much taller than the typical Mayan; where they would drown, he would merely feel uncomfortable.

When he caught one of the pebbles, it stung his hand. He saw with a bit of a shock that the pebbles were flint. If a sufficient enough number of them fell as the mineral oil rose; a sparking flint could set fire to the oil.

Raymond waded back to the spot underneath the hole in the ceiling and hoped for Henrietta's return.

After what seemed like hours, a line dropped out of the hole. It hung about three feet above his head. The liquid about his waist impacted his ability to jump and it took several tries before he grabbed the line. He felt it give a bit and then stop.

He heard Henrietta curse.

"*Mon Dieu*, you are a heavy one! Hurry, my sweet, hurry"

Raymond felt the line giving as he climbed. Although it did not register at first, he realized that he was not climbing a robe but a line made of soft cloth.

Once he had poked his head into the tunnel mouth, what he saw almost made him lose his grip. The beautiful and voluptuous Henrietta de Marigny crouched in the tunnel, completely nude but for her boots and the line tied around her waist.

She gave him a look that was part annoyance and part amusement.

"My darling, I promise you that you may have a much longer and closer look, but you are so damned heavy, please hurry before you pull us both down."

Henrietta held herself in the tunnel with all of her might, her arms and legs quivered with effort and exertion. He swung himself into the tunnel and braced himself. With his greater size, it was less of an effort. He crawled up to Henrietta and told her to rest on him for a moment. Without a word, she let herself fall against his broad chest and curled up against him, breathing heavily.

Raymond knew that Henrietta was nearly exhausted because she only gave him a tired smile when noticing him where his eyes rested.

Henrietta lay against his chest for a few moments before she reluctantly pushed herself up. She was very tired and needed to pause every few minutes and support herself against Raymond. He kept his eyes on the walls when she leaned back against him, since bracing himself against the tunnel walls was hard enough without additional distractions. As they climbed, Raymond asked, "What became of the other rope?"

Chest heaving with exertion, she breathed, "The tunnel is only one of our problems."

After they had laboriously climbed most of the way out of the narrow tunnel, Henrietta stopped and slowly turned around to face Raymond.

"Hold me up."

She tied the other end of the line around his waist, then crawled out of the tunnel mouth and turned around backwards. Henrietta disappeared. Raymond climbed further up and saw that the tunnel ended in a small stone ledge, a semi-circle about two feet wide and long. There was a three-inch lip around the edge of the semi-circle. The small ledge projected over a sheer cliff He peered over the edge and saw Henrietta was climbing down the mountain face. Looking downward, she did not see him and shouted:

"Get as close to the edge as you can!"

The rope tautened as all her weight pulled on his waist. She cursed in a very unladylike fashion.

"I'm climbing back up!"

When there was enough slack on the line, Raymond stood and pulled Henrietta up to him. When she was near enough, he grabbed her about the waist and sat down on the ledge with her on his lap. Untying the rope from his waist, he very carefully removed his shirt and draped it over her abraded shoulders. He knew that she might be warm and perspiring but would be chilled as soon as her body cooled.

Henrietta smiled as he draped the shirt over her shoulders and leaned back against his chest to provide him with warmth.

When she had sufficiently regained her strength, Henrietta said:

"I hurried out the tunnel and nearly fell to my death. I tumbled over the edge but caught the ledge's lip with one hand. The rope around my waist came loose and the tablet fell down, nearly pulling me down with it. When I tried to pull myself up, I soon found that the tablet was caught on something below. It wouldn't work loose and I had to untie the rope from my waist so I could get back onto the ledge. Since I was worried about you, I hurriedly made a rope of my clothing and rushed down to rescue you".

After they had rested a few moments, Henrietta slipped off of his lap and began sliding into the shaft.

"I'm going back into the tunnel so you'll have plenty of room to disrobe."

"What! Why do I need to take off my clothes?"

"I can nearly reach the tablet to work it loose but I need three more feet; your shirt and pants should provide that extra three feet."

"I have a longer reach. I can climb down the cliff and get the tablet"

Henrietta shook her head forcefully.

"There's nothing to tie the rope onto and I'm don't think I have the strength to bear your weight again."

Grinning wickedly, she poked him in the stomach with her finger.

"So my fine Monsieur, it is alright for me to stand about naked, yet you re-fuse to return the honor. For shame!" She shrugged out of his shirt. "Here is your shirt, should I also remove your pants?"

Raymond held up a hand, "Thank you Mademoiselle, I believe I can man-age that by myself"

"Of course you can, but it surely would not be as fun," she said with a gig-gle and went back into the tunnel.

Raymond disrobed and tied his shirt and pants onto the rope of Henrietta's clothes. She emerged from the tunnel and looked him over. Her brow arched and she gave him a quizzical look.

Following her gaze, Raymond quickly, retorted. "It's chilly up here!"

Henrietta laughed and blew him a kiss.

"That was not a critical look, *mon chéri!*"

Raymond moved into the tunnel to give Henrietta room to climb over the ledge and down the cliff face. He moved closer to the edge to give her as much line as possible and also to watch her progress. Once she had the tablet in her hands, he began hauling her up the cliff.

Once she was back on the ledge, she hugged him tightly and then sat down to disassemble the rope she had made. When she was finished unraveling the rope, she handed him his shirt and pants, remarking:

"You'll have to get back in the hole while I get dressed."

They took turns dressing on the small shelf of stone. Henrietta's clothes were ripped and torn from having been scraped against the stone walls of the tunnel and from being used as a rope.

Raymond averted his eyes from a hole in her shirt from which something rather interesting protruded, and looked for a way down the mountain. Below the shelf loomed a sheer cliff face, naked granite rock stretching hundreds of feet straight down. Beyond this spread a wooded area and a river that cut through the canyon. Above them was another sheer cliff; however, directly above the shelf was a groove cut into the rock face. This was about six inches wide and two deep. He believed that this was how the mineral oil had been channeled into the tunnel. The groove did not look as though it would provide any hand or foot holds, so climbing up would not be any safer than climbing down the sheer rock walls.

Henrietta had not noticed any handholds or ladders near the shelf when she had climbed down the line to retrieve the tablet. However, just under the shelf there was a foot wide projection of a cliff face that stretched around the curve of the cliff.

Raymond tied the tablet to his back, lowered Henrietta down to the small cliff that jutted out from the cliff face and climbed down to join her. Hugging the cliff face, they slowly and carefully worked their way around the sheer cliff.

For once, fortune smiled upon them. Just beyond the curve, the foot-wide projection widened to become a large cliff. After walking a short distance across the larger cliff, they found a trail leading down to the wooded area and the river below the mountain. Raymond was not certain, but believed that they were on the opposite side of the mountain from where the temple and their camp were located.

As they walked down the trail, Raymond said:

"I wonder if there will be a welcoming committee of hostiles when we reach the foot of the mountain."

Henrietta gave him a puzzled look, wondering if he were being facetious.

Smiling, Raymond said, "For all of your brilliance, you are naïve sometimes, or else you focus so intently on the project at hand that you ignore peripheral evidence. Once the first trap was sprung, I realized that it explained some of the puzzling marks and stains on the tunnel walls, which suggest that the traps have been sprung before. Since they were active for us, they must have been reset. The lack of skeletons is also telling. This points to an active presence in the temple, probably a cult of some type. Hopefully, by surviving the traps we have proven that we deserve the tablet. I doubt it, however."

Henrietta gave him a wan smile and squeezed his thick shoulder affectionately.

"My cheery hero!" With a wink and a grin, she added, "Well, don't you worry. I'll protect you and won't let any beautiful High Priestess have her way with you."

The trail ended abruptly at a spire of rock that jutted over the river. There had been a rope bridge connecting this rock spire to another across the canyon; however, it had been cut.

Henrietta looked all around the spire after they had rested for a moment. It was late afternoon and the Sun would be setting soon. She threw a rock over the side of the cliff.

"It seems we must either climb down or jump."

"Well, I know I could certainly use a bath. Last one to the other side of the river is a rotten egg!"

With a laugh, Henrietta dove off of the cliff to the river some fifty feet below.

"Damn the woman!" Raymond cursed her impulsiveness. There was no way to know how deep the river was or how strong it was! He made certain the tablet was securely tied to his back before he made his leap.

Henrietta landed with a large splash and sank. She broke the surface seconds later, grinning and waving up at Raymond. He watched her swim a few feet and then stand up in waist-high water. She slogged through the water towards the river bank. Raymond was so distracted by how fetchingly her ragged wet clothes clung to her body that he failed to see five men erupt from the woods and grab her. Or rather make the attempt to do so. Despite being petite, Henrietta was rather strong and knew how to fight. She held them off. However, she was severely outnumbered and it was only a matter of time before she was captured.

Raymond Mystère quickly untied and unwrapped the rope securing the tablet to his waist and jumped off of the cliff.

The cold water and a bad landing knocked the breath from him, yet he burst out of the water and hurried like a demon to where Henrietta was being dragged. Using the tablet on the end of the rope as a flail, he began to knock down the men surrounding Henrietta.

Although magazine serials and adventure novels always had cultists dressed in antique or outlandish garb, these men were dressed like ordinary Guatemalan peasants. The weapons that they wielded were no more exotic than knives and machetes. Raymond had knocked down three of the five men with broken heads or broken bones. They either fell into the river water in relative silence or splashed about frantically trying not to drown while crawling to shore.

Raymond did not have the luxury of following their progress. One of the men standing between him and the shore held a large knife that he waved about menacing. Another man held Henrietta in his arms, a machete against her side. He placed the edge of his machete against her throat.

Raymond stood stock still.

"Give us the tablet, Señor and we will let the *muy bonita chiquita* go."

There was no hesitation on Raymond's part; he pulled the tablet to him and untied it.

Henrietta saw what he intended to do and struggled but the man held her fast, although he inadvertently nicked the smooth skin of her neck.

"Raymond! Raymond! That tablet is priceless, don't trade it for me. You don't even know that he will keep his word"

"Ah, I like the fiery ones! They are so good to tame!" exclaimed the one nearest to Raymond.

Raymond addressed the man holding Henrietta, "Do you swear by Vucub Caquix that you will allow the girl and I go unmolested, if I give you the tablet of my free will?"

With a sour look, the man holding Henrietta spat, "Si!"

Raymond tossed the tablet onto the riverbank next to the man who held Henrietta captive. He gave Henrietta a fierce push that tossed her back into the river. She landed hard and had the wind knocked out of her. Just as Raymond moved towards her, the other man let loose a shout of triumph. He rushed over to Henrietta and grabbed a-hold of her long, wet hair and dragged her to the shore. Sticking his knife in his mouth, he ripped off her ragged shirt and grabbed her naked breasts.

Raymond frantically waded through the river towards her, shouting at the man with the tablet. "Is this how you honor your vow!"

"Hernandez, stop! Leave the girl alone!" yelled the man holding the tablet.

Hernandez waved him off and began to pull down his pants. The late afternoon sun flared golden bright across a machete blade as it flashed through the air and buried itself in Hernandez back. With a scream, Hernandez yanked the blade from his back and tossed it into the river. Raymond dove for it.

When Raymond emerged from the river with the machete in his hand, he saw the two men involved in a knife fight.

"…turn on me, Aguirre!" screamed Hernandez.

"We swore an oath before Vucub Caquix and I will keep that vow!"

"To Hell with Vucub Caquix and you. I will take the woman and then I will take the tablet and sell it to some rich Americano museum." Hernandez stabbed Aguirre in the leg and received a knife in the throat in return. Aguirre picked up the tablet and staggered off onto a trail in the woods next to the river.

Raymond rushed over to Henrietta. He watched her calmly try to arrange the tattered remnants of her shirt into some type of covering for her breasts. She gave up with short curse, throwing the tattered cloth into the river. When Raymond reached down to give her a hand up, he received a swift kick in the stomach that sent him sprawling backwards into the river.

Anger made her usually humor filled luminous blue eyes blaze like gas jets. "Why the Hell did you do that! You idiot! That tablet was irreplaceable. He will probably hide it where we can never find it."

Raymond stood up and took off his wet shirt, wadding it up he flung it into her face with enough force to knock her down. With a scream of rage, she flung the shirt aside, she sprang to her feet and launched herself at him.

With a laugh, Raymond caught her about her waist and picked her up so that her face was even with his while holding her at arms' length. She beat her fists against his oaken arms. "Let me go, you big lummox! Let's get after him before he gets too far."

"He kept his word, I will keep mine."

"So your honor will cost us dearly!" she shouted angrily, her flaming eyes burned into his.

Gazing into the endless depths of those incandescent orbs, Raymond smiled and said, "No, if I had not made the vow, what I would have lost would have destroyed me. There was no choice. I do not care if it had been the Ark of the Covenant or King Arthur's sword; nothing is worth endangering your life. My hands hold the only treasure that means anything to me, everything else is just old trash."

Raymond gathered Henrietta to him. She gasped as their wet bare flesh met and as her bosom was compressed against his muscular chest. Her eyes blazed once again but not with anger. She hungrily sought his questing lips.

With a dreamy smile she leaned back, "Well, it certainly took you long enough to say that you love me. I've only been waiting for years."

Years! Raymond frowned, "You only started to show an interest in me recently."

Henrietta laughed and took his cheeks in her hands, "You are such a lunkhead! Of course, I have been in love with you from the first and I knew that you loved me. I became tired of waiting around for you to court me so I had practically throw myself at you. It was getting to the point where I thought I might have to club you over the head like an Amazon and drag you into bushes."

She kissed him once more, breaking the kiss reluctantly. With a wistful smile she said, "We should try and get back to camp before dark."

Raymond set her down on the river bank. She picked up his wet shirt and put it on. Grabbing one of the fallen machetes in one hand, she grabbed his hand in her free hand and began walking down the trail that Aguirre had taken.

They had traveled about two miles when they found Aguirre's body. Laying next to him was the tablet. The cut in the leg that Hernandez had given him had severed his femoral artery and he had bled to death.

As Raymond picked up the tablet, Henrietta bowed to the man who had held a knife at her throat. "Thank you, this will be a fine wedding present, Monsieur."

"Wedding present?"

"*Oui*, there should be a priest in one of the nearby villages. Hopefully he can perform the ceremony tonight." Taking his free hand in hers, she looked up at him and gave him a sly grin. "Otherwise, the wedding night will precede the ceremony."

2. The Lost Treasure
(Paris, Late 1929)

Oaths that would make a sailor blush followed the sound of a pen clattering across a paper strewn desk. The pen flew to the floor and skidded to a stop against the shoe of Raymond Mystère, as he stepped into Henrietta's small office. Another stream of curses erupted from a pair of lips better suited for kissing than cursing.

Delicate feminine fingers balled up sheets of paper as if Henrietta were attempting to throttle something. She tossed the balls of paper over the drafting desk where they bounced against the wall and landed next to a trash can overflowing with wads of paper.

Catching sight of Raymond, Henrietta struggled to calm herself. With a visible effort to keep from screaming, she spat out at him.

"*C'est impossible!* No matter how I translate it, all I get is gibberish."

Raymond picked up the pen and handed it to her, "You should not let yourself get so upset, especially…"

"Especially because of the delicate condition that you put me in!" she exclaimed angrily, pushing herself away from her drafting table. The gesture would have been more dramatic if there had been room for her chair to sail backwards, as it was it moved only a few inches before clanging into the back of a file cabinet. As she struggled to extricate herself from between her chair and the drafting table, Raymond took the opportunity to once again view his treasure.

As always Raymond felt a catch in his throat as he saw the full beauty of his wife. Her voluptuous form had grown even more so in these past few months since their wedding night. Henrietta's petite form dramatically showed the fullness of her pregnancy as she stepped towards her husband. Since her office was rather small this was only a matter of a couple of feet.

Raymond laughed and picked her up by her expanded waist.

"Ah, now, my sweet, if I remember correctly, once we had reached our camp, it was you who followed me into my tent and had your way with me. It was, in fact, several days before you gave any thought to finding a priest."

Henrietta's anger evaporated and a merry light came into her bright blue eyes. Tossing back her long mane of raven hair, she grabbed onto Raymond's neck and hugged him tightly. Leaning back, she gazed into his face and grinned saucily, "You know I don't think that anyone in the camp believed my story that we needed to be quarantined together."

"Not with all the noise you made," Raymond said and cut off her sarcastic reply with a passionate kiss.

"Well, if I had waited for you, I would still be an old spinster rather than a happily married woman." She hugged him again.

With a sour expression, she nodded her head in the direction of her drafting table. "My happiness would be absolute, if it were not for that damned tablet we found. It is driving me mad." Smiling softly, "And being the size of a steamship does not improve my disposition or patience."

"Yes, indeed you are a heavy one!" Raymond joked and regretted saying it immediately as he saw a flash of hurt and anger flicker through Henrietta's eyes.

"I meant, of course, that there is much more of you to love", and kissed her quickly. She responded perfunctorily at first but then with growing heat, holding the kiss until they both had to break for air.

Stroking his hair, she had a pensive expression as she gave him a familiar look, "I am getting nowhere with the translation today. Perhaps we can take an early lunch."

"Where do you want to eat?" Raymond asked, knowing full well that eating was the last thing on her mind.

Henrietta just grinned and replied with another passionate kiss. "I'll get my things and we can head on home."

Raymond put Henrietta down and she unbuttoned her smock, revealing her modest white blouse and calf length black skirt.

Even in her advanced state of pregnancy had not abated Henrietta's sexual appetite. In fact it seemed to have whetted it. Not that Raymond was complaining.

Raymond and Henrietta had finished their summer dig and returned to the Sorbonne University in Paris where they were now associate professors of antiquities. In between her other duties, Henrietta had taken it upon herself to translate the tablet that they had discovered. She was the acknowledged expert on Meso-American antiquities, whereas Raymond Mystère's expertise was in African and Asian antiquities. She often teased him about why he had decided to accompany her on the dig to Central America, saying that his theory about there being a Mayan-African connection through the Olmec culture was just a smokescreen, a flimsy scholarly excuse to be with her. Raymond wryly had to privately admit that there was more truth to Henrietta's claim than he would let her know.

While Henrietta went to the cloakroom to get her coat, hat, gloves and purse Raymond looked over the pile of material on her drafting table. There were rubbings of the tablet, drawings of the various Mayan pictoglyphs with their phonetic translations and photographic enlargements of sections of the tablet. Once of the pictures caught Raymond's eye.

As Henrietta returned to the table he said, "This is an odd-looking Mayan. Why, he could walk down the Champs Elysées without turning a head since he is wearing a fedora and an opera cloak."

With a puzzled look Henrietta took the photo into her white-gloved hand and studied it. Rolling her eyes and giggling, "You have a vivid imagination, my darling. This is obviously a *payi'aj* and across his shoulders is a *q'ub'el*. Next, you will tell me that he is the Man in the Moon."

Raymond smiled and then said, "Well, isn't this the Moon next to him?" pointing to a circular object near the pictoglyph of the man.

Henrietta shook her head with a smile, "No, the photograph did not pick it up, but there is another circle inside this one, so it is a hole or entrance or possibly an eclipse."

"So it could be the Moon," Raymond insisted with a grin. "What does the symbol under it say?"

With palling amusement Henrietta shuffled through the papers on the desk. "They are not Mayan words, or at least not Mayan words that we know. The rest of the tablet is also of an unknown Mayan tongue which bears no resemblance to the Quecha language. According to my best translation, the symbols under the disc come out as *ekakundala* and the symbols underneath the man are *duhrmrra*."

Startled, Raymond said, "Could you repeat the first word?"

Frowning, Henrietta did so.

"Again, please, more slowly." Raymond said as he closed his eyes to concentrate on her words.

"Are we playing a game? If so, I had a much more enjoyable game in mind for this afternoon," Henrietta asked with a laugh yet her comment fell on deaf ears, as Raymond began to rifle through the papers on the desk and sound out the phonetic symbols Henrietta had written.

Throwing them down on the drafting table he turned to her with a stunned expression.

"*C'est incroyable!* Maybe Churchward is correct, or not entirely wrong. Perhaps your brother is not the crank we always thought him to be!"

With an expression of equal parts exasperation and amusement, Henrietta put a gloved hand on his cheek and said, "My darling, what are you babbling about? I know this tablet drives one crazy, but I thought it took a while."

"These words seem to be Vedic. There are some scholars who believe that Vedic is the oldest living language; some of the more esoteric scholars even believe that it is a remnant of the language once spoken on Mû and Lemuria. My grandfather, Doctor Mystère, claimed that his vehicle, the Electric Hotel, was based on ancient Vedic designs. If so, perhaps they were from the supposedly advanced civilization of Lemuria. Some believe that the civilizations in Meso-America, Africa and Asia were colonies of Lemuria or Mû, or that they were begun by survivors of them."

Henrietta gazed at him, unsure if he were playing a joke on her or not. With a laugh, she said, "Certainly you are not suggesting that this is true, are you?"

"No, I do not believe that the Meso-American and other cultures were colonies of Lemuria, but if Lemuria existed, then I believe that it is possible that refugees may have founded some cultures that became part of an existing culture or were taken over by a newer culture; possibly both. Looking at your phonetic transcriptions, many of these words seem very familiar. If they are indeed Vedic, then we may be able to translate the tablet."

With an exaggerated sigh, Henrietta put down her purse and pulled off her gloves, playing along with Raymond's game. However as they began to work, she soon realized that there were indeed correlations between the pictoglyphs and the translation that Raymond provided.

They worked all through lunch up until it was time for their afternoon classes and then returned to continue the translation. Working long into the night, they finally finished. Raymond read the transcribed text.

Fifth World of the Sun
Tenth Age of Man
Spirits of evil unbound
Dark riders across the west
Justice of the last king
Reforged in virtue,
The one ring.

Henrietta shook her head, "Even in translation, it does not make sense; at least, I cannot make any sense of it right now. Let's start fresh in the morning. I am starving and tired."

Raymond felt guilty about making his very pregnant wife working so hard. When he became overly solicitous, Henrietta grinned and hugged him as tightly as she could. "As you can feel, I am not made of glass. I am solid and sturdy, not a fragile little thing."

After a quick supper at a late night bistro, Raymond and Henrietta went directly to their little apartment on the Left Bank. Exhausted, Henrietta fell asleep quickly. Yet, sleep would not come for Raymond. The image of the Mayan with the hat and cloak kept swimming before his eyes. The words of the translation reverberated in his mind as he tried to discern their meaning. He had flashes of imagery, of a great evil defeated, of great battles lost and won, of a red eye destroyed in fire, yet whose gaze and influence lingered long after its destruction.

Perhaps because of his background, Raymond Mystère was not like many of his colleagues who dismissed anything not rationally explained by science. His father, Cigale Mystère, had many odd adventures as a youth and Raymond's adoptive grandfather, Doctor Mystère, was a Hindu Prince who was part scientist and mystic whose adventures had often delved in areas not readily explained by hard science.

Raymond had the nagging feeling that it was not by mere fortune that he and Henrietta had found the tablet. His grandfather's teachings about destiny and karma had an undeniable influence on him. Raymond believed that people had series of pre-set destinies; however, the choices that they made in this life determined which destiny they would achieve. So there was pre-destination and yet also free will.

Raymond and Henrietta had been placed on a life path together; with her lying next to him, it seemed as though they had always meant to be together. If so, finding the tablet was part of this destiny. Yet, what greater purpose did the tablet serve?

A couple hours after she had fallen asleep, Henrietta felt a great call of nature as pregnant women are prone to have. Returning to bed, she noticed Raymond awake and staring at the ceiling. Crawling into bed, she lay down upon his chest and stared at him with a bemused expression.

"Can't you sleep, my darling? It is that damned tablet! It is a puzzle that drives one mad! Were it not for the fact that it finally brought us together I often wished we had never found it."

"Yet, it did bring us together, so it cannot be so bad, hmm? Yet, why did we find it? You're an expert on Mayan writing, and I know Sanskrit. I was only there because you were there." Her eyes gleamed with love light, yet Raymond also noted that a flare of triumph also danced in her eyes. Grinning, he said, "Very well, I admit it. You were the reason I went on that particular dig. Yet I was there and it was the combination of our efforts that removed the tablet from the Mayan temple and brought it here. It was the unlikely combination of our particular translation skills that allowed us to decipher the document."

"Do you suspect a hoax of some type?" Henrietta asked as the thought suddenly crossed her mind.

"No, I do not think that it can be a hoax, there are too many anomalies. The fact that the tablet is not stone but of an unknown metal. The tablet had been forged rather than carven, the words burned into the metal sheet. This lightweight yet extremely durable metal resists all efforts to analyze it, only a diamond will chip it. Yet it is pitted with age, so it has to incredibly ancient. I feel that something else it at work here. Something like divine providence."

At Henrietta's quizzical smile, he added, "I know that, as scientists, we often put our faith in the divine on the backburner. Yet we are both religious people, we both attend Mass, albeit irregularly and we were married before a priest, and we pray on occasion. So to us science and faith are not mutually exclusive. I feel that there is something at work here, something that brought us together so that we could find the tablet together."

Henrietta wrinkled her forehead at that and smiled softly. "I am not certain what you are asking me, if you are asking me anything. I do believe that we were meant to be together, that our destiny is to be together. I disagree however that we were brought together just to find an ancient tablet. I do not know whether it was destiny, fate or even the Hand of God but I do know now, as I have almost since I met you, that my life and yours would be spent as one."

"Don't you feel in the slightest bit cheated, as if you had no choice in the decision?"

Henrietta placed her face just above his and stared into his eyes her eyes sparkling with amusement and affection. "Oh, my darling, I know that I had no choice in the matter. When I first saw you, I was entranced; when I heard you speak, I was infatuated, and when we had our first argument, I was in love. I knew even as we argued that we would wed and I would have your babies. And since here I am laying on top of you, big as house with our child, I know that fate has proven kindly." Her face became serious and she said, "As for being cheated? No, I never felt I was cheated because what I felt was fated to be actually came to pass. Do you feel cheated or trapped? Did I rush you into marriage? I did not expect to start a family so soon but I was happy it turned out that we would, because it seemed another piece of evidence that we were meant for each other."

"Or that you are a fertile as a bunny," Raymond joked but Henrietta's face became even more serious.

"Are you truly thinking about the tablet or is it that you have second thoughts about our marriage or about having this child?"

Raymond had become used to the fact that Henrietta's often mercurial mood changes were accentuated by her pregnancy but sometimes he was caught by surprise.

"Nothing I will ever learn will ever compare to the joy that was mine when I learned that you loved me. Nothing that I may discover will ever amount to the wondrous discovery I make each morning when I awaken and find you next to me."

Henrietta stared him for a long moment and then softly kissed his forehead. "Since you cannot get that tablet out of your mind on your own, I think I can help you forget it for a while."

Leaning back, she straddled him for a moment, taking time only to pull loose the tie at the neck of her nightgown. She slowly unbuttoned his pajama top and began kissing her way down his chest. True to her word, Raymond did not think about the tablet for hours.

Raymond and Henrietta consulted with other experts on Mayan and Vedic languages to corroborate their translations. Once their work had been confirmed, they were encouraged to publish their preliminary findings. Although most antiquarians did not give credence to the diffusionist connection between the Mayans and Vedic India, for the most part the responses were favorable, encouraging them to continue their investigation to discover the truth about the mysterious tablet. There was one stinging rebuke from Professor Henry Jones, who not only scoffed at their work, but felt that he had wasted his time even trying to teach them anything. Raymond took his acerbic remarks with a grain of salt, considering Jones' well-known Grail obsession.

Since Raymond and Henrietta were among the more popular associate professors, the Dean prevailed upon them to give a public lecture about their adventure of discovering the tablet and discussing their findings.

The lecture was well attended by many students, their parents, alumni and interested parties.

After the lecture, one of their students, Jean Aubry, introduced Raymond and Henrietta to his father, Comte Jacques de Trémeuse. The dark, lean appearance of the Comte struck Raymond with such familiarity that he was prompted to ask if they had met before. Trémeuse smiled mysteriously and told Raymond that, to his knowledge, they had not met. He then invited Raymond and Henrietta to his estate outside of Paris for the weekend, as he was interested in their research and would like to discuss it in greater detail. He also thought the young couple might enjoy a weekend away from the University.

Raymond and Henrietta had a pleasant train ride through the countryside from Paris to the La Frondaie estate, located on the Seine, near Fontainebleau. The Comte, who drove his own automobile rather than using a chauffeur, met them at the Fontainebleau-Avon train station. Although Raymond did not say anything to Henrietta, he had the unpleasant feeling that they were being followed. He did not spot anyone specifically following them, but rather attributed this sensation to his years as a young adventurer accompanying his father. Cigale and Raymond Mystère were often followed, either by the authorities or by persons with ill intent.

Raymond and Henrietta spent an enjoyable weekend with the Comte and his family, meeting his wife Jacqueline and their two boys. Also up for the weekend was an old family friend, Prosper Cocantin, his wife Daisy, and their young son Jacques. Cocantin was the owner of the renowned detective agency, *Celeritas*. Their adopted older son had joined the family business and was busy with an investigation.

Little Jacques Cocantin was almost enough to give Henrietta second thoughts about having a baby. He was a bundle of energy, but an extremely clumsy child, forever falling down or knocking something down. His parents indulged him, believing that their child was extremely delightful. Jacques Cocantin spoke in an odd accent, which his parents attributed to his having French and Swedish parents. This accent became all the more pronounced by Jacques's slow and deliberate manner of speech. Even at an early age, young Jacques had a rather self-important and arrogant attitude and believed that his pronouncements were of the utmost importance to everyone around him. He told the Mystères that digging up old bones was all well and good, but he was going to work for the people of France by becoming a police officer and eventually Chief Inspector of the Sûreté!

Raymond found it very hard not to laugh at the pompous little boy, especially after, having announced this to Raymond, young Jacques strode out of the room with exaggerated dignity only to trip over one of his toys which he had left laying on the floor.

On Saturday afternoon, Jacqueline de Trémeuse took her boys and the Cocantins to the cinema to give her husband a chance to talk with the Mystères.

Over lunch, the Comte gave the Mystères a bit of background of why he was so interested in their work.

"This estate is the result of the second fortune of my family," he explained. "The first was wiped out due to the unethical business practices of a banker named Favraux. Unable to bear the shame of being bankrupt, my father committed suicide."

Henrietta was both saddened and a bit frightened by the flash of dark anger that illuminated the Comte's eyes. He gave them a bitter smile, "Shortly thereafter, a messenger arrived and told mother that one of the investments, a mine in Africa, had yielded up a very rich vein of gold. Mother had made her two boys, Roger and I, vow to avenge our father's death by destroying and killing Favraux."

Trémeuse's story twigged something in Raymond's memory. And he began to wonder if perhaps he had made a mistake bringing Henrietta to this estate.

Jacques de Trémeuse noticed his guests' unease and waved his hands at them and smiled, "Sorry, if I caused Madame Mystère to doubt my sanity. My father's death and Favraux's treachery are still quite painful memories. Let me assure you that, despite our vow, we did not kill Favraux, although we did bring him to justice. Before that, Roger and I spent years learning various skills that gave us the means to penetrate the web of lies and deceit surrounding the banker. We became adept in the arts of disguise, mastered many of the sciences and studied many of the techniques of investigation. While we studied, mother directed the family fortune, diversifying it from the gold mine into many lucrative ventures. So we would not follow our father's mistake of letting others steer our finances badly, we were directed to learn everything we could about our business ventures. To this end, I spent six months working in the African gold mine."

He smiled a bit at the memory. "…And I do mean working, not just supervising," he continued. "One day, while I was on a drilling team opening up a new branch tunnel, the wall being drilled suddenly crumbled, revealing a large cavern. After some initial exploration, my engineers and I soon ascertained that this was not a natural cavern but an ancient mine shaft. The shaft lead upwards for some distance, but did not reach the surface; a cave-in had long ago had sealed this mine shaft. Although we expected this section of the mountain to have already been emptied of gold and precious stones, we explored it. The ancient mine shaft branched off and went downwards for some distance before abruptly ending in a stone wall of polished granite. Against this wall were granite receptacles, each containing clay tablets covered in writing. One of the receptacles also contained a large tablet made of metal. This metal tablet was also covered in writing, yet also contained several pictoglyphs. Two of these pictoglyphs resonated with me. One was the image of a lean man wearing a slouch hat and a cape; the other was that of a golden ring. Upon closer examination, I discovered it was not simply the image of a golden ring, but an actual golden ring set into the tablet. As my fingers brushed up against it, the ring rolled out of the tablet and landed at my feet. When I tried to put it back into the tablet, it no longer fit! The ring was a simple gold band with an engraved interior. This script inside, however, seemed different from what was on the tablet."

As Trémeuse related his story, the Mystères forgot the aura of menace that had seemed to come over the Comte at its beginning. They looked at one another, smiled and grabbed each other's hands. They could tell by the pulse throbbing that both of their hearts were pounding with excitement.

The Comte noted the effect that his story had on the two archaeologists and decided not to drag it out for much longer.

"Roger and I knew that this was a momentous archaeological discovery, but since our mission of vengeance against Favraux was the first and foremost goal of our life, we kept silent about it. Disruption of the gold mining operations could not be allowed; the money was needed to fund the mission. I placed the ring into my pocket and had that section of the tunnel placed off limits. However, I kept having dreams about the tablet with the caped man and the ring and so had I had it retrieved later. My dreams subsided once the tablet was in my possession; however, the image of the caped man stayed with him and, when the time came for me to exact our vengeance on Favraux, I adopted a guise very similar to the pictoglyph, and wore a slouch hat and a cape."

"As I thought, you're Judex!" Raymond exclaimed.

Jacques de Trémeuse acknowledged Raymond's insight with a small smile and short bow.

"Once our mission had been brought to an end, we tried, without success, to have the tablet translated. When Jean told me about your discovery, naturally I was interested, especially when I learned that the symbols underneath the caped man meant Justice. Judex was of course Latin for a judge, the arbiter of justice. It was like an affirmation of my destiny!"

"So this tablet is identical to ours? Do you have it in your possession?" Henrietta asked with mounting excitement.

"Yes, but it is not identical to yours. It is similar, but different." Smiling, Jacques de Trémeuse, stood up. "I will not torture you any longer. Please follow me."

Trémeuse led the Mystères into his library where the metal tablet was lying on a table. It was made of the same type of metal and measured the same dimensions as their tablet. It was, as Trémeuse had stated, also quite different. Although both tablets had the same pictures of the man wearing a hat and cape, and the circle next to the man, they were in different locations. On the Mystères' tablet, these symbols were in the center of the lower portion of the tablet on the Trémeuse's tablet, these symbols were on the center of the top section. The Mystères' tablet ended just under the captions below the pictures of the man and the ring, but Trémeuse's tablet had several lines of script and then a blank expanse underneath the picture of the man and the ring. The major difference between the two tablets, however, was that the script on Trémeuse's tablet was entirely different from that on their own tablet.

Trémeuse said, "Alas, the most renowned linguists in the world do not recognize the language, nor could they decipher it. Do you know it?"

Raymond and Henrietta looked at each other with huge smiles. She said with a slight giggle, "No, but can start a translation."

Trémeuse gave them a puzzled look, not quite certain if they were putting him on for his long-winded story.

Raymond explained, "By using our tablet, we may be able to decipher the script on yours, if the captions for the pictures are the same. Of course, we will have to deduce most of the script, and it will take some time, but eventually we should be able to read the other clay tablets that you found in your mine. Will you allow us to take the tablet to the Sorbonne for further study?"

Trémeuse stood regarding them with piercing gray eyes for a moment. Raymond almost felt as thought they were on trial and Trémeuse was the judge. Finally, he said, "I will allow it, but I want my family's name kept out of any discussion of the tablet, and I want the location where it was discovered to remain a secret. I also wish to remain involved."

Trémeuse noticed the looks that the Mystères exchanged out of the corner of their eyes, a look meaning that savants had to suffer the eccentricities of patrons for the sake of science. "I'm not simply throwing my weight around; I am somewhat skilled at cryptography."

Trémeuse knew his next statement would not be greeted with enthusiasm, but he knew something about obsession and recognized the signs. They needed a break from their work, "Also I insist that we begin next week; for now, let's enjoy the weekend." Although Raymond and Henrietta burned to start translating the new tablet, they put aside their academic roles for the rest of the weekend.

Shortly after their startling luncheon with Jacques de Trémeuse, the other weekend guests returned from their trip to the cinema. Young Jacques Cocantin was sopping wet, having somehow managed fall into the fountain in front of the house as he exited the motorcar.

They spent the rest of Saturday and Sunday morning dining, playing table tennis, lawn tennis, croquet and card games. Raymond and Henrietta left the Trémeuse estate with some regret, but were very excited to return to Paris and work on the tablet. Jacques de Trémeuse had some business affairs that prevented him from accompanying them, so he joined them late Monday.

When Trémeuse brought his tablet into their laboratory, the business of its translation took on unexpected twist.

They laid the two tablets on a table, one above the other, separated by about two inches, to see how similar they were. With the exception of the script used, the bottom of the tablet found by the Mystères, and the top of tablet found by Jacques de Trémeuse, were identical.

When Raymond moved the tablets closer together to get a better sense of the exactness of detail, something amazing happened. The two tablets moved under their own power, as if drawn together by a powerful magnetic force. Once they were butted against each other, the crack separating them faded and their surfaces blurred over, as if subjected to some vast heat, yet the metal remained cool to the touch.

The two tablets had become one smooth piece of metal!

All three of them touched the smooth surface of the metal plate. However smooth it was, it felt as if ants crawled just beneath its surface. After a moment, lines and shapes began forming. When it finished reshaping itself, the script for the new tablet was now in the unknown language that had been upon the Trémeuse tablet but the blank expanse had been replaced by a map. And below it was a new line of script!

"If I had not seen it with my own eyes, I would have never believed it!" Raymond exclaimed.

"It is almost as if the tablet were magical," Henrietta said, her eyes wide with wonderment.

"Or the product of a science much more advanced than ours," Raymond said.

Jacques de Trémeuse was also surprised, but not shocked by what had happened. Raymond regarded him for a second and then asked with an edge of suspicion. "You are not entirely surprised that this happened. Why?"

Trémeuse looked at the Mystères pensively, pursed his lips and said, "I was astonished, but not entirely surprised that tablets did something unusual. You may recall gossip that Judex had the ability to become invisible or cloud the minds of people around him. These were based in part on my mastery of the art of disguise and an innate ability to charm and persuade people. Yet, a good deal of that legend derives from the fact that I could indeed turn invisible for a short period of time and also influence people near me. This ability derived from the ring that I found in the gold mine; how it worked, I have no idea. So that the metal of the tablets could reshape itself wasn't entirely a shock."

They quickly made rubbings and took photographs of the new tablet, in case it decided to revert to a smooth plate of metal. The transformation was not the setback it could have been, since Raymond had already translated the main portion of the Mayan symbols. His translation provided their Rosetta stone. The new script turned out not to be phonetically rendered in Vedic Sanskrit, but rather in an unknown language reminiscent of Basque or Algonquin.

It took them two weeks to create a transcription of the known words, because the word order, in a few instances, had changed. While their work progressed, Raymond's sense that they were being watched increased. He mentioned it to Trémeuse, who admitted that he had also had this odd sense of being under scrutiny. They agreed not to mention it to Henrietta and to make certain that she was protected at all times.

After completing the translation of the known section of the tablet, they decided to go out for a celebratory dinner. Once they reached the car, however, Henrietta discovered that she had forgotten her purse. Raymond ran back to their office to retrieve it, while Jacques de Trémeuse kept her company.

Raymond opened the office door and surprised one of the janitors reading the translation, his mop and bucket set off to the side of the drafting table.

"Hey, that's private research!" Raymond shouted at the nosy custodian.

The janitor grabbed the end of his mop and swung it at Raymond. Hot soapy water and wet slippery mop strands covered his face, filling his eyes, nostrils and mouth. Raymond flung the mop from his face, snorting and gasping for air, as he rubbed the stinging water from his eyes. He saw the janitor sweep the papers onto the floor and throw a match on them. He then grabbed the tablet. Raymond ran forward, kicking over the bucket of hot water. He tackled the janitor, who lost his grip on the tablet. The tablet flew across the room to smash against a blackboard. The blackboard's slate cracked and fell to the floor in a shimmer of black shards.

Raymond slipped in the water on the floor which allowed the janitor to struggle free of his grip. He lashed out with a kick to Raymond's stomach and ran out of the room. Raymond struggled to his feet and ran after the man, but he had disappeared in the University's dark corridors.

The mop water had put out the fire that the man had started. Much of the translation had been burned, but it would be a relatively easy task to recreate it now that they had memorized the script. Raymond stayed in the room, knowing that Jacques and Henrietta would come back when he did not return.

After they arrived, he quickly explained what had happened. They could only guess that an artifact hunter had decided to take the tablet for his own, and this is why they were being followed. Still, why he would destroy their work?

To ensure the safety of the tablet and their work, Jacques de Trémeuse suggested that they continue their research at a property he owned called Chateau-Rouge. It was well fortified, so the tablet, their research and themselves would be safe from attack.

When the Dean was informed of the attack, he investigated the matter. It turned out that the real janitor had been killed the night before Raymond was attacked and replaced by an imposter The Dean bade them to take a few weeks off. He was concerned about Henrietta's well-being, as well as the University's reputation.

Chateau-Rouge turned out to be an old castle, mostly in ruins. However, Jacques de Trémeuse led them into one of the towers, which contained a modern elevator that descended into a complex built beneath the ruins. This, Raymond realized, was the secret lair of Judex!

In addition to Jacques and his brother providing protection, Trémeuse had also hired the Celeritas Agency to provide additional help.

A couple of days into their research, Jacqueline de Trémeuse insisted on taking Henrietta shopping for baby clothing and clothing that the new mother could wear after the baby was born. Since Jacqueline was about Henrietta's size, she could try on the clothing for her. Raymond thought that it would be a pleasant diversion for his wife and insisted that she go. The person who drew the delightful duty of accompanying the ladies was Michel Cocantin. He followed them at a distance so as not to intrude.

Michel Cocantin, the former "Licorice Kid," was now a young, well-dressed man about town, who flirted with the shop girls and customers while keeping a sharp eye on his charges. However, there was one place he could not go. While Jacqueline and Henrietta went into a changing room, he sat outside, slowly chewing on a piece of licorice. After what seemed to a protracted time, he knocked on the door. Receiving no answer, he burst into the room, kicking in the locked door. He found Jacqueline de Trémeuse lying in an unconscious heap on the floor. A quick check ascertained that she was breathing steadily. A hole had been cut into the dressing room and into the one next to it. Michel ran through the holes and out to the rear door of the shop. He spotted Henrietta being forced into a black sedan by two men dressed in dark suits. Michel ran forward to help her, but skidded to a stop when one of the men placed a wicked looking blade against Henrietta's bulging stomach.

Michel raised his hands to show that he meant no harm. The man holding the knife flashed him a quick grin. Once Henrietta was inside the car, the man reversed his grip on the knife and flung it at Michel. Michel stopped the knife from entering his abdomen at the cost of a slashed arm. He chased after the car trying to staunch the flow of blood. The license plate of the car had been blackened out.

Michel ran to a phone to tell Jacques de Trémeuse what had happened.

After Michel had called Trémeuse, Jacques and Raymond hurried to the hospital where Jacqueline had been taken. She had recovered from her chloroforming, but Michel was still laid up. The slash on his arm had taken several stitches and he was fighting off the effects of some drug that had been smeared upon the blade. Before succumbing to unconsciousness, he described the men who had abducted Henrietta.

Jacques de Trémeuse hissed when he heard the description.

Henrietta's abductors did not take long to make their demands known. Notes were sent to the Celeritas agency and also to the Trémeuses' home.

Raymond was to bring the tablet and all of the work pertaining to it to a location outside of Paris. He was to come alone. Henrietta would then be freed.

Raymond could understand why a collector of antiquities would want the tablet, but why would they want all of the research as well?

"I suspect the people we are dealing with are the so-called 'Men in Black,'" explained Trémeuse, "an organization comprised of influential people throughout Europe; politicians, military men, scientists and even leaders of various criminals organizations. My enemy, the banker Favraux, might have been a member and to exact my justice on him, I had to make it appear as though he were dead, otherwise I might have had to deal with the entire organization. However, some members got wind that he was still alive and tried to retrieve him. It turns out that, by removing the banker I had also dealt a serious blow to the Men in Black because Favraux had handled some of their finances.

"Fortunately, the members of the Men in Black often work at cross purposes. There is a constant internal struggle for power and control of the organization. One of their branches is rumored to acquire and destroy artifacts such as the tablet, and to suppress research on then. Apparently, they have certain doctrinaire beliefs about the history of the world, and work to ensure that this history remains the only history known to all. Their agents persuade researchers or people who find artifacts to forget all about them—or else they disappear. They must have our tablet in their sights. This meeting will be a trap. If captured, you may be subjected to various forms of persuasion to ensure that you forget all about the tablet."

Raymond's anxiety about Henrietta quadrupled. "Then, Henrietta is in danger, even if we give them the tablet!"

Trémeuse nodded gravely. His eyes flashed with a fierce fire and a grim smile crossed his face. "Fear not, my good friend. I will find her. It is time for Judex to take up the hunt for justice once more. If you are brave and steadfast, we will rescue your wife and keep the tablet out of the hands of this insidious organization. You shall go to this meeting alone, as they request, and give them the tablet and all the papers they wish. While you are meeting with them, I will be rescuing Henrietta. Once she is safe, I will send a signal for my other agents to move in on your position. I cannot promise you, however, that your captivity will be pleasant, however short it may be."

Raymond readily agreed to the plan, as long as there was chance that Henrietta would be safe.

Since Michel Cocantin was still in the hospital, his father volunteered to accompany Raymond to the rendezvous. Despite Cocantin being a dear friend, Jacques knew that he was often inept and suggested instead that his services would best be served by remaining at the Celeritas Agency to relay any messages.

Jacques de Trémeuse dressed in a black slouch hat, a black tunic and a black cape. The resemblance between him and the man on the tablet was uncanny. Then Judex gathered up his pack of dogs and set them on the scent of Henrietta.

Raymond arrived at the broken down windmill where he was to meet Henrietta's captors an hour before the meeting was scheduled to take place. Already, there were two black sedans parked outside.

As he exited his automobile, the driver's doors to both of the sedans opened up. Out of each car came a man dressed in black. They walked towards Raymond and motioned for him to walk forward. About twenty paces from Raymond, the two men stopped and made a gesture for Raymond to also stop. One of them then walked towards Raymond, while the other held a pistol on him. When the man was near to Raymond, he said, "Drop the stuff in your hands and back away!"

Raymond did so. The man strode over to him and thoroughly and professionally frisked him for weapons. Satisfied that Raymond was unarmed, he picked up the tablet and the briefcase of papers. He carried them to the other man and placed them at his feet.

The gun was passed over and the materials were examined. Once finished, the examiner nodded at the man holding the gun.

"Thank you for bringing the cursed object to us. We will make certain that the Devil's work is destroyed, or forever lost. Unfortunately, forbidden knowledge also resides in your heads, so regretfully you and your lovely wife will have to die. Since you've been tainted by the works of Satan, we are, in a sense, saving your souls."

Raymond instinctively started for the man, but his sense of self-preservation jerked him back. "Henrietta is pregnant; you will also be killing an innocent baby."

The Man in Black looked shocked and offended, "Monsieur, we do not kill the innocent. Mademoiselle Mystère will be allowed to live until she bears the child, then, most regrettably, she will be eliminated. The child will be trained as a soldier of the black."

Raymond wondered why the man just did not shoot him.

As if reading his mind, the man said, "My associates are bringing in your accomplice. It would be better for us if it appeared as though you and he had a falling out and shot each another."

Raymond looked behind him, expecting to see Roger de Trémeuse, Jacques' brother who was supposed to be watching over him. However, it was a thin man, accompanied by a small boy, who appeared, being urged along a dirt road by two more Men in Black. Both the thin man and the young boy stumbled several times on their way down the road.

It was Cocantin and his son, Jacques.

Cocantin was made to stand by Raymond. Cocantin shrugged and said, "I could not in good conscience allow you to beard the lions by yourself. And Jacques wanted to see how real detectives worked."

When Raymond explained that they were going to be shot, Cocantin paled and looked nauseous.

Jacques clung to his father. Cocantin's long fingers covered the boy's head. "Certainly, you do not intend to kill my boy! He is somewhat feeble mind-ed, and will forget all about you in a moment."

Cocantin yelped in pain as Jacques bit him. The Men in Black laughed.

"Be at peace, Monsieur, we will not harm the boy. He will be raised as one of our own."

Jacques was forcibly pulled from his father's leg and made to stand by the Man in Black holding the tablet.

Two of them raised their pistols. Raymond realized that they needed two guns to be fired, so that Cocantin and he would not have bullets from the same gun in both of them.

There was a high shrill shriek as young Jacques Cocantin ran over to the gun men and drove his small fists into the crotches of the Men in Black as they fired. Bullets whined past Raymond and Cocantin. The two gun men were off balance from the pain in their midsections. Taking advantage of this, Raymond launched himself at one of them, fully expecting to be shot. As he grappled with one of the men, and desperately grabbed for the gun, he heard a shot. Raymond drove his fist into the man's crotch much harder than young Jacques ever could. The man retched with pain. Raymond's fingers found the gun, but did not have time to get a proper grip on it. He grabbed it around the barrel. Then he heard two more shots and a car's motor turn over. He slammed the gun against the head against the man he was fighting and was gratified when he slumped into unconsciousness.

Raymond spun the gun into a proper grip as he stood up. Two of the other Men in Black were lying on the ground, shot through the chests. Cocantin was sat there, stunned, as he tried to stop the bleeding from a wound in his shoulder. Jacques ran after one of the black sedans speeding off down the road, but tripped over his own feet and went sprawling in the dirt road, covering himself in dust.

Raymond noticed that the tablet and the briefcase filled with their research were gone. Sighing with disappointment, he walked over to Cocantin and exam-ined the wound. A gash had been cut into Cocantin's shoulder by a bullet that had otherwise missed him. Raymond tore off a piece of one of the dead men's shirts and packed the wound. He then used the ties of the dead men to truss up the unconscious Man in Black.

By the time he had finished, Jacques had returned. He ran over and em-braced his father.

"Where did the little hero learn Vo Thuat?" a voice spoke up from behind. Raymond spun around with his gun at the ready to discover that he was aiming at Roger de Trémeuse, standing there, grinning, cradling a rifle in his arms.

Cocantin smiled and ruffled young Jacques hair. "A young Annamese boy with the unlikely name of Cato has been teaching him a few tricks."

A raven cawed overhead and circled above them. It banked and flew down to land on Rogers shoulder.

Roger de Trémeuse put down the rifle and opened the message attached to the bird's leg. He smiled at Raymond and said:

"Henrietta is safe and en route to Chateau-Rouge. But Pierre is dead."

At Raymond's blank look, Roger explained, "Pierre was one of our best dogs; my favorite whom I raised from a puppy. The bastards!"

Roger wrote out a note, attached it to the raven's leg and sent him on his way. He then began going through the sedan that had been left behind. He spoke to them as he carried out his investigation.

"It is a good thing that young Jacques acted when he did. I could not fire before because you two were blocking my shot. When Cocantin fell to his knees, and Raymond moved to attack, I was able to take out two of them. Unfortunately, I only winged the other one and he took off with the tablet and your papers... This car is clean and I am certain that they will carry no identification papers. Let's get Cocantin to a doctor so he can be stitched up."

That evening, everyone assembled at the Trémeuse villa for a quiet dinner that Jacqueline hoped would help sooth their pains. Henrietta clung to Raymond as they sat on a divan as if she never wanted to let him go. Her ordeal had been torturous because they had told her that Raymond was dead, and she and her baby would be killed if she did not tell them all about the tablet. She felt guilty because she had readily given up the translation, but no one blamed her. Her captors had then laughed at her and told her they would let her go after she had whelped. They had then locked her in a room.

Henrietta fell into an exhausted sleep in Raymond's arms. As he held her, he listened to Jean Aubrey regale young Jacques Cocantin with the tale of her rescue.

"Judex took his dogs to the spot where Henrietta had been abducted and put them on her scent. The dogs ran after the scent. To Judex' surprise, they stopped after a few blocks and surrounded a small apartment building. The kidnapers were so sure they wouldn't get caught that they holed up short distance from where they had taken her."

Jacques interrupted and displayed the distinct lack of tact so common to children, "Maybe they had to find some place close because Henrietta is so fat and could not go far." Fortunately for young master Cocantin, Henrietta remained asleep.

"The dogs then led Judex and I to an apartment inside. The raucous barking and baying caused many heads to pop out of opened doors like so many jack in the boxes. One of these opened doors was the apartment before which the dogs had regrouped. They rushed inside en masse, bowling over the man who had opened the door. Judex and I followed them. There was a fierce growling, a sharp cry of pain, and then the piercing whine of a dog in pain.

"I grabbed the man who had been knocked down by the dogs and gave him a couple of good whacks to the chin. Judex ran after the dogs, his gun at the ready. Henrietta lay on a bed, her hands tied to the posts. She looked otherwise unharmed. A man sat on the floor, propped against the bed, clutching his throat as blood poured over the edges of his fingers. A large mastiff lay next to him. Judex's heart sank as he noticed the knife in the dog's side. He hurried over to the dog; it was panting heavily, his eyes rapidly dimming. Eyes stinging, Judex patted the dog on the head, 'Good Pierre, good boy.' The dog gave his hand a weak lick before breathing his last.

"Judex then stepped over the man to untie Henrietta and remove her gag. Her first response was to spit at the dying man on the floor. When the dogs had burst into the apartment, that brigand had grabbed a knife from the kitchen and was about stab her. Pierre had launched himself at the villain and torn out his throat before he could carry out his evil deed. But the villain stabbed our valiant companion as he fell.

"Judex untied Henrietta and helped her to her feet. Amidst the pack of dogs, they walked over to where I was slapping the face of the man I had just tied up. He roused but then, suddenly, slumped again. My slaps had no further effect. Judex placed his hand on the man's carotid and said, 'He is dead.'

"Shocked, I said, 'But I did not hit him that hard.'

"Smiling grimly, Judex opened the dead man's mouth. One of his bottom front teeth was broken. Judex said, 'He had poison in his tooth. It is a common thing among the more fanatical of the Men in Black.'

"We quickly left the apartment in case the villains had sent more men, and drove back towards Chateau Rouge. Judex sent one of his pet ravens to search for Roger and deliver the message that Henrietta was safe."

3. Lost Tales Found

The Men in Black had won a victory in stealing the priceless tablet, but the Mystères still had copies of their work. They would be able to use it to decipher the clay tablets that Jacques de Trémeuse had found in the gold mine back in 1905. Thus, this was one ancient secrets about which the Men in Black would not be able to suppress knowledge. Yet, it bothered Jacques that if all the Men in Black wanted to do was to suppress the knowledge, why had they wanted the Mystères' research notes? They could have just destroyed them after killing the them. There was something else about the tablet that the Men in Black was interested in discovering.

They poured over their notes and recited the lines of the script found on the tablets.

Fifth World of the Sun
Tenth Age of Man
Spirits of evil unbound

Dark riders across the West
Justice of the last king
Reforged in virtue,
the one ring.
Light leads to light
Like leads to like
Ages replayed
Cycles turn not true
Three great lands drowned
Due to fear, greed and hate.
The Bird in its nest
Protects the ivory gate
Lost tales newfound

Yet, the meaning eluded them. Cocantin offered to look over the papers with his trained detective eyes; perhaps he could see something that the amateurs had missed. Although the Trémeuse family and the Mystère family doubted his deductive abilities, a fresh perspective might turn up something, so they agreed to let him take a look.

As Cocantin poured over the papers, often nodding his head thoughtfully, little Jacques amused himself by alternating skipping about the room and looking over the papers that his father was finished with. He continually sang a song refrain, "Three Drowned Lands," based on the song refrain, "Three Blind Mice."

While looking at one of the papers, he said, "Three drowned lands. One, two, three! One, two, three!" Jacques then stabbed his finger at the piece of paper. More than slightly annoyed, Raymond took the paper out of the boy's hands and put it back in the pile of papers. He noticed that Jacques' grubby little fingers had left three faint smudges on the sheet.

Raymond started to rub them off, but found himself riveted in place. Jacques had seen what the adults had failed to see! The paper he had held was the rubbing taken of the map that had appeared on the joined tablets. There were three spots on the map, which had been hidden among the topography.

The map was of a single land mass surrounded by water. The three smudged spots spanned its entire breadth.

Inspiration suddenly struck Raymond and he began tearing through the atlases in the library to find one that had maps of a comparable size to the one on the rubbing.

While Roger and Jacques looked at Raymond as if he had gone mad, Henrietta looked at him with an amused smile.

"What are you looking for, my darling?"

"Gondwanaland!"

Her eyes lit up with comprehension. "Of course!"

While Raymond searched through the atlases, Henrietta explained to the others about Gondwanaland. Some theorized that the present day continents had once formed a single land mass named Pangaea. When Pangaea had broken up, it had formed two smaller landmasses: Laurasia and Gondwanaland.

Jacques de Trémeuse nodded. "I remember reading about this. However, this took place millions of years ago, if I recall."

"That is true," Henrietta explained as Raymond continued his search. "However, despite the lack of geological evidence, there is some anecdotal evidence of other larger, continental masses that have formed and broken apart in more recent history. There are tales of the legendary continents of Hyboria, Lemuria, Mu, and, of course, Atlantis. Remember that these tales of drowned lands may not necessarily be actual continental landmasses, but may pertain simply to islands that sank, or became part of larger landmasses due to shifting tides or water sources. There may not be any solid connection between the three drowned lands, except through the commonality of being drowned lands. A metaphoric connection may have been created by the writer of the tablets."

Raymond Mystère finally found what he had been searching, which was a map of the world where the continental landmasses were of a similar size to the ones in the rubbing. He placed the rubbing on top of the map and used a pin to mark the three spots that Jacques Cocantin had found. Removing the rubbing, he hissed in shock. One of the picks was the approximate location of the Mayan temple that he and Henrietta had found. Another was in Central Africa. Carrying the atlas over to Jacques de Trémeuse, he asked him if this was anywhere near his mine. Trémeuse nodded slowly, comprehension dawning on his face.

However, when Raymond and Jacques located the final pinprick, they discovered that it was in the middle of the South Pacific, far from island chains or any known landmass.

"If this last one refers to a genuinely sunken land, why do the other points are on landmasses?" Trémeuse mused aloud.

"Perhaps, they refer to the repository of knowledge from the drowned civilizations?" Henrietta said, also puzzled by the last location.

"Or it refers to both a depository of knowledge and a drowned land," Raymond said thoughtfully, tracing the paths of the areas mentioned with his finger. "For example, the land where we found the tablet may have been the depository of knowledge from Atlantis. Yet, at the same time, that area where we found the Mayan temple was also near the region described by Ventidius Varro as Atala, which had ties with Atlantis, as well as being mistaken for it. The area in Africa could have been the depository of knowledge about the sunken civilization that gave rise to the idea that Atlantis had colonies in Africa. I suspect that there was an African civilization that was the true parent of such lost cities as Zu-Vendis, Kor, Opar and Zimbabue. So, possibly, the last location refers to a land what was in the Pacific and was lost, such as Lemuria or Mu. Perhaps we are not looking at an expanse of ocean, but rather a fragment of a lost continent, an island."

"Exactly!" Henrietta said, slapping her hands on the table. "Yes, it all makes sense. A script that has yet to be deciphered, that some claim is akin to the ones found in the Indus valley. The rumors of being part of Lemuria. The location has to be—Easter Island!"

She jumped to her feet, or rather made the attempt to do so. Off balanced by her gravid stomach, she fell back into her seat. Mustering her dignity, she slowly pulled herself to her feet.

"It is imperative that we travel there and rescue whatever treasures were left before the Men in Black discern the riddle, and either destroy or forever hide the artifacts of this lost civilization."

"Time is of the essence, I agree, but you are in no condition to travel with us!" Raymond exclaimed, alarmed that Henrietta would even think of going with them.

Henrietta put her hands on her hips, leaned back and looked upwards to meet her husband in the eye. "Did you think that I was going to give up my career? Did you think I would be shut up in a house taking care of babies and keeping house while you were wandering about the world? Was that part of your plan, make Henrietta pregnant so you can go running off without her, hmm?"

"No, of course, I did not expect you to stay home forever, but you must admit that you are in no condition to travel, when you are so close to giving birth."

"Nonsense! Babies have been born while women have been traveling for thousands of years. I am going, and that is final."

Raymond threw his hands in the air, knowing it was useless to argue with Henrietta once she had made up her mind.

Jacques de Trémeuse quickly made the arrangements for an expedition to Easter Island. To gain access to the island, however, he had to deal with Compañia Exploradora de la Isla de Pascua, which leased the island from the nation of Chile, which had annexed it. This was the company had turned the island into a large sheep farm. Ostensibly, Trémeuse, through one of his firms, would be looking to buy wool and mutton.

The fastest route was to travel across Europe and Asia by train and then book a fast steam ship in China for Easter Island.

As Henrietta was packing her bag for the trip, she suddenly dropped the clothes she had been folding and gasped. She clutched her swollen stomach. Raymond raced to her side.

Henrietta smiled at him to show that she was not in any danger. She took his hand and placed it against her. He felt a tremor.

"Your son is playing football in there." With a slightly sad and wistful smile she began to unpack her bag.

Raymond looked at her questioningly. "No, I am not about to deliver but nonetheless, I am not going with you. Yes, I will miss the adventure, but I won't regret doing so. I was caught up in the thrill of the chase and forgot where my priorities lie. This is child of ours is much more important to me than all the lost cities in the world."

Raymond began unpacking his things and had to jerk his hands out of the case when Henrietta slammed it shut.

"You are going! Jacques will not be able to find what we seek without you. As much as I will miss you, I don't want those bastard in black to steal any more knowledge from the world"

Henrietta finished packing his bags and then after a long kiss sent him on his way.

Raymond traveled alone by train to St. Petersburg. He met Jacques de Trémeuse there. They hoped that, by traveling separately, they would keep the Men in Black off of their trail. From St. Petersburg, they traveled to Moscow and took the Trans-Siberian railroad to Peking. From Peking, they traveled to Shanghai, where they chartered a fast steam ship to take them to Easter Island. The ship was *The Pious Woman*, owned and operated by Captain Owen Kettle. He was old banty sea dog whom Trémeuse did not entirely trust, but believed could be bought. He bought the ship from Kettle with the condition of selling it back to him for a nominal sum.

Easter Island rarely saw ships since it was so isolated and because it did not have a natural harbor. It was also notorious for the number of ships wrecked near its shores. Captain Kettle was reluctant to get too close to shore and so Jacques de Trémeuse and Raymond Mystère set out for the island on a cutter that they had to buy for an additional sum from Captain Kettle. He informed them that the ship could probably wait for them for two days, but no longer, otherwise they would use too much fuel and not be able to reach another harbor.

Since most of the shore of Easter Island was made of rocky, craggy cliffs and rocks, Trémeuse and Raymond landed at Cook's Bay, near the village of Hanga Roa, the only place of human habitation on the island. The story of Easter Island was, in many ways, a tragic and cautionary tale. The original settlers had found an island rich with lumber and wildlife. They cleared and cultivated the land. As the population boomed, they carved the megalithic heads for which the island was famous. In doing so, they depleted many of the forests using logs to move and support the heads. As the forests shrank, the topsoil washed away and this led to the shrinking of arable land. The wildlife had also dwindled with the forests. Food sources became depleted and the human beings started to fight for resources. Many blamed the giant heads for their troubles, and many of the megaliths were broken in the lean years. Although some inhabitant resorted to cannibalism, the population continued to shrink. Eventually, it had become small enough that, even the island's limited resources, could only support few people.

Hanga Roa had a wall around it and a locked gate that limited the natives' access to the main portion of the island. They were confined to the village and needed permission to leave it so that they could not decrease the livestock roaming freely. The sheep and cattle were owned by Williamson and Balfour, and the natives were not allowed to eat them, but had to subsist on what they cultivated in the gardens, and on fish and on supplies provided by the company on a semi-annual basis. Although Jacques de Trémeuse seethed at the injustice of making the inhabitants of Easter Island prisoners on their own home, he realized that there was little he could do about their situation.

Raymond could sense the barely contained rage that burned in Trémeuse's heart as they walked through the village. The villagers greeted them cordially and enthusiastically. They were dressed in the ragged remnants of clothes from Europe or South America.

They were escorted to the Manager of the Island, its de facto governor. Mr. Edmunds, described in Katherine Routledge's book *The Mystery of Easter Island*, had since retired and been replaced by Señor Ortiz, a Chilean representative of Williamson and Balfour. His residence was outside of the village. Trémeuse noted that Ortiz carried two sidearms on a holster. He was accompanied by two men toting powerful rifles.

Trémeuse and Raymond also noted that, at the approach of Ortiz and his bodyguards the native accompanying them had evaporated.

Ortiz waved them into his small house "Welcome, gentlemen! Would you like some coffee, or perhaps something stronger?"

Both Jacques and Raymond took coffee and sat in the manager's office.

"The Company contacted me by radio about your visit," said Ortiz. "We are currently experiencing a glut of sheep and would be happy to provide Monsieur le Comte with as many as he needs."

"Excellent," replied Jacques. "I'd like to look them over as soon as possible. My friend here is a scholar, and has prevailed upon me to ask if we could visit some of the sites described in the recent book about Easter Island."

Ortiz frowned but said, "If you wish to waste time looking at the pagan statues made by the heathen savages of the island, it's fine by me. However, one of my guards must escort you about the island."

Then, Ortiz insisted on hearing the latest news from South America and Europe before allowing them to leave.

Jacques and Raymond spent the rest of the day examining sheep. There were three sheepherders patrolling the island, men with shotguns who watched over the various flocks. During the course of their examination, they came upon the corpse of a sheep that that been killed and butchered. The sheepherders had apparently not seen this particular wolf. Raymond and Jacques' companion, Hernandez, made a note of the location of the sheep.

When they returned to Ortiz' house, Hernandez informed him of the butchered sheep.

Ortiz sighed and smiled grimly. "Hernandez, go get one." Lighting a cigar, he then added, "Now, Monsieur de Trémeuse, I will demonstrate why Williamson and Balfour can guarantee any amount of sheep that your company would care to order. Great measures are made to keep the flocks safe from the depredations of the natives. Please come with me and see."

They walked to a spot just outside the village gate. There were two upright poles set into the ground.

Hernandez returned in a few moments. He and the other guard marched a native boy of about eight years old up to the poles. The boy was quickly tied to the posts. When Hernandez uncoiled a long bullwhip, it became apparent to Trémeuse and Raymond what was about to transpire.

"Ortiz, this is not necessary. I will pay for the sheep rather than have this boy beaten."

Ortiz was adamant however. If leniency was to be shown, even this once, the natives would gorge themselves on the sheep until it was all gone. "Despite however many sheep you can buy, I have to think of the long-term establishment of order on the island," he gave them a grim smile added, "If either of you interfere, you'll be shot, guests of the company or not."

The boy shouted at Ortiz: "I did not kill the sheep, Señor!

Ortiz sneered, "It does not matter who did the actual killing; everyone in the village is guilty. You are the scapegoat for their sins."

Raymond and Jacques were forced to stand by while the boy received fifteen lashes with a bullwhip. Yet, that was not the end of his punishment. He was to be kept tied to the posts overnight and then, starting the next day, would work a week in the company's gardens.

After the whipping, Raymond and Jacques excused themselves, stating that they were exhausted from their trip. However, they sent a couple of bottles of French wine for Ortiz and his men to share. Jacques also made certain that the guards also received one. Jacques and Trémeuse then repaired to their tent which they set up a distance from the Manager's home. Once darkness had set, however, Jacques de Trémeuse donned his Judex outfit.

Raymond chuckled, "Why are you bothering with that? Ortiz will know it was one of us who freed the boy."

Jacques smiled, "It just feels right just that Justice should come to this island, even if only for one night."

Judex and Raymond made their way to the Manager's house and the bunker that that guards shared. As they had hoped, all were snoring away from the doped wine.

They had planned to make friends with the natives, and then dope the company's men, but the brutal beating had altered those plans. They now had only one night to find where the third tablet was hidden.

They quickly went to the poles where the unfortunate boy was tied. Judex cut his bonds. Raymond slung the unconscious boy over his shoulder as they made their way to the locked iron gates of the village. Judex quickly picked the lock and they entered the village.

The people of the village had watched their progress. Some of the older people gasped at Judex's appearance, but they did not have time to make inquiries. Judex handed the boy off to a couple of the village men.

"Take the boy to the ship off shore of the island," he instructed. "They will make certain that he receives medical attention."

He wrote a note to the Captain. Some of the villagers set off carrying the boy to a boat.

"The Manager and his men are sleeping and will sleep for the better part of a day," he said next. "We are seeking a tablet made of metal that may have been hidden in a cave."

But the villagers knew nothing of the tablet.

An old villager dressed in a rumpled flannel shirt and blue jeans said, "I am Raraku, I will lead you to our greatest treasure that we have, so far, hidden from all other treasure seekers."

When Jacques and Raymond set out, they noticed that the entire village was following them.

Judex was afraid that they would be in the way. "While we appreciate the company, we do not need you all to help us."

Raraku laughed and said, "No, señor, they are just traveling with us a part of the way. When the boy is found gone, Ortiz will be enraged. My people must hide in the secret caverns until his wrath has passed."

A few miles past the Manager's house, the main body of the villagers departed and headed for the smallest of the three volcanic mountains.

Raraku took Raymond and Judex to Orongo, a deserted village on the far side of the island, consisting of fifty stone buildings. They were built in two rows on a cliff, overlooking the ocean. There, directly out from the village, were three islets.

Raymond and Jacques knew from their reading of the Routledge book that Orongo had been the center of the Bird cult, which had grown to prominence during the desperate years of Easter Island, when birds had become a vital source of food. The island's ecological devastation had caused the social order to break down. The hereditary rule of kings had been abandoned for rule by lottery. Each year, the men competed to be the first one to bring a bird's egg back from one of the nearby islets. The winner would be the ceremonial leader for a year.

"Even though I am now a Jesus man," said Raraku, "I still honor the old ways, as do many of my generation."

This is why when Jacques had come into their village dressed as Judex, many of the older people had reacted in awe. His large nose, dark hat, dark cloak and pale face had made him seem like a human version of the sooty tern. This was the species of bird that the egg hunters had sought, which had black and white upper parts, as if it wore a hat and cape. Jacques's appearance had seemed to them to be the living embodiment of *tangata-manu*. In fact, some ancient carvings predating the Bird cult strangely looked very much like Judex.

Rakaku led them to a cavern beneath the village of Orongo. This was the place where the village elders would listen for the birds. Once inside, Raraku slowly felt his way among the petroglyphs on the wall. He pressed his fingers against one. There was a small clicking sound. He knelt down to the floor and pulled a small section of stone upwards. A three foot by two foot slab of stone swung upwards as if on oiled hinges.

Raraku crawled into the opening and said, "Follow me!"

They crawled into a larger cavern which narrowed into a natural tunnel leading downwards. Raraku went down this tunnel, which widened after about twenty feet. The walls were carven with petroglyphs. On the rear wall was a petroglyph of a bird-man. He had an egg where his navel should have been. Stacked on an altar below it were dozens of small wooden slabs. These were covered with a script which Raymond recognized as Rongorongo, the written language of Easter Island. He also noted, with shock, that it was similar to the script found in Mohenjo Daro in the Indus Valley. It was also similar to the script on the tablet found by Trémeuse in Africa.

This was the treasure of the Rapa Nui. Jacques and Raymond spent a while searching the area for a possible entrance into another chamber. Raraku left them to their studies to check up on the rest of the villagers.

Jacques continued to look about the chamber while Raymond studied the wooden tablets for a possible clue. The language was tantalizingly close to that of the African tablet, but not identical. Raymond was so intent upon examining the tablets that he nearly dropped one when he heard a scream.

Their first thought was that Ortiz and his men had recovered from the drug and found Raraku. They hurried out of the chamber through the tunnel and into the antechamber. Raymond was shocked to discover one of his former associate professors flanked by three members of the Men in Black. One stood behind Raraku's slumped form and held the native up by clasping him under the arms. Raraku was unconscious and it appeared as though the fingers on his right hand had been broken. One of the Men in Black grasped the native's other hand. The third man had his arm fastened about the waist one of the young woman from the village; his other arm was about her neck.

"Ah, young Raymond Mystère," said Dr. Rene Belloq, "if you would be so kind, hand over that tablet, and we won't kill the girl or the old man."

With a girl's life at stake, Raymond could do nothing else. Belloq accepted the wooden tablet with a superior smile. Raymond remembered why he had never liked him.

"Now, gentlemen, sit on the floor with your hands underneath your legs," ordered the Frenchman.

Raymond had heard that Belloq had turned his knowledge and skills to treasure hunting and looting. While some of his fellow academics had dismissed these as stories, he had had little trouble believing them now.

"You killed a sheep yesterday," said Judex. "Since you did not put to shore at Cook's Bay, I'd guess you and your companions scaled the cliffs and kept watch on us with telescopes or binoculars."

Belloq looked a bit startled at Trémeuse's statement, but replied with a bit of wry humor, "I prefer my lamb to be prepared by a chef, but it was sufficient for a meal on the run."

"A boy was cruelly beaten because you killed that sheep. You will answer for that crime here or in Hell."

Belloq laughed, "Monsieur de Trémeuse, that is the least of my sins. I have powerful friends and I shall never have to pay for my crimes." Smiling contemptuously, he added, "And I certainly do not fear the wrath of your non-existent God!"

Turning to the Men in Black, Belloq continued, "I am going to examine the next chamber, gentlemen. If anyone tries anything heroic, kill these two innocents."

Belloq pushed past them to crawl down the tunnel into the far chamber. Raymond looked to Jacques to see if he planned on jumping the three Men in Black. Jacques shook him off. It was too much of a risk to take with the lives of the two Islanders.

After about an hour of searching, Belloq returned with two more wooden tablets in his hands.

Belloq spoke to the Men in Black, "If there is a third tablet, it is not here. I know that we will not get anything out of Monsieur le Comte de Trémeuse or Monsieur Mystère, even if we torture them. A pity his pregnant wife was not along, Mystère would've cracked then. The girl and the old man have told us all that they know. We can search some more, but the people on this wretched island probably know less than we about their origins. They might be useful in showing us some hidden caches however…"

The man holding Raraku dropped the native on the floor like a sack of potatoes. "This one will not tell us anything; he is dead."

The girl screamed and struggled against the man holding her. His laugh soon became a scream as she bit him on his face. Nails extended, she attacked Belloq. The archeologist shot her in the midriff with a pistol and quickly turned to train it on Mystère and Trémeuse who had moved when the girl had attacked.

Raymond could not contain himself any longer. "Belloq, how can you work with these evil suppressors of knowledge?"

The Frenchman looked at Raymond and shook his head in wonderment. "You are so naïve, Monsieur Mystère! First, they pay well. Second, they only suppress certain types of knowledge. Besides, they allow select people in their employ to view their secret archives. Like Dr. Faust, I would, and perhaps already have, sold my soul for wealth, power and knowledge." His eyes and face became filled with loathing. "You and your fellow so called scholars are welcome to spend your days sifting through dust, languishing in extremes of temperatures, so you can pull out a few ancient bones and perhaps some scribble, something that no one will ever read. I prefer to use my talents more profitably."

Raymond was as shocked as everyone else in the room when Judex suddenly disappeared.

One of the Men in Black then bent over backwards, as if grabbed by a pair of unseen hands.

Belloq calmly fired four shots in the direction of the struggling guard. As the bullets slammed into the man, Judex suddenly appeared directly behind the dead guard. He slumped forward, blood leaking from his chest and head.

Raymond moved to help him but was stopped by Belloq's pistol.

"That was a nice try, Monsieur le Comte, but I, too, have trained at Rache Churan."

Belloq smiled expansively and bowed slightly to Jacques, yet his gun never wavered. "Many thanks for giving us the treasure of Easter Island and, of course, for providing us with a means to translate these tablets. It will be interesting to see what secret knowledge they reveal."

Belloq waved the Men in Black out of the cavern. With a wild laugh, he said, "Too bad the world will never know the secrets of Easter Island." He kept his pistol trained on Raymond as he stooped down to crawl out of the rectangular hole in the wall.

As soon as Belloq had exited the cavern, the stone slab was pushed back into place, sealing Raymond and Jacques inside.

Raymond rolled Jacques over to see how badly he was injured. He had taken two shots directly to the chest. However, he had been wearing a chainmail vest that had stopped the bullets. The wound to Jacques's head was merely a graze. He was in much better condition than Raymond had thought; most of the blood had, in fact, come from the guard.

When Jacques regained consciousness, they searched for a way out of the cavern. The slab door could not be moved. They went into the other chamber and, once again, began to feel about for hidden doors for a couple of hours, but in vain. Frustrated, they sat down to rest.

Raymond was moved to ask Trémeuse, "Did you study at Rache Churan?"

"No, I cannot say that I ever heard of the place."

"I heard of it from my grandfather. It is a monastery in Tibet where mystic and mental powers were learned. However, these skills take great discipline and from what I know of Belloq, I doubt that he had the wherewithal to make it through the front door, much less through any of the training. René has always been a venal and materialistic man with very little discipline. He was always pretentious and prone to make exaggerated, or entirely fictitious, claims about himself and his work. You heard him rant about scribbling that no would ever read? Belloq let his ambition and lack of discipline ruin his academic career. He published a series of monographs about ancient Egypt and Babylon; the only problem was that he falsified and fabricated his data. His bogus work was exposed and he was dismissed from his academic post."

Raymond found himself staring at the picture of the bird-man who bore a startling resemblance to Judex. His attention was drawn to the egg-shaped navel. He got up and examined it more closely. He discovered that it had been covered over with a thin layer of clay. Using his fingernail, he cleaned it off.

Inside the egg was a small circle.

"You told us that you found your ring inside the tablet, right?"

"Yes," Jacques said. "I think, however, that we should concentrate on getting out of here first; then, we can think about the research."

"I am just wondering if anything would happen if you put your ring in the circle on the bird-man."

To humor Raymond, Jacques pushed his ring into the small hole in the center of the egg. He did not expect anything to happen. After a minute, his doubts seemed to be justified and he took the ring back. Once it was back in his hand, however, the wall behind the statue quivered. Lines took shape, forming a rectangle on the wall. With a slight grinding of stone, the rectangle behind the statue moved upwards, creating a doorway.

Raymond and Jacques walked into a room which contained two pedestals, each about four feet tall. On one, sat a round glass ball which looked like a fortune-teller's crystal ball; on the other, lay three very thick books. One was bound in red leather, one in a shimmering cloth, and the third was covered in same metal that the Mayan and African tablets were made.

Trémeuse moved towards the crystal ball as if it called to him. He placed his hands on its cool surface. The transparent interior clouded as if filled with white smoke. The white cloud coalesced into the figure of an old man. With a shock, Raymond realized that the old man looked as though Jacques de Trémeuse might look in old age.

"My child," said the figure in the crystal ball. "I call you my child yet the generations that separate us are so vast that they cannot be counted. Yet mine lineage was imprinted with my essence so that it would continue, however dispersed or diffused, the Kingdoms of Man became. You are a Telcontari, a member of the house of Elessar Telcontar. This is why you look as you do, and why you have strong sense of right and wrong. This was done with a singular purpose, so that the knowledge of my Age would not be lost, so that the triumph of Good over Evil would not be forgotten. When the time was right, and the possibility arose that the Evil One might once again ascend to create a dark empire, we made certain that our history would be discovered anew by one in whom my essence was strong. We set in motion certain events so that our history would be saved by people whose histories paralleled ours, as similar events cycled through history. Even with the vast power of this *Palantir*, which now holds but enough energy for this last message, we could not foresee how long it would be before our lost tales were found. The stamp of my essence led you to the tablets of precious *mithril*, which in turn led you to this *Palantir*. I now charge you to take Book of Thain, the Book of Kings, and the Book of Mazarbul, to the one who can best translate them for your people.

"We do not know his name, only that he is a descendent of the Ring Bearer. The ring of power you hold was once an instrument of evil. It was melted down in the fires of Mount Doom, and the evil inside it was extinguished from this plane of existence. The lump of melted gold was found by a raven and brought to me. Although the evil is gone from the ring, it still has some slight power which can only be wielded by a descendent of mine in the cause of justice. Other rings may yet survive, and may call out to my descendents; this ring shall rule them all. So long as this ring that you wield is used for the cause of justice, mine other descendents may use their rings in a similar fashion. Just as you serve the cause of justice, you have no doubt fought against the minions of the Dark Lord, the Black Riders. Even though their Lord has gone, he seeks always to re-establish his reign and blanket the world in darkness. Guard well against the Dark Lord and his minions. Stride forth and serve justice and the light."

The image in the glass ball faded. The clear glass darkened and cracked. Raymond and Jacques picked up the three books. These were written in scripts unrelated to the other languages that Raymond had seen in the course of this adventure. They were unlike any script he knew. He rolled his eyes in frustration.

The door that had let them in had closed. They found an exit in the back of the chamber, which led to a narrow passageway that wound around for several miles before exiting just above the crater lake of the extinct volcano in which Orongo had been built.

It was noon when they started their way back towards Cook's Bay. However, in the distance, they saw Ortiz and his men riding horses towards them. Trémeuse and Raymond ran back towards Orongo.

Once at the cliff, they made the decision to climb down. The further down they climbed, they noticed a dinghy tied up at rock, previously hidden from view by an overhang. As they made their way to it, they heard another series of shouts behind them. René Belloq and his men were scuffling down the cliff after them. Jacques and Raymond jumped into the boat and began to row away. In the bottom of the boat were the wooden tablets that Belloq had taken from the cavern. There were also a few other artifacts that the Frenchman had helped himself to as well, such as a bundle of reeds known as a *pora*, which had been used by member of the bird man cult when they swam to the islets.

The Men in Black and Belloq shot at Raymond and Jacques. Bullets sang in the air, splashed into the ocean, and plunked into the wood of the boat. This spurred them to row even faster.

Ortiz and his men reached the top of the cliff. They began firing upon Belloq and the Men in Black. One of them was hit and fell into the ocean with a splash. The other two hurried down the cliff and began swimming after the boat. Suddenly, one of the Men in Black screamed as a shark took off his leg. Calculating the odds, Belloq put his hands up in surrender and walked towards Ortiz. The Manager's men then concentrated their fire on Raymond and Jacques. Their rifles did more damage than the Men in Black's handguns. The rowboat started to take on water. They spotted *The Pious Woman* and rowed towards it with all their might, but it was not enough. Their boat became so heavy that they could no longer move it. Having little choice, Jacques and Raymond jumped into the water, placing the wooden tablets and the books on the bundles of reeds. They swam towards the ship, pushing their packages before them.

Captain Kettle was quite shocked to see them but recovered rapidly. "Boys, escort these fine gents to their cabins. I have to get us underway." But Trémeuse grabbed the Captain by his shoulder, spun him around, and punched him to the floor.

"As the owner of this vessel, I am assuming command. Captain Kettle is to go to the brig. The charge is piracy." Raymond gaped at this turn of events. "Did you see any other ships about? No, because Belloq and the Men in Black did not follow us in another vessel, but rather paid Captain Kettle to hide them on board *The Pious Woman*. The dingy we were in was from this ship. Keep an eye out for any member of the crew that might be a member of the Men in Black." He turned to Kettle. "I am a bit surprised; I had heard you might be unethical, but loyal to your employers."

Captain Kettle grinned around a bloody lip. "I was; they paid me first."

Despite his vigilance, Raymond awoke early one morning to discover that someone had broken into the Captain's cabin and opened the safe, taking the books and wooden tablets. From the bridge, he looked about the ship and spotted someone throwing things off of the bow. Raymond ran down and tackled him. The sailor fought back with desperation. He pushed Raymond aside and jumped overboard.

The member of the Men in Black had succeeded in throwing aboard all but six of the wooden tablets from Easter Island. A search for them failed to find them. Fortunately, the three ancient books that they had been charged to take care of were still safe.

Raymond and Jacques took turns watching the three books and the tablets for the rest of their voyage to Shanghai, to Beijing, and on to Paris.

As the train pulled into the Gare de l'Est, Jacques said, "Raymond, we will never have any rest until the three books are out of our hands. Do you have any idea who Elessar Tolcontar had meant to translate the books?"

"No, unfortunately not. But perhaps Henrietta will."

Michel Cocantin met them at the station and winked at Raymond and punched his arm. "You're a papa, but I'll leave the details to Henrietta."

He drove them both to the de Trémeuse estate.

While Henrietta presented Raymond with his son, he regaled her with the tales of their adventures.

Henrietta paced, "Damn the Men in Black for their interference and their destruction of this precious knowledge. At least, they will not be able to translate the tablets from Easter Island." She looked over the three books that they had brought back with them. "It is really amazing. I would never have believed your tale if I hadn't seen the tablet change before my eyes. These books are really odd as well. I recognize the script, or at least part of it. Although I have never met him in person, I have corresponded with a professor of Anglo-Saxon literature at Oxford who has such a love of linguistics that he made up his own languages. He sent me examples of these. One of these books from Easter Island is written in his made up language."

"Perhaps he is really not creating languages, but remembering them!" Raymond picked up Henrietta by her narrowed waist and said, "He is welcome to them. We will have enough to do translating the clay tablets from the mine and the wooden tablets from Easter Island."

"Khokarsa," Henrietta said with distraction as she hugged her husband with all her might. It suddenly hit her that she came to losing him.

"Geshundeit!" Raymond said

"No, silly, that seems to be the name of the sunken island civilization mentioned in the African tablets. However, we have years to talk about that. For now…" her eyes glowed as she bent forward to give Raymond a promissory kiss as she slipped from his arms.

She then picked up the baby and cradled it in her arms, kissing him on the forehead as she said, "Little Monsieur, I think you will have a knack for being in the wrong place at the wrong time."

Epilogue

The Mystères sent the three books to the Oxford professor of Henrietta's acquaintance. These books formed the basis for a group of histories which were published under the guise of fiction to escape visitation from the Men in Black; yet, everyone who has read these works know them to be more than mere fiction. Some even believe the tale of Numenor to be his version of Atlantis, rather than the story of an island empire that existed ages before Atlantis.

The tablets from the Trémeuse mine were, unfortunately, not as complete as the Mystères would have hoped. They formed incomplete epics about the Khokharsan empire that flourished on an island in the central African sea approximately 12,000 B.C. This island empire also drowned. One particular epic about a hero named Hadon was popularized by an American author whose work was recommended to the Mystères by the Ironcastle family.

The wooden tablets that Raymond Mystère had rescued from the Men in Black turned out not to be in the Rongorongo script found on all of the other tablets, but rather on a script similar to that found in the Indus Valley.

These tablets formed the epic tale of a warrior-King named Thongor who lived in ancient Lemuria. According to this history, Lemuria possessed technology and magic similar to that described by the ancient Vedas.

Upon discovering that the Men in Black were part of age-old organization with insidious plans for humanity, Jacques de Trémeuse spent the next few years taking up the mantle of Judex with more vigor. His son took up the fight when Judex apparently perished in a final battle in a dirigible tethered to the Eiffel tower. However, there could be but one Judex, so his descendent, Frederic-Jean de Trémeuse better known as Frederic-Jean Orth, became L'Ombre.

Despite his influence and wealth, Jacques de Trémeuse was not able to exert enough pressure or influence to change the situation of the people on Easter Island. The Chilean government remained steadfast in treating the island as a territory, and the natives as unwanted interlopers on the island. Jacques de Trémeuse did secretly fund the Franco-Belgian expedition to Easter Island in 1934. An ethnologist named Alfred Métraux wrote about the information he gathered on Easter Island and his books resulted in focusing the world's attention on Easter Island. However, even this was not enough to free the natives of Easter Island. and it took decades for them to be able to once again freely move about their homeland.

Young Martin Mystère grew up to be the renowned Detective of the impossible, part private investigator and part archaeologist. Among his more acclaimed investigations would be the true stories behind Stonehenge and the Tunguska explosion in 1908. His greatest enemies were always the Men in Black.

Young Jacques Cocantin grew up to become Chief of the Sûreté, succeeding to the position after his predecessor, Chief Inspector Dreyfuss, had become mentally unstable. When Jacques heard that Hollywood would be making a film about his famous case against Sir Charles Litton, the jewel thief known as the Phantom, Cocantin was very pleased until it became apparent that the film made him out to be a buffoon. He demanded that his name be changed, and so it was. However, many people in the know have stated that the actor's depiction of Jacques Cocantin was uncannily accurate.

Dr. René Belloc would learn, quite dramatically, that he should have feared the wrath of God.

.

Late 1929. This time, Judex crosses the path of a most unexpected hero, or anti-hero depending on how one looks at it: Felifax, the Tiger-Man, created by none other than Paul Féval, fils, the son of the great writer who gave us the Black Coats. Felifax's appearance in this story takes place between Book 1 and Book 2 of his own saga, translated by Brian Stableford, and collected in a single volume in its Black Coat Press edition.

Christofer Nigro: *Eye of the Tiger-Man*

Three dark-attired men strode purposefully down the evening streets of the Marais neighborhood in Paris' third Arrondissement. The area's characteristic gray-toned architecture, the work of master architect Baron Georges Eugène Haussmann, perfectly blended with the darkness of the hour, granting the trio of criminals a sense of confidence that their activities were sufficiently camouflaged.

As operatives of the dreaded "Black Coats" organization, they knew that they dared not fail in their mission, but were enticed to try by promises of great riches and elevated status should they succeed. They were well aware that they had little to lose, save their lives, but to the likes of them, a life of unending poverty and insignificance in the great scheme of things was tantamount to no life at all.

The designated leader of the gang, Pierre, led the others to the steps of a bleak-looking house that sheltered more than mere tenants. For one of its empty rooms was used by the Black Coats as a storage depot for modern firearms that were later sold at a lucrative profit to any aspiring criminal who could afford them. Such weapons made the lawless elements a greater danger to the Parisian police whose job it was to curtail their activities. These three had been sent to retrieve a portion of the inventory in preparation for such a sale.

"Are you sure this is the right place?" Tréval, one of the gang, asked Pierre.

"Of course, I am!" Pierre snapped back. "Do you think the boss would have put me in charge of this retrieval if he thought me a fool?"

Tréval and the third man, Francois, declined to reply as Pierre brandished a special key and opened the front door leading into the house.

The trio was astounded to see an even darker-clad figure enveloped by a cape and wearing a slouch hat standing before them in the entranceway, with two ominous-looking firearms pointed in their direction.

"*Bonjour*, gentlemen," Judex said with all due irony.

"Oy!" was the only response Pierre could muster.

"And *au revoir*," the vigilante concluded as he depressed both triggers and sent two projectiles of hot lead into Pierre's knees. "Perhaps you should reassess your statement about your boss not hiring a fool to lead the rest of the fools."

"*Sacrebleu!*" Tréval hollered as he and Francois fled the steps in opposite directions, leaving a bleeding and crippled Pierre to his fate.

"I trust that I have no need to ask you to remain here," Judex remarked at the screaming Pierre as he began pursuit of Tréval up the darkened boulevard.

Running up the street as fast as his legs could carry him, Tréval could see that the neighborhood was bereft of all other people, save for a single young pedestrian who was casually walking in his direction, seemingly oblivious to the goings-on's.

As the panic-stricken criminal passed the young man, the youth unexpectedly extended his right leg and tripped Tréval. Such was the malcontent's speed and surprise that the breath was completely knocked out of his lungs as he hit the ground with a loud thud.

"*Excusez-moi*, Monsieur," the young man said with just a hint of sarcasm. "Forgive my notorious clumsiness."

Finally regaining the ability to breathe properly, Tréval rolled onto his back, only to have Judex's heavy dark boot thrust upon his throat, painfully blocking his airways.

"Prepare to meet justice," the vigilante said to the indisposed Tréval, his firearm pointed directly at the criminal's forehead. "I would refrain from all unnecessary movement while I take you into my custody and determine your sentence."

A gagging sound indicating compliance was all that his captive could utter in response.

Judex then turned to the young man standing beside him, a lad of about 19 attired in baggy trousers with a cap upon his head.

"Your tips are as on target as my gun shots, Kid, just as they always have been."

The Licorice Kid shrugged his shoulders in an expression of false modesty. "Well, what can I say? I'm a useful little curmudgeon. Did I just earn an increase in my fee? Information brokering doesn't come cheap, ya know."

"Maybe," Judex replied, not noticing François peeking out from a nearby pillar and holding a small blowpipe in his hands.

"That rapscallion cost us everything," Francois whispered to himself as he aimed the tubular device and used a blast of exhalation to project a thin needle at great speed towards the Licorice Kid.

The needle stuck in the side of the youth's neck, as Judex turned around just in time to recognize François as he fled around a corner. Unfortunately, the criminal departed too fast to hit with a bullet even from one with his extraordinary draw speed.

"Ow!" the young man yelped as he removed the needle from the side of his neck. "What was the big idea...?"

No sooner had those words escaped from his mouth than he suddenly appeared to turn a shade of sickly green, as his eyes rolled into his head and he collapsed to the ground.

"Michel!" the vigilante yelled, referring to the Kid by his adopted name, Michel Cocantin.

He immediately bent before the young man to check his pulse. It was detectable, but extremely weak.

"Hah!" Tréval choked out of his swollen throat. "You see what you get for trifling with the Colonel. He will kill all that you hold dear, and then he will remove your entrails and force feed them back to you..."

"Be silent!" Judex exclaimed as he kicked the criminal in the face with his boot, shattering his septum and sending a huge spurt of blood from both nostrils. Needless to say, Tréval was silent after that.

But sadly, so was the Licorice Kid.

A few short hours later, the Licorice Kid lay in a bed at the Trémeuse Estate on the outskirts of Paris. In his company were Jacques de Trémeuse, Judex's *alter ego*, his adopted parents, detective Prosper Cocantin and his wife, Daisy, and Jean Aubry, Judex's step-son, who grasped the young man's hand while sitting beside his bed.

Cocantin did his best to hold back the shedding of tears and to secure a brave front for the ailing young man whom he loved more than life itself. But seeing the Kid in the throes of agony from the poison in his system proved beyond his ability to restrain his tears for long.

Nevertheless, the Kid's bravado was greater than even the immense pain he suffered. "Don't count...me out yet, Dad," he said, while clenching his teeth to offset the effects of the spasms he suffered as the poison ripped through his circulatory system. "You know I'm...too... stubborn to...give up."

"Please, hush and reserve your strength," Jean told his friend. "My father will get you help. He'll make you all better. Right, father?"

Judex wanted to reply in the affirmative more than anything else in the world, but lying was not in his soul; nor was conceding to fatalism, however.

"Let me go and check with the doctor," was his studied reply.

Jacques left the room where great efforts were conducted to keep his long-time young ally as comfortable as possible. He made his way to the downstairs laboratory where Doctor de Villiers-Pagan had been performing a thorough analysis of the Kid's blood sample.

Villiers-Pagan had helped him—as well as several of his more outlandish friends—several times in the past, and although he shunned publicity, he was known in some circles as a true miracle worker. Jacques knew it was a good idea to have such a lab constructed in one of the lower levels of his multi-leveled mansion for just such emergencies. His sophisticated forensic lab doubled quite well as a makeshift medical lab in situations like this.

Quietly entering the lab, he observed Villiers-Pagan glaring into an expensive microscope. His attention was totally focused on the blotch of the Kid's blood smeared on a small glass slide. The Doctor noticeably frowned as he looked at the results of a chemical drop he had introduced to the sample moments earlier.

"Is there any progress, Doctor?" Jacques asked in a somber tone.

"I fear not, Monsieur le Comte," Villiers-Pagan replied. "That poison appears to have been extracted from a rare botanical source that isn't native to this continent—but exactly what type, I have no idea yet. It's quite potent, however, and its cells have resisted every chemical curative I know. I fear your young friend doesn't have much more than a week to live, at most. I suggest making the proper preparations for his passing, and turn our efforts towards alleviating the great pain he will suffer as the toxin proceeds towards its inevitable course."

"Are you certain you have exhausted every possible avenue? There must be an antidote! And if there is, you can rest assured I will leave no stone unturned to procure it."

"My good man, if there were such an antidote in existence, the only one who could possibly know about it would be those who created the poison in the first place. But from what I understand of the Black Coats, generosity is not one of their defining characteristics."

"I will find the man who poisoned the Licorice Kid and I will see to it that he tells me where I can find the antidote. In the meantime, please concentrate on keeping my young friend comfortable, as you suggested, Doctor."

"I will do that, of course. But how can you locate the man who created this poison?"

A very somber expression suddenly took over Jacques' visage. "I have my ways of finding what I need to know."

Hours later, François awakened to find himself trapped in a small chamber with stone walls. It was empty, other than the cot he lay upon. An object resembling a large mirror was situated near the ceiling, well out of his reach. He rubbed the left side of his face, which was swollen from the blow that had rendered him unconscious.

The criminal began to panic and recite several silent prayers to a God he scarcely believed in as he came to a full realization of his predicament.

"Welcome back to consciousness, François Marchand," said a deep, raspy voice emanating from an invisible speaker. "I am Judex, and you're in my custody, courtesy of a former partner of yours who was only too eager to provide your location after a few moments of conversation with me. You are no doubt quite hungry, so I will allow you to eat before we get down to some very important business. A tray of food will be dispensed through an opening at the bottom of the door to your left. Eat it quickly, and then we shall talk."

His entire body trembling with terror, François wasn't sure he could keep any food down as a tray containing potatoes, peas, and a cup of water was indeed pushed through the small opening by unseen hands a few seconds later. But with the hunger gnawing at his stomach, after so many hours since his last meal, he knew he would do his best to consume the meal. Within mere minutes, the repast was ravenously devoured.

"Now that your stomach is satisfied, François," the daunting voice continued through the speaker, "we will get to the purpose of your captivity—as if an explanation was actually a mystery to you."

"What happened was an expected consequence of crossing the Black Coats!" François shouted. "Had I not done that, the Colonel would have ordered a far worse reprisal. *S'il vous plait*, I was simply the dispenser of his retribution; I am not the one to blame! And if you refuse to release me, the Colonel's men will locate this place and free me, while you and all others within will be killed!"

"I greatly look forward to the day when your Colonel and I shall finally meet, but that is not your concern here. You are a failure to the organization, and you would fare no better in the hands of the Colonel than my own, your little move towards revenge notwithstanding. And that is why you are here. I will grant you a degree of leniency in exchange for providing me with the antidote to the poison you injected into my friend."

"Monsieur, nothing you could possibly do to me would be worse than what the Colonel would do if he got his hands on me for telling you. So keep me here indefinitely, or execute me at your discretion, I'll not tell you a thing."

"I beg to differ," Judex calmly replied as François suddenly grasped his stomach area with both hands.

A searing pain of extraordinary severity spread through his lower abdomen. He felt as if his stomach had been cut open, a demented fiend had inserted both hands into the incision and had begun sadistically twisting and ripping his entrails to pieces. François screamed in agony as he desperately squeezed his belly in a fruitless attempt to relieve the pain.

"François, that horrific agony you're now experiencing is courtesy of a special pain-inducing chemical I sprinkled over your food and drink. It won't kill you, but it will continue to bring you unending and ever-worsening pain until I am so merciful as to provide you with the antidote. And in order for me to do so, you must first provide me with the *other* antidote."

"Aaagghhh, curse you to Hell!" François screamed as a feeling akin to a disgraced samurai committing *seppuku* tore through his lower extremities. "I won't—*I cannot*—tell! Please, have mercy!"

"You mean, like the mercy you showed my friend? If he is to suffer without a cure, then so shall you. The difference will be that the hand of Death will grant him the mercy you denied him in a short time, but not so with you. The poison causing you such agony is not lethal, which makes it all the more horrible. So any degree of mercy you will receive is not for Death to give, but me, and me alone. And if you wish to receive any such mercy from me, then first you must be willing to give it for my friend."

For several more moments, François made a herculean effort to withstand the fiery sensation ripping through his guts like a blazing inferno. He screamed so loud that his larynx grew as raw as tenderized meat, and he repeatedly pummeled the wall beside him with extreme fury to keep the pain at bay. All such efforts proved ineffectual, and he lay on his cot flailing his arms and legs while begging God to free him from this indescribable nightmare.

"Do not beg God, beg *me*, you fool! I'm the hand of justice in the material world! Tell me what I want to know! Tell me, or suffer the tortures of Hell long before you actually die!"

After a few more minutes of pain-wracked effort, his innards beginning to feel as if they were enduring an acid bath, François could take no more.

"All right, god damn you! I'll tell you, just please make it stop!"

"Tell me first!"

"The antidote can only be found in a rare plant found amidst the jungles of India! Just outside the city of Benares! It's called *'Leaves of Mercy'* by the natives! Now pleaaassseee…!"

"*Tres bien*," Judex said quietly. "I will begin my journey to Benares this evening, to procure a sample of the plant, and test its curative extract on my friend. If it works, then will I give you the antidote to the poison which is now torturing you."

"What? No, you must give me the antidote now! Such a trip will require days! I cannot take another second of this! Pleeaaasseee…!"

"My friend will have to suffer for the same amount of time as you do. And if such a journey turns out to be wasted, then you will pay a greater price than he will in the end, for I will not grant you a single moment of reprieve from your agony. Enjoy your next few days, François, as I put the truth of your words to the test."

Judex then switched off the speaker system, and François's ever-escalating screams of anguish were lost behind the sound-proofed walls.

Jacques de Trémeuse strode through the streets of Benares following a 42-hour flight via the fastest aircraft on which his fortune could buy him passage. After a short period of rest and meditative techniques, he had beaten the effects of jet lag, and was at full operational capacity. He was attired in a light-colored outfit with the wide-brimmed hat that was typical of the garb Europeans often wore while visiting this sub-tropical environment to ease the effects of the extreme levels of heat and humidity. Moreover, he had disguised his facial features with a gray beard and mustache, with the hair at his temples and eyebrows colored a similar shade, to complete the masquerade.

As was the case during a previous journey to India, he was deeply affected by the degree of squalor that marred the streets as he headed towards the village of Bhavanour. This was in marked contrast to the impressive examples of iconic statuary of the great Hindu deities like the majestic Shiva, the bizarrely four-armed Vishnu, and the terrifying personage of Kali the Black—her girdle being adorned with human skulls—that were evident in all the temple architecture. He saw several such temples dedicated to the worship of these strange but amazing deities, so different but no less enthralling than the pantheon he studied from classical Greek mythology. He had difficulty understanding a culture that would embrace such beings in prayer, but as an individual who was often said to worship the concept of justice as if it was a divine force of the universe, he found himself able to relate to the native Indians on some metaphysical level beyond his immediate understanding.

The information Jacques had purchased upon his arrival proved quite accurate, and he soon found himself at the steps of the highly regarded convent of Shiva Ardhanari. It was the home and headquarters of Sourina, reputed to be the most highly revered Brahman in the nation, and a staunch ally of the occupying British government. His knowledge of the outlying jungles and their native flora was said to be second to none in this region—save for a legendary being of great heroism called "Felifax," who was allegedly the scion of Kali herself. But Judex had no time for legends, and was obliged to seek out a person of confirmed existence who could be readily located. Sourina was that person.

Using a forged card identifying him as a member of the British parliament named Reed Stratton, the undercover vigilante walked into the temple. He did his best to keep his attention off the multitude of scantily-clad *bayaderes* who jubilantly danced about, as well as the fierce gazes of the sacred tigers kept in cages within various sections of the convent with animal-tamers seeing to their maintenance. When he finally found a temple attendant who spoke English—a tongue he long ago had learned—Judex insisted that urgent business from the British authorities required an immediate audience with Sourina.

He was quickly pointed to the special chapel where Sourina conducted his personal meditations for any number of hours during the day. "Lord Stratton" was instructed to politely ask one of the guards outside the chapel to inform the temple leader that he needed to break meditation to address important government business.

Approaching the two guards, the disguised Judex spoofed a friendly smile and displayed his bogus government identification card.

"Lord Reed Stratton, here to see honorable Sourina on urgent government matters," the vigilante said in a surprisingly convincing British accent. "I understand he is deep in his daily meditations right now, but rest assured I wouldn't interrupt him were this not an urgent matter."

One of the two guards who was so chosen for his position due to his fluency in English responded, "Very well, sir. But would you please allow us to look over your card first? We are instructed to be very careful in admitting anyone who arrives unannounced, even esteemed officials of the British government."

"Why, of course," Judex replied with another phony smile as he handed over the card as requested.

The guards gazed at the card carefully, with the one who could not speak English telling his fellow something in Hindi that was accompanied by an expression of concern.

Damn it, Judex thought to himself. *I knew I should have used my usual Swiss forger instead of rushing up things in Paris!*

"Sir," the English-speaking guard said, "I dislike the thought of inconveniencing you, but..."

"Then don't!" Judex exclaimed in his usual French as he delivered an open finger strike to the guard's throat with astounding speed. The man hacked uncontrollably as Judex followed up his brutal assault with a front kick to the man's diaphragm that sent him clear to the ground.

The second guard shouted something in Hindi and went for his blade. Just as he drew it, however, Judex executed a side kick to the man's right leg that sent his bone clear through the skin. Dropping the blade and gasping in shock and agony, the guard was in no condition to defend against Judex's reverse punch to the nose, sending him to join his comrade on the floor.

"Forgive me for this, gentleman, as I am aware both of you were simply doing your jobs, but the life of a very good man is at stake, and I cannot abide by the usual niceties."

With the apology given to the two barely conscious guards, Judex entered the chapel. There he found Sourina deep in meditation on his knees in front of an exquisite, ten-foot statue of Kali in one of her destructive aspects, each of her multitude of arms holding either a blade or a severed human head by the hair, and her tongue extended almost serpent-like from her mouth. This statue was decorated with numerous precious jewels, each of which the wealthy vigilante instantly recognized as being worth a small fortune. Sourina was so intent on his meditative trance that he apparently didn't notice Judex's entrance, or the sound of his earlier scuffle with the guards.

That turned out to be another lie, however, as Sourina quickly jumped to his feet and drew a long curved blade. The formidable Brahman was startled when the strange white man before him drew a firearm at even faster speed and shot the blade out of his hand before he could thrust it into the interloper's chest.

"Pardon me, Monsieur Sourina," Judex said. "I presume you are fluent in French, *non?*"

"I am," Sourina replied in the vigilante's native tongue. "Now please state your business here, for there are far more guards in this temple than the two you dispatched outside. And know that I am a good friend of the British government."

"I do not care about any of those things, Monsieur. I came here for some simple information, the providing of which should not impact on you in any way. Tell me the truth, and I promise you will not have the misfortune of laying eyes on me again in the future. Refuse, and I will get persuasive until you inevitably give me what I seek. No guard or government official can help you more than you can help yourself here, not as long as I hold you at gunpoint."

Appearing to think the matter over for a few moments, Sourina responded with, "This all depends on what you seek. So what is it, outsider?"

"I seek a rare curative plant called *'Leaves of Mercy'* by the forest dwellers."

That plant is utterly sacred to the vanaprasthas *who live within the tiny locale where it grows in a very small cluster of patches,* Sourina thought to himself. *If he attempts to procure it, they will cut him to pieces if the monkeys do not do so first, and even this man will be no match for such obstacles, especially if the rumors of whom they have befriended ring true. The best way to gain Kali's rightful vengeance for this fool's temerity in intruding upon her sacred temple is to simply tell him the truth.*

"That sounds like an easy request," Sourina said with a barely detectable grin. He then dispensed the precise location of the plant to the vigilante, even being so generous as to draw him a detailed map. "You have my word on the honor of Brahma himself that this information is entirely correct."

"I'm sure you are aware of the consequences of giving me anything *less* than fully accurate information," Judex impressed before further surprising Sourina by departing through a window several yards above the ground floor to avoid having to injure any more guards.

And here I believed only my surrogate son Felifax could navigate in such a manner, the Brahman mused to himself. *I pray to Kali that you shall soon have a grave misfortune of your own in meeting the tiger-man, interloper.*

Shortly afterwards, Judex was trekking through the rain forests outside of Benares. He was garbed in a modified version of his dark uniform: this attire had a green-tinted camouflage motif that aided him in blending with the foliage. The wide-brimmed hat had flattened edges to help keep the sunlight from occluding his vision, and protecting his head and face. The uniform had thin plastic tubing grafted into its inner fabric that contained a specialized fluid which acted as a natural coolant. As a result, he wasn't leaking a single drop of perspiration in the scorching tropical environment. The stealth techniques he learned long ago in Tibet, along with his military survival training, would serve him as well in these surroundings as in a Himalayan mountain range or a European battle zone. His firearms were likewise modified, in this case to fire bullets nearly silently, so as not to attract any sort of unwanted attention should he be forced to discharge them.

Following the detailed directions drawn for him by the scheming Sourina, Judex waded through the deep jungle towards his goal, careful not to disturb any of the dangerous beasts known to inhabit it. Such creatures ranged from those as small as spiders, whose venomous bite could kill a grown man, to big cats, powerful enough to easily render a human being limb-from-limb. Other than swatting away some unidentified flying insects of large size, the only other animal life of concern he encountered were monkeys that sometimes darted from unexpected places. Occasionally they would acknowledge his presence by screeching at him and baring some imposingly sharp teeth for a moment, before skittering away. He had a firearm at the ready just in case one or more of these intimidating little primates decided to go beyond mere bold posturing.

His concerns appeared to be justified after approaching the intended destination, when a large monkey rushed out of a nearby brush *not* past him but *towards* him. Its sharp teeth and claws were extended fearsomely as it charged. Such were the vigilante's reflexes, however, that the beast succeeded in nothing more than getting its brain blown out the back of its head by a bullet. Just then, another leaped out of a tree about a dozen feet above Judex, determined to rip his throat with its fangs. Again, the vigilante's reflexes proved on the mark as he grabbed and hurled the primate from his shoulders after no more than a second of feeling the impact of its weight. The beast leaped at him from where it was thrown, only to be stunned by a quick side kick to its face with Judex's thick, weighted boot, and then having the top part of its head blown off by gunfire before it could recover. A third monkey was shot out of an overhanging tree branch about 15 feet off the ground about two seconds later when the vigilante noticed it situated there, in obvious preparation to pounce.

Upon that deed being done, another dozen monkeys ran screeching in the opposite direction, having taken the measure of this strange intruder in their neighborhood and deciding that he was a target best avoided. *Strange how these monkeys only attacked when I reached this specific area, where the* Leaves of Mercy *are to be found,* Judex mused. *But this region is said to be mostly avoided due to the fierce warriors that jealously protect its botanical treasures, so it's possible that the fauna here may not be as acclimated to a human presence as their counterparts in most other areas of the jungle. It's a mystery that cannot concern me now, however.*

As Judex approached ever closer to the patch of priceless flora he sought, he concentrated on breathing techniques and meditative visualizations that didn't detract from his keen sense of awareness, but which placed him in a calm state of mind where he was prepared to face anything. He was well aware that all his stealth training may not be enough to avoid a confrontation with the warrior denizens indigenous to this rarely visited area of the Indian jungle who knew the environment far better than he did. Though an ostensibly urban avenger like himself rarely faced adversaries of this sort, he reminded himself that, during one of his few excursions in such a locale before, he successfully survived an assault by the ferocious South American cannibal tribe known as the Shamatari, albeit not entirely unscathed. He knew how fiercely territorial warrior tribes could be.

As he hid behind a large tree and approached a clearing, he finally saw one of the very few patches of wild-growing *Leaves of Mercy* that bloomed amidst a small row of trees. He was certain his identification was correct thanks to detailed descriptions of the plants provided by his contacts. The proverbial coast appeared clear, but he still needed to avoid overconfidence and make the several yard dash it would take to acquire the plants, and then get out of that area as fast as a human who had not taken Professor Gibberne's infamous "accelerator" drug possibly could.

Taking a deep breath, Judex began jogging towards the desired botanical patch. No sooner had he run just a few yards, however, than he became aware of a large stone being hurled at him a mere split second before it would have become impossible to dodge. He bent his body backwards just far enough to avoid having the side of his head smashed. A second later, a bronze-skinned man with flowing black hair and wearing nothing but an animal skin *lamba* rushed towards him wielding a heavy wooden bludgeon. Before the warrior could attempt a swing, Judex hit him with an elbow strike to the bridge of his nose, crushing the cartilage in a small but dramatic eruption of blood, stunning the assailant; he followed this up with a spear hand poke to the man's solar plexus that sent him to the ground, unable to draw a breath.

In a fantastic display of his reflexes, Judex caught the next hurled stone thrown at him with his right hand. In a blur of motion, he drew his firearm and shot in the exact direction from which the two stones were thrown, hitting the warrior hidden on a low-hanging branch directly in the throat. The man uttered a horrific gagging sound and coughed out a stream of blood as he fell several yards to the ground.

Before the vigilante could make another move, he was struck on the back of his left leg by a long staff, causing him to drop his firearm and fall to his right knee. As he turned to recover his weapon, he saw that this particular stick had a blade apparently made of sharpened stone affixed to the end, and it was pointed a mere inch before his face.

"Cease and desist, or I will puncture your eye, intruder!" his assailant yelled to him in English.

Judex saw that the man holding him at blade point was an older but quite fit member of this warrior tribe, his flowing mane of dark hair streaked with silver, as was his long, straggly beard. His skin was somewhat wrinkled as a sign of age, but his great musculature was still readily apparent.

"You speak English?" Judex asked rhetorically in the same language.

"It was taught to us by a valued friend as useful to know," the older warrior replied. "The region outside the trees has been conquered by outsiders from a faraway land who speak this language, and you are clearly one of them, come to steal our treasured gift from the gods."

"I presume you are an elder of this tribe?"

"I am, and since the furry ones of the forest didn't claim your life as expected, I was forced to have my own tribal warriors make the attempt. And my elder position will not prevent me from standing at their side and facing the same danger they do."

"That is… quite noble of you. And I assure you that I am not like those other outsiders. I hail from a different land, and I am here to acquire your sacred plant to help a very good man who has been stricken ill for risking his life against evil-doers."

"I regret to hear of your friend's plight, but the *Leaves of Mercy* belong to my people alone. It has been our tradition for many generations to never share them with those outside our tribe, as the gods would be very angry if this rare gift was squandered in such a way. We are the guardians of these treasures, and you are therefore refused. You also killed one of my men with the tiny metal spears that weapon of yours fires, and you will be held accountable for that by my people's laws."

"Forgive me, honored one, but I have no time for negotiating with your narcissistic ways."

Upon that pronouncement, Judex made another astoundingly fast move by grasping the staff and striking the warrior elder's right leg with his own in a swift simultaneous movement. This resulted in the older guardian being knocked off of his feet and divested of his weapon.

"You will not have our treasure!" the older man shouted at the stranger who now held him at bay with his own bladed stick.

"Yes, I will," Judex told him defiantly.

"No, you will not," countered another voice from behind.

Judex turned to find himself facing one of the most impressive specimens of humanity he had ever seen. A single glance screamed 'warrior of the highest caliber' to the seasoned dispatcher of justice. This newcomer was clearly quite young, perhaps no older than 19 years of age, and was tall of stature with light bronze skin, short sandy blonde hair, and muscles rippling from all four limbs and torso. He too was dressed in just a loincloth, and wielded a Hindu ornamental blade in one of his hands.

"You are…?" Judex asked.

"My name is Rama, but you may call me Felifax, as many have come to do," said the powerful-looking youth in a strong voice. "The people of this area are my friends, and the natural treasures of this region will not be exploited by the intruders from Britain."

"I am not from Britain, but France," Judex reassured him. "And I do not come here to exploit anything. A very good man has been poisoned while in the act of battling evil-doers, and I was told by a physician that only the extract of that plant can save him. He is my friend, I owe him my own life many times over, and I will not leave here without a sample of the plant."

"Do the noble men of this jungle, not being friends of yours specifically, have lives of less value than your friend?" Felifax queried. "Are they but 'savages' to you, as they are to the British conquerors? You can kill one of them to obtain what you want, because it's easier to take *their* lives than to lose someone whom you have personal affection for, right? That is not nobility, but the very definition of the narcissism you accused the elder of having."

"I won't let one who has risked so much for me and the pursuit of justice die!" was Judex's final exclamation before raising his purloined staff and commencing an attack on Felifax.

The tiger-man deftly dodged the first strike, and retaliated with a slash of his blade, tearing the tunic of Judex's uniform and drawing a trail of blood on his chest. This act immediately won the vigilante's respect, as few men could so easily inflict an injury upon him, however minor. In another blur of motion, Judex delivered a feint with the staff to trick Felifax into dodging to his left, which the vigilante exploited to deliver a roundhouse kick to the jungle hero's jaw. Felifax's face recoiled with the blow, but much to Judex's surprise he remained on his feet. He spit a wad of blood from his torn lip and rushed towards Judex. The vigilante swung the staff at his opponent—a move Felifax anticipated—and the jungle champion ducked downwards in mid-rush to avoid the blow. He managed to tackle Judex thanks to this cunning feint of his own, and lifted his opponent as if he were a rag doll, slamming him on the ground with great force.

His breath forced from his lungs by the impact, Judex found himself lying on his back as Felifax leapt on him, pinning him beneath the weight of his muscular form and placing his blade to the vigilante's throat. In another surprising move, Judex fought against the temptation to quit and slapped both of Felifax's ears with his cupped hands, nearly rupturing both of the jungle man's eardrums with the air forced through the alimentary canals. The jungle hero leapt upwards and howled in pain. Taking advantage of this momentary gain, Judex gathered as much strength as he could muster, and delivered a side kick to the stunned Felifax, sending him several yards back against a tree.

Swiftly retrieving the staff and forcing himself to stand via a huge effort of will, Judex prepared to resume the battle. However, a pang of great concern pervaded his psyche when he saw that Felifax was likewise still standing.

Behind him, the elder warrior friend of Felifax grabbed Judex's gun where it lay, pointed it at the khaki-attired intruder, and fired. However, though he knew how to discharge a gun, he was not trained in doing so, and the blowback of the weapon surprised him, causing him to miss his target by a large degree.

Judex detected the air displacement caused by the bullet, and he turned and angrily stabbed the older warrior in the stomach with the bladed end of the staff. Blood poured out of the wound as Judex retracted the weapon, and the older man put his hands over the injury and fell to his knees.

"No!" Felifax shouted, as the bestial side of his genetic make-up took hold. Judex looked back at the jungle man to see a sight that actually caused him to wince with greater concern than before: Felifax began growling like a wild animal as his eyes suddenly changed to resemble the greenish-yellow orbs with slit-like irises reminiscent of a feline, and brownish stripes akin to those on the coat of a tiger suddenly began forming on the young man's skin. The jungle hero had now truly become a tiger-man!

With a loud roar that echoed across the forest and sent several flocks of birds fleeing from the branches they perched on, Felifax charged Judex with animalistic fury. Realizing he was not likely to survive a head-on attack, the vigilante jumped to the side to evade the charge. Rolling back to his feet, Judex swung his staff, striking the enraged son of Kali twice in the face with two blinding flashes of motion. Much to his consternation, however, the tiger-man shrugged off the blows by shaking his head like an animal, and caught the staff when his foe attempted to strike him a third time. He then pulled the stick from Judex's grip with little effort, and broke it in two, tossing each half aside. Though genuinely given pause, Judex reminded himself that he had fought and survived the likes of Dracula, and would certainly overcome this jungle-borne adversary, no matter how formidable he may have turned out to be. The urban warrior took on a fighting stance as he prepared for his opponent's next move, and eager to answer the challenge, Felifax gave another ear-splitting roar as he prepared to charge again.

Both ceased in their tracks, however, when the elder warrior suddenly limped between them and shouted, "Stop!" In defiance of his stomach wound, he exerted enough pressure on it with his hands to staunch the severe bleeding just enough to prevent him from losing consciousness. The fact that he was on his feet in this condition displayed an amazing degree of will and fortitude that caused both champions to heed his order.

Felifax was still in feral mode, and he longed to taste his adversary's blood, not cease his attack. He growled again, his mouth frothing in anticipation of another leap at Judex's throat, but the elder warrior remained obstinate.

"Rama, you must come out of your animal state," he told him in Hindi. "The wound inflicted on me was not deep enough to puncture anything vital, and I will recover with the help of some of the clotting salves."

The words of his friend, strongly in tune with the forces of nature, affected Felifax on a deep level. Within moments his feline characteristics and feral mindset subsided, with his handsome human features and affable personality returning.

"Both of you, listen to me!" the elder said in English again. "Rama, when I saw you two fight, I could sense the true nature of this man's spirit. He is not motivated by selfishness; his main folly is desperation, not malice. I believe he fights for the forces of justice just as you do, even if in a different manner. I now realize that despite our generations of tradition, we must be willing to share our great treasure with him so he can save the life of another noble man. If we deny him, then we become no different than those who refuse to share their resources with others who need them. If we cannot prove we are better than our adversaries, then we become no more worthy of the gods' blessings than they are."

Pondering the words of his valued friend for a moment, Felifax replied, "You speak wisely, as you so often do, Elder Rakki. But one of your tribe died at this intruder's hands."

"He was slain in self-defense," Rakki noted. "He was a warrior who knew the risks, and had attempted to take our intruder's life just before losing his own. This man reacted as a warrior would have, and not in a pre-meditated manner. He initially attempted to take the plant by stealth, not murder."

Felifax turned to gaze at Judex again. "Who are you, stranger?"

"You can call me Judex," the vigilante answered. "And I do apologize for the life I took from this tribe, for the injuries I inflicted on the other two, and for my conflagration with you. I can tell you are not some primitive savage as the British government likes to describe the jungle tribes, but a man of great nobility and honor. I am well aware that not all tribes, or individuals within them, can be considered 'noble,' but many of you certainly are. You have my solemn promise that I will not make the extract of your sacred plant available on a wide basis, but will only use it to cure my friend. He is a good young man around your age, Rama, and I believe if you met him, he would earn your respect as he has mine."

"Then take your sample, and leave," Felifax said with authority. "I don't mean to be brusque, but I would see an end to this, and I need to tend to my injured friends and prepare the burial of our fallen guardsman, just as you no doubt need to make haste in getting the plant back to your friend in the far off land of France."

Judex nodded in agreement before extending his hand to the tiger-man. Felifax accepted the gesture and shook in a powerful grip. Judex was well aware that the nature of their meeting, and the life he took from the tribe during the melee, would prohibit these two disparate warriors from forging anything beyond an uneasy understanding at this time.

But as the two went their separate ways, and Judex took the small sample of the botanical treasure he needed to save the Licorice Kid, he was pleased to see that champions of justice could be found in many lands across the globe. This gave him further hope that his endless and thankless mission, with all its attendant sacrifices and tragedies, was not a futile endeavor.

*1932. In this small metafictional exploit, Rick Lai, the translator of the two orig-
inal Judex novels, attempts to deconstruct the notion, once put forth by Philip
José Farmer, that The Shadow and The Spider were one and the same—a concept Farmer himself later rejected. If Judex is the first of the dark cloaked,
slouched hat avengers, then how does he cohabit with his American progeny?
And can their fantastic WWI adventures be reconciled with History?*

Rick Lai: *Judex Rules*

New York, 1932

In 1963, Georges Franju released his remake of a classic French serial,
Judex. The English version of the film contained this foreword:

"During the First World War, moviegoers were enthralled by a series of serials from France made by Louis Feuillade—the D. W. Griffith of France—
recounting the fantastic exploits of Fantomas, a super-criminal, and his archenemy, Judex, a super-detective."

Anyone familiar with Judex would have been appalled. Judex wasn't the
adversary of Fantomas. The nemesis of the master criminal was a totally different man named Juve. What nobody realized at the time was that the foreword
had revealed a startling truth about the universe.

In May 1937, the man in the black hood and robe was alone in the rigging
of the *Hindenburg*, the prized dirigible of Nazi Germany. Soon, the airship
would be docking to the mooring mast of the Lakehurst Naval Station in New
Jersey. The hooded man just set a bomb to explode. The timer was scheduled to
ignite the bomb in five minutes. That was just enough time for him to escape
with a parachute.

The saboteur had boarded the dirigible in Frankfurt posing as a member of
the crew. He lived to spread terror and destruction. He hated Germany because
of all the carnage it caused in the Great War. He had been a soldier in the
trenches during that conflict. The saboteur reached for his parachute when an
ominous voice interrupted him.

"Prepare to face justice, Fantomas!"

The speaker was a man with burning eyes. He wore a black hat and cloak.

"Judex!" shouted the hooded Fantomas. "How did you get here?"

"I followed your bloody trail across Europe to this airship. Disguising myself as an American businessman named Shaw, I booked passage. It took me
time to identify you. Now you shall pay for your crimes against my family!"

Judex leaped at Fantomas. One of the dark avenger's hands grabbed Fantomas by the throat. The other hand yanked off the master criminal's hood.

"No! It can't be you!"

These were the last words ever uttered by Judex. The bomb exploded incinerating him and his antagonist.

To fully comprehend this confrontation in its proper context, we must go back five years earlier.

Mike Volny was one of the top gangsters in Chicago. They called Eliot Ness and his federal agents the Untouchables because they couldn't be bribed, but Volny was the true "untouchable." No crime stuck to him. Twice in 1931, he had stood trial for murder in Chicago. Both times he had been acquitted. Now one year later, he was about to expand his underworld empire. Realizing that the demise of bootlegging was inevitable with the upcoming presidential election, Volny was about to branch out into narcotics.

The gangster had come to New York to make a deal that would give him an endless supply of illegal drugs from the Middle East. Volny had chosen New York for the site of the meeting because Ness had been putting pressure on him in Chicago ever since his second acquittal.

Volny was scheduled to meet his Middle Eastern contact at Malay John's. Before World War I, this establishment had been a gambling hall and opium den. In 1932, it was a speakeasy. There was a secret room in the basement that was soundproof. Many a murder had been done inside it. The Irish-American proprietor also owned a bar, known as Malay Jack's, in the Limehouse district of London. Regardless of whether he was call John or Jack, this unscrupulous individual arranged meetings between members of the criminal elite from two continents.

The man who Volny awaited was the most powerful drug trafficker in the Middle East. He was called Ali of Cairo, alias El-Iblis ("The Demon"). He presided over a monstrous organization that dealt in drugs as well as human slaves. Volny had never met him, but there would be no difficulty in recognizing him. Ali was rumored to be the ugliest man on Earth. He was an elderly hunchback with a pockmarked face.

Together with his two bodyguards, Volny waited impatiently for Ali of Cairo in the secret room at Malay John's. Suddenly, there was a knock on the wall from outside. The gangsters pulled out their guns. Volny hit the switch that caused the secret door in the wall to slide open.

In the doorway stood a hideous figure. He was a hunchback in a black hat and cape. His ugly face reminded Volny of John Barrymore in Dr. Jekyll and Mr. Hyde. The hunchback had grotesque teeth and long white hair.

"You know who I am?" asked the stranger.

"You're Ali of Cairo," replied Volny.

"May I come in?"

"Certainly," replied the Chicago gangster. He was surprised that Ali hadn't brought any bodyguards with him. Volny and his underlings holstered their weapons. The hunchback entered the room. Volny closed the panel. After sitting down in the chair, the hunchback took out a cigar. Volny reached into his pocket to pull out a cigarette lighter.

"There's no need," replied the hunchback. "I prefer my own." He took out a lighter and lit the cigar.

"You know my offer, Ali," stated Volny. "What are your terms?"

"My terms are very simple. Death!"

Before Volny or his bodyguards could respond, a revolver appeared in the hunchback's hand. Three shots rang out. Standing over the corpses of Volny and his associates, the hunchback pressed the base of his lighter against their brows. The emblem of a red widow spider was imprinted on the forehead of each cadaver.

Some minutes later, there was a knock on the wall. Holding his revolver, the caped hunchback hit the switch to open the secret door. Standing outside was a pockmarked hunchback flanked by two bodyguards.

"Araneus!" shouted the real Ali as the other hunchback opened fire. Soon there were three more dead bodies with branded foreheads. Reaching the ground level floor, the hunchback ran outside. He was seen by several witnesses later interviewed by the police.

The newspapers had a field day. The *Daily Register* called the assassin "the Red Widow Slayer," while the *Gazette* dubbed him "the Hunchback of New York." The biggest media sensation was made by a controversial radio personality.

The sound of a telegraph key sounded on the radio.

"Good evening, Mr. and Mrs. America from border to border and coast to coast and all the ships at sea. Let's go to press. This is Walter Winchell.

"Mike Volny, the man voted most likely by the Chicago police to make a witness turn up dead, is no more. His bullet-riddled body was found last night in the basement of a New York speakeasy. Among the five other corpses next to him was Ali the Demon, the so-called 'King of Narcotics' wanted by Scotland Yard.

"The foreheads of all the bodies bear a scarlet mark. It resembles the red widow spider of Florida. This is the fourth such incident in New York within the last two weeks. In all four cases, the victims had ties to organized crime. All bore this modern Mark of Cain on their brows. Witnesses have identified the murderer as a hunchback wearing a black hat and cloak. Who is the Red Widow Slayer?

"It is my privilege to have as my guest the man who will unmask the killer. He is the noted British criminologist, H. Ashton-Wolfe. He is the author of the 'Secrets of the French Police' series currently appearing in the pages of *Ameri-*

can Weekly. In the early 1900's, Mr. Ashton-Wolfe served with the French police in both Paris and Lyons. RKO Pictures will be releasing a movie based on his exploits this December. He will now publicly reveal the identity of the gangland killer terrorizing New York City."

"The killer is Hanoi Shan, the most dangerous criminal ever to plague Paris," stated an aristocratic voice. "Prior to the Great War, he murdered people with monstrous centipedes. This Chinese hunchback adopted the alias of 'the Spider.' So far, I have recorded six of my encounters with Hanoi Shan during my time with the French police in the pages of *American Weekly*. Some of those stories can be found in my books, *Warped in the Making* and *The Thrill of Evil*."

"But you wrote that Hanoi Shan was dead!" interjected Winchell. "He had been fatally shot by a member of his own gang!"

"The French police were deceived. Hanoi Shan faked his own death in 1910. Thus he began a complex scheme to eliminate his underworld rivals by posing as a cloaked vigilante."

"You're claiming that there were similar slayings before the Great War?"

"Yes, the clue lies in the fact that Hanoi Shan now wears a black hat and cloak. Reports of a similarly clad vigilante surfaced in Paris as early as 1913. This enigmatic individual was called Judex, Latin for 'judge.' He was also christened 'The Mysterious Shadow.' Judex was suspected of persecuting a prominent banker, Maurice-Ernest Favraux. In late 1918, there appeared in Monte Carlo an almost identical vigilante called Umbra, Latin for 'shadow.' During the 1920s, there were sporadic reports of Judex in France and Umbra in remote corners of the world. There are also rumors of a caped vigilante leaving a mark on dead criminals in India. This man calls himself Araneus, Latin for 'spider.'"

"I'm confused by all these names, Mr. Ashton-Wolfe. Exactly what are you saying?"

"Judex, Umbra and Araneus are the same man! All these vigilantes are Hanoi Shan!"

In a room lit by a blue light, the radio was turned off by a hand wearing a ring with a purple girasol. "What utter nonsense!" exclaimed the listener. He sat down at a desk and wrote the following with a large quill pen in a journal.

My legacy has been stolen by an interloper. I am the son of Théophraste Lupin and his second wife, Darlla Rassendyll. I should have been born Kenton Lupin, but the persecution of the Black Coats forced my parents to adopt a surname that was an anagram of my mother's first name. Josephine Balsamo and her associates orphaned me at an early age. Luckily my older sister found me. She raised me to respect law and order. How different my destiny would have been if our accursed brother, Arsène, had located me instead.

My sister never intended for me to become a vigilante like my mother. She wanted me to be an aviator, but the vengeance of the Black Coats once again altered my fate. I had no choice but to seek out my mother's sanctum hidden be-

neath the Paris Opera House. There I found her private annals detailing her ac-
tivities as the Revenant. In my quest, I was aided by my stalwart cousin, Ragging
Rassendyll. He insisted on his older half-brother, Dick, joining us. I foolishly
agreed. I'm not paying the price for that decision.

Ragging, Dick and I all read my mother's annals. Recruited by the British
Secret Service, I was on assignment in Russia when the Great War begin. Both
Ragging and Dick became pilots for the Allied cause. When President Wilson
brought our country into the war, we all transferred to the American Expedi-
tionary Force. Ragging continued to fight in the air, but Dick was assigned to
the trenches. He has developed a sadistic addiction to violence. Perhaps it was
witnessing the constant slaughter of his fellow soldiers that unhinged Dick's
mind. I do not know. Despite my boast to fully comprehend the nature of my fel-
low men, Dick has always remained an enigma to me.

After the war concluded, Ragging, Dick and I have drifted apart. Ragging
stayed in the army. Dick went to India. Immediately after the war, I launched a
new campaign against the Black Coats. In Monte Carlo, I assumed the alias of
Umbra. I adopted a Latin nom de guerre to honor my mother's first Acolyte,
Julia de Trémeuse, and her firstborn. Since that time, I have used variations of
Umbra in multiple languages. Inevitably, I settled in New York, the city of my
birth. I have a wonderful setup here. The Police Commissioner denies that I ex-
ist. One of his detectives secretly cooperates with me. Now Dick has returned
from India. That lunatic threatens to screw up everything. Like myself, Dick had
been inspired by my mother's records to become a vigilante. Just as my moth-
er's records prompted me to contact Jacques de Trémeuse, they caused Dick
and his brother to do the same. Impressed by Judex as I was, Dick has adopted a
Latin alias.

His hunchback disguise was inspired by Henri de Lagardère, the duelist
who slew opponents with a thrust to the forehead. Lagardère pretended to be a
hunchback in order to infiltrate the entourage of a stock market manipulator.

Of all the crime-ridden states in the Union, why did Dick have to come to
New York? Couldn't he have chosen New Jersey? Why does he have to wear a
hat and cloak like me? With all his money, you'll think Dick could afford an
original costume! This flagrant copycat loves publicity. His branding of corpses
with the mark of Araneus will make it impossible for any vigilante to work in
this city. The police will be forced to track him down. There's even talk of re-
placing the Commissioner. The ordinary cops have always ignored me. Soon
they'll mistake me for Dick and try to shoot me.

I have no choice but to end this madness. Dick must die!

"How long have you had these visions?" asked Jacques de Trémeuse.

"Since 1914," replied Captain "Ragging" Rassendyll. An accomplished ace
in World War I, Rassendyll had earned his nickname due to his constant playing
of a jazz song, "Ragging the Scale." Last year, Rassendyll had achieved fame by

fatally shooting an escaped gorilla that had gone on a rampage in New York. Now he was in the city to attend a birthday party in his honor hosted by the Police Commissioner, a war veteran whose cousin had flown with the Captain in France.

A special guest invited to the same dinner was the Comte de Trémeuse. Before Europe had been consumed by bloodshed, he had been the cloaked vigilante known as Judex. When Germany threatened his native land, the Comte and his younger brother had selflessly enlisted in the French army. The Comte had fought alongside both the Captain and the Commissioner in Europe. Peace had permitted the nobleman to resume the outward existence of a wealthy aristocrat while secretly administering his own brand of justice.

"The visions nearly drove me insane. Fortunately, Kenton correctly diagnosed my problem in 1917. I was viewing events from a parallel world."

"What are you talking about?"

"There is at least one alternate reality in which most of us exist on an Earth with a different history. Kenton had discovered a portal to this parallel world in the state of Maine. There was another Captain Rassendyll in this alternate reality. I was witnessing events in the life of my astral double during my waking hours. With Kenton's help, I managed to get these visions under control. He persuaded Captain Philip Strange to use his hypnotic powers to stabilize my affliction. Now I only relive my otherworldly twin's life when I sleep. According to Kenton, my condition is not uncommon. He believes many people, especially professional writers, experience visions of this parallel world in their dreams."

"How does this other Earth differ from our own, Ragging?"

"The war lasted years longer. The Germans had the most horrible arsenal imaginable. Their scientists invented everything from giant insects to zombies."

"What about your family. Is it the same in this parallel world?"

"Dick was still my half-brother, but we have another sibling, Al Rassendyll. He corresponds to my cousin, Kenton. Al is the Umbra of this world."

"What about Kenton's mother, Darlla Rassendyll?"

"She was murdered in 1879 by the Black Coats."

"Do I exist in this parallel Earth? If Darlla died, there would have been no one to prevent my mother's suicide."

"Actually, your mother's double was rescued by Jean Lamotte, the Revenant of this second Earth."

"Interesting. On our world, the Black Coats murdered Lamotte, and Darlla became the Revenant to avenge him. The opposite must have happened on this other world."

"Precisely, Jacques. Since this alternate Darlla Rassendyll was a distant cousin, my doppelganger investigated her decades-old death with his two siblings. As in our world, the Revenant's annals were discovered beneath the Paris Opera House in 1910."

"I gather that my own history was the same in this parallel world?"

"Not quite. The chronology of your life is different. Your vendetta against Favraux reached its climax in 1916 instead of 1913. However, the outcome was identical. You married Favraux's daughter. Another variation is that your brother suffers severe bouts of depression due to all the horrors he saw in the war."

"What about this Al Rassendyll? He must have a different personality than our Kenton."

"Al doesn't feel as comfortable hiding in the shadows like Kenton. Al still wears the hat and cloak, but would rather solve mysteries openly like Philo Vance and Ellery Queen. Remember Kenton's magician friend? Al doesn't have Walter for a confidant. Instead, the Umbra of that world confides in a far different person."

"Who?"

"His loving brother, the parallel Captain Rassendyll. Since I'm psychically linked to my alternate self, I sometimes have insights into the activities of the Umbra of our world."

"Since you'll telling me this, I can only conclude that Al is doing something that you disapprove of. You must fear that Kenton is behaving in a similar fashion."

"Al intends to kill his world's Araneus. The other Umbra can't stomach a rival vigilante."

"Then Kenton must have the same murderous intentions regarding your half-brother."

From an alleyway across from the Sovereign Hotel, the man known as Araneus waited in an alleyway. Soon three notorious gangsters, Lucky Luciano, Meyer Lansky and Joe "the Teacher" Kulak, would be arriving in the same car. Araneus intended to ambush all of them.

As the gangsters' vehicle parked in front of the hotel, Araneus readied his automatic revolvers. Suddenly a ghostly laugh erupted from the shadows. The bogus hunchback turned around. "Umbra!" he shouted.

"To paraphrase your illustrious French predecessor," answered the laughing intruder, "since you would not come to me, I must come to you. I have a gift for you." Emerging from the back of the alley, Umbra carried a large oblong box. He opened it revealing a pair of eighteenth century swords. "Pierre d'Artois has authenticated these blades. They were once Lagardère's. You may have one of them."

Araneus chose one of the swords. He examined it closely. "Magnificent! I assume this act of generosity comes with a catch."

"You're perceptive as always, Monsieur Araneus. You have trespassed on my territory. Such an offense is unforgivable. There is only one way for gentlemen like ourselves to settle this dispute."

"A duel to the death! You appeal to my artistic nature, Monsieur Umbra!"

Umbra grabbed the other sword. "Then you accept my challenge?"

"Of course. En garde!"

In a dark alley in New York, two men in black hats and cloaks parried back and forth.

"You must find that false hump cumbersome," taunted Umbra blocking one of his antagonist's thrusts.

"It never hampered Lagardère," answered Araneus. "Why should it bother me?"

"You copy Lagardère's methods too closely—even the mark on the forehead." Umbra dodged another thrust.

"Actually I got the idea from your mother mutilating the shoulders of her vanquished enemies. I just mixed her modus operandi with Lagardère's."

"You will never equal Lagardère. You don't known his deadly thrust, the Botte de Nevers." Umbra was now gaining the upper hand in the duel.

"Only Vautrin ever learned that secret."

"You're wrong. I know it."

Umbra was about to fatally stab Araneus in the forehead when another man in a hat and cloak tackled him. Before Araneus could react, he was seized from behind by Captain Rassendyll.

"Who dares interfere?" demanded Umbra.

"Judex!" announced Jacques de Trémeuse.

An hour later, a meeting occurred in Captain Rassendyll's study in his New York residence. Judex sat at a desk. Standing before him were Umbra and Araneus. Seated in another chair was the Captain in full military regalia. The other three men still wore their hats and cloaks.

"Dueling is a relic of the past," declared Judex. "Three of us render justice wearing the hat and cloak. I am the most senior of the trio present. My sobriquet means 'judge.' Today disputes between gentleman are settled by judges. I implore you, my two friends, to accept me as an independent arbitrator."

"I accept," stated Umbra.

"As do I," acknowledged Araneus.

"Monsieur Umbra, state your grievance."

"With the exception of the Gray Seal before the war, I was the first vigilante to take up permanent residence in New York City. I claim no monopoly on fighting crime, but such work must be done in secret. The flamboyant methods of Monsieur Araneus invite retaliation from the underworld. Like Favraux, most malefactors prefer to commit their misdeeds in the dark. However, a new breed of criminal has begun to arise. Fantomas was the first of this ilk. These men are flagrant exhibitionists who delight in killing the innocent. Recently, I slew in this very city a Fantomas imitator, a dark master of evil who wore a black hood and robe. He tried to devastate the city with bombs. Human monsters like

Fantomas are a rarity in this city, but they would soon become commonplace if my colleague makes New York his base of operations. He would attract these sadists like a magnet. Thousands of innocent New Yorkers would perish every month. I have no more to say."

"Monsieur Araneus, it's your turn," instructed Judex.

"Crime is a disease that will never be cured. Its progression can only be stalled. The folly of Prohibition has mutated crime into a virulent plague. Monsieur Umbra argues that I will spark an abundance of Fantomas copycats. The emergence of such Lords of Terror is already inevitable. Desperate times calls for desperate measures. These human predators must not be slain in the shadows. They must be slain in the open. They must be marked as the unjust. No one man can combat these outlaws. I have as much right as Monsieur Umbra to protect New York from criminal scum. I rest my case."

"You have both been very eloquent," concluded Judex, "but there is one issue that neither of you addressed. The role of the indigenous police must be considered. The police will not tolerate a vigilante openly usurping their duty to combat crime. Already there is a citywide manhunt for you, Monsieur Araneus. The Commissioner is diverting major resources that should be combating the gangsters of this city. What is your response to that inconvenient truth, my friend?"

"Once the Commissioner fails to apprehend me, he will be replaced. The new Commissioner will probably be a personal friend of mine. That fact shall work to my advantage. He'll turn a blind eye to my activities."

"Monsieur Umbra, you're permitted a rebuttal," proclaimed Judex.

"I know the man of whom Monsieur Araneus speaks. He is a man of honor who would never countenance the slaughtering of criminals by a self-appointed executioner. If he became Commissioner, he would pursue my rival with an unprecedented religious zeal. To be successful, vigilantes must shroud themselves in secrecy."

"Monsieur Umbra's counter-argument is sound," decided Judex. "In my early days as a vigilante, Monsieur Araneus, I was as brazen as you are. I wrote threatening letters to my archenemy declaring my existence. If Favraux, in his guise of a respectable banker, had taken those letters to the police, I would have found myself in a needless battle with the law. Fortunately, he did not. Eventually, I reached the same conclusion as Monsieur Umbra. To be successful, vigilantes must shroud themselves in secrecy.

"Alas, Monsieur Araneus, I must rule against you. Your presence here would make crime more rampant by creating an unhealthy diversion for the police. Furthermore, the criminals here would find a way to turn your presence to their advantage. Like the Black Coats, they know how to make innocents *pay the law*. You would find yourself constantly being framed for their crimes. You must leave this city."

"Won't I ever be permitted to return?" asked Araneus. He looked at Captain Rassendyll. "I do have relatives here."

"The restrictions on your presence in New York will be totally up to the discretion of Monsieur Umbra," said Judex.

"I shall be generous in victory," volunteered Umbra. "There are times when I'm forced to fight crime outside of New York. Generally, I'll take a jaunt to Maine, Florida, or some other state, but sometimes I travel to another country. Someone will need to protect the city in my absence. An occasional visit by Araneus to New York would be beneficial under such circumstances."

"You'll be able to contact me in Los Angeles," said Araneus. "The growth of the movie industry there is attracting the interest of organized crime. I shall make that city my headquarters in the United States."

"In deference to your decision, I shall scrupulously avoid Los Angeles in the future," promised Umbra.

"I have one suggestion, Dick," noted Captain Rassendyll. "We should stop all this wild talk that you, Kenton, and Jacques are the same man. Kenton effectively phased out his Umbra alias long ago. He only employs it with those of us who know him from the old days. You should abandon your own Latin alias."

"You're quite right, brother. I'll start using the English equivalent."

That night, Captain Rassendyll dreamt of his counterpart in the parallel Earth. As in our world, Umbra and Araneus fought a duel in a New York alley. However, the Umbra of this world wasn't the man who should have been christened Kenton Lupin. He was Dick's half-brother. Al Rassendyll was no match for the phony hunchback. Araneus would have fatally stabbed his sibling if Judex and Captain Rassendyll hadn't intervened. Mimicking the events of our world, the quartet gathered in the Captain's study to hear a ruling by Judex,

"We live in violent times, my friends. Soon criminals will be armed with weapons as lethal as those invented by the Kaiser's scientists in the Great War. New York will become a battlefield as bloody as No Man's Land. An exceptional man must protect this city. Alas, Monsieur Umbra, you are not the man to undertake this mission. You are ill-suited to the hat and cloak. Only Monsieur Araneus has the nerves of steel to meet vicious violence with vicious violence. You may remain in this city if you desire, Monsieur Umbra. Nevertheless, you must be subject to your older brother's orders, just as my younger brother, Roger, is subject to mine."

The dream ended there, but there were events that unfolded later. Depressed by Judex's decision, Al Rassendyll took a brief European vacation. In France, he sought solace with Roger de Trémeuse. Al and Roger had been friends since they served together in the trenches of the Western Front.

"It's difficult being the younger brother to a man like Dick," said Al. "I now understand why he and Jacques get along so well. They're both arrogant snobs."

294

"You have to be more sympathetic to Jacques," advised Roger. "He's suffering a severe mental strain due to all the humiliating defeats at the hands of his archenemy."

"Archenemy? Wasn't Favraux defeated?"

"He was. Even though Favraux drove our father to suicide, Jacques spared his life in order to marry the corrupt banker's daughter. Favraux was permitted to live out his life in lonely retirement. The banker was later found murdered. For years, my brother has been futilely chasing his father-in-law's killer. He doesn't want anyone interfering in this vendetta. That's why he hasn't told you or your brothers about it."

"Who killed Favraux?"

"Fantomas."

"Didn't Fantomas drown with Inspector Juve in 1912?"

"That was the first Fantomas. Years after that fiend's death on the *Titanic*, a secret admirer of Fantomas took his idol's name. This second Fantomas is as ruthless as the original."

Returning to America, Al Rassendyll moved to Los Angeles. Following his half-brother's abandonment of his cloaked alter ego in the 1940's, Al resettled in New York. There he befriended a writer named Bruce Elliott. Many of Al's exploits were chronicled by Elliott.

In 1973, Jacques de Trémeuse reached his ninetieth birthday. Shortly after that milestone was passed, he was visited at his estate near Fontainebleau by an old friend from the United States.

"I've been reviewing my correspondence with Ragging over this parallel world," observed Jacques. "The discrepancies are amazing. Rocambole actually created that vigilante society called the Knights of the Moonlight. Not only was Chéri-Bibi much older, but he overthrew a tyrannical government that launched a new Reign of Terror in France. In the 1840s, Fergus O'Breane destroyed all the cities in Australia and threw Ireland into a ruinous civil war. In our world, O'Breane merely raided British ships near Australia and then died shortly after returning to Ireland."

"It's our reality that concerns me, Jacques," admitted the American. "I need your advice. All my secrets are about to be exposed by this man." The speaker handed Jacques a photograph.

"Isn't this that brilliant American author who penned that novel where everyone in the history of mankind is reincarnated on another planet?"

"Yes, Jacques. He's written two biographies about distant relatives of mine. Both contained genealogical charts of our large family. Dick's ancestry was cited in one of them."

"How does that affect you, Kenton?"

"This writer tried to track down Dick. Instead, he found his half-brother. Ragging Rassendyll pulled an elaborate prank. Borrowing from H. Ashton-

Wolfe's wild speculations, Ragging pretended that he, Dick and I are all the same man. The American writer repeated that falsehood in his biographies."

Jacques laughed. He pointed at the photograph. "That won't fool a man with his intellect for long. He'll gradually realized that he's been conned."

"He already has. He's discovered Ragging's true relationship to Dick. Ragging will be unmasked as Dick's half-brother in a revised paperback edition of one of the biographies. This writer demands that Ragging tell the truth about me. What should I instruct Ragging to do?"

"The parallel world provides the solution. You don't exist there, Kenton. Your role in history was transferred to another man. Ragging can identify the shadowy vigilante of New York as Al Rassendyll."

"Perfect!"

"Technically the story isn't a lie," stated Jacques gazing at the writer's photograph. "Hopefully this man will never write anything about my family."

"Actually he told Ragging a very interesting theory about your family."

"What?"

"In fairness, the gentleman in question has been misled by the faulty introduction in the English version of Franju's film about you."

"I never saw the English version. What did it claim?"

"The foreword confused your alter ego, Judex, with Juve. You were falsely identified as the archenemy of Fantomas."

"What does that have to do with my family?"

"You're forgetting Juve's ancestry."

"*Mon Dieu!* Juve and Fantomas were brothers! This man is going to claim that Roger and Fantomas are the same person!"

"Don't worry," assured Kenton. "My cousin convinced him that Roger isn't Fantomas."

Neither Kenton nor Jacques suspected the horrible truth. On the parallel Earth, Roger de Trémeuse had assumed the identity of Fantomas. Roger's mind had been driven insane by the monstrosities of World War I. In order to avenge his father's suicide, he killed Favraux. In May 1937, this alternate Fantomas and his brother perished fighting each other aboard the *Hindenburg*.

John Gallagher is a distinguished British artist who offered to illustrate a series of covers for books that never existed for Tales of the Shadowmen 8. *Two of these involved Judex in a fight with Bernède's other creation, the villainous Belphégor, with accompanying text by Jean-Marc Lofficier.*

John Gallagher: *Judex vs. Belphegor*

1: LE CRIME — Arthur Bernède
2: LA VENGEANCE — Arthur Bernède

1935. As official ceremonies take place at Mont Saint-Michel to celebrate its new status as a historic treasure, the French President is mysteriously assassinated under impossible circumstances: shot by a ghostly apparition. Meanwhile, Micheline du Bec, the fiancée of Judex's son, is kidnapped. A 50-year-old Judex is forced to again take up the mantle of crime fighter. His investigation reveals the mastermind behind the murder and the kidnapping: Simone Desroches, a.k.a. Belphegor, a ruthless, amoral scientist who is seeking the location of the Sword of the Archangel Michael who slew the Dragon of the Apocalypse. Micheline is the key to finding the Sword, hidden on the Mount by her ancestor.

What if...? The manuscript for Judex contre Belphégor *was found unfinished (except for a few pages) in the papers of Arthur Bernède upon his death in 1937. Written 20 years after* Judex *and 10 years after* Belphégor, *this mythic encounter between two "monstres sacrés" of the French cinema immediately became a best-seller. Plans to film it were abandoned due to a disagreement between the heirs of Bernède and those of Louis Feuillade (co-creator of* Judex*).*

ARTHUR BERNÈDE

JUDEX CONTRE BELPHÉGOR

DEUXIÈME ÉPOQUE : LA VENGEANCE

"LES ROMANS MYSTÉRIEUX"
EDITIONS JULES TALLANDIER

1935 Romain d'Huissier is the author of several French RPGs and the co-anthologist (with Julien Heylbroeck) of collections of short stories taking part in the Hexagon Comics universe, as well as Hexagon: Dark Matter, *a novel taking place in that same universe, recently published by Black Coat Press in a translation by Matthew Baugh, who also translated the following story. Romain has spun here a thrilling espionage yarn pitting two French champions, Judex and a secret agent known as The Chinese Fish (because of his ugliness), against their German counterparts...*

Romain d'Huissier: *A Ticket for Thule*

All seemed quiet among the warehouses that dotted the industrial area on the banks of the Seine. Night fell slowly and the early autumn darkness crept between the buildings, chased here and there by the faint light of an electric street-lamp. Suddenly, the sound of engines broke the silence. Two trucks appeared and navigated the maze of alleyways, as if looking for a specific address. They finally stopped in front of a large building, their headlights illuminating the legend which adorned the pediment: *Ironcastle Foundation.* Fifteen men emerged, dressed in black and wielding pliers and bolt-cutters—heavy enough to cut through the security fence and the padlock on the door. They operated quietly, professionally, quickly gaining entrance into the building.

Some distance away, a man watched them furtively. As he hid in the shadows, he reached into his jacket and drew a gun from its holster. The man had an ungainly appearance, but dressed with some elegance. His name was Georges Sauvin and his slightly protuberant eyes had earned him the nickname of "the Chinese Fish." More to the point, he was an agent of the French Secret Service. He had been on a case for several days and all signs had led him to the Ironcastle Foundation warehouse—an unidentified German spy in his sights.

Sauvin smoked in silence. He'd hoped he would only have to deal with a few men, half a dozen at most, not the fifteen thugs who had come. So much for his arrogance, which had made him imagine he could manage this alone. With a sigh, the agent was in motion. Slipping from shadow to shadow, he reached the building's entrance which the criminals had entered a few moments earlier.

It took Sauvin's vision a few seconds to adjust to the darkness inside, but the noise told him what was going on. Apparently, the thieves were breaking open crate after crate, looking for something. When they didn't find anything interesting in one, they moved on to the next. Operating in small groups, they were quickly turning the inside of the warehouse upside-down. The Chinese Fish decided to try a bluff and stepped into view, pointing his gun:

"Don't make a move! The warehouse is surrounded by the Secret Service. You can't escape!"

Dead silence followed this announcement as the bandits stopped working to stare at the newcomer. Time seemed to stand still and Sauvin thought his bluff would work. Then reality took over and one of the robbers pulled a gun, followed by several others. The French agent scarcely had time to utter an expletive before plunging behind a crate, bullets buzzing past his ears.

Leaning out intermittently from his shelter, he fired back—it was time to find better cover. Sauvin, an accomplished marksman, wounded three enemies during this brief exchange, incapacitating them. But that was not enough to tip the balance; the Chinese Fish was outnumbered and could only prolong the inevitable. His ammunition was not inexhaustible.

Under the cover of their comrades' gunfire, the other bandits resumed hastily breaking open the crates one by one. The ground was strewn with straw and valuable artifacts; yet, these seemed of little interest to the burglars.

Suddenly, a mysterious shadow appeared before them and the electric lights overhead seemed to dim. They looked up and froze with fear at what they saw: a man facing them, his face hidden by the shadow of his hat, his body draped in a black cape fastened with a silver clasp.

Judex!

The brigands hesitated a moment as the apparition moved silently toward them. Then, they resumed fire despite the dull terror that caused their hearts to pound. Brandishing their guns, they fired and fired again, but in vain. Judex continued to walk calmly forward and the bullets were lost in the folds of his cloak or in the shadows surrounding him.

With one leap, the vigilante found himself in the midst of the criminals. Without giving them a chance to react, he lashed out with fists and feet with all the speed of an accomplished *savate* artist. His foot smashed a knee here; his fist broke a jaw there; he parried a blow from a set of iron bolt-cutters from his right; he dodged the butt of a pistol from his left. In the space of a breath, and almost silently, Judex had put many of his adversaries out of commission.

Sauvin had realized that the pace of enemy fire was diminishing, but he didn't understand why. Boldly, he rose, ready to fire, and swept his gaze across the warehouse. He saw what had disturbed his attackers: the black-clad Judex, on the other side of the warehouse, wreaking havoc in the opposing camp. Yet, this had not stopped the other bandits from continuing to search the premises. A cry told the Chinese Fish that they had finally laid their hands on what they wanted. He just had time to see them raise a heavy granite tablet before he was targeted again and forced to drop to the ground.

As he retreated, step by step, from the burglars' redoubled gunfire, Sauvin tried to find a way to block the men who had seized the artifact from reaching the door. Noticing the fight at the back of the warehouse, he shot two of Judex's opponents before gesturing to the man in black:

"This way!"

A brief glance was all it took for the vigilante to understand. Disappearing into the darkness, he slipped away from the men surrounding him to reappear at the door. He glanced outside and shook his head. Sauvin got the message when he heard screeching tires, then the sound of an engine fading into the distance. The robbers had fled with the fruits of their theft—the very thing they had been looking for.

The shooting was not over yet: there were still a half-dozen armed opponents. Judex drew two pistols from his cape and, standing boldly in the open, fired methodically. Leaping from cover, Sauvin came to his aid, and their crossfire quickly neutralized the criminals. Several of them were still alive and the Chinese Fish would have them questioned by his office to learn more about their purpose. With any luck, they would give him a lead on the German agent he had been stalking for weeks.

While Sauvin made a phone call from the warehouse's mysteriously empty sentry box, Judex examined the remains of the boxes the burglars had ripped open. Crouching amid the debris, he tried to understand the reasons for this crime. Among the objects he scanned, there was a great deal of gold and precious stones; a treasure that bandits would not normally have ignored. The chest which had held the stolen tablet was no different from the others and, obviously, had contained nothing else.

Sauvin approached Judex and the vigilante turned to face him.

"My men are coming soon to take these fellows," he said, pointing to the bandits who still lived and had been bound. "I hope to draw some useful leads from them."

"You have the first clue here," Judex said—he spoke in a monotone, his voice ageless but deep—"I've found a code on the crates indicating their source, followed by a serial number. The listing on the box whose contents our visitors were interested in is *Middle East: SUM3X.*"

Sauvin tried to outstare the other man, without success.

"Yes, I guess the Ironcastle Foundation must keep track of their possessions. I'll go there right away.

Hearing the noise of cars outside, Sauvin glanced through the door.

"In the meantime, I hope I can count on your testimony so that..."

When his gaze returned to Judex, he was gone, as if swallowed by the shadows.

Two days later, Sauvin waited patiently in a room at the headquarters of the Ironcastle Foundation in the heart of the seventh arrondissement. He had landed an interview with Hareton Ironcastle himself to get the famous French-American adventurer's insights on the stolen tablet. As he sat in a comfortable chair, the Chinese Fish kept going over the events of recent days. For several weeks, his contacts in France had been whispering about the presence of a dangerous German agent in France; one of the best. Present in Paris for some unknown reason, he kept to the shadows, and the French Secret Service had not discerned much about his plans; their information was scattered and mostly unusable. But Sauvin had managed to piece together the puzzle from tenuous clues and had gleaned that the Ironcastle Foundation was involved. Little by little, he had backtracked to the warehouse plundered two days earlier.

Sauvin went over the various elements in his mind. First, the Ironcastle Foundation. It had been founded over a decade earlier by the explorer on his return from a particularly epic adventure in darkest Africa. Its purpose was simple: it financed expeditions across the globe in order to push the boundaries of human knowledge. Hareton Ironcastle's considerable fortune allowed him to pay substantial sums for the daring projects which had the good fortune to catch his fancy. The Foundation reserved the right to ten percent of the riches recovered, plus a copy of all the knowledge discovered on these adventures. According to the Secret Service, the Foundation was completely transparent: legally registered, it paid its taxes, declared its assets and collaborated with various academics, mostly historians and ethnologists.

Judex on the other hand... he was a different story. An unfathomable mystery, the most famous urban legend of Paris, a vigilante of who punished criminals under the cover of night. Elusive, perhaps immortal... Once before, the Secret Services thought they had discovered his identity, but it was probably a sham, the man they suspected was over 45 years old, while the apparition called Judex seemed ageless. Maybe it was a dynasty? An identity that was handed down from master to disciple? Perhaps there was more than one Judex? The riddle was insoluble. Not that it unduly disturbed Georges Sauvin; after all, this mysterious shadow was working on the right side.

An impeccably dressed secretary came to get the Chinese Fish, pulling him out of his reflections. She told him that Mr. Ironcastle was ready to see him and guided him through a maze of corridors his office. Sauvin thanked the young woman, not without an appreciative glance in passing, and then entered.

Hareton Ironcastle's office was a cave of treasures. Vast and ornate, it offered visitors a change of scenery that was abrupt, dramatic and primitive. The walls were covered with strange trophies, glass cabinets exhibited objects from every continent. Exotic carpets on the floor formed a surreal mosaic. A powerful fragrance projected the mind to some far off place by the rhythmic pounding of phantom drums. It took Sauvin several seconds to regain his composure. Hareton Ironcastle was behind his desk; he had risen at the Chinese Fish's entrance to greet him. The man's appearance matched his reputation—colossal. Though he was more than 50, the explorer had kept his impressive physique and imposing presence. He was a titan, with long blond hair and eyes as blue as icy fjords that he had inherited from his Viking ancestors. The plainly dressed man held out his large hand with a smile. Sauvin shook it, feeling the vitality of the adventurer's thousand exploits.

"Mr. Sauvin, it's a pleasure to meet you," Ironcastle said, a slight trace of an American accent in his voice. "Thank you for your diligence in trying to solve this crime."

"Please, I should to thank you for seeing me so quickly. I know you're very busy. I was sorry to hear of the death of the warehouse guard."

The watchman, who should have protected the Foundation building, had indeed been found dead at his home the night before, which explained his absence during the break-in. The giant nodded, sat back and invited the speaker to sit at turn opposite him.

"I have all the information in our possession. The stolen property was discovered during an expedition led by my nephew in person, on one of the supposed sites of ancient Sumer. It was the only artifact intact, hence its interest to us.

Ironcastle took several photos from a large envelope. Sauvin leaned over and examined them one, by one; the tablet it was shown from all angles.

"Here are pictures of the tablet, taken on site. It is made of granite and covered with cuneiform writing typical of the period. I assigned some linguists to work on it after the theft, thinking it might be helpful. According to them, the text speaks of a legendary land beneath the earth; an unknown country - to which, it seems, this tablet is a map.

"Interesting," the Chinese Fish muttered. "However, I can't figure why these antiquities would be of any interest to German Intelligence."

"But I know," interrupted a sepulchral voice that seemed to come from nowhere.

Immediately Hareton Ironcastle was on his feet, his muscles taut like a wary animal's. Sauvin reflexively raised his hand to his gun, but paused when he saw who had surprised them—Judex! The man in black stood in the corner of the office. It was impossible to say how he could have entered without being noticed. He advanced a few steps to place himself in the light and the Chinese Fish signaled Ironcastle to sit down.

"Well," said the giant, "that's a funny way to invite someone in!"

"I have some information for you," Judex said, ignoring the remark. "I know the sponsor—the German spy sought by the French services. And I know the reason for his act."

Sauvin whistled admiringly.

"In two days, you learned more than our agents have in several weeks of investigation?"

Judex gave a sinister smile, and even the intrepid adventurer, Ironcastle felt a shudder down his spine.

"I have my methods. And let us say that the criminals we let escape preferred to speak before being submitted to them."

Sauvin squirmed uncomfortably in his chair. Perhaps the vigilante was on the right side, but nothing about him was warm or reassuring.

"Very well," Ironcastle said, squaring his chair. "We will listen to you."

Judex was silent several moments for effect. Finally he said a name, just one.

"Jan Mayen."

This revelation had the effect of a thunderclap. Sauvin appeared dismayed.

"Mayen? The German hero? I knew he was in France, on a diplomatic mission at the embassy, but I would never have suspected he was our man... That makes sense, after all, It explains why it was so difficult for us to see."

"It wasn't clear, even for me," said Judex. "He is a well protected man who enjoys powerful relationships. He was ideally placed to commission what might pass for a simple burglary."

"There remains the question of 'why'," Ironcastle said in a thoughtful voice.

Judex turned to him.

"I think the name Sun Koh will tell you something—enough for you to understand this whole affair."

"Sun Koh?" Sauvin wondered aloud. "The adventurer who claims to be the last Atlantean?"

"Yes," Ironcastle said. "I've had trouble with this individual. For some years, he has been on the trail of the legendary Thule, also known as the Hollow Earth."

The Explorer stopped, eyes widened with understanding.

"Precisely," Judex said. "The Hollow Earth, to which the stolen tablet is a map, according to your linguists. And it is common knowledge that Jan Mayen works for Sun Koh.

A long silence ensued, as each man took in the full impact of these revelations. Sauvin slumped in his chair, a look of despondency on his face.

"If it is actually Jan Mayen behind all this... then we are powerless. He is protected by diplomatic immunity, and even if we could gather evidence against him, the law could do nothing."

Again, Judex's smile sent shivers down his spine.

"I couldn't care less about the law; I am only concerned with justice. And I have decided that this tablet shall not fall into the hands of the man called Sun Koh."

Before the others could answer, the man in black took a few steps back and his cape seemed to merge with the darkness, wrapping him in a cover of shadows. He disappeared without a sound, leaving Sauvin and Ironcastle alone in the office.

A strange aircraft split the heavens heading toward Germany. It was neither a plane nor a Zeppelin, although its shape was vaguely reminiscent of the latter. The ovoid ship progressed rapidly, driven by nothing less than an atomic reactor. Famous throughout Europe, it was the craft developed by Jan Mayen.

The latter, strapped into a suit halfway between a uniform and an explorer's garb, stood in the cockpit, watching the men who maneuvered his ship.

Mayen was satisfied. The mission that had brought him to France was a great success. He had been able to capture the Sumerian tablet that his employer, the fascinating Sun Koh, desired so passionately. The artifact would bring him closer to his goal: the conquest of Thule, and the establishment of an underground empire to accommodate his pure race as the world was covered with ice; a new Atlantis reserved for the elect. It was now time to return to Berlin for further operations.

Suddenly there was a powerful roar. The man in the cockpit looked at each other in surprise. Mayen moved to the window and saw what it was: a streamlined plane, whose pilot was protected by a glass bubble. And Mayen recognized the pilot immediately.

"Judex," he whispered, with a hint of a smile.

The German loved challenges. In reality, he had felt almost disappointed that his mission had been so easy. It had been his fond hope that the famous Judex would try to thwart his plans again. It was immediately confirmed as a chattering, like the sound of maddened insects, indicated that the plane was under fire. The bullets pierced the fuselage of the aircraft, frightening the crew.

"Calm down!" ordered Mayen. "Get to your posts; prepare to fight back!

The crew rapidly got themselves organized. Their machine gun turrets were aimed at Judex's plane and opened fire.

Shortly after leaving the Ironcastle Foundation, Judex had gone to the Château-Rouge, his secret lair. In this half-ruined fortress, he stored all his material—his weapons in the fight against evil. His possessions included a sophisticated aircraft, equipped with the latest advances in propulsion and weapons; a fighter surpassing anything owned by the militaries of the world.

The sound of engines broke the silence as Judex took off in his powerful craft. Through his underworld contacts, the vigilante had discovered that Jan Mayen had left France on the same day. Using sophisticated navigation equipment, he soon found the German's strange ship, and immediately opened hostilities.

Making his first pass on the enemy aircraft's flanks, Judex riddled the fuselage with bullets. A trail of smoke leaked from the canopy and the man in black smiled; his equipment was all he'd hoped. Starting a wide, banking turn for a second pass, the vigilante saw flashes from the front of the airship, indicating retaliation—just in time!

With an oath, Judex dove, avoiding the first burst. With a touch of his thumb on a red button he fired, but his bullets were lost in the sky. The plane shook, struck by enemy fire and his flight became erratic, less assured. With a quick glance Judex assessed the damage to his right wing. He adjusted his grip on the handle accordingly and rushed straight at the enemy aircraft. He didn't swerve an inch as he emptied his magazines and a fierce gleam of defiance shone in his eyes.

Jan Mayen had to shout to be heard by the crew. After weathering a series of near misses, Judex's plane had recovered and was diving at the airship at full throttle. Mayen swore, grabbed the helmsman and threw him to the ground, taking his place. Bracing himself against the crank, he tried to change course and take his ship out of the path of deadly Parisian vigilante but it wasn't possible. With a deafening crash, the plane slammed into the airship and lodged in its side. A powerful jolt ran through the ship while a series of explosions were heard in the rear of the vessel, which began to dive toward the ground.

Rising, Mayen could only see damage. Several of his men, without waiting for orders, donned parachutes and jumped into the void. Mayen ran a hand through his hair and felt blood beneath his fingers. His sight blurred for a moment. When his mind refocused, he saw a man stood in the cockpit, facing him. The hat, black cape, the aura of assurance: Judex himself! However, the vigilante's right arm hung limp at his side, a thin trickle of blood flowed down to drip from his fingers.

"Ach!" Mayen said in a heavy Germanic accent, pleased. "Obviously not as invincible as all that."

He took out a Luger from the holster on his belt and pointed it at the apparition. Judex did not move as the aircraft inexorably dove to the ground. Mayen felt a trickle of sweat run into his eyes; Judex had cut off his access to his cabin, where the tablet lay. He was out of time; his only priority could be to get out alive.

"Go to Hell!" The German adventurer's weapon belched fire.

Suddenly, Judex came to life, diving to avoid the bullet. His injury kept him from springing far enough to tackle Mayen. The German took advantage of those few seconds to grab a parachute and jump through a window in a shower of glass. Judex rose unsteadily and walked. The shock had affected him more than he wanted to admit. With a blank look, he watched the ground rushing toward him faster and faster, until the final impact.

The explosion was deafening and provided food for gossip in all the surrounding villages. Fortunately, the ship had crashed in the Ardennes forest, far enough from any dwelling that no lives were at risk.

The French Army quickly secured the site and searched every corner of the gutted wreck. The military, however, found no body there.

A few days later, when Georges Sauvin opened the door of his office, he discovered a granite tablet inscribed with cuneiform markings.

The Chinese Fish smiled as he returned to his seat.

(Translated by Matthew Baugh)

1939. The first "Affair of the Necklace" is, of course, the historical case from the 1780s involving Queen Marie-Antoinette and Cardinal de Rohan, which contributed to discredit the French Monarchy before the Revolution. Alexandre Dumas used the story as the basis for his novel The Queen's Necklace *(1849-50), a sequel to* Joseph Balsamo, *in which his version of Cagliostro plays a much greater and more romanticized part. In 1906, Maurice Leblanc used the same necklace as a springboard for a short-story (included in Black Coat Press' edition of* Arsène Lupin vs. Countess Cagliostro*) in which young Arsène steals it from the wealthy Dreux-Soubize family. This is the third, and heretofore untold, Affair of the Necklace...*

J.-M. & Randy Lofficier: *The Affair of the Necklace Revisited*

It was the smells that Richard Benson remembered the most. The smells of wood smoke and chestnuts that heralded the early days of winter in Paris.

War had been declared, but other than the bellicose and chauvinistic articles in *L'Echo de France* and *Le Matin*, one never would have guessed it. There were no military operations, the Germans being occupied in the demolition of Poland, while the French felt totally safe behind their impregnable Maginot line.

The journalists had coined a name for it: the "*drôle de guerre*" or "Phoney War," but to someone like Benson, attuned to even the tiniest shift in the zeitgeist, it was but the ominous calm that precedes the furious storm.

The American still remembered the intoxicating smells of freedom and futures unbound that had filled the French capital two years before, during the *Années Folles*, when he had taken his wife, Alice, to a Picasso exhibit at the World's Fair. They had met the famous painter's paramour, the photographer and poet Dora Maar, who had tried to teach Alice the knife game.

But all that was in the past now. Alice, and their daughter Alicia, were no longer of this world; they existed only as memories, just as tragic to him as Picasso's *Guernica* had been that night, when it had been unveiled.

So much death, so much blood.

And what of him, the survivor? Like the dead soldier in Picasso's painting, he wore the stigma of his martyrdom on his face. He had become a mockery of a man who found succor not in painting bloody visions of a dead horse and a bull, but in the purging of the world's vilest elements.

But it didn't stop the nightmares. Nothing did.

And now, the melancholy smells of Paris had contributed to the loss of another chunk of his past which, like a giant iceberg breaking away from the shelf, would disappear slowly in the impenetrable, murky waters of the past.

Benson chased away the memories and turned into a small street two blocks south of the Luxembourg Gardens. It ended in a cul-de-sac with an imposing building that had known better days. It was an austere bourgeois house that belonged to his friend and business associate, Pierre Duchêne.

Benson had last met the tall, bearded Frenchman in the Congo, where he had been trying to launch an oil company that he wanted Benson to invest in. In the American's opinion, Duchêne was an unusual Frenchman in that he treated the natives with remarkable grace and generosity. This, more than anything else, had convinced him to invest in the venture, and he had never regretted it; since then business had boomed.

Now, Duchêne, unaware of the profound changes that had transformed Benson's life forever, had asked his partner to come to Paris to discuss a "pressing business matter." Filled with curiosity, Benson had cabled his acceptance and date of arrival.

In the declining light of the day, the façade of Duchêne's house exuded a quiet air of finality, as if it was trying to repel an intruder, or at least warn him away. Benson shrugged off the feeling, climbed the five steps of the *perron*, and rang the bell.

A butler appeared and invited the American inside. Monsieur Duchêne, he said, was in the library. Would Monsieur Benson please follow him? Monsieur Benson had no objection.

Guided by the manservant, the American climbed a great marble stairway lined with old-fashioned, dusty oil paintings, which he presumed were a gallery of Duchêne's ancestors. He was then introduced in the library, after which the butler discreetly shut the door behind him. The long room smelled of leather and old books, and was lit only by a desk lamp.

Duchêne, who had been at work sitting behind a large and beautifully carved mahogany desk, rushed to greet his friend.

"Richard. You have come. I am so glad to see you," he declared effusively.

"The same here, Pierre."

"How long has it been? Five years, *non*? Much too long anyway. I've been meaning to come to New York, but you know how it is with business. It is the most demanding of mistresses."

"I wouldn't know."

"*Bien sûr*! I forget. You are married now…"

"Alice and Alicia were killed six months ago…"

Benson generally felt no desire to tell the world the details of the tragedy that had cost Alice and Alicia their lives. So he normally used the white lie of a "tragic plane accident" to ward off even well-meaning inquiries.

The Frenchman's face at once became crestfallen.

"*Mon Dieu*! I didn't know. I am so sorry…"

"But the people who did it paid for their crimes. Their death was avenged."

"That is good," said Duchêne, shaking his head. "That is good indeed."

"Life must go on, as they say. Why did you call me, Pierre?"

309

"I have the most wonderful business opportunity to present to you Richard. One must act quickly—not too quickly however. It will be best to discuss this in the morning, when our spirits are fresh. Besides, tonight, I have been invited to a most interesting soirée... I thought you might like to join me?"

Benson sighed internally. A Parisian function was just about the last thing he wished to attend. But he perked up when he heard Pierre say:

"...The unveiling of the Queen's Necklace."

The gala was held at the *hôtel particulier* of the Comte and Comtesse de Dreux-Soubise, a stately mansion located in the posh Faubourg Saint-Germain.

The evening was already in full bloom when Duchêne and Benson arrived, dressed in the best of tuxedos. All of Paris' high society was in attendance: businessmen and politicians, archbishops and dons, bankers and generals. Duchêne quickly left Benson to his own devices to go and shake hands with various friends and acquaintances.

Alone and not feeling very social, the American drifted towards the dais where the Necklace was being exhibited, resting on a bed of dark purple velvet in a glass case carefully guarded by two policemen. It was a resplendent piece of jewelry with four heavy tassels, festooned with diamonds, and a smaller piece comprised of even more beautiful, glittering stones arranged in pendants.

"It is a marvelous, *n'est-ce pas?*"

Benson turned and saw a beautiful young woman, with luscious black hair and sapphire blue eyes, dressed in a stunning Schiaparelli gown, standing there, holding a glass of champagne.

"I am your hostess, the Comtesse de Dreux-Soubise," she introduced herself. "And this is my husband, Comte Renaud."

"Richard Benson," the American introduced himself, offering a light *baisemain* to the Comtesse and a slight nod of the head to the older man with a square and rubicund face who had just joined them.

"Glad to meet you, Mister Benson," said the Comte, smiling. "We have already received several offers from your country to exhibit the Necklace. I'm always delighted to do business with Americans. Your people are so, er, straightforward."

"I'm quite sure folks will be lining up for blocks to see it, Monsieur le Comte. So it is Queen Marie-Antoinette's legendary necklace?"

"Only a reconstruction, I'm afraid, but the best we could do under the circumstances. The original was stolen by Jeanne de La Motte in 1785, who dismantled it and sold the stones to British jewelers. I, myself, am descended from the unfortunate Cardinal de Rohan, who had thought to gain the Queen's favor by offering her such a magnificent gift. It's taken my family several generations to put it back together..."

"I had heard it had been stolen again—by the notorious Arsène Lupin?"

The Comte raised an eyebrow at the evocation of what was obviously a painful memory.

"You are well informed, Mister Benson, Yes, that scoundrel Lupin stole it from my late uncle in 1880, but even he eventually felt compelled to return the mounting to us, its rightful owners—a publicity coup, if you ask me. It has taken the Dreux-Soubise another generation and over 30 years to locate and acquire the right kind of stones to restore the Necklace to its original glory."

"I am impressed, Monsieur le Comte," said Benson, truthfully. "I hope you are well insured."

"Such a jewel is more than an heirloom," said the Comte, somewhat haughtily. "It is part and parcel of French History. You cannot put a price on it."

Benson thought that he knew several people in the less savory diamond districts of Antwerp and New York's Nassau Street who would be eager to do just that, but he decided it was wiser to remain silent.

The Comtesse saw that the Comte had intended his remark to be a light rebuff of the American's honest intentions and stepped in.

"Don't be offended by my husband, Mister Benson," she said in a sweet and compassionate tone. "He is very sensitive when it comes to the Necklace. His uncle was shot by Zigomar when he tried to steal it many years ago. He'd give his life to protect it. I'm sure that, with what happened to your wife, you can understand his feelings?"

Benson nodded. "Of course, it is I who must apologize if I unintentionally gave any offense."

"We shall talk no more of it," said the Comte, back to his jovial self. "I am, in fact, interested in hearing your opinion about the Winstons, Mister Benson..."

QUEEN'S NECKLACE STOLEN!

The *Paris Herald Tribune*'s headline immediately caught Benson's eye as he exited his hotel near the Rue Monge the next morning at around 11 a.m.

He had left the soirée at an appropriately late hour. He had lost sight of Duchêne in the growing excitement of the night, and decided to walk back to his hotel alone. His friend was probably busy gathering more investors for his new business venture—whatever it might be. It was around 2 a.m. when the American had stepped inside his hotel, having enjoyed the long stroll down the Boulevard Saint-Germain.

At once, Benson bought a paper and sat at a café to read the article. Past the usual hyperbole, the facts were as follows: the two policemen making up the daytime watch had come on duty at 6 a.m. and had found the body of one of their colleagues strangled in the tiny bathroom adjacent to the exhibit room, and that of the other guard stabbed near the display case which was, needless to say, empty. The doors of the exhibit room were supposed to have been locked at all times, and since the two policemen could not have killed each other, the only logical conclusion was that someone had come into the room and done the deed.

According to the article, the two policemen were above suspicion, so the notion of them being bribed by an outsider had been quickly dismissed by the police. The thief and murderer had to be someone whom they trusted. The Commissioner in charge of the investigation, Monsieur Gilles, had immediately insisted on talking to the Dreux-Soubise and their staff. But he had met with yet another unexpected discovery: the Comte had disappeared!

The Dreux-Soubise slept in separate bedrooms and the Comtesse reported having said good night to her husband when they had retired for the night at around 3:30 a.m. However, the Comte's bed had not been slept in. Could he have murdered the two policemen and scampered away with his own property? As illogical and insane as it was, it seemed the only possibility.

Benson shook his head in an almost instinctive gesture of denial. He couldn't accept that version of events. Everything in him screamed that there was more to it than what he had just read; there was a darker and more sinister plan at work... But he couldn't figure what it was. He finally decided to let the matter rest for the time being and, since the weather was unusually sunny for the season, walk up to the Luxembourg gardens and his friend Duchêne's house.

The *Paris Herald Tribune* was only a morning paper with a single edition. By the time Benson reached the Luxembourg, the *Matin* had come up with a new edition which shouted (literally in this case, as it was being advertised by a young street vendor): *"COMTE DREUX-SOUBISE ASSASSINÉ!"*

Benson's French was more than adequate for reading a newspaper and, a quick purchase and several minutes later, he learned that Commissaire Gilles had been anything but idle. The body of the Comte had been discovered, stuffed in a trunk in a baggage room rarely visited by anyone. What was even more amazing, however, was that all medical signs indicated that Monsieur Dreux-Soubise had been murdered—stabbed, no doubt by the same dagger as the policeman—*no later than 1 a.m!* So it couldn't have been the Comte who had killed the two policemen and stolen the Necklace. More disturbing—*to whom, then, had the Comtesse said good night?*

The writer for *Le Matin* was hysterically blaming, *en masse*, the legendary Fantômas (presumed dead), Belphégor (ditto), Ténébras (ditto) and a host of other criminal masterminds of the past, or their ghosts, but in truth knew nothing for certain, and wrote even less.

One line, however, caught Benson's eye. It was a quote attributed to Commissaire Gilles, a simple statement that said: "It is as if the murderer *had the ability to change faces.*"

Benson thought long and hard about this. He was lucky that no one in the French police knew of his presence in the City of Lights. His visible interest in the Necklace the night before and his unusual abilities might have easily branded him as their number one suspect.

What Benson didn't know was that there were other, more sagacious, guardians of the Law in Paris than the police...

Benson took a shortcut through the Luxembourg Gardens. The trees were devoid of leaves, and only the evergreen bushes and the lawns reminded him of past springs in Paris. He saw a white dove flutter by and land gracefully on a skeletal branch. He sighed when he stopped briefly to admire the view of the Pantheon. That, too, evoked other painful memories of Alice. Alicia had played here, launching her small boats in the basin, watching them float slowly away, waiting for her daddy to go recover them in his bare feet...

Shutting the windows of the past, Benson hurried toward Duchêne's house. Something he now remembered from the previous night was puzzling him. A theory of the crime was forming in his mind. His friend might hold the key to the mystery, he thought.

The cul-de-sac was empty, except for a black mastiff rummaging through a trash can, looking for scraps of food.

Once at the house, the American knocked at the door. Twice. Three times. Strangely, no one came to answer.

He tried the handle. The door wasn't locked.

Benson entered the house, which appeared to be deserted. He yelled a couple of times, but got no reply.

Worried, he climbed the stairs with the grace of a jungle cat and proceeded toward the library, where he thought he might find Duchêne.

Stealthily, he opened the door and took a step inside the room.

At that moment, he felt a blow on his skull which was like the explosion of a thousand lights inside his head.

Benson dropped the floor, unconscious.

When he awoke, he was no longer in the library, but inside a small, damp cellar, solidly tied by a rope to an iron ring embedded into the masonry. The ground was wet. Water was seeping from under a square metal gate located at ground level on the wall to his right. Benson easily guessed that if it was raised, water—from the sewers, judging by the smell—would quickly fill the tiny cell and drown its occupant. As it had, in fact, killed the previous occupant, whose foul-smelling and putrefying body, half-eaten by rats, lay discarded on the soil.

Despite the sorry state of the corpse, the American could still identify the unfortunate victim.

Pierre Duchêne.

But if Duchêne had been dead for what looked like at least ten days, who, then, had he met and talked to the day before?

The murderer, of course. The man whom Commissaire Gilles had said, *had the ability to change faces.* The man whom the Comtesse de Dreux-Soubise had said good night to, instead of her husband, who already lay dead in the baggage room. The man who, looking just like the Comte, had had no problem getting the two guards to open the door to let him in—and then, had killed them both savagely.

The door, which was situated on the opposite wall, made of ancient oak and reinforced with iron, suddenly opened with a groan.

Pierre Duchêne walked in, holding a torch—except it wasn't Duchêne, but a ghastly imitation with an unspeakably evil grin on his stolen face.

"I see that you're awake, Mister Benson. Good. It is fitting that you die slowly and painfully," said the murderer.

"Have you come to gloat?" asked the American.

"Actually, no. I'm here to collect samples."

"Samples?"

The man began touching Benson's malleable face, rubbing away the makeup, revealing the pallid complexion beneath.

"Amazing," he muttered. "And this is entirely natural? A consequence of your tragedy? You didn't take any drugs? Undergo any operation?"

"Not as far as I know," said Benson, acidly. "What about you? Because, if I guessed correctly, you and I have the same power. You used yours to impersonate Duchêne, then at the soirée, you murdered the Comte and took his place. From that point on, it was child's play to kill the guards and steal the Necklace."

"Fine detective work. I'm sure you'll be greatly missed," said the man, who had begun to carefully remove skin cells and hairs with small metal instruments and put them into tiny glass vials. "As you surmised, my own condition is entirely artificial…" His face began to shift and change into that of a man in his fifties with almost no chin and a thin, aristocratic nose.

"My real name is Baruch Jorgell," he said, while continuing his macabre task. "I belong to a criminal society called the Red Hand. My abilities are, indeed, the result of a series of operations performed by our master, Dr. Cornelius Kramm, who has rightfully been nicknamed the 'Sculptor of Human Flesh.' We make a point of keeping tabs of new crime fighters, and when we heard about you and your, er, talent, we decided to kill and impersonate your friend Duchêne in order to lure you to Paris. First, my masters thought you would make an excellent culprit for the Necklace Affair. After all, one of the oldest mottos of our organization is to always *pay the law*. But also, Dr. Cornelius wanted to study you—I mean, your body—to see if we couldn't manufacture more people like you and me. You see, my creation, too, was something of an accident, a successful but wholly unintended side-effect of the operations. But think what a criminal army of faceshifters could achieve… The mind boggles!"

Having finished his grisly task, Jorgell got up and walked to the door.

"I will come and recover your body later. Good-bye, Mister Benson. I hope you're not afraid of rats."

The door shut. Two minutes later, Benson saw the grate slowly being lifted by a cable buried within the wall. The foul smelling waters of the Paris sewers began to invade his cell.

And the rats, too.

Try as he might, Benson could neither break his bonds, nor pull the ring out of the wall. The death trap was centuries old, and had often served its grisly purpose, without fail. Duchêne's body was there to attest it. The American reflected that his crime-fighting career had come to an abrupt end, far sooner than he had anticipated. He knew that he had now fully solved the mystery of the Queen's Necklace robbery, but it was unlikely that he would ever share the truth with anyone.

A more aggressive rodent made a move toward him and Benson used his feet to stomp on it, keeping the others at bay—for the time being.

Suddenly, a massive black form swam through the opening, pushing its way through several rats, the necks of which the creature broke with its powerful jaws. Benson thought he recognized the mastiff he had seen earlier wandering about the cul-de-sac. But what was it doing here…?

Having disposed of the vermin, the dog paddled quickly towards the American and started to chew on his bonds. In seconds, Benson was free. The dog then delivered a powerful lick to his face, creating light ripples in his malleable skin. The Avenger didn't know what say.

"Er, *bon chien*," he finally muttered, petting the animal on the head.

The animal nodded, as if he acknowledged the compliment, and ran to the door. Benson followed him. Jorgell had been so certain of his victim's fate that he hadn't bothered locking it.

In the corridor outside, Benson first turned the metal wheel that controlled the raising and lowering of the gate, then ran swiftly and silently up an ancient flight of stone steps, the black mastiff on his heels.

He arrived in a wine cellar, stepping out of a secret passage hidden behind a movable bottle rack, and, running up another flight of stairs, came out of a small door located on the ground floor under the main marble stairway.

His timing could not have been better, for Jorgell stood on the threshold, with a small suitcase standing next to him, preparing to lock the main door behind him.

When he saw Benson and the dog running towards him, the murderer muttered a curse and swiftly pulled a gun from his pocket. Benson knew that it is only in Hollywood serials that villains missed the hero. He was too far to stop Jorgell, and there was no place to hide in the straight and narrow corridor. The man from the Red Hand would probably hit him with the first shot. He could only hope that it wouldn't be fatal. And that the dog would get him.

Suddenly, just as Jorgell prepared to shoot, a white dove flew in and scratched his face, pecking at his eyes, hurting him, forcing him to instinctively raise his arms to chase the bird away. Several shot were fired. In the air. Harmlessly. Then Jorgell fell with a thud.

Benson had been right.

The dog had gotten him.

The American took the suitcase and opened it. It contained some papers and makeup products, but no necklace, no jewels. He wasn't surprised, because he had a good idea where the Necklace was.

Then, he heard the bells of the neighboring Saint-Sulpice church toll 10 p.m.

"If I hurry, I'll be just in time," said the Avenger.

The night train to Antwerp was scheduled to leave the Gare du Nord at 10:28 p.m. At exactly 10:25 p.m., a man who looked exactly like Pierre Duchêne stepped aboard. He strolled through the first class sleeping car, spoke in whispers to a steward, then proceeded toward a numbered compartment.

He slid the door open and said:

"I'm afraid your trip to Antwerp will have to wait, Madame la Comtesse."

The Comtesse de Dreux-Soubise appeared surprised to see him.

"Jorgell? What are you doing here? You were supposed to take care of the American..."

"I thought it was you, but I needed to be sure," said the Avenger, erasing Duchêne's features from his face and remolding it into his usual likeness.

The Comtesse's eyes grew wide and her jaw dropped slightly as she heard the whistles in the station outside. The train didn't move.

"Yes," confirmed Benson. "Commissaire Gilles' men are already here. Tonight, you will sleep at La Santé. After that..." and he slowly drew his hand across his neck.

The Comtesse fainted.

Benson took a hat box from the baggage rack and opened it. Even under the feeble lights of the train compartment, a myriad sparkles filled the air.

"The Queen's Necklace has been found," murmured the Avenger.

The day after, Benson sat at a café overlooking Notre-Dame, sharing a glass of wine with the mysterious, dark-clad avenger known as Judex. He was a tall man, with dark hair and steel grey eyes, which could become very soft when he felt compassion. He also looked much younger than he ought to have been, but Benson didn't feel it was any of his business to inquire about that.

"Thank you for all the help," he said, pointing at the dove perched on a nearby Colonne Morriss and the black mastiff sleeping peacefully at his master's feet, "and also thank you for trusting in my innocence and letting me finish with my investigation."

"It was quite natural," said Judex. "I never believed for a minute that you could be guilty. I am, however, interested in learning how you exposed the Comtesse so quickly?"

"Easy. When we met, she made a mention of my wife being shot by a gangster. The only person I had told was Duchêne—I mean, Baruch Jorgell. So it came to reason that he must have told her, and she inadvertently let it slip. That proved they were in it together."

"I see," said Judex, nodding slowly. "I predict a bright future for you in our common field of endeavor, Monsieur Benson. Shall we toast to it?"

Judex raised his glass. "To Justice," he said.

"To Justice," replied the Avenger.

The glasses shone briefly in the Parisian sunlight and clinked. Somewhere in Heaven, Alice's spirit smiled.

Late May/early June 1940. In the same way that the great Anthony Boucher told a story of Arsène Lupin during WWII (reprinted in our collection The Many Lives of Arsène Lupin*), we had to have some tales about Judex in Nazi-Occupied France. Our Australian contributor, David McDonald, is the first to project our Dark Avenger into these troubled times...*

David McDonald: *Shadows from the Cold*

A shadow hung over Paris, immovable by the bright light of day or by the glittering streetlights that lit the night. The City of Lights was no stranger to shadows; in better days, they provided shelter for a thousand young lovers and enfolded scores of bohemian cafes and bars in their embrace. But these shadows were different, and brought no pleasure to the Parisians who scurried about their business with slumped shoulders and downcast eyes. Even the man who watched the night-time crowd from a concealed rooftop felt ill at ease, though he had made the shadows his home. For him, shadows had always been his refuge and his fortress, from which he ventured forth to dispense justice upon the wicked. These shadows, though, were not a simple absence of light, but an absence of hope.

Despite the clearness of the skies, thunder rumbled to the east of the city, as it had for days. Every day, the dull roar seemed a little closer, and the demeanor of the people on the streets showed that they knew it was only a matter of time before the storm broke upon the city itself. This was no natural phenomena; the thunder was the sound of guns as the German Army drew inexorably closer. Occasionally, some odd convergence of air and temperature would cause one of the peals of thunder to echo as if miles closer, and each time furtive glances flashed towards the east. Such was their distraction there were numerous small collisions as two oblivious pedestrians collided, but even their arguments seemed muted and subdued, as if they were scared to attract too much attention and bring down whatever calamity hung over them like hammer waiting to drive in a nail. Only the man on the roof seemed able to focus on the task at hand.

His keen eyes followed the young woman gradually working her way across the square, weaving through the milling crowd with quiet grace. To anyone else, she might have seemed just another young woman hurrying home, but his hunter's instincts could see the tension in her shoulders, the way they hunched almost imperceptibly as if waiting for a blow to fall. And there, far enough behind as to deceive the casual observer, two men shadowed her. Despite being dressed in the rough garb of laborers, it was obvious to the watcher's finely honed senses that these were no mere workers, or even the common thugs who preyed upon their fellow citizens. The men were a different kind of beast. The way they carried themselves, like wolves cutting through a herd of sheep,

318

gave away their true nature. The people around them sensed it too, pulling away as if a mere touch might be dangerous, clearing their path through the cluttered square.

There was no such respect shown to the young woman, who had to fight her way through the crowd, and her shadows were rapidly gaining. He could see she was well aware of this, her head moving around as she sought an escape route, finally settling on a dingy alley way. Judex cursed softly, knowing that it circled almost completely back on itself before ending in a tall, brick wall. As she hurried towards he was already moving across the roof tops, a flickering shadow that left no trace of its passing, hoping he would get there in time. As he ran, he flicked his arms out sharply, releasing a hidden buckle on both forearms. The comforting weight of two black wooden poles slapped against his palms, and he slowly slid them out until they were completely free of his sleeves. His thumbs found hidden catches at the base of the rods and pushed on them, spring loaded cross bars flicking out and forming a shape like a cross with one arm broken off. By the time he reached the roof alongside the alley way, the cross pieces were nestled in his palms, the poles running the length of his forearms, rounded tips protruding past his clenched fists.

As fast as he was, he was almost too late. Peering over the edge of the roof that overlooked the dead end, he saw that the two men had beaten him to it. They had cut off the alleyway, and were cautiously advancing on the young woman from the square. One of the men had a deep gash in his face, a flap of skin hanging loose, but surprisingly little blood. As the man on the roof watched, the wounded man pressed the flap of skin back into place with no sign of pain. He took his hand away, revealing unmarked skin, and resumed his advance on the young woman. She had her back against the wall, her arm extended in front of her, a wicked looking knife weaving circles in the air. There was something odd about the knife; the man's eyes wanted to slide off it, the air around shimmering with an unsettling haze. The two men menacing her obviously felt it too, hanging back just out of her reach.

One of them reached out, and dug his fingers into the crumbling brick of the alley wall, pulling out a chunk of stone. With the speed of a striking snake, he hurled it at the young women, who barely had time to react, managing only to move far enough that the stone merely clipped her shoulder. The force of the blow was still enough to send her staggering back, the knife clattering to the ground. The man of the roof top had seen enough and he leapt into the street below, his long dark cloak fluttering about him like the wings of some nocturnal predator. His black leather boots came down squarely between the shoulders of the closest man, not only breaking his fall but sending his enemy to the ground. Using the momentum of his impact, the man in black leapt to his feet and, using the cross piece as fulcrum, sent the pole in his left hand arcing towards the head of the other assailant.

319

The was a low, flat crack as the other man effortlessly caught the pole in the palm of his hand and pulled it, hard, sending its wielder flying into the other wall.

For a moment Judex just lay there before slowly pulling himself to his feet, using the wall as a support. Fortunately, his weapons had not fallen too far from his reach and he gathered them up and waited in a low combat stance as the thug advanced on him. That one brief encounter had shown him that he could not hope to match the other man's strength, or allow him to dictate terms. Before the thug could get within grappling range Judex sent the poles flicking in from opposite directions, the pulled out of the feints as the other man lashed out. Ducking inside the man's reach, he used the rounded ends at his fists in short sharp jabs, hitting the thug with a devastating combination of blows; solar plexus then short ribs then kidneys as he darted behind his attacker.

The other man merely grunted, then whirled with frightening speed and attacked the man in black. Judex caught the first of the thug's blows with the pole laid across his forearm and winced at the cracking noise of wood splintering, a noise that could have easily been his bones. Knowing that he was in fight that would end with him either dead or maimed unless he did something about it, he ducked inside the next wild blow and drove the end of the other pole into the other man's throat. There was a sickening crunch of cartilage and the thug dropped to his knees, clutching his throat and heaving desperately for air. Before Judex could move in to finish the thug, he caught a flicker in the corner of his eyes. He spun around just in time for the other thug to grab him by the throat, and found himself lifted and slammed into the brick wall, feet flailing a good two feet above the cobblestones.

The thug's grip was like an iron band, and he barely flinched as his struggling victim drove his boots into whatever parts of the thugs body he could reach. Judex could feel the blood pounding in his temples as he fought for air, but the thug was monstrously strong and nothing he did seemed to shift him. Finally, Judex managed to catch the other man's gaze, and stare deep into his eyes. He focused, trying to mesmerize his attacker, to convince him that were allies, that this was all some sort of misunderstanding. Anything to give that split second of distraction he needed to escape the thug's death grip. For a moment the other man's eyes softened, then *something* shifted in them and the pupils flared a bright red. Judex recoiled as far as the thug's grip would allow. There was something else, something inhuman, looking out through the thug's eyes and whatever it was, it was evil of type that even Judex had never before encountered. He opened his mouth to speak, but before he could voice his question, the red light flickered out, and the other man's eyes rolled back in their sockets. He gave a ghastly rattle, and then collapsed bonelessly to the ground, sending Judex crashing to the cobble stones.

Still dazed, he looked up to see the young woman pulling her knife from the back of the thug's skull. She spat on the corpse and walked over to where his

320

companion was still choking. Startled, Judex realised his entire fight with second thug had taken mere minutes, though it had felt like an eternity when those pincer-like fingers had been wrapped around his neck. Without a second's hesitation, the young woman grabbed the choking man's hair and pulled back his head, and drove the blade in under his chin and up into the brain. The man shuddered and fell backwards, now only a lifeless lump of meat. She spat on the corpse and then wiped her blade on his shirt, sheathing it with a smooth motion than spoke of years of experience.

Judex stared at her, discomfited by the brutal nature of the execution, for executions it was. She turned, and caught his look.

"What?" she snapped. "They were trying to kill us. Should I have kissed him better?"

Judex was a little taken aback by her vehemence. "That may be so, but you just executed an unarmed and injured man."

Her laughter had a jagged edge, and he could tell that she was at the very edge of breaking under some terrible nervous strain.

"That was no man. Not anymore." Her voice bore traces of an Eastern European accent, from the higher echelons of society if he had to guess.

Judex couldn't argue with her statement. Even without the two men's strength and speed, what he had seen in those eyes would haunt him for days. Still, he couldn't help but be uneasy with such casual killing.

"You may be right, but it is never good to be too quick to kill."

"Thank you for that pearl of wisdom."

Judex wondered why she hadn't used that tone on her attackers; it seems as edged as the knife she had wielded to such effect. She turned and began to walk away.

"Hold on!" He hurried up to her and grabbed her shoulder, only to freeze, the point of her knife suddenly appearing far too close to his throat. "Hey there, calm down! I am not going to hurt you."

She gave him an assessing look. Judex couldn't help but notice how blue her eyes were, or the golden shade of her hair. It was hard to reconcile such beauty with her violence. After a moment, the knife disappeared.

"What do you want?"

"Well, a thank you would be nice, for start." He smiled at her to show that he wasn't angry. "Though I should be thanking you for saving me there at the end."

A small smile appeared on her face. "That's true, I did. But, thank you for intervening when you did, I thought they had me." She shuddered slightly.

"And who are they?" he asked. "*What* are they?"

"Look, I really do appreciate you help, but you don't want to get involved in this. Just jump back up on that roof, or whatever it is you do, and forget all this happened."

"I don't think so," he said. "I want to know what is going on. Are more of those things going to come after you? You don't really think I'd leave anyone to face that alone, do you?"

"I can take care of myself. I don't even know who you are, anyway."

"That is easily remedied!" He gave her an elaborate bow. "I am Judex, welcome to my city."

She laughed despite herself. "Well, Judex, if that is your real name—something I doubt—I am Karolina"

They began to walk out of the alley.

"So, tell me about these men."

She hesitated. "You wouldn't believe me if I told you."

"You'd be surprised by the things I've seen, Mademoiselle."

"Still..."

Her voice trailed off, and he realised that it was not about whether she thought he would believe her, but about whether she could trust him. Putting himself in her shoes he couldn't blame her. She was in a strange city, and had just been attacked, and he was a stranger. Sighing, he turned to face her. He hated doing this, but he couldn't see any other choice. She obviously needed help, and he had to find a way of giving it to her.

"Look at me."

Startled, she looked up and he locked gazes with her. Exerting his gifts, he focused his mind on her.

Trust me.

Trust me.

Trust me.

Karolina gave a small shake of her head, and frowned.

"Have you heard of the Thule Society?" she asked.

He shook his head. "No, I can't say I have."

"They have been around for hundreds of years, men willing to seek out dark secrets if they would bring wealth or power. They were relatively harmless, crackpots mainly. But then along came Hitler and his Third Reich."

"Hitler? What does that madman have to do with this?"

"Hitler has long been obsessed with the occult. When he came to power everyone wanted to gain his favor, and the Thule Society came to him offering him their accumulated knowledge. He gave them to his pet, Himmler, and he made them in an arm of the SS. With his backing, and the resources of the Reich behind them, they were able to make real progress with their research." She stopped, a funny look on her face. "Why am I telling you all this?"

"Don't worry, you can trust me," he said. Before she could think about it too much, he went on. "And those men, they were from the Thule Society?"

"Yes. But they aren't men, not anymore. I am not sure what has been done to them, but it's like they are possessed. They have been hunting me since I fled

Poland. Day and night, every time I thought I had lost them they would find me again."

Her voice broke, and Judex realized that she was near tears, the stress and fear catching up with her.

Trying to distract her, he continued his questions.

"So, why are they so determined to catch you?" He cleared his throat uncomfortably. "I mean, don't take this the wrong way, but what is so special about you that they would send these...creatures after you?"

"My father was in the *Biuro Szyfrów*, part of the intelligence service. He managed to acquire information not only on the Thule Society, but on the codes that the Germans use, their Enigma machine. He knew if he could get that to our Allies in Britain they would be able to gain vital intelligence on the German war effort."

Judex whistled softly. If she was telling the truth, that information was priceless. Britain and her allies needed every advantage they could get, and Judex knew that the fate of France was entwined with their friends across the Channel.

"And your father?"

"Someone betrayed him. Before he was captured, he passed the files onto me, and a knife he had taken from a dead Thule. They are very hard to kill, but that blade is spellwrought and deadly." Judex could verify their assailants' unnatural abilities, he ached all over. "He led them on a wild goose chase while I escaped."

Now she was crying. Judex took her in his arms and she buried her face in his chest, her sobs shaking them both.

"He died to save me. I can't let him down."

"It's OK. I will get you to England. You have my word."

She smiled up at him, her eyes filled with trust. Judex just hoped that trust wasn't unfounded.

"So, let me get this right. We are in a city about to be invaded, that has the might of the *Wermacht* camped on one side, and a sea filled with U-Boats on the other, and you are asking me to try and smuggle some blonde you met in an alley way across the Channel?"

Judex couldn't help but smile. The small women in front of them still bore traces of her Australian heritage, and not least of them was her forthrightness. Expressive eyes flashed under dark hair as she lectured Judex. He raised his hand placatingly.

"Na..."

She cut him off before he could finish.

"It's Andrée here, remember?"

"I'm sorry. *Andrée*, I wouldn't ask you this if it wasn't important, but the information this woman is carrying could change the course of the war."

"This woman can speak for herself!" There were red spots on Karolina's cheeks. "I told you that I can take care of myself. If your friend won't help me, I will find my own way to England."

Andrée laughed. "No need to get your knickers in a knot, love. We will help you. We'd do anything that will cause Jerry problems, wouldn't we, boys?" The rough men gathered in the room nodded. "Anyone who was paying attention saw this invasion coming. That's why I am here, helping organize cells to resist the occupiers once the city falls. When I am done here, I will go home and do the same there because it is only a matter of time before Marseilles falls too."

Karolina glared at the other woman. "You are not the only ones resisting the Germans, you know."

"Please, we are all friends here," Judex said. "We share a common enemy, and I am sure they would love us to be fighting amongst ourselves."

After a few more moments of glaring, both women nodded. Judex wasn't silly enough to believe that they were now best of friends, but hopefully the peace would hold until Karolina was gone.

"As I was going to say before we went off on a tangent, you are in luck." Judex winced at Andrée's pointed tone. "There is a vessel leaving tonight, a fishing trawler owned by smugglers. They are already taking over a general to confer with the Poms, so you will be in exalted company."

Karolina hesitated and then leant over and took the other woman's hand.

"Thank you, Andrée, I really do appreciate this."

Andrée squeezed her hand in return. "That's okay, dear; we will get you to safety and thumb our nose at Jerry while we are at it!"

Her voice hardened as she began issuing a stream of commands. Men scattered from the room, until only two were left.

She nodded at the smaller of the two, a thin, angular man with a wispy moustache.

"This is Stefan. He has a sense of direction like a homing pigeon and he is very handy with a garrote. He will get you to the docks."

"And his friend?" Judex asked.

The second man was huge, a head and a half taller than Judex, and twice as wide across the shoulders. His face had the battered look of a bouncer, and his trench coat bulged suspiciously.

"This is Anton. He is my explosives expert, but I sometimes wonder why he bothers when he could knock stuff down with his fists."

Anton grinned, revealing there or four missing teeth.

"Andrée exaggerates, *mon ami*. I am a gentle giant." He opened his coat to reveal a bandolier of explosives strapped to his vest. "But, yes I do like my little toys."

"Now, these men will take you to the ship, and make sure that our Polish friend has no problems getting on board," Andrée said. "Judex, after this you will owe me…"

She was cut off by the sound of splintering wood, coming from the front room. It was followed by gunshots, then the screams of men in terrible agony.

Judex swore and headed towards the noise, followed closely by the two other men.

"No, take the girl. You have to get that information to the right people!" Andrée moved to block their way, a pistol in each hand. "We will hold them off here."

"No! I am not going to abandon you," Judex snapped. "We will deal with them here and now."

"Don't be an idiot. The ship can't wait, and another chance might not come for weeks.

Judex's shoulders slumped. She was right.

"Take care, Andrée. I know your story doesn't end"

She grinned wolfishly and kicked the door down, guns already blazing. Her exultant laughter was still echoing in their ears as the hurried through the streets towards the docks.

As they stepped out of the streets towards the docks, they could see the trawler was already loaded and waiting. Before they could move it towards a shadow detached itself from the darkness and blocked their way. The figure was dressed in the same rough garb as the other thugs, but his eyes marked him as something more. All humanity gone, they were pools of glimmering crimson and even Judex shivered as his gaze fell upon them.

"You've led us a merry chase, Karolina! But, it ends here."

Karolina took a step forward and fixed him with an icy glare. Judex could not help but admire her poise, she seemed every inch the aristocrat and he wondered exactly who she was, back home.

"Never! I haven't come this far to be stopped now. I will complete my father's mission."

The creature's laugh was like fingernails on a chalkboard.

"So brave, just like your father. I wonder if your heart will taste as sweet as his did?"

Karolina let out a moan of anguish, and would have charged the creature had no Anton grabbed her arm. Judex moved past her.

"You will have to deal with us first," he said. "I will not let you have her."

"Nor I," Anton rumbled from behind him.

"Nor I." Stefan had moved up beside Judex, and his voice was steely with resolve.

"Who are you to defy one of the Thule? We have discovered powers beyond your imagination."

"I heard you were just crackpots, Himmler's little lap dogs," Judex said.

The creature snarled. "You are trying to provoke me, to distract me. It won't help you. Perhaps once we were...limited in our knowledge. But we have found allies in the spaces beyond who have taught us much. And, we only grow stronger as the war goes on. You would not believe the treasures we have found as we conquer old kingdoms. Libraries modering in forgotten castles in the forest of Eastern Europe. Dark artifacts hidden away, dragged into the light, prizes that will win us this war."

"It's a shame you won't be around to see it. Stefan, go! Now"

The smaller man grabbed Karolina's arm, and as Anton and Judex charged at the Thule, he dragged her towards the ship. Before the creature could stop them, Anton was upon him, a huge fist smashing into the Thule's chin. The creature didn't even stagger, lashing out with a blow of its own that sent the big man flying.

"You will have to do better than that. Who are you, mere men, to challenge a creature of the shadows?"

Judex laughed. "Ah, but this is my city. The shadows here belong to me."

He launched himself at the creature, sending it staggering with a flurry of blows, the hard wood of his weapons smacking against flesh. The creature was fast, but Judex did not stay still long enough for it to touch him, targeting its joints and the soft tissue of throat and groin. But the creature shook of each blow, taking punishment that would have felled a dozen men, and Judex knew it was a only a matter of time before he made a mistake and one of its blows landed. He risked a glance over his shoulder, and saw Stefan helping Karolina onto the trawler. The moment's distraction was all the Thule needed, and a wicked blow sent Judex crumpling to the splintered wood of the dock.

He looked up at the Thule standing over him. It raised its boot over Judex's head.

"First you, then the girl."

Judex watched the creature's foot descend, seeming to move in slow motion, every stone and piece of grass caught in the tread standing out in vivid detail. Judex closed his eyes, waiting for the blow, but it never came. Instead, there was a crunching noise, like a sack of grain falling from a high shelf onto a stone floor. When Judex opened his eyes, the creature was gone. The sound of struggling came from his right, and he turned to see Anton wrestling with the Thule, his vast strength barely enough to keep it from tearing out his throat. As Judex watched, the Thule began to bend the big man backwards, inch by inch.

"Run!" Anton shouted. His voice was strangely distorted, and Judex saw that there was a wire trailing from a small, oblong box in his mouth, disappearing under his jacket.

Judex turned and ran for the edge of the dock. Behind him he heard a muffled shout.

"Pour la Liberté!"

As Judex dived, the world behind him turned to fire.

By the time Judex dragged himself from the chilly waters, the ship was far out to see, and Stefan was sitting on the dock weeping. Judex staggered over and sat next to him, putting his arm around the other man.

"Karolina?"

Stefan stared at him blankly for a moment, then blinked away his tears.

"Yes, she made it."

Judex let out a breath of relief. "Thank God. If it weren't for Anton..." He trailed off. "He was a brave man."

"I hope that that it was worth all this. Anton, my friends, who knows what happened to Andrée," Stefan said. "And for what?"

"*Mon ami*, we may have just won the war."

Late 1940. This is another story that pits the seemingly ageless Judex against the Nazi menace, and which also serves as a prequel to one of the best-loved movies of all time...

Travis Hiltz: *Ilsa's Crossing*

The town was silent as the grave, its citizens "relocated" by German troops several days ago. The shops, homes, churches and offices stood, their windows dark and lonely, as they waited for the townspeople to return. At the head of the main street was a modest white church; there, two uniformed figures huddled in the bell tower. Both wore the uniforms of United States Marines.

They were the duo whose exploits in China had earned them the nickname of the *Fighting Devil Dogs.*

Lt. Tom Grayson peered through the narrow window in the bell tower, using his binoculars to watch over the forlorn-looking town. His compatriot, Frank Corby, sat, his big form huddled up on the floor, back to the wall, his head pillowed on his folded arms.

Grayson nudged him with the toe of his boot. Corby started and frowned at his friend.

"Hey, Tom," he complained in a hushed tone. "You mind? I need my beauty sleep."

"I'm not spending the rest of the war in a prison camp because the krauts heard your snoring," Grayson replied. "The train has left with the refugees. Keep an eye out. I'm going to go rouse our 'package.' I want to start moving once it's dark."

Corby nodded, and sat up, accepting the binoculars and moving to the window.

Grayson made his way down a narrow flight of stairs to a cluttered, dusty storage room below the tower. On top of an old trunk was a huddled form, wrapped in a tattered blanket. He paused a couple steps away, took off his helmet, and ran a hand through his short, blonde hair. He reached towards the blanket, then paused again and frowned. He then straightened up and coughed lightly.

The blanket-wrapped shape shifted and a small, light-skinned hand reached out.

"Hmm...what?" A soft, accented voice asked, quietly.

"Mrs. Lazlo?" Grayson said, quietly. "We are going to need to leave soon. How are you feeling?"

The figure sat up, and the blanket fell away. Ilsa Lazlo was a slim woman, nearly his height, and refined-looking. Despite the smudges of dirt and rumpled work clothes, Grayson still felt a bit awkward in her presence. At the same time, he had grown to admire her inner strength; she had never complained at any step of their journey. He kept thinking of a porcelain figurine with a core of iron.

She adjusted a dark beret over her luxurious blonde hair and nodded to the marine.

"I'm fine, thank you. Lieutenant," she murmured, getting to her feet. "The train has left…?"

"Yes, Ma'am," Grayson nodded. "It's on its way. The refugees are all safe, but unfortunately, we're going to have to get across enemy lines on our own, and the Jerry's have got more troops moving into the area."

"More troops?" Ilsa asked. "Why here?"

"Wish I knew," Grayson shrugged. "Such a sleepy little town to be getting so much attention. Gather your things, I'll fetch Corby and we'll move out."

Grayson headed back up into the tower and kneeled down next to Corby.

"How do things look?" he asked.

"Better by the minute," Corby replied, taking the binoculars away from his eyes and handing them to the other soldier. "A couple more trucks just showed up. Looks they are bringing in supplies and some kind of equipment."

"Something's going on here," Grayson said, peering through the binoculars. "It can't all be about catching her."

He sat back and pushed back his helmet in order to scratch his head.

"What have we stumbled onto, Frank?"

"Beats me," the other man replied, taking his canteen off his belt. He took a swig and then grimaced at the brackish water. "Do we have a plan?"

"Sort of," Grayson said. "If we go through that little neighborhood off to the west of the main square, we'll have a lot of cover and can make for the forest. That, or the river, are our best… our only chance."

"We gotta get her out of here, Tom," Corby said, in a low, worried tone.

"Think I don't know that?" Grayson muttered, moving back to the stairs. "Grab your gear. We need to move."

Soon the pair of marines and their charge had made their way down through the church and out a small back door, into a narrow path that cut through a small cemetery. Hidden from enemy troops by the church on the one side, and the wall surrounding the cemetery on the other, they made their way, quietly down the path. Then, moving through the village in the opposite direction from the German encampment, they kept the buildings between them and their pursuers, until they had nearly reached the stretch of woods to the west. They ducked into doorways, cut through empty shops, and generally kept to the shadows as they went.

They made their way single file, the young woman from the Resistance between the two American soldiers. The dark, cloudy night, the abandoned buildings, and the knowledge that the Germans were hunting them, gave the quaint village a sinister air. Every sound and hint of movement was an additional burden to the trio's already tortured nerves.

"OK, let's hold up here for a second," Grayson said in a hushed tone. "Thought I heard something. Corby, stay here with Mrs. Lazlo."

Grayson inched his way to a t-junction and peered both ways. The street was wide, with houses on the one side and a waist-high brick wall on the other. He crossed the street quickly and crouched in a doorway. Peering down the street, he could make out distant hints of movement, a shifting patch of shadow, and the occasional flash of light.

"They're moving through the town," he muttered. "Looking for us—or are we just unlucky…?"

Keeping low, Grayson crept closer, making his way down the row of houses, in the hopes of catching a glimpse of the German troops and getting some idea about what they were really doing in the village—and if he, Corby and Ilsa had a chance of avoiding them.

Three houses from the end of the row, Grayson snuck into a doorway and inched over. At the end of the street was another road. He caught a glimpse of headlights and the rumble of a large vehicle moving past. He ducked back, and in that instant, a gloved hand clamped onto his shoulder, followed by another over his mouth.

"Monsieur," an accented voice said close to his ear, "you appear to be lost."

Grayson froze. Momentarily startled, he tensed, ready to fight his way free.

"I am not your enemy," the voice added, not losing its quiet, reassuring tone.

The young marine realized that the accent was French. He relaxed a little, his instinct telling him that something unexpected was going on here, and that he needed to listen. Fighting was not was going to get him any answers.

"Shall we talk?" the stranger asked, feeling the American soldier's body untense. "We may be able to help each other."

The hands holding Grayson let go and the marine turned quickly, ready to strike out if needed. He didn't point his sidearm at the other man, but he didn't return it to its holster either.

He was facing a slim man of uncertain age, dressed all in black. The newcomer wore a short cloak and a slouch brimmed hat that partially obscured his features.

"Who are you?" Grayson demanded. His nerves and the need to whisper made the question come out as a growl.

"I am Judex," the man in black replied. "You are a long way from home… Lieutenant, is it?"

"Lieutenant Tom Grayson. What's going on here?"

"I was hoping you could tell me," Judex replied, a rueful smile cutting through the shadows. "If you are not investigating the Germans' unusual activities, then may I ask, why are you here?"

Grayson peered at the man in black, his suspicion struggling with a strange urge to trust him. His outfit was reminiscent of those worn by the mystery men from the comic books. At the same time, he felt that this stranger was most likely the only ally the trio was going to find.

"I was sent here to assist the Resistance," Grayson explained. "They needed our help moving some refugees and wounded soldiers."

"Interesting," Judex said, rubbing his chin thoughtfully. "There is more occurring than either of us thought. We do need to talk, but we should move to more convivial surroundings."

Judex made an "after you" gesture towards the door behind him.

"I'm not alone," Grayson explained. "There are others… back that way"

"Go fetch them," Judex said, losing his charming host tone, for one that brooked no disobedience. "We have a limited window for escape. Quickly!"

Grayson nodded and, keeping low, scurried back the way he had come. He reached a doorway and peered through the darkness, trying to catch a glimpse of Corby and Ilsa Lazlo. The deepening shadows made it near impossible. He could hear the distant sounds of the German troops and trucks getting closer. It still felt as though they were just sweeping the village, rather then deliberately heading his way, but, to his anxious mind, that was small comfort.

He crept up to the edge of the road and waved his hand in a signal to Corby. Spotting no sign of response, Grayson frowned and made a quick, frantic dash across the road and ducked behind a low stone wall.

"Where did you get to, Frank?" he muttered to himself.

Hearing the sound of shoe on gravel, he raised his sidearm and quickly sprung around the corner, only to find himself staring down the barrel of Corby's rifle.

"Jeez, Tom," Corby muttered, lowering his weapon. "You just about ended up scaring me outta three years' growth."

"I lost sight of you and couldn't risk using a light to signal. The Germans are right at the end of the street. Where'd you go?"

"We decided to move back from the road when we heard the trucks," Corby replied. "What's going on?"

"Damned if I know," Grayson told him. "But I may have found us some help. Where's Mrs. Lazlo?"

"Right here," Ilsa replied, stepping out from behind Corby. She tucked her pistol back into the man's belt she wore.

"Stay low and keep moving," Grayson advised, quietly.

They quickly and discreetly made their way to the edge of the street. Grayson dashed across the road first. Once across, he scanned the road and surrounding neighborhood anxiously. He then gestured for Ilsa to join him. She nodded, took a breath and ran to his side. When she was halfway across, the lights at the far end began to move. The young woman from the Resistance kept her gaze on them without slacking her pace, and she was soon kneeling besides the blonde marine.

Grayson held up a hand to signal Corby to stay still until the lights had moved and were lost to sight. Then, Corby sprinted across the road and the three made there way hurriedly back down the street.

Stepping through the doorway, the trio found themselves in a small, dark shop.

"Where's this mystery man of yours?" Corby asked, stationing himself by the window and peering intently out into the night.

"I am here," Judex said, stepping out of the shadows. "We must move quickly. Come, follow me!"

He led them through the shop and out the back door, which opened on a backyard, surrounded by a low stonewall, in need of repairs. There was a small, weathered shed at the far corner, towards which the man in black made his way.

"I need to retrieve something," he explained, pulling out a wooden peg that acted as a lock on the shed's door. Inside, lying on the dirt floor was a German soldier, trussed up like a prize Christmas turkey.

"Jeez!" Corby breathed.

"If you would be so kind...?" Judex asked the burly young marine, with a gesture towards his prisoner.

Corby looked at Grayson, who nodded in reply. The larger man frowned, handed his rifle to Ilsa, and hefted the captive over his shoulder.

The odd quintet then made their way through a series of deserted homes and yards, until they reached a narrow dirt road on the edge of the village. Nestled in the shadows was an old black roadster. Its polished surface seemed to draw in the faint moonlight, and it shone as if it were made of obsidian.

"You do know they kept making cars after 1929, right?" Corby muttered to their cloaked guide.

"It is lovely," Ilsa added. "But isn't it a bit inconspicuous?"

"A bit of faith," Judex said, stepping up to the car and patting the hood. "She has served me well."

With a slight dramatic flourish, Judex opened the passenger side door and Corby, the bound German and Ilsa bundled in. He and Grayson slid into the front. Judex donned a pair of driver's goggles, pulled several switches and the car rolled off, down the dark and rutted lane.

"Um...are you going to risk lights with the Germans all over the town?" Grayson asked, looking nervously at their surroundings.

"Are we coasting?" Corby asked. "I don't hear the engine...?"

"The lights and the engine are on," Judex replied, with a self-satisfied smile. "My brother and I spent many years tinkering with her and, if you'll pardon a touch of bragging, there is no other car like her in the world."

"How do you get the engine that quiet?" Corby asked, his tone a mix of puzzlement and wonder.

"The headlights are ultra-violet and you have special glass in the head-lights and your goggles," Grayson said, a touch of awe creeping into his voice.

Judex nodded in acknowledgement and approval of the young marine.

"What about the quiet engine?" Ilsa asked.

"That's a bit more complicated," Judex replied. "And I need to concentrate on the road."

They traveled in silence, every turn and bump causing the three passengers to grip their arm rests and whatever handhold they could find. The tension built up with every dark object that sped by. They all realized that that they were en-trusting their very lives and freedom to a man none of them had ever met before, relying on the flimsy fact that he had given them his word that he could see in the dark.

All three passengers let out an audible sigh of relief when the roadster slowed and turned. Grayson could no longer glimpse the thin, crescent moon and guessed they must be parked in some building, a barn or garage.

"It's a cave…?" Ilsa breathed, looking around.

"Where are we?" Grayson asked.

"Anybody else smell licorice?" Corby asked.

"To answer your questions," Judex said, stepping out of the car, "this is my home and as for the smell…Michel, these are guests, stop lurking."

A man in his thirties stepped out of the shadows. He wore the kind of rag-ged makeshift uniform common among members of the French Resistance and a shapeless cloth cap that failed to contain his shaggy black hair. He slung his rifle over his shoulder, freeing his hands to light a lantern.

After the darkness of the drive, the lantern shone like the sun to Ilsa and the marines, who stood still, allowing their eyes to adjust. Grayson caught a glimpse of two other men pushing closed a stout oaken door and setting a cross-bar in place.

Grayson and Corby exchanged a nervous glance, looking from the two men at the door, to their host and the licorice-smelling man holding the lantern. Ilsa must have spotted the look and managed to interpret it. She leaned in and placed a hand on Grayson's arm.

"We are safe." She said, in a hushed tone. "He is Judex. He is a friend to the Resistance. Please, trust him."

Grayson gave her a thoughtful frown and, looking at Corby, got only a shrug in reply. Both men were aware that they were dangerously short on choic-es, and every decision they had made so far seemed only to be taking them in stranger, not necessarily safer, directions.

The marine turned to find Judex watching them, as though he could over-hear their silent debate and was willing to wait until a decision had been reached. Grayson felt as if he was looking across a chessboard at the man in the black cloak and hat. He had the odd feeling that Judex had already mapped out the entire game in his head, while he was still struggling to remember if he was playing white or black! Having nothing more to go on than Ilsa's claim that Judex could be trusted, he and Corby decided to go along.

"Can you help us?" Grayson asked.

"I think so," Judex nodded. "More accurately, I think we can help each other. Let us move upstairs. It'll be more comfortable and we have much to discuss."

He gestured for Michel, directing him towards the bound German soldier in the car.

Corby moved to help, but Judex waved him away. Retrieving another lantern from a shelf carved into the stone wall, the vigilante lit it and then gestured for the trio to follow him. They walked the length of the cave, until, at the far end, they reached a narrow set of stone stairs.

The stairs corkscrewed through a structure that gave the marines the impression that were in a hollowed out mountain. They passed several landings, which lead off into corridors of stone. Several merged with wood paneled rooms.

"Place is a castle," Corby muttered, as they climbed. "Or some kind of pirates' den."

At the third landing, Judex left the stairs and lead them through a set of doors.

"Ladies on the left, gentlemen on the right," he said, with a slight bow. "Get some rest and I'll arrange for food to be brought to you."

"I'd rather have some answers," Grayson said, pointedly.

"And you will," the cloaked man replied, grimly. "But there is work to do first."

The two men locked gazes for a moment, and while Grayson wasn't entirely sure what he saw there, it was something that he was willing to trust.

An hour passed. While Corby was happy to savor resting on a mattress, enjoying a sandwich and waiting for orders, Tom Grayson paced the modest guest room as if it was a cage.

"Tom, you gonna sit down before you fall down?" Corby asked. "We both need the rest and this is the first real food we've had in a couple days."

"I know, I just don't like this," Grayson said, sitting down on the other, small bed in the room. "We don't exactly have many options, and this Judex character got us away from the krauts, but still…"

"He looks like something out of a cliffhanger serial," Corby nodded. "But, Mrs. Lazlo…Ilsa… trusts him."

"And I suppose we do need to trust her," Grayson said, reluctantly.

"What's that all about?" Corby asked, sitting up. "She was our contact with the French Resistance! She helped us get those refugees outta here before the Nazis moved in! How can you not trust her?"

"It's not that… Not really," Grayson said, slowly shaking his head. "There's just… something about her…"

"Makes you want to protect her," Corby nodded.

"The most dangerous kind of woman there is," Judex said, quietly from the doorway.

Both marines started. The cloaked man had crept up on them undetected and neither could have said they had even heard the door open, let alone how much of their conversation had been overheard.

"Lieutenant, if you'd care to join me," said Judex. "We may be able to obtain the answers we both seek and can then form a strategy."

Corby glanced a question, and Grayson gave a faint shake of his head, as he got to his feet. He followed Judex down the corridor again, but in the opposite direction. They reached another flight of stairs and traveled downwards until Grayson began to wonder if they'd gone even deeper than the cave garage where they had first arrived.

"Quite a place you've got here," the marine said, as they moved from wood-paneled corridors to stone tunnels. The lower they went, the more primitive the architecture became. After several minutes, Grayson would not have been surprised if a medieval peasant or caveman had passed them. Coming to a small, low-ceilinged chamber, Judex paused before a stout, oaken door.

"We seem to have two separate problems, or perhaps objectives," Judex said. "And they have, at this time… overlapped, shall we say?"

"You mean because, whatever plans we had got derailed by the Germans suddenly deciding to take this town?" Grayson asked. "Any idea why? We planned our route through this area because they'd been ignoring the place."

"Yes, their sudden interest in the village, and whether or not my home being located so near it, might be a contributing factor has been much on my mind. Tonight, when your party and I crossed paths, I had decided to do something about solving the mystery. I am including you in my efforts, but I must ask that, no matter what you see, you do not interfere."

"If you think it can help with getting Mrs. Lazlo to safety, I'm willing to trust you."

Judex nodded and then opened the door and took the young marine inside. The room was narrow and dimly lit, the walls and floor bare rock, the only furnishings were a dark, wooden desk with a matching chair. On it was a metal keyboard, like that from a typewriter, set into a shallow metal box. Wires led from it up the wall to a large flat sheet of mirrored glass.

Judex sat down at the desk, turned a dial, and casually flicked several switches. A low hum came from the device. Grayson stepped up and stood behind him. Peering at the glass, he saw the captive German soldier in a bare cell, sitting slumped on a crude wooden bunk.

"Now, let's see what our guest has to say," Judex said. He removed his gloves, flexed his fingers and began to type.

Grayson was amazed, when he looked from Judex back up to the glass and saw words forming across its reflective surface.

335

"What the…?" He muttered. "How…wait, don't tell me, you and your brother put this together after you were done with the car?"

"Something like that," Judex replied, not looking up from his typing.

Grayson had trouble following the words on the glass; it looked as if they appeared reversed so the soldier could read them. All Judex's questions concerned the German's reasons for moving troops into the area.

Upon first spotting the writing on the mirror, the captive soldier looked up in stunned amazement. He slumped where he sat and shook his head defiantly, as Judex continued to type and the letters grew brighter. Try as he might, the soldier could not keep his gaze from being dragged back to the words on the glass.

Minutes ticked by and, slowly, the soldier's eyes became fixated on the glass, his features grew slack and his body swayed slightly.

"Stationed here… to set up… compound. Were told to clear the village… any able bodied men were to be held for workers," he muttered.

Judex nodded and typed.

"Command says it is to be munitions plant many of us think that is just story…" the soldier continued, in a drowsy voice. "Soldiers and scientists brought in, but few workers."

"What are they up to?" Grayson asked, under his breath.

Judex's face was shrouded in shadows as he silently typed away, intent on interrogating the soldier, so the American's question merely hung in the air, unanswered.

"Have converted mill and barns into work areas," the German continued, in his dazed monotone. "Told more troops… be arriving in three days. We were to have things established for the rest of the science staff… within the week… along… along with… trucks... last of… equipment…"

The soldier swayed, fell forward, and seemed to momentarily snap out of his trance, before losing the struggle and collapsing onto his bunk.

"Strong willed," Judex muttered, sitting up and taking his hands away from the keys. "And just enough information to be worrisome."

"I'm not even going to ask about… *that*," Grayson said, gesturing at the glass from which the last of Judex's words were fading. "The Germans have some big project they are setting up here… is that what's happening?"

"It seems so. You and Madame Lazlo were just unlucky to wander into the middle of this. Whatever efforts we take to get you to safety run the risk of drawing a great deal of unwanted attention to our Resistance activities here."

"So what are the Germans doing?" Grayson asked. "If it's not a munitions plant, what is it?"

"A scientific research station," Judex said.

"Researching what?"

"Dangerous things," Judex said, getting to his feet, and moving towards the door. "Events are moving faster and in a most perilous direction than even I had anticipated."

"Look here…" Grayson said, reaching for a wooden stool, before noticing his host was walking away. He shrugged and quickly followed. "I don't understand half of what's going on, and your inability to give me a straight answer is not helping. Corby and I have a job to do. You say you can help us, but all you do is talk in riddles! We are not green cadets; Corby and I could help you, but I've got to know what's going on before risking my mission or the people I'm charged with."

"You are right, Lieutenant," Judex replied, turning around to face the young marine. "I have grown used to having my word obeyed, and that tends to have an effect on one's common courtesy. The Resistance contacted me, not just to help them, and to let them use my home as a base of operations, but also because I have a talent for clandestine work and a gift for dealing with… unusual problems and puzzles. I believe one of the tasks I've been involved in, tracking down the Boroff Papers, is connected to this new 'munitions plant'."

"Boroff…?" Grayson muttered. "I know that name…"

"A scientist, both famous and infamous," Judex nodded, continuing to walk. "Along with their interest in the occult, the Nazis have been pursuing numerous projects involving fringe science. Professor Boroff worked with them until greed and obsession prompted him to flee Europe and, by all accounts, he met a bad end in your country."

They strode up several flights of narrow stairs before coming out onto a plain stone balcony. It was at the back of Judex's home and looked out, not at the nearby town, but rather at a stretch of woods with a stream snaking through it.

"I'm guessing he left stuff behind," Grayson said, struggling to catch his breath and organize his thoughts.

"Several… caches of his papers were discovered after Boroff fled and the Germans used them and materials confiscated from several other scientists," Judex explained.

"And that's why we are dealing with things like War Wheels, electro-beams and zombie soldiers," Grayson nodded, leaning on the stone railing and gazing out into the night-shrouded wilderness. Despite all the craziness and uncertainty going on around him, it was kind of nice to just stand for a moment and take in the peacefulness of the night and the surrounding woods, to feel the wind on his face, and to hear the distant sound of the stream. A brief feeling of peace came over him, quickly followed by an avalanche of thoughts and ideas. After several minutes, he glanced up at his host.

"What?" Judex asked.

"That stream…" Grayson muttered. "It connects to the river that leads into Paris, right? The Seine…?"

"Yes, I have a small boat that I've made use of to travel clandestinely."

"Then, you could take Mrs. Lazlo the rest of the way to Paris," Grayson said, turning to face the older man.

"Could I...?"

"Look, I'll be honest, Corby and I are stumbling around here and Mrs. Lazlo is a city girl. With whatever the Germans are setting up, we don't stand a chance of getting out of here, but you do. You know the area, you have the resources and contacts, and you have a gift for moving about quietly and getting in and out of places. So, the best chance of us dealing with our respective problems is to swap."

"Swap...?" Judex muttered. "You mean, I would escort Madam Lazlo to her rendezvous in Paris, while you and Sergeant Corby would deal with the research station... Hmm..."

"Look, you can handle the stealth, while a couple leathernecks like Corby and I are best suited for a problem that can only be solved with some rough stuff."

"Yes, it has a certain logic that is hard to dismiss," Judex shrugged. He stroked his chin thoughtfully. "But what you would be taking on..."

"...Is no worse than what Uncle Sam asks of me on a daily basis," Grayson countered. "The main problem is breaking the news to Mrs. Lazlo. She may look elegant and delicate..."

"But is not the sort of woman to..." Judex began.

"To approve of being talked about like she is a child or a parcel to be delivered," Ilsa Lazlo said, stepping out of the shadows in the doorway.

Both men looked sheepish, suddenly transformed into errant schoolboys caught by a stern teacher.

"So, have you two decided who is to be my chaperone yet?" She asked, her lovely mouth a tight line.

"Look, Mrs. Lazlo..." Grayson began and then paused, frowning thoughtfully. "Getting you to Paris is my mission, and I'm sorry if your feelings are hurt, but it's more important that you reach your rendezvous than how happy you are about the travel arrangements."

He then squared his shoulders, preparing for the onslaught, which thankfully, never came.

"You are right, about your mission and my... responsibilities," she said, "but I am not a parcel, nor a child. I have worked with the Resistance and have contacts that can help you. This is not some boys' adventure story and I am not to be treated like a damsel in distress."

Grayson glanced over at Judex and the cloaked man nodded in approval at Ilsa's speech.

"You're right," Grayson said. "We are all in this together. The priority is to get you to Paris. That's not changing."

338

"I will need Madam Lazlo's assistance in planning our route," Judex said. "I can escort her to the city, but will need her knowledge to reach the rendez-vous."

Ilsa favored the mysterious crime fighter with a small smile and then turned her gaze to the young marine.

"And you will need the help of the Resistance, if you are to go ahead with the attack on the German's research compound," she said. "You and Sergeant Corby cannot expect to do it by yourselves."

"I can also provide you with some more information on what equipment and personnel they may have there." Judex added.

Soon, Grayson was back in the room he shared with Corby, sitting on the bed, a plate of bread and cheese on one side of him, a small stack of papers on the other. The more he read, the more furrowed with thought and worry his brow became.

Corby was still sprawled on the other bed, also peering over a scrap of paper. He gave a silent whistle, shook his head, and lowered the paper to look at his friend.

"And you volunteered us for this job?" he asked, incredulously.

Grayson looked up, frowned at Corby, and then went back to studying the rough sketch map of the area.

"It's the best chance we have of getting both plans to succeed," he replied. "You've had a look at Judex's men."

"Have you seen this list of stuff Judex thinks the Jerries are trying to build...? Haverlyte rays, robot bombs and some chemical that will dissolve through steel and rock...! Almost makes me miss the days when all we had to worry about was getting shot."

"Don't worry, there's a good chance that'll happen too," Grayson said with a grim smile. " But, I think, with the info Judex has managed to put together, we may have a chance of keeping the Germans busy, getting Ilsa safely to Paris, and maybe surviving the whole shindig."

"Can't wait to hear this plan," Corby said, sitting up.

"Look at this," Grayson said, handing him a torn scrap of paper. "See that gobbledygook at the bottom?"

"Yeah, looks like some big math problem."

"Judex thinks it's part of the Boroff formula... the stuff that melts rocks. If they actually have some of the stuff at the research lab..."

"Then we could use it to do our job for us," Corby nodded. "Pretty good thinking, Tom."

"Just 'cause we've got a chance, doesn't mean it'll be easy."

"If it was easy," Corby said, with a shrug. "They wouldn't send us to do it."

The following day was spent resting up for the coming tasks and preparation of both of equipment and men. Grayson and Corby helped the half-dozen Resistance fighters get their eclectic collection of weapons together and in top shape; they, in return, gave the two American soldiers the lay of the land and the best routes to use in reaching the mill yard, and the best ones for retreat.

As dusk began to creep across the sky, Judex, Ilsa and the two marines gathered in a small grotto beneath the Frenchman's home. The room was all stone, with a low ceiling. The far end was a slab reaching out into an underground stream. Moored to the stone dock was a small wood-paneled motorboat. Like Judex's car, it was a vehicle that had been quite stylish and popular roughly thirty years ago.

The quartet stood in the grotto, a mix of emotions playing across their features, as eagerness for action after all the hiding and waiting, clashed with the anxiety. There was no expectation that they would meet again, let alone survive the night's activities.

No one knew quite how to say good-bye, or at least did not want to be the first to say it. Judex stood back, knowing that, as a recent addition to the group, he had taken no part in what they had gone through to reach this place. So, he allowed them their moment.

"I won't be so trite as to say I've enjoyed our time together," Ilsa said, giving them a hint of a smile, "but, I am grateful for all you have done for the Resistance and for me."

"Any time," Corby nodded, with a self-conscious shrug.

"Just doing our job, Mrs. Lazlo," Grayson said. "Get to Paris and your rendezvous. Don't let yourself get distracted worrying about a couple of old 'devil dogs' like us."

She ducked in quickly, but gracefully and gave each a brief, chaste kiss on the cheek.

"Stay safe," she murmured. 'The world does not have so many brave men that it can afford to lose any."

With that, Ilsa turned and joined Judex. He helped her step over into the motorboat and then turned to the two marines.

"Gentlemen," he nodded, with a grim smile. "I hope to find you safe when I return."

"Good luck!" Grayson said.

"Bring us back a souvenir," Corby added.

Judex stepped into his seat, slid on his goggles, and the boat moved away, as silently as its land-based relation had earlier.

It went down a low stone tunnel that opened up into the river. Ilsa sat on one of the two benches that lined the side of the boat, just behind Judex, as he steered them down the dark waterway. The trees and bushes clustered close to the edges, in a few spots forming an arch over the river.

Soon, Judex's château was merely a hulking mass of shadow. Ilsa hugged herself, feeling a chill that was only partly from the cold.

"So," Judex said, his voice quiet, but still managing to startle his passenger in the dark. "Where shall you be going next?"

"I'm sorry…?"

"I know enough to know that you and your husband will be unable to stay in Paris," he continued, his tone casual, while his eyes scanned the landscape intently. "I'm guessing Paris is only a stopping point, not your ultimate destination."

"Yes, you are right," Ilsa sighed. "Victor is hoping we can get to Lisbon… though, I doubt it will be a direct trip. There has been talk of having to go through North Africa… I don't know…"

"Brave heart," Judex told her. "I have learned that the journey can be a long and serpentine one, but if you stay strong, you will reach your destination. Belief in a cause, or another person, can make a man a giant, but as you may have read in the Bible, it takes but a single stone to topple a giant."

While they were intended to be soothing, Ilsa could also feel the trace of sadness that ran through the mysterious man's words.

She glanced thoughtfully out into the night, and started when she caught a glimpse of movement on the riverbank. She reached out a tentative hand to touch Judex's arm.

He glanced over at her and she mouthed:

"There's someone in the trees."

She gestured towards the bank, while with her other hand, she drew her pistol. Then, she saw a second shadowy blur of movement. Glancing nervously about, she saw a third shape on the opposite bank. A form pushed through the branches, just as the Moon peeked out from the mass of clouds.

"It's a dog…?" Ilsa whispered, confused. "There are several of them…?"

"Yes," Judex said, unfazed and concentrating on his steering. "Nothing to fear, they are here to watch over us."

"You know…?" She started to ask, feeling a bit baffled.

"They are friends of mine," Judex smiled. He gave a sharp whistle and suddenly there was a pack of dogs, three on each side of the river. "Long before I allied myself with the Resistance, I had soldiers of my own."

Ilsa could only make out their shapes; she could see that the dogs, a mix of sizes and breeds, all stood, like proud sentinels, following the boat's progress.

"Are they going to follow us all the way to Paris?" she asked.

"No, only until this branch joins the river," Judex chuckled. "Once there, we should be safe to make the rest of the journey 'unchaperoned.' There are blankets under the bench. Make yourself comfortable. We will be breakfasting in Paris."

Under the watchful eyes of the dog pack, the motorboat made its silent way down the river and into the night.

So, time passed; awash in the fear and grief of war, the few remaining families and lone refugees huddled down for the night in their various hiding places, hoping to snatch a few moments of rest. The German troops and their conscripted workers had settled down either to sleep or patrol the makeshift compound.

All were unaware of the plans and activities of the American marines and their French Resistance allies.

The inhabitants of the area stayed in sleepy ignorance until shortly after midnight. The first hints that something was occurring were sounds of distant gunfire, followed by shouts in both German and French. Then a noise washed over the landscape, somewhere between the roar of an animal and a massive ocean wave. It lasted for several minutes, a steady rumble that never seemed to peak. A tremor passed through the Earth as the sound began to fade away. More shouts could be heard, but they seemed to be of people in distress, rather than the earlier sounds of conflict.

When the sun came up, where the German compound had been was now a hole in the ground, several hundred feet across and, at its center, fifty feet deep. Parts of several small outlying building and several dozen dazed soldiers and workers were all that remained.

On a wooded hill, away from the hole in the ground, the two American marines and the licorice-smelling Resistance fighter lay sprawled on the ground, bruised, battered, struggling to catch their breath.

"Suppose you're gonna blame this on me," Corby muttered, before coughing and wiping at a gash on his forehead with his sleeve.

Grayson turned his head, squinted at his friend, and, wincing, struggled to sit up.

"Yeah, I think I am," he said, rubbing his upper arm. "I did warn you about Boroff's formula and then you go and shoot the biggest tank of it... What did you think 'disintegrator gas' meant?"

"It was dark and all those Nazis shooting at me threw my aim off. Anyway, that research base isn't a problem anymore..."

"Then we just have to hope Judex's boys can get us back across the line."

"And we can go back to just worrying about guys with guns, instead of this crazy science stuff," Corby grunted. "You think Ilsa and Judex made it to Paris OK?"

"Sure," Grayson nodded, lying back down. "They'll be fine. The Resistance will make sure she and her husband get together and then get them out of the country. I don't think they'll have any problems once they reach Casablanca."

1959. In the story that follows, Matthew Dennion pays homage to George Franju's ground-breaking 1960 horror film, Les Yeux sans Visage [Eyes Without a Face]*, staring Pierre Brasseur as the surgeon with a disfigured daughter, tragically played by Edith Scob who, coincidentally, played Judex's wife Jacqueline in the 1963 remake.*

Matthew Dennion: *Faces of Fear*

She was sweating profusely as she ran, not just from the exertion of sprinting at full speed but because the enormous boiler room she was in was giving off a tremendous amount of heat. What made it worse was how the sweat stung as it slowly worked its way into the cuts all over her body. *I shouldn't be here,* she thought. *How did I even get here? This whole thing is insane.* Behind her she could hear the sound of metal scraping against metal. She stopped for a second turned and could see sparks in the darkness. *I shouldn't be here. Where is here anyway?* She began to cry as she ran. Where was her father? The last thing she could remember was her father taking her to the clinic.

"The clinic!" she said aloud "I am in the clinic!"

The girl ran over the recent past in her mind to see if she could remember how she got where she was.

"I was in a terrible car accident; my face was horribly scarred and disfigured. My father took me to his clinic to treat my wounds. My face was disfigured to the extent that I was forced to wear a plastic mask to conceal it. I was having terrible dreams about becoming a monster. I began to see a horrible, burned and mutilated face every time I closed my eyes. When the dreams got worse, my father sent for Dr. Crane, from the psychiatric hospital, to see if he could help me out. He treated me with medication for a few days but the dreams only got worse. The dream was no longer just the burned face, the face started to become something more!"

She began to form the picture of the creature in her head and, as it formed, her steps seemed to get slower and slower. It was as if she was running in ankle-deep mud. The floor beneath her seemed to be changing or melting.

The scarping sound behind her got louder and closer as she screamed in terror. Her head snapped back just as someone grabbed her hair from behind and she came to a dead stop. An awful smell assaulted her like flesh burnt and decayed. Were she not so terrified, she would have vomited.

A series of blades appeared next to her masked face. Two of them slowly reached over, punctured the plastic mask and cut into her already burned cheek. As the blood fell from her, she noticed that the floor directly in front of her dropped. Suddenly, she was standing on the end of scaffold in front of long drop.

"What's going on? This can't be happening! This can't be real!" she screamed.

The girl could feel something rough next to her face, as a raspy voiced joked: "Oh, it's real Christiane, real enough to leave you scarred for life!"

She was pushed from behind and fell head-first into a chasm. It felt like three stories before she came to hard stop, hitting another steel floor.

As she hit the ground, her mask went skidding in the darkness. Shaken and bruised, she turned on her back to look up at who—or what—was after her. She could only see a silhouette of what looked like a man with a red and black stripped sweater and some kind of fedora hat. Then, she noticed his hands—or his one hand to be specific. The fingers were elongated and thin. As she was looking, the man lifted the misshapen hand and a glint of light reflected off of it. Her body went rigid as she realized that those weren't misshapen fingers but blades. The man continued to lift his gloved hand to his mouth and lick her blood off the steel.

The man cackled; he arched his body back in the throes of ecstasy. His voice echoed elation as he looked down at her.

"Your fear!" he said. "It's more powerful than all of the other children I've consumed combined! Devouring your soul will make me a virtual god!"

He laughed in a high pitched cackle as he jumped down in front of her. Yellow eyes stared at her as the demon reached down and wrapped his bladed hand around her chin.

"You know, ever since that S-Mart flunky used that dammed *Necronomicon* to send me hurtling through time, I've been so lonely trying to make my way back to my children. Lucky for me, I found you and now, look at us—don't we make quite the pretty pair!"

The monster howled at his mocking remark, while he raked her ravaged face with his knifed fingers. The girl pulled away, got to her knees, and started to run. She didn't know where to go, but she had to get away from him.

She was running again, crying, looking for any hope of salvation. In the distance, at the end of the pitch black corridor, she could see a blood red light in the darkness. She ran for it as the man—or whatever he was—behind her mocked her and chased her down and down the endless corridor.

The girl kept running toward the light, until she came to a dead end. She was now bathed in the light. She looked for somewhere to escape, to keep running, but the walls seemed to go straight up forever, with a series of pipes and bars connected to them.

She had thought that the light would save her, that she would get out, leave this torture behind, but now, she was trapped again and the creature had caught up with her.

He slowly wiggled his bladed fingers as he stalked towards her.

"Just keep telling yourself, it's only a dream," he sneered as he approached, laughing his high-pitched laugh.

She bent down and curled into a ball against the wall as the laugh echoed all around her, but, suddenly, it started to sound deeper and hollow, and come from somewhere above her.

The creature suddenly stopped in his tracks, as the deep laugh erupted again.

This time, it was no echo.

Both the monster and the girl looked around as the laugh continued. Neither seemed to know where it came from. The creature swung his bladed hand through the air and screamed:

"Who are you? What are doing here? You can't be in here—this is my world! The dream world! Only I can enter this girl's head! She's mine!"

But the eerie laugh only increased in speed and was so chilling that it gave even the creature pause. Then a deep voice answered:

"The dream world in people's minds may be yours, but I can see directly into their souls! Judex judges men by the acts they commit, and I find you to be an abomination!"

Christiane was still scared, but she could have sworn that the creature chasing her was even more terrified of the voice than she was!

The voice started again:

"This girl has suffered enough! Your suffering, however, is just beginning. You have taken your last life!"

Christiane looked up and saw a massive cloaked figure swoop down from seemingly nowhere. As it descended, she could see a man's face under a tight fitting hat. The light suddenly tightened and focused on the creature like some kind of blood-red spotlight. The creature lifted his bladed hand into the air as Judex crashed into him. Christiane watched as the two figures tumbled into the darkness...

Suddenly, she shot upright in her bed. She was back in the clinic, but her cheeks and back were still bleeding from where she had been cut in her dream.

Panting, she looked next to her and was even more terrified than she had been in her dream. The psychologist, Dr. Crane, was standing next to her bed with a maniacal look on his face. He was looking at her charts, but was smearing them with blood.

The girl became terrified as she realized the doctor had her blood all over his hands. She screamed in terror.

The lights turned on as her father came running into the room. He ran as quickly as he could over to the bed.

"Crane, what have you done?"

Two orderlies came through the door. Dr. Genessier yelled at them:

"Get him out of here!"

The orderlies quickly restrained Crane. Genessier snarled at the psychologist:

"Crane, why would you do this to my own daughter? She's your patient, for God's sake!"

"It wasn't me, Genessier," shrieked Crane. "Not me! Don't you see her fear! Her own fear did this to her! Never did I think my serum would lead to such levels of terror!"

Genessier couldn't understand what Crane meant until he looked at Christiane's I.V. bag.

"What is this? What have you been treating her with?"

The psyhologist smiled as he said: "My masterpiece, Genessier! Don't you see? Now, I can study fear at its full potential!"

As the psychologist was forcibly dragged away, Genessier shouted: "You're through in this country, Crane! I'll see you deported for this!" Then, he turned to his daughter. "Are you OK, my dear?"

Christiane was sweating as he began to treat her wounds. The girl had a stunned appearance about her.

"What happened?" she whispered. "I thought it was all a dream."

Her father sighed. "It seems Dr. Crane was experimenting on you with some kind of fear toxin; he attacked you in your sleep to increase the level of terror you were experiencing."

Genessier's eyes began to tear up as he removed Christiane's plastic mask. He fought hard to keep his reaction to a minimal when he gazed on his daughter's hideous face. Whatever Crane had done to her had caused fresh wounds to appear on her already damaged face. The previous condition would have made the healing process difficult, but with the additional damage, Genessier knew that he would have to take drastic steps to restore his daughter's beauty.

Raising his eyes toward the ceiling, he made a vow to himself that he would right these atrocities wrought on his beloved Christiane no matter what the price.

Suddenly, a red light flashed across the room, catching all of the people in the room by surprise.

In the bed next to Christiane, the hand of the wounded man sharing her room moved slightly. As it slid out from under the cover, a bright red ring could be seen on one of his fingers.

Genessier, however, was more fixated on the printouts from the electroencephalogram connected to the man. The printouts flashed a series of activity. The doctor looked at one of his assistants.

"Orloff, check that equipment. That man has been brain dead since he came in here with those gunshot wounds last night."

"But his hand—it moved from under the sheet?" Orloff stammered.

"With all of the commotion in this room," Genessier sneered, "I'm surprised it was only his hand and not his whole body that fell out of the bed! Now, please check the equipment."

As Orloff approached, the electroencephalogram the printouts went buzz-ing again. "Well, well, he seems to be doing much better suddenly…"

Christiane started at the man's ring and wondered:

It's the same color as the light in my dream! It was just a dream wasn't it?

Dennis Power imagined that the secret origins of Judex went as far back as the Dawn of Time itself. In this fitting epilogue to an anthology devoted to a character that is as surely as archetypal and timeless as any other, we journey to the farthest future...

Jean-Marc Lofficier: *The Earth abideth forever*

A billion years in the future stood the city of Diaspar. Humanity had long since left Earth for the stars, and those who had chosen to remain behind stayed forever immured within its great walls.

In Diaspar, the Central Computer created bodies in which those people lived, and stored their minds at the end of their allotted lifespans, before recreating them to live again, and again.

From time to time, a Unique awoke, one who had had no previous lives. They were anomalies. Most were harmless eccentrics or bold pioneers capable of opening much needed new vistas in an otherwise unchanging pattern; only a few, a very few, were truly dangerous.

Danker was one of them.

But Yarlan Zey, the genius who had built the Central Computer, had had the foresight to predict even this, and had devised a cure.

As Danker wrapped his hands around his girlfriend's neck and began to squeeze, in a secret vault, deep within the Central Computer, a switch moved, seemingly of its own accord.

Judex awoke.

Credits and Sources

Acolytes of the Shadows

Co-Starring:	Created by:
Julia Orsini	Arthur Bernède & Louis Feuillade
Darlla Rassendyll (The Man in the Felt Hat)	Rick Lai based on a character created by Gaston Leroux & the works of Anthony Hope
Erik	Gaston Leroux
Gloria Scot (Joséphine Balsamo II)	Maurice Leblanc
Léonard	Maurice Leblanc
Monsieur Nemo (Prof. Moriarty)	Arthur Conan Doyle
El Hichmakani (The Persian)	Richard Francis Burton and Gaston Leroux
Lucien Gévrol	based on Emile Gaboriau
Antoine Dragone (Anthony Draco)	Stephen Kandel and Ray Russell
Henri Jaraud (Henry Jarrod)	Crane Wibur and Charles Belden based on Alexandre Dumas
Jean Lamotte	
Jacques Lefèvre	Pierre Gendron, Arnold Phillips & Werner H. Furst
Gaston Morrell	Pierre Gendron, Arnold Phillips & Werner H. Furst
The Black Coats	Paul Féval
Colonel Bozzo-Corona	Paul Féval
Gentlemen of the Night	Paul Féval
Josine (Joséphine Balsamo III)	Maurice Leblanc
Sabine	Rick Lai
Dr. Villagos	Fortuné du Boisgobey
William Rassendyll	Anthony Hope
Armande	Emile Zola

Arnaude Kent Rassendyll	Rick Lai based on the works of Walter Gibson and Anthony Hope
Lee family	Richard Marsh
Eugène Rougon	Emile Zola
Leon Fauchery	Emile Zola
Anna Karenina	Leo Tolstoy
Count Corbucci	E. W. Hornung
Vautrin	Honoré de Balzac
Priests of Erlik Khan	Robert E. Howard

Previously published in *Shadows of the Opera.*

The Quality of Vengeance

Co-Starring: **Adapted by:**
Pazuzu William Peter Blatty

Judex ab Chaos

Co-Starring: **Created by:**
Quentin Durward Walter Scott

Mask of the Monster

Co-Starring:	**Created by:**
"Gouroull" (Monster of Frankenstein)	Mary Shelley and Jean-Claude Carrière
Jules Maigret	Georges Simenon
Louise Maigret née Léonard	Georges Simenon
The Léonard family	Georges Simenon
Dr. Cornelius Kramm	Gustave Le Rouge
Fritz Kramm	Gustave Le Rouge
Jules de Grandin	Seabury Quinn
Dr. Lorde	Cyril Berger
Inspector Gauthier	Matthew Baugh
Sherlock Holmes	Arthur Conan Doyle
C. Auguste Dupin	Edgar Allan Poe
Joseph Rouletabille	Gaston Leroux
Sâr Dubnotal	*Anonymous*
Balaoo	Gaston Leroux

Previously published in *Tales of the Shadowmen* No. 1.

Lost and Found

Co-Starring:	Created by:
Kaspar Gutman	Dashiell Hammett
The Vampires	Louis Feuillade

Previously published in *Tales of the Shadowmen* No. 2.

Two Hunters

Co-Starring:	Created by:
Nikolas Rokoff	Edgar Rice Burroughs
Paul d'Arnot	Edgar Rice Burroughs
Lord Greystoke (Tarzan)	Edgar Rice Burroughs
Jane Porter	Edgar Rice Burroughs

Previously published in *Tales of the Shadowmen* No. 3.

The Gargoyles of Notre-Dame

Co-Starring:	Created by:
Sâr Dubnotal	*Anonymous*
Gianetti Annunciata	*Anonymous*
Doktor Von Meyer	Seabury Quinn
The Gargoyles	Clark Ashton Smith
Blaise Reynard	Clark Ashton Smith
Séance participants	Matthew Baugh
Mitra	Robert E. Howard
Viritrilbia	C. S. Lewis

Penumbra

Co-Starring:	Created by:
Philippe Guérande	Louis Feuillade
The Vampires	Louis Feuillade
M. Oreno	Louis Feuillade
The Waynes	Bob Kane & Bill Finger
Kent Allard	Walter Gibson
Ribaudet	Arthur Bernède & Louis Feuillade

Joseph Rouletabille	Gaston Leroux
Cigale Mystère	Paul d'Ivoi

Previously published in *Tales of the Shadowmen* No. 1.

What Rough Beast

Co-Starring:	Created by:
Hugo Danner	Philip Wylie
Sâr Dubnotal	*Anonymous*
Gianetti Annunciata	*Anonymous*
Doktor Von Meyer	Seabury Quinn
The Colossus	Clark Ashton Smith
The Ghouls	H.P. Lovecraft
The Ape Demon	E. Hoffman Price
The Tentacled Demon	Seabury Quinn
Abednego Danner	Philip Wylie
General Broulard	Humphrey Cobb
Nathare of Vyones	Clark Ashton Smith
Tom Shayne	Philip Wylie
Joiry	Catherine L. Moore

Previously published in *Tales of the Shadowmen* No. 7.

Justice and Power

Co-Starring:	Created by:
Leo Saint-Clair (The Nyctalope)	Jean de La Hire
Korrides	Jean de La Hire
Dr. Cerral	Maurice Renard
Colonel Fontaine	*Historical*
General Anthoine	*Historical*
Rémy Baudoin	George Lucas

Previously published in *Night of the Nyctalope*.

The Beast Within

Co-Starring:	Created by:
Dr. Cornelius Kramm	Gustave Le Rouge
Prosper Cocantin	Arthur Bernède
	& Louis Feuillade

Michel Cocantin (Licorice Kid)	Arthur Bernède
	& Louis Feuillade
Bertrand Calliet	Guy Endore
The Pitamonts	Guy Endore
Aymar Galliez	Guy Endore
Dr. Dumas	Guy Endore

Every Rose

Co-Starring:	Created by:
Maciste	Gabriele d'Annunzio
Gina	Hayao Miyazaki
"Gouroull" (Monster of	Mary Shelley and
Frankenstein)	Jean-Claude Carrière
Béatrice	Nathaniel Hawthorne
Rappaccini	Nathaniel Hawthorne
Magistrate Buratti	based on Massimo Carlotto
Professor Teone	based on Hugo Pratt

The Ultimate Prize

Co-Starring:	Created by:
Prosper Cocantin	Arthur Bernède
	& Louis Feuillade
Michel Cocantin (Licorice Kid)	Arthur Bernède
	& Louis Feuillade
Gabrielle Deslys	*Historical*
Dracula	Bram Stoker
Jules Maigret	Georges Simenon

The Dreadful Conspiracy

Co-Starring:	Created by:
Inspector Ménardier	Arthur Bernède
Francis Ardan (Doc Savage)	Guy d'Armen/Lester Dent
Berthelaux	Vincent Jounieaux
Andrew Blodgett Mayfair (Ham)	Lester Dent
Theodore Marley Brooks (Monk)	Lester Dent
Monsieur Ferval	Arthur Bernède
Jules de Grandin	Seabury Quinn
Leclerc	based on Dennis E. Power
Ivana Orloff	based on Henri Vernes
Ming (The Yellow Shadow)	Henri Vernes

The Shin Tan	Henri Vernes
Inspector Pujol	Claude Desailly
Inspector Terrasson	Claude Desailly
William Harper Littlejohn	Lester Dent
John Renwick	Lester Dent
Thomas J. Roberts	Lester Dent
Judge Coméliau	Georges Simenon
Doctor Lyndon Parker	August Derleth
The Si Fan	Sax Rohmer
Anton Zarnak	Lin Carter
Chantecoq	Arthur Bernède
Chevalier Auguste Dupin	Edgar Allan Poe
Comtes de Boehm-Orloff	Paul Féval
Commissaire Valentin	Claude Desailly
Doctor Septimus	Edgar P. Jacobs
The Mega Wave	Edgar P. Jacobs
The Depository Bank of Zurich	Dan Brown

The Talisman

Co-Starring:	Created by:
Henry "Indiana" Jones	George Lucas
Baroness Hilda von Einem	John Buchan
The Companions of the Rosy Hours	John Buchan
Hercule Poirot	Agatha Christie
Mocata	Dennis Wheatley
Sâr Dubnotal	*Anonymous*

Training Day

Co-Starring:	Created by:
Professor Challenger	Arthur Conan Doyle
Grun	Robert J. Hogan
Lorenzo Prunesti	Chester Gould
Don Luis Perenna (Arsène Lupin)	Maurice Leblanc
Chen Zhen	Ni Kuang
Pai Mei	Quentin Tarentino
Kent Allard (The Black Shadow)	Walter Gibson
Bruce Wayne	Bob Kane & Bill Finger
Jules Maigret	Georges Simenon
Huo Yuanjia	*Historical*

The Judex Codex

Co-Starring:	Created by:
Raymond Mystère	Dennis E. Power based on Doctor Mystère & Martin Mystère
Doctor Mystère	Paul d'Ivoi
Cigale Mystère	Paul d'Ivoi
Martin Mystère	Alfredo Castelli
Henrietta de Marigny	Dennis E. Power based on H.P. Lovecraft
Etienne-Laurent de Marigny	H.P. Lovecraft
Henri-Laurent de Marigny	Brian Lumley based on H.P. Lovecraft
Henry Jones	George Lucas
Thomas Swift	Victor Appleton
John Kenton	Abraham Merritt
Pierre d'Artois	E. Hoffmann Price
Miskatonic University	H.P. Lovecraft
The Tcho-Tcho	August Derleth
Jean Aubry	Arthur Bernède & Louis Feuillade
Prosper Cocantin	Arthur Bernède & Louis Feuillade
Daisy Torp-Cocantin	Arthur Bernède & Louis Feuillade
Michel Cocantin (Licorice Kid)	Arthur Bernède & Louis Feuillade
Jacques Cocantin / Jacques Clouseau	Arthur Bernède & Louis Feuillade and Blake Edwards & Maurice Richlin
Cato	Harry Kurnitz
The Men in Black	Modern Folklore, developed by Alfredo Castelli
Ventidius Varro	H. Warner Munn
Khokarsa	Philip José Farmer
Zu Vendis	H. Rider Haggard
Kor	H. Rider Haggard
Opar	Edgar Rice Burroughs
Zimbabue	Charles R. Saunders
Captain Owen Kettle	C.J. Cutcliffe Hyne
René Belloq	George Lucas

Rache Churan	Sax Rohmer
Elessar Telcontar	J.R.R. Tolkien
The Palantir	J.R.R. Tolkien
The One Ring	J.R.R. Tolkien
J.R.R. Tolkien	*Historical*
Philip José Farmer	*Historical*
Hadon of Opar	Philip José Farmer
Ironcastle	J.-H. Rosny Aîné
Thongor	Lin Carter
Frédéric-Jean Orth (L'Ombre)	Alain Page
Charles Dreyfuss	Harry Kurnitz
Sir Charles Lytton	Blake Edwards
	& Maurice Richlin

Eye of the Tiger-Man

Co-Starring:	Created by:
Michel Cocantin (Licorice Kid)	Arthur Bernède
	& Louis Feuillade
The Black Coats	Paul Féval
Colonel Bozzo-Corona	Paul Féval
Jean Aubry	Arthur Bernède
	& Louis Feuillade
Prosper Cocantin	Arthur Bernède
	& Louis Feuillade
Daisy Torp-Cocantin	Arthur Bernède
	& Louis Feuillade
Dr. de Villiers-Pagan	Jean de La Hire
Surina	Paul Féval, *fils*
Professor Gibberne	H.G. Wells
Felifax	Paul Féval, *fils*
The Shamatari	Ruggero Deodato

Judex Rules

Co-Starring:	Created by:
Georges Franju	*Historical*
Fantomas	Pierre Souvestre
	& Marcel Allain
Juve	Pierre Souvestre
	& Marcel Allain
Mike Volny	Harry Kronman
Eliot Ness	*Historical*

Malay John / Malay Jack	Frank L. Packard and Sax Rohmer
Ali of Cairo	Sax Rohmer
The Spider (Araneus)	R.T.M. Scott & Norvell Page
Walter Winchell	*Historical*
H. Ashton Wolfe	*Historical*
Hanoi Shan	H. Ashton-Wolfe
The Shadow (Umbra)	Walter Gibson
Théophraste Lupin	Maurice Leblanc
Darlla Rassendyll	Rick Lai
The Black Coats	Paul Féval
Joséphine Balsamo	Maurice Leblanc
G-8 (Ragging Rassendyll)	Robert J. Hogan
Al Rassendyll	Philip José Farmer & Bruce Elliot
Henri de Lagardère	Paul Féval
King Kong	Merian C. Cooper & Edgar Wallace
Philip Strange	Donal E. Keyhoe
Pierre d'Artois	E. Hoffmann Price
Vautrin	Honoré de Balzac
Philo Vance	S.S. Van Dine
Ellery Queen	Ellery Queen
Joe Kulak	Mort Thaw
Lucy Luciano	*Historical*
Meyer Lansky	*Historical*
The Gray Seal	Frank L. Packard
Rocambole	P.-A. Ponson du Terrail
Chéri-Bibi	Gaston Leroux
Fergus O'Breane	Paul Féval

A Ticket for Thule

Co-Starring:	Created by:
Hareton Ironcastle	J.-H. Rosny Aîné
Georges Sauvin (The Chinese Fish)	Jean Bommard
Jan Mayen	Paul Alfred Müller
Sun Koh	Paul Alfred Müller

The Affair of the Necklace Revisited

Co-Starring:	Created by:
Richard Benson	Paul Ernst

Pierre Duchêne	Jean-Marc Lofficier
The Dreux-Soubize	Maurice Leblanc
Commissaire Gilles	Jacques Decrest
Baruch Jorgell	Gustave Le Rouge
Alice Benson	Paul Ernst
Alicia Benson	Paul Ernst
Arsène Lupin	Maurice Leblanc
Zigomar	Léon Sazie
Fantômas	Pierre Souvestre & Marcel Allain
Belphégor	Arthur Bernède
Ténébras	Arnould Galopin
Dr. Cornelius Kramm	Gustave Le Rouge
And:	
The Queen's Necklace	Alexandre Dumas & Maurice Leblanc

Previously published in *Tales of the Shadowmen* No. 8.

Ilsa's Crossing

Co-Starring: — **Created by:**

Co-Starring:	Created by:
Tom Grayson	Franklin Adreon, Ronald Davidson, Barry Shipman & Sol Shor
Frank Corby	Franklin Adreon, Ronald Davidson, Barry Shipman and Sol Shor
Professor Boroff	Franklin Adreon, Morgan Cox & Ronald Davidson
Ilsa Lund / Lazlo	Julius & Phillip Epstein
Michel (Licorice Kid)	Arthur Bernède & Louis Feuillade

Faces of Fear

Co-Starring:	Created by:
Christiane	Jean Redon
Freddy Krueger	Wes Craven
Dr. Crane	Bill Finger & Bob Kane
Dr. Genessier	Jean Redon
Dr. Orloff	Jesus Franco

Previously published in *Tales of the Shadowmen* No. 7.

The Earth abideth forever

Co-Starring:
Diaspar

Created by:
Arthur C. Clarke

SF & FANTASY

Henri Allorge. *The Great Cataclysm*
Guy d'Armen. *Doc Ardan: The City of Gold and Lepers*
G.-J. Arnaud. *The Ice Company*
Charles Asselineau. *The Double Life*
Cyprien Bérard. *The Vampire Lord Ruthwen*
Aloysius Bertrand. *Gaspard de la Nuit*
Richard Bessière. *The Gardens of the Apocalypse*
Albert Bleunard. *Ever Smaller*
Félix Bodin. *The Novel of the Future*
Louis Boussenard. *Monsieur Synthesis*
Alphonse Brown. *City of Glass; The Conquest of the Air*
André Caroff. *The Terror of Madame Atomos; Miss Atomos; The Return of Madame Atomos; The Mistake of Madame Atomos; The Monsters of Madame Atomos; The Revenge of Madame Atomos; The Resurrection of Madame Atomos*
Félicien Champsaur. *The Human Arrow; Ouha, King of the Apes; Pharaoh's Wife*
Didier de Chousy. *Ignis*
Captain Danrit. *Undersea Odyssey*
C. I. Defontenay. *Star (Psi Cassiopeia)*
Charles Derennes. *The People of the Pole*
Georges Dodds (anthologist). *The Missing Link*
Harry Dickson. *The Heir of Dracula*
Jules Dornay. *Lord Ruthven Begins*
Alfred Driou. *The Adventures of a Parisian Aeronaut*
Sâr Dubnotal *vs. Jack the Ripper*
Alexandre Dumas. *The Return of Lord Ruthven*
Renée Dunan. *Baal*
J.-C. Dunyach. *The Night Orchid; The Thieves of Silence*
Henri Duvernois. *The Man Who Found Himself*
Achille Eyraud. *Voyage to Venus*
Henri Falk. *The Age of Lead*
Paul Féval. *Anne of the Isles; Knightshade; Revenants; Vampire City; The Vampire Countess; The Wandering Jew's Daughter*
Paul Féval, *fils. Felifax, the Tiger-Man*
Charles de Fieux. *Lamékis*
Arnould Galopin. *Doctor Omega; Doctor Omega and the Shadowmen* (anthology)
Judith Gautier. *Isoline and the Serpent-Flower*
Léon Gozlan. *The Vampire of the Val-de-Grâce*
G.L. Gick. *Harry Dickson and the Werewolf of Rutherford Grange*
Edmond Haraucourt. *Illusions of Immortality*
Nathalie Henneberg. *The Green Gods*
V. Hugo, P. Foucher & P. Meurice. *The Hunchback of Notre-Dame*
Romain d'Huissier. *Hexagon: Dark Matter*
Michel Jeury. *Chronolysis*
Gustave Kahn. *The Tale of Gold and Silence*
Gérard Klein. *The Mote in Time's Eye*

Fernand Kolney. *Love in 5000 Years*
Louis-Guillaume de La Follie. *The Unpretentious Philosopher*
Jean de La Hire. *Enter the Nyctalope; The Nyctalope on Mars; The Nyctalope vs. Lucifer; The Nyctalope Steps In; Night of the Nyctalope*
Etienne-Léon de Lamothe-Langon. *The Virgin Vampire*
André Laurie. *Spiridon*
Gabriel de Lautrec. *The Vengeance of the Oval Portrait*
Alain le Drimeur. *The Future City*
Georges Le Faure & Henri de Graffigny. *The Extraordinary Adventures of a Russian Scientist Across the Solar System* (2 vols.)
Gustave Le Rouge. *The Vampires of Mars; The Dominion of the World* (w/Gustave Guitton) (4 vols.)
Jules Lermina. *Mysteryville; Panic in Paris; To-Ho and the Gold Destroyers; The Secret of Zippelius*
André Lichtenberger. *The Centaurs*
Jean-Marc & Randy Lofficier. *Edgar Allan Poe on Mars; The Katrina Protocol; Pacifica; Robonocchio; Tales of the Shadowmen 1-9*
Xavier Mauméjean. *The League of Heroes*
Joseph Méry. *The Tower of Destiny*
Hippolyte Mettais. *The Year 5865*
Louise Michel. *The Human Microbes; The New World*
Tony Moilin. *Paris in the Year 2000*
José Moselli. *Illa's End*
John-Antoine Nau. *Enemy Force*
Marie Nizet. *Captain Vampire*
C. Nodier, A. Beraud & Toussaint-Merle. *Frankenstein*
Henri de Parville. *An Inhabitant of the Planet Mars*
Gaston de Pawlowski. *Journey to the Land of the 4th Dimension*
Georges Pellerin. *The World in 2000 Years*
Ernest Pérochon. *The Frenetic People*
Pierre Pelot. *The Child Who Walked on the Sky*
J. Polidori, C. Nodier, E. Scribe. *Lord Ruthven the Vampire*
P.-A. Ponson du Terrail. *The Vampire and the Devil's Son; The Immortal Woman*
Henri de Régnier. *A Surfeit of Mirrors*
Maurice Renard. *The Blue Peril; Doctor Lerne; The Doctored Man; A Man Among the Microbes; The Master of Light*
Jean Richepin. *The Wing; The Crazy Corner*
Albert Robida. *The Adventures of Saturnin Farandoul; The Clock of the Centuries; Chalet in the Sky; The Electric Life*
J.-H. Rosny Aîné. *Helgvor of the Blue River; The Givreuse Enigma; The Mysterious Force; The Navigators of Space; Vamireh; The World of the Variants; The Young Vampire*
Marcel Rouff. *Journey to the Inverted World*
Han Ryner. *The Superhumans*
Brian Stableford. *The New Faust at the Tragicomique;The Empire of the Necromancers (The Shadow of Frankenstein; Frankenstein and the Vampire Countess; Frankenstein in London); Sherlock Holmes & The Vampires of Eternity; The Stones of Camelot; The*

Wayward Muse. (anthologist) *The Germans on Venus; News from the Moon; The Supreme Progress; The World Above the World; Nemoville; Investigations of the Future*
Jacques Spitz. *The Eye of Purgatory*
Kurt Steiner. *Ortog*
Eugène Thébault. *Radio-Terror*
C.-F. Tiphaigne de La Roche. *Amilec*
Théo Varlet. *The Golden Rock. The Xenobiotic Invasion; The Castaways of Eros; Timeslip Troopers* (w/André Blandin); *The Martian Epic* (w/Octave Joncquel)
Paul Vibert. *The Mysterious Fluid*
Villiers de l'Isle-Adam. *The Scaffold; The Vampire Soul*
Philippe Ward. *Artahe*
Philippe Ward & Sylvie Miller. *The Song of Montségur*

MYSTERIES & THRILLERS

M. Allain & P. Souvestre. *The Daughter of Fantômas*
A. Anicet-Bourgeois, Lucien Dabril. *Rocambole*
A. Bernède. *Belphegor; Judex* (w/Louis Feuillade); *The Return of Judex* (w/Louis Feuillade); *The Shadow of Judex* (anthology)
A. Bisson & G. Livet. *Nick Carter vs. Fantômas*
V. Darlay & H. de Gorsse. *Arsène Lupin vs. Sherlock Holmes: The Stage Play*
Séamas Duffy. *Sherlock Holmes in Paris*
Paul Féval. *Gentlemen of the Night; John Devil; The Black Coats ('Salem Street; The Invisible Weapon; The Parisian Jungle; The Companions of the Treasure; Heart of Steel; The Cadet Gang; The Sword-Swallower)*
Emile Gaboriau. *Monsieur Lecoq*
Goron & Emile Gautier. *Spawn of the Penitentiary*
Steve Leadley. *Sherlock Holmes: The Circle of Blood*
Maurice Leblanc. *Arsène Lupin vs. Countess Cagliostro; Arsène Lupin vs. Sherlock Holmes (The Blonde Phantom; The Hollow Needle); The Many Faces of Arsène Lupin*
Gaston Leroux. *Chéri-Bibi; The Phantom of the Opera; Rouletabille & the Mystery of the Yellow Room; Rouletabille at Krupp's*
Richard Marsh. *The Complete Adventures of Judith Lee*
William Patrick Maynard. *The Terror of Fu Manchu; The Destiny of Fu Manchu*
Frank J. Morlock. *Sherlock Holmes: The Grand Horizontals; Sherlock Holmes vs Jack the Ripper*
Antonin Reschal. *The Adventures of Miss Boston*
P. de Wattyne & Y. Walter. *Sherlock Holmes vs. Fantômas*
David White. *Fantômas in America*
Pierre Yrondy. *The Adventures of Thérèse Arnaud*

SCREENPLAYS

Mike Baron. *The Iron Triangle*
Emma Bull & Will Shetterly. *Nightspeeder; War for the Oaks*
Gerry Conway & Roy Thomas. *Doc Dynamo*
Steve Englehart. *Majorca*
James Hudnall. *The Devastator*

Jean-Marc & Randy Lofficier. *Royal Flush*
J.-M. & R. Lofficier & Marc Agapit. *Despair*
J.-M. & R. Lofficier & Joël Houssin. *City*
Andrew Paquette. *Peripheral Vision*
Robert L. Robinson, Jr. *Judex*
R. Thomas, J. Hendler & L. Sprague de Camp. *Rivers of Time*

NON-FICTION

Stephen R. Bissette. *Blur 1-5. Green Mountain Cinema 1; Teen Angels*
Win Scott Eckert. *Crossovers* (2 vols.)
Jean-Marc & Randy Lofficier. *Shadowmen* (2 vols.)
Randy Lofficier. *Over Here*

ART BOOKS

Jean-Pierre Normand. *Science Fiction Illustrations*
Raven Okeefe. *Raven's L'il Critters; Rave's Faves*
Randy Lofficier & Raven Okeefe. *If Your Possum Go Daylight...*
Daniele Serra. *Illusions*

HEXAGON COMICS

Franco Frescura & Luciano Bernasconi. *Wampus*
Franco Frescura & Giorgio Trevisan. *CLASH*
L. Bernasconi, J.-M. Lofficier & Juan Roncagliolo Berger. *Phenix*
Claude Legrand, J.-M. Lofficier & L. Bernasconi. *Kabur*
Franco Oneta. *Zembla*
L. Buffolente, Lofficier & J.-J. Dzialowski. *Strangers: Homicron*
Danilo Grossi. *Strangers: Jaydee*
Claude Legrand & Luciano Bernasconi. *Strangers: Starlock*

www.ingramcontent.com/pod-product-compliance
Lightning Source LLC
Chambersburg PA
CBHW060414030726
47495CB00003B/572